She gathered her skirts together and sat him at her feet. Her face grew serious. “The time has come for us to have a conversation. You are old enough now.”

Eager for a word with her, the child drew near. “Yes Mother.”

“All people, even some adults are not good. There may be bad people with intent to harm you.”

His lovely eyes widened. “How Mother?”

“There are sick people in the world that may touch you in a bad way,” she said. “If this should happen, don’t be afraid to let me know right away, no matter what they tell you.”

“But, how will I know?”

She sighed and cleared her throat. “Well, if it feels bad, it probably *is* bad.”

“Oh.” He fell silent, thoughtful. “But…what if it feels good?”

What if it Feels Good?

a novel by

D. J. McLaurin

Taylor Nicole Publishing
South Holland, Illinois

ISBN-10: 0-9794038-0-4
ISBN-13: 978-0-9794038-0-4
LCCN: 2007902733

Edited by Susan Mary Malone
Cover design by www.barrondesigns.com

To my mother
Mable (Muh) Smith
Who taught me to dream

For my sister
Demeatris (Dee Dee) Townes
For inspiring me to write this book

For my sister
Mary Ann Maddox
The world's best one-woman cheer squad

Acknowledgments

With my first keystroke, I'd like to acknowledge God and thank him for the many blessings he has bestowed upon me and my family. He has given me a wealth of distinctive experiences, providing enough material to write for the rest of my life.

Editor, Susan Mary Malone: You are incredible. Editor, Marc Schwertley: You truly are a gentleman and a scholar. Editor and Consultant, Lissa Woodson: Without you I would still be at the gate, trying to get out.

To all my quasi-editors who read this novel when it was 600-1000 pages still—Demeatris Townes, Mary Maddox, Teri Hoskins, Theresa Posley, Betty Harris, Lenette Gullens, Belivia Fleming, Rosemary Wright, Brenda Cowens and Betty Turner—thank you so much for your comments, suggestions, enthusiasm, criticism and just being generally good sports.

I could never recall the names of all who inspired or influenced me in this journey. Those of you who provided continued encouragement to trudge on—Quiana Smith, Marla Byrd, Viola Jackson, Sharese McGhee, Cassandra Richardson, Barbara Johnson, Cynthia Schwertley and Christopher Levy—my gratitude has no boundaries. To my brothers, Marvin and Clyde, I love you guys.

Thanks to the creative team: Barron Steward, Cover Designer and Michael Slaughter, Website Designer.

Smooches to my daughters Teri and Taylor who genuinely believe that mom can do anything. And most importantly, a resounding thank you to the man who showed me what romance is *really* like, my husband, Bernard McLaurin for your patience, your generosity, your affection and devotion, I love you, I love you, I love you...

Part One
Age of Discovery

Chapter One

Men were attracted to him. At just fourteen, Michael could see it. Of course, not every man was attracted to the youthful sweetness of the innocent, but there were enough of them to make a lucrative living. If he could stomach the consequences. He couldn't, but Michael Joseph Bagley was now in more trouble than he had ever bargained for. He had no choice.

Porter had given him this particularly brilliant idea that would, at least, give Michael a headstart. Michael had known Porter for as long as he could remember being on the streets. His friend was constantly hatching one scheme or another. Michael had yet to see one that really worked. Still, the lure of what a quick fifty dollars could get him, a one-way ticket to someplace else, as far away from the police's reach as possible, was too good to ignore.

Even Michael had to gasp at the number of kids inside Dana's Diner. Many were hanging around the jukebox or lounging around the entrance trying to look both cute and sexy, while the luckier ones lunched at tables draped with red and yellow checkered cloths with men who, upon first inspection, might have passed for their fathers. Upon second inspection though, the ferocity with which the youngsters ate what was often their first meal in days matched the hunger in the eyes of the pedophiles that lay calmly in wait, their food untouched...watching.

Several gazes found him almost instantly. He settled on a handsome, bronze-skinned businessman in a lovely suit, sipping coffee and reading the business section of the *Detroit Free Press*, and moved toward him, deftly sliding into the empty seat at the bar near his table. This way, his back was to the customer but he could still hear him.

His stomach rumbled in response to the sweet smell of grilled onions and beef that permeated the room. A greasy menu was banged onto the counter in front of him. Offended, he looked up into the disapproving face of a middle-aged waitress that looked like she had stepped out of a 50's sitcom. Her name tag read 'Delilah.'

Her eyes widened. When he followed her line of vision to the blood still on his undershirt, he said, "my nose," and removed the shirt his cousin Pooch had given him, then the undershirt, which he rolled into a ball and placed on the counter. Shrugging into the shirt again, he buttoned it to the neck, hoping she wouldn't call him on the lie.

"You're new," she said.

"No."

"I haven't seen you around here." She screwed up her sharp eyes and twisted a pouty, red mouth while she waited for him to answer.

"So?" He shrugged.

The waitress leaned forward, her face close to his. For a moment, her eyes were soft. "Why don't you scat?" she said with a sigh.

They locked gazes and, briefly, Michael thought he had a sampling of what it would feel like to have a grandmother or even a real aunt, someone who cared. He swallowed, clearing his throat. Thoughts like these could ruin his prospects. "I'll have the double-decker with cheese and a coke float."

Her eyes hardened as her body straightened, lips pursed so tight they looked like a belly button.

"Salt and pepper on the fries," he added for effect.

A smirk replaced the look of motherly concern. "You'll need it," she said. Her eyes darted over his shoulder.

The businessman cleared his throat.

"Looks like you'll be working hard for this one." She snatched the menu from Michael's hands and smiled at his flushed face.

Michael bit back a retort. Known for his smart mouth, he had to keep his head and not go scaring people off when he needed money. Breathing in deeply, Michael scanned the place. A boy about sixteen years old got up from the table without paying and left the diner. Pretending not to notice, the guy sitting closest to him took a last sip of his coffee. That was the routine...so obvious. Michael rolled his eyes in disgust when the man threw two twenties on the table seconds later and followed the boy out.

Michael was just beginning to ponder how he should start when his food arrived. The pungent scent of beef and sweet onions wafting into his nose made him want to attack the plate. Always hungry, he couldn't appear to be desperate. It would be bad for negotiations.

"You shopping?"

The voice startled him even though he had been waiting for the customer to speak. "You buying?" he responded, being careful not to look around. He stuck a fry in his mouth and chewed slowly.

"Maybe."

Michael's heart contracted in his chest. He had to be smart from this point on if he were to score.

The voice came again, "How old are you?"

"Old enough,"

"Don't play with me."

Michael craned his neck.

"And don't look at me!"

Michael whipped his head back to his plate. Before, he had liked the man's voice. It was controlled and decisive, the way he imagined his father's voice would be, if he could have chosen a father. He felt a stab of regret at what he was planning to do before that asshole comment simply made playing his part easier.

"Um…eighteen," he said smoothly, then added, "I just turned eighteen."

"Good. How much?"

"Fifty."

"For what?"

"For whatever." He should have asked for more.

They didn't speak again before Michael finished his meal.

Scowling, Delilah slid the bill onto the counter next to his plate. Behind him, he felt the customer rise. He could hear his own heart pumping blood.

"I'll take that," the man said, placing two crisp ten dollar bills on the counter—way too much money, which disappeared into Delilah's hands.

"Thanks." Michael gulped, slid off his chair and walked casually, he hoped, to the door. He could break and run at this point, his belly was full of free food, but the meal was only gravy. He waited outside in the brisk air. The sun had set into the silver-blue horizon like an egg sunny-side up.

When the customer came out moments later, he was smiling congenially as if they were going to a ballgame. He was tall and good looking. His nails were clean and his watch was made of real gold. Damn! He really should have asked for more money.

"Aren't you the looker," the man said, ogling him. Michael cringed, feeling like a used car. "My ride's over here."

He followed the man a short distance to a parked silver Lexus. Michael hesitated at the open door. His stomach felt hollow. He wished he could have told his mother his plans, but the less she knew about it, the better. Besides, she'd have talked him out of it. He stole a glance at the businessman, who had been watching him. This was his final chance to bail, but that fifty bucks had his name on it. He breathed in deeply and sank into the passenger seat.

They drove to a secluded spot behind Kurt's Auto Parts, a chaotic junk yard of useless, rusting metal. The man began fumbling with his zipper. Michael instinctively turned his head away. "Uh…you've gotta pay first," he said, his voice quivering.

The guy stopped fumbling and looked at him a long time. "Okay," he said after a moment. He produced a wallet and removed a fifty dollar bill, handing it to Michael who wanted to shout. Instead, he calmly folded it and placed it in his shirt pocket.

"Take your pants off." This was important, according to Porter. This would give him an advantage.

"I don't need to take my pants off," the guy said, frowning as he peered at Michael. Then he tugged at the grey slacks until they were bunched around his hips.

Michael held his breath and shut his eyes against the bulging erection. "What's your name?" he asked, stalling for time.

"Mister." Panting, the man's face had taken on a pained look of urgency. He had morphed from a respectable-looking businessman into a creepy deviant. "Come on, touch me!"

"Sure." Michael had the money in his pocket and, though he hadn't got the guy to lower his pants as much as he'd have liked, it would have to do. The car door flew open and Michael rolled out of it, nearly falling to the ground.

"Hey punk!" the guy yelled, but Michael was already pounding the pavement.

He ran and ran, thankful for the burst of energy provided by his recent meal. He dared to turn around and nearly pissed himself. The guy, blazing a trail behind him, wasn't far off the mark.

Michael picked up speed. His lungs burned. His legs ached. He hadn't eaten a bite since the previous evening. He had youth on his side, but today's meal wouldn't carry him far. He stole another glance, alarmed to find that he was nearly caught. He tried to change his course and was tackled to the ground. The force knocked the wind out of him. Gasping for air, he thought he might pass out. The cold steel of a gun's barrel was pressed against his head for the second time that day.

"You little shit!" the stranger growled. His eyes burned with anger, but a sinister smile curved his lips on one side. His breath smelled of weak coffee. "Think you can rob me?" He yanked the fifty dollar bill from Michael's pocket and stuffed it inside his own. "This'll teach you!"

To Michael's absolute horror, the guy tugged at his jeans. *He's gonna rape me*. Nausea swept over him. He didn't want his cousin Pooch or his mother to know they found him with his pants down and his brains blown out. Exhausted, he wasn't even sure where he was.

Without this money, he would be caught. Visions of an earlier confrontation with another gun-wielding lunatic flickered about in his mind. He had fought with his mother's boyfriend and the gun had gone off. It was an accident...wasn't it? The police wouldn't see it that way. Maybe he should just let him…

"No," he heard himself say.

The man fumbled, trying to keep his pants up with just the one hand. The gun slackened in his other hand as he lost his focus.

"No!" Michael knocked the hand away. The gun went flying. He came up hard with a knee to the groin. The guy folded. Vomit spewed from his mouth. Michael delivered a punch to the face. The man twisted and writhed in pain.

Michael knelt over the guy and began to feel around for his wallet. Had he put it in his pants or his shirt pocket? A grip on his wrist forced him to stumble backward to free himself. This guy was stronger than he imagined. He might be a cop—or worse.

Michael ran. Better to be caught by the cops than this psycho. He hadn't made it far when gun-fire rang out. "Holy Christ!" he prayed, "Save me…"

When he just couldn't run anymore, he cut through an alley and ducked behind a row of metal garbage cans. There he stayed, listening to the combination of sounds—the cries of babies, the laughter of children, the hiss of foods frying—all signaling the apartment life around him.

Darkness had fallen when his legs stopped shaking enough to venture out. He crept toward the street and looked around. Minutes passed before he could figure out where he was. He expected his attacker to jump out at him from around every corner.

"Fuckin Porter and his bright ideas!" he mumbled. Hurrying, he didn't stop until he saw the familiar bridge, affectionately called the 'pass,' a shelter to him and many of his friends. He picked his way through makeshift barricades, boxes, tattered tents and old sheets erected on discarded clothes-racks until he found Sam and Myrna Longbottom, an older couple who had become more than friends.

Mrs. Longbottom moved so that he could slip in between them. They smelled of old age and fresh dirt. She stroked his face as if she knew he had been through something. "Rough day?"

So they had heard. Word must be on the street that he was a murderer. He laid his head against her bony chest in answer, trying hard to hold back his tears. If only they knew how close he had come to never seeing them again.

Sam patted him on the arm. "The cops were here, but we didn't tell them nothin'," he said in his gravelly voice.

"Twice they came," Mrs. Longbottom added. "They've been questioning everybody."

"Someone must've told em' they'd find you here." Sam cast a rheumy glare at those sleeping nearby. "Any one o' these derelicts will sell you out fo' a dime."

"But I don't think they'll be back tonight," Mrs. Longbottom assured him. "Try to get some sleep."

"I can't. I have to move on."

"To where?" Sam asked, wiping a shaking hand across his furrowed brow.

He had no money. Pooch had no money. Porter's help had almost gotten him killed—again. Perhaps his mother...

"Have you eaten?" Michael asked as the thought struck him. He had been gone all day and they depended on him. They were too old to walk the couple of miles to the shelter that might provide them at least one meal a day.

"Oh, sure honey." Mrs. Longbottom smiled, but he knew she would lie about it for his benefit. "What about you? I could fix you up something."

Michael blinked back tears. There was nothing. In her old age, she liked to pretend. To her, he was the grandson she never got a chance to care for. "No, thanks." He lay, absorbing the sounds of homeless night life. Ms. Melinda's baby started to cry. June and Fuzzy, high on something, had begun their nightly brawl. Bottle Ben had returned, the squeak of his rusted grocery cart ripping the darkness. He wished hunger and exposure were the *only* problems he had.

Mrs. Longbottom peered out from beneath the underpass and announced, "Looks like rain."

She was right. He could smell it. That was the last thing they needed.

Michael sighed. Why didn't he just give up, lie down and let death take him? Why did he fight to survive day in and day out? Why did he ask God to save him? He should have just let that man shoot him. Maybe it would have gone quickly. He closed his eyes savoring the short reprieve before daybreak would bring a new set of problems.

"It's already raining," he whispered.

Chapter Two

Michael Bagley rose before the sun and waited behind Blaine Thompson's liquor store until he heard her beat-up Chevy shudder to a halt. He emerged from the shadows just as she removed her key from the door. Eyes wide, she jumped, prepared to scream, but released a sigh of relief the instant she recognized him.

"Get in here!" She grabbed his arm and shoved him inside. "The cops are looking all over for you!"

"I know. Look, I hate to ask, but I need money."

Without turning on the lights, she moved to the back of the store where she kept the safe. He watched the gentle sway of her hips, the way her long auburn hair fell down her back, and the way the white cotton sundress molded to her lush curves.

"Good thing I hadn't gone to the bank yet," she said as she worked the combination. She returned quickly and pressed a wad of bills inside his hand. Petite and fine-boned, she appeared child-like in the shadows. "What happened, Michael? Did you really shoot Jaye?"

"I can't talk about it now. I need a favor."

"So, what else is new?" she scoffed, but the lines around her mouth deepened as she peered at the fourteen-year-old.

"Can you house a few of my friends in the back for a few days, just until I can figure something out?"

Blaine crossed her arms Indian-style. "Not again!" she scolded him. "I don't want those filthy motherfuckers in my store. The last time you brought them here, I fought lice for a week!"

He moved forward, touching her arm. "Come on, Blaine!"

She sighed and closed her eyes, but soon opened them to lock gazes with him. "All right, but only a few days."

Michael smiled.

"And you owe me!"

"Thanks." He moved silently in the dark and picked up a few supplies: a snack cake, a bag of chips, a pack of cigarettes. "I owe you for these too."

"Where will you go?"

"I don't know. I figured I'd get on a bus and just keep going. You seen my mother?"

Blaine shrugged. "She doesn't talk to me, but I heard she's going out of her mind with worry." Her grey eyes brightened. "Hey, won't you lay low at my place for a few days?"

"Too dangerous. Everybody knows I'm fucking you. Soon the cops'll know it too, if they don't already."

"The police have already been there." She moved to the door and peered out. "I said I hadn't seen you and they knew I was telling the truth. I told them you'd be a fool to come to me."

"I don't know—"

Blaine swung around to face him. "You can't just hop on a bus! You've got to let things cool down. Nobody really cares about Jaye! It's not like he died or anything."

"He's...alive?" Michael asked, his surprise mingled with his relief.

"They're saying it's a tough call, but he might pull through. This'll blow over in a week. Even if he dies, nobody'll blame you. Jaye's a creep."

"But he's...my father." Their gazes locked briefly before drifting away. Neither of them believed that.

"Anyway," Blaine continued, "the cops are only doing their jobs. They don't really care about what happens to him." Before Michael could argue, she thrust her house key into his hand. "Wait on the floor inside the car. If I don't open the store now, things will look suspicious. Give me a couple of hours. I can take a break as soon as Sandi comes in."

Her eyes, moist with pain, scanned him, taking in the tattered clothing, the worn-out sneakers and the shock of black hair in need of a cut. For a moment, Michael wanted to tell her what happened yesterday. Nearly being raped and beaten by a total stranger had set his nerves on edge. But then again, she would pose questions he was none too ready to answer.

For lack of a better option, he took the key and started for the back door.

"Wait!" She ran to him. For a moment, they just looked at each other. "You have your pills?"

He had begun taking the pills at his mother's insistence. They helped him wage an increasing battle with depression, or they were supposed to.

"No, I left them at mom's. Can you get my cousin to bring them?"

"Okay. Here." She removed a compact and sponge from her purse and began blotting at the distinctive birthmark underneath his ear. "They'll be looking for this."

When she was done, he hesitated. She nodded for him to leave and he started again for the door.

"And, hey!" Blaine called after him. He turned and found her smiling, but her eyes were wet with tears. "Just so you know, little boy, you're not fucking me, I'm fucking you!"

Chapter Three

It started out as being one of his better days. On his cousin Pooch's birthday they got tickets to a Duke Spencer concert. Michael had been a Duke fan as far back as he could remember.

During his long walk to Pooch's house, Michael's feet began to ache, so he stopped at old Mrs. Benneton's porch where he sat and ate a candy bar. He ran into Chauncey, a notorious Turk (one of the toughest gangs) and begged for a shower. He could have showered at Pooch's, but whenever he could avoid his aunt Melanie, he did.

After showering and changing, he met up with Pooch for the concert. They pulled into the theatre parking lot in Pooch's rented car. Never had they seen so many people in one place. All races, all ages, both sexes, all sizes; Duke-mania was more far-reaching than they had imagined.

"Look Mike!" Pooch pointed at a larger-than-life figurine of the Duke himself. The statuette was clothed in all white and leaning on a guitar that dazzled with what seemed like a million twinkling lights. The two boys looked at each other and grinned.

They were led to seats third-row center from the stage.

"How much did you pay for these puppies?" Michael asked Pooch.

"Don't worry about it." Pooch smiled. "Let's just call it an early birthday present for you and a late one for me."

"Check out the females here!" Pooch began, but Michael could no longer hear what he was saying as the lights went out and the crowd jumped to its feet. The entire stage went up in fireworks and a distorted voice over the intercom system began to introduce the star attraction. Wind machines blew from every direction so that hair and clothes flew all over. The whir of helicopters flying overhead nearly drowned out the screams of the crowd. Then, from the center of the room at the very top of the high-vaulted ceiling, Duke Spencer was being lowered. Mid-air, Duke began to take slow, deliberate steps toward the stage. The sound system blasted his latest hit, "Crowd Pleaser," on high volume.

For the next two hours Michael stood transfixed as he watched his idol put on the performance of a lifetime. By the time Duke sang his final song, "Shock Treatment," Michael broke from his trance and joined Pooch and the rest of the crowd in a frenzied dance party. When Duke finally disappeared into thin air in a magnificent magical trick signaling the end of the show, Mike shook himself like a man rousing from sleep. Just before Duke disappeared in a puff of smoke, Mike could've sworn he winked at him.

They decided to go see Gherri dance at the Lynx, which stayed open til 4. Pooch had a serious crush on Gherri, who used her position to get her under-aged friends complimentary admission.

Michael's mother, Sarah, also danced at the Lynx. As the club's main attraction, she would strip down to nearly nothing and twist her near-perfect body into unfathomable positions. Sarah was the last act of the night, and if Michael knew his mother, she probably hadn't even left the house yet.

"Crash at my house. Give yourself a break today. You can go back to the pass tomorrow," Pooch suggested as they stepped out of the smoke-filled club into the brisk morning air.

"Naw, I'm gonna hang out at Mom's for the night. The house is probably empty by now and they don't normally get back before ten."

He shouldn't have gone there in the first place; he and Jaye had been enemies since the day they met. Jealous of Sarah's relationship with her son, Jaye found ways to separate them, from scheduling her gigs so that she was away from him for long periods to physically locking him away in his room; but as Michael got older, he opposed Jaye more and more. Jaye responded with beatings and torture that grew worse as the child aged.

Sarah's fear of Jaye rendered her powerless to help Michael. She admitted she was half-glad when Jaye put Michael out on the streets at thirteen. At least she knew her son wouldn't be killed at the hands of her own boyfriend.

There was shouting when he arrived. Sighing, he contemplated turning around. The doorknob jiggled and Sarah swung the door open, clutching a robe to her chest, her mouth falling open in surprise. "What are you doing here?" she cried.

"I thought you'd be at the club by now. I wanted to take a nap. Guess my timing is fucked—again." He turned to go.

"Wait!" Sarah stole a glance behind her. "I'm...having sort of a party."

"I thought you had to work."

"I'm off tonight. Look, you can stay...just for the night; but Michael, you have to promise me you won't say anything to Jaye. Promise you won't do anything!"

Had it not been for the lateness of the hour, he would have left straightaway; instead, he headed for his old bedroom. With no chance of sleeping, he cranked up his music to drown the laughter, shouts and swearing coming from below. He knew what was going on and it incensed him.

Michael picked up his bag. If he didn't leave right away, there would be trouble.

"Stop, you asshole! You're hurting me!" Sarah screamed.

Michael dropped his bag and hurried to her bedroom where Anne, another dancer, met him at the door. "She's a grown woman, Michael. Don't give Jaye a reason!"

"I can't stand by while he fuckin' beats my mother to death!"

"He's not beating her!" Anne moved to block Michael's entry.

"Well, well." Jaye emerged, a thunderous expression on his face. He pushed Anne aside. "The prodigal son has come home to roost."

Two men struggled to hold his mother to the bed. Shoving Jaye against the door, Michael ran over, grabbed one and threw him to the floor.

"Hey!" the guy yelled, "what is this?"

"Don't worry, Pops," Jaye said. "I'll handle this punk."

Michael went for the other guy, but Jaye hit him from behind with something hard.

Sarah screamed. "Stop it! Stop it!" She cried. "Don't hurt my baby!"

Michael and Jaye fell across furniture, knocking things over. Glass splattered everywhere as stuff came crashing to the floor with them. Mike freed his arm and began hitting Jaye as hard as he could with his fist. Jaye kneed Mike in the stomach, doubling him over. While Mike clutched at his belly, Jaye pulled out his pistol, whacking Michael across the face. Mike sank to the floor, the room swaying around him. Blood streamed down the side of his face. He opened his eyes as Jaye grabbed his hair and drug him toward his mother, the pistol pressed into his temple.

"No, no, no, please, please, I'll do anything!" Sarah begged. "Let him go Jaye, he'll never come back; I'll make sure of it, please!"

Michael clenched his eyes shut. His head was pounding, his mouth was dry, and blood dripped onto his clothes.

"Hold those legs!" Jaye ordered.

"You bastard, I hate you!" Sarah fought and kicked with all her might, but Jaye had shoved Michael's face into his mother's crotch. Horrified, Michael threw his head back and knocked Jaye off his feet again. He lunged in fury at Jaye, when a sudden force met him and he lay crumpled on the floor, his mother's desperate cries fading into darkness.

He recalled walking down the road, his shirt splattered with blood, his face swollen. He spotted Chauncey sitting on the hood of his car drinking with his friends, Fleet and One-eyed Booker.

"I need some heat," Michael said.

Chauncey hesitated, scratching the top of his head. "Look, you get caught, you ain't seen me, you hear?"

"Yeah."

He searched the strip as dawn burned away. An area popular for prostitution, Jaye was known to hang out there. Michael found him in his old Chevy, parked on the corner of Laurel and Hoyne streets. He approached the car cautiously. Jaye wasn't alone. The pretty girl next to him, in just her bra and a mini-skirt, couldn't have been older than Michael.

He bent so that his face was in the open car window. The smell of alcohol on Jaye's breath was so strong, Michael could lean against it. A sinister grin spread across Jaye's face. "Well, what have we here?"

The rest was a jumble of events. Michael raised the small handgun—Jaye grabbed at it—the air exploded with sound...

Before Michael realized what was happening, Jaye slumped over into the young girl's lap. She covered her breasts with her bloodied blouse and shut her eyes, screaming.

"And that's what happened," Michael finished.

Blaine and Pooch watched him intently.

"We've got to come up with a plan." Blaine stood and began to pace.

At times like this Michael liked Blaine. He had been sleeping with her the past year. An old friend of his mother's, she was kind to him when he was a little kid. She made her move on him one day after he had delivered groceries to her home. He relied on her for food and shelter when he had no place else to go.

A knock at the door made the three of them start. When the knock came again, a muffled voice called out something about a warrant.

"Don't run," Pooch pleaded to Michael's retreating form. "It's too late. You'll make it worse."

Blaine hugged him and went to the door.

Chapter Four

It had been days, though it seemed like weeks. He couldn't comprehend the trouble he was in. He went over bits and pieces of the last moments prior to his arrest in his head. He remembered walking with the gun dangling from his fingers.

Chauncey strolled by, casually taking it from him. "I'll take care of it."

He found himself at Pooch's, where Pooch gave him a fresh shirt and hustled him away before Aunt Melanie, could find him there. Then there was Dana's, the john that would have killed him and finally Blaine's house, where he was apprehended.

"Bagley!" a burley policeman called out. Michael looked up questioningly through the bars of his cell. "You have visitors."

He was handcuffed and taken to a small waiting area where his mother and Pooch sat at a steel table. Pooch's pug, little face was streaked with tears.

"Oh, baby," Sarah wailed as she reached out to him.

The officer flung his arm out between Michael and Sarah. "Don't move so suddenly ma'am," he instructed her. "Stay seated, please."

Sarah threw her arms around her son anyway, sobbing. "How are you baby? They haven't hurt you, have they?"

He only gazed at her.

"Don't you worry, I'm working on getting you out of here!"

"I'm so sorry, mom."

"Michael, listen to me. It was an accident."

Michael blinked. An accident?

"I have an old friend," Sarah continued. "I'm going to get in touch with him, and he is going to help you. You just hold on now! You hear me?"

"Time's up!" the officer announced.

Pooch reached out and grabbed Michael's hand.

The officer took Michael by the arm to lead him away.

Sarah leaned further over the steel table to press her lips to his. She held on to him until he was pulled away from her.

* * * *

Days or months or weeks might have passed. Michael couldn't tell. His concentration was trained on getting through each meal, each chore, each night. With no sign of Sarah or Pooch, he began to lose hope. Then his name was called and he was led again down the long brick corridor, to a dim little room as cold as a freezer. Everything around them was brick and steel.

His respite at seeing his mother was short-lived as he took in the man seated beside her. His hands were smooth, sporting a single diamond of at least two carats. His nails were clean and his hair was freshly cut with precision. The man's fingers danced nervously over a pen and pad and the uncertainty in his handsome face belied the confidence in his erect posture.

They sat in little steel chairs that, certainly, must have been meant for pre-schoolers. The man and his mother sat on the same side of a long steel table that would separate them from Michael. Sarah's face was drawn with grief.

The guard walked over and placed his hand on Michael's shoulder and with a downward shove, forced him into the waiting seat. The boy shot a hateful glance at him. Fire burned deep within his dark eyes. Then, just as suddenly, the fire went out and he sat as if dumb, gazing at his reflection in the table.

"I brought someone here to see you, Michael." Sarah spoke quietly and carefully as if she might frighten him if she spoke any louder. "He's going to help us." She shot a glance at the man, but he offered no words. After a brief silence, Sarah tried again. "Honey, can you just look at us, please?"

Michael sat, sullen. He felt the man's eyes studying him.

"This is Steven Doyle, a friend of mine. He's a great attorney—never lost a case. He flew all this way to see you, honey. He wants to ask you some questions. Can you just talk to him?"

Michael raised his dark head and looked squarely at the man, who returned his gaze.

"I know this is hard for you," Steven said. "Just try to remember everything you can, don't leave anything out, no matter how small. Tell me, in your words, what happened."

Michael looked at his mother. She nodded. He closed his eyes and tried to collect events he had spent so much time trying to forget.

Steven pulled out a tape recorder.

As Michael spoke, they scrutinized each other. He tried to get a glimpse of the notes Steven jotted onto his pad; the man obviously wasn't listening to his speech. Abruptly, Steven closed his pad and dropped his pen, causing Michael to halt mid-sentence.

"Go on," he urged.

Michael continued. He closed his eyes, more to escape Steven's probing gaze than anything. When he finished talking, he opened his eyes to find him staring. Michael and Sarah exchanged glances.

"You okay?" Sarah asked Steven.

"Uh, yeah, uh—" Steven seemed to struggle. "Is that a fresh bruise on your cheek?"

Michael reached up and touched his face as if he was unaware of the bruising. "I don't know," he said softly.

"Times up!" the guard roared. Steven began to collect his tape recorder.

"That's it?" Sarah asked. "That's all? You're not going to *do* anything?"

"Sarah, I have to go back and review my notes. I have to think about this—" When Michael looked away, he said, "Look, I don't think they should have you in this facility with hardened criminals; you're still a minor. I'm going to work on getting you moved."

Michael sighed with gratitude.

"And we need to make sure that your injuries are being taken care of," he continued. "Here, let me see your cheek again."

Steven reached in his pocket for a mini camera he managed to get through. Michael turned his left cheek and Steven gasped, dropping the camera, shattering it to pieces.

Chapter Five

There couldn't have been a more perfect day for a cook-out on the terrace. The sun, a yellow ball in the sky, bathed them in pleasant warmth. A soft, fragrant breeze from his surrounding garden played in his hair and Joe Simpson's mood ran high as he prepared to light the grill. His friends Jake, the doctor (with his wife Marie), Dominic, his accountant and Steven, his attorney and partner, were all present. His best friend, Chachi, was still out of town and Renee, Chachi's girlfriend, had gone to meet him, as she often did when he was on the road. Lydia, Joe's wife, was running late.

Joe glimpsed Dominic grab Steven by the arm and pull him into the house. They had been at if for a while, their faces flushed in anger, their heads close together. Joe had hoped they'd work it out alone.

An hour and several glasses of champagne later, Joe wore his white chef's hat and tossed burgers high into the air. "Jake, you got the drinks?" he called out.

"Got it." Jake sprang to his feet and ran over to tend the bar.

Steven walked over to Joe at the grill and watched him remove charred burgers onto a platter.

"Not Chachi's burgers, huh?" Joe admitted. He had never been a great cook.

"I heard a little charring adds flavor and texture," Steven joked.

Dominick pounced between them. "Hey, I'm starved. You've got to put a move on it, man," he said to Joe, but his gaze was on Steven. Steven sighed and looked away.

"I'm doing my best!" Joe whined in defense. "Here, have a burger." He pointed to the platter with his spatula. "Condiments are—well, you know how we do it."

Dominick grabbed a burger and stuffed it between two buns. He grabbed Steven by the arm and led him away. Joe inched closer to them, straining to hear.

"What are you up to now?" Joe heard Dominic say.

"Leave me alone! I know what I'm doing," Steven spat in return.

They moved out of his range of hearing, but Joe's curiosity peaked.

Steven walked briskly over to Joe and whispered in his ear. "Dude, call me at home tonight. I need to talk to you. Right now, I've got to run." He headed for the exit.

"Whoa, whoa, whoa—" Joe called out, waving his spatula. "Wait a minute guy! Where are you going all of a sudden?"

"Call me," Steven called behind him.

Joe looked over at Dominick. Something was not right. "Steven!" he shouted. "Do you have something to say to me?" Joe removed his chef's hat and began untying his apron as Steven slowly returned. They all stood quietly for a few seconds.

"Yeah," Steven said finally. Was he doing the right thing?

Joe tossed the apron into a grassy area nearby. "Let's get this over with now, before my wife gets home."

Joe sat with his legs sprawled and his face cradled in his hands. He felt like sobbing. Marie sat with Joe and put her arm about him. Dominick stood with his back to the rest of them and angrily puffed at a cigarette.

Jake sat stupefied. "I can't believe this is happening again. What does it take to make this woman go away?"

"You know, Sarah brought this on herself," Steven said. "I'm not asking anybody to do anything for her, but we are not innocent bystanders in this thing either."

"Oh?" Joe's face emerged from the cradle of his hands. "Sounds like you've become a little cozy with the two of them."

"Look. I'm not here to defend myself. I told you there is nothing between me and Sarah and I don't have to justify anything else."

"Yeah, well, you sound real defensive to me," Dominick scoffed.

Joe held up his hand to silence him. "Okay," he said calmly. "I'm sorry. I'm not accusing you of anything. I'm just upset." He took a couple of deep breaths and tried again. "I guess I don't know what you're asking me, or what I am supposed to do now. It's obvious she doesn't want me to have a relationship with the kid or she would have told me this news a long time ago."

"She said she had been threatened."

"Aw, bullshit!" Dominick blurted.

"Will you calm down?" Joe insisted.

Dominick waved his hand in the air.

Steven continued, "She didn't say who or what, and I didn't press her. She is only concerned that her son does not go to jail. She's not even asking for your money."

Joe frowned. "He killed a man, isn't he supposed to go to jail?"

"I did not say he killed anyone!" Steven yelled. "Look," he said more calmly, "it's obvious we won't get anywhere on this today. I think I need to leave before something is said that we can't take back." He rose. "Take a moment to think about it. Call me when you're ready to talk."

"All right, tell me what you need me to do." Joe's voice trembled.

Steven sighed. "I'll need Jake to provide me with a vial of your blood for the test."

"Done."

"Then I'll need to brief you on what's going on. We're due in court in a week."

"A Week!"

"Yeah. I'm sorry for the short notice. Everything had to move kind of fast." They both fell silent.

"You really think he's my son, Steven?"

"Yeah," Steven breathed.

"I mean, why? Does he look like me, or something?"

"He looks more like Sarah, but now that I've seen him a few times..."

"Shit," Joe murmured.

"He's got a lot of your mannerisms. But what sealed it for me—"

"What?"

"He has the *mark*."

Joe's mouth bobbed like a fish. "My God, Steven! David doesn't even have it! This is bad. Lydia—"

"Lydia loves you. She will not give up on you for something that happened fifteen years ago."

"How can we keep this on the low?"

"Well, if everything goes as planned, I'm hoping the judge will grant Sarah custody. You will need to provide support for Michael."

"Of course, if he's my son, of course I'll support him."

"Good. And you don't have to, but it would sway the judge if you could pay for the medical care of the victim. Looks like he'll never walk again."

"Okay. What else?"

"If things go smoothly, Lydia won't have to know until you're ready to tell her. You can take your time to decide what kind of relationship, if any, you want to have with the boy." Steven paused. "You do want to meet him, don't you? You don't want the first time he sees you to be in the courtroom, do you?"

"I don't know anything yet. I can't see anybody. Right now, I just want to get this court thing behind me and keep Sarah out of my space long enough for me to figure out what to do."

Steven's voice softened. "Are you angry with me?"

"I'm not angry with you. I just don't trust this whole thing with Sarah involved. I don't want this shit to get out of hand like it did the last time. But I'll give you what you need. Who knows, the test could come back negative and then there's no problem after all."

"She's changed a lot, Joe."

"We'll see. I'll get with Jake."

"Okay. I'll keep you posted."

Chapter Six

Two months at the Darwin Kelly Home for Adolescent Boys had done wonders for Michael. The glow of health had returned to his skin and his clothes fit better. Now he leaned over the side of his bed and tried to peer at the photograph of the distinguished gentleman by candlelight. His mother had given it to him after a lengthy discussion, explaining to him the circumstances surrounding his arrival in the world. He couldn't believe the man in the photograph was his father. He looked regal and confident. What would they talk about? He had been sure his mother would tell him that Steven was his father. There was just something between them, a special connection.

He thought he heard footsteps and quickly blew out the candle, cramming the photo underneath his mattress.

Michael was a bit disappointed that he hadn't met his father yet. He thought he'd at least have gotten a phone call. Steven tried to make him understand the pressure he was under and assured him that they would meet in time.

Michael shifted underneath the bedding, too nervous to sleep. He had so many questions. Oh well, he'd get one wish granted soon enough. They were due in court tomorrow.

* * * *

Testimony went back and forth for three days and Michael still had not seen evidence of the man in the photograph. He had a new respect for Steven, who was a different man in the courtroom.

On the fourth day, Steven approached the District Attorney with a plea bargain. Though things were going in their favor, he didn't want to chance a verdict, so he offered the court a situation in which Michael would get counseling and probation and then, of course, be released into the custody of his mother and the supervision of his father who had agreed to, going forward, provide for the two of them until his son's adulthood. Sounded good. But the judge had to approve the plea. He announced to the two sides that he would render his decision the following day

The next day the judge summoned all parties to his chambers. They waited anxiously in the halls outside the huge double doors.

"Where is he?" Michael whispered. "You said my father would be in court today."

"He promised," Steven said as he looked around. The flight from New York to Detroit was a relatively short one. Joe should have been there.

They were escorted inside the judge's chambers by armed guard, but Michael was asked to wait over thirty minutes in a separate room. Once he was returned to chambers he saw neither Steven nor his mother inside. He was asked to take a seat in a large, wide leather chair.

The judge disrobed in an attempt to appear less intimidating, but Michael knew that his life was in this man's hands and was terrified of being interrogated alone.

"Michael, I'm Judge John Monohan. I've spoken to each of your parents this morning." Michael stiffened. "They seem to agree that together they can raise you into a respectable, law abiding citizen. I am convinced that you, with the right guidance, can be a contributing member of this society."

Unable to speak and not knowing what else to do, Michael nodded.

"Up until now you've lived a life without structure. In your new environment, you'll have to go to school."

With eyes downcast, Michael nodded again.

"This is a new chance for you. The drop-out rate among homeless children is staggering. I've spoken with your counselors and they have apprised me of your superior learning ability. Taking that into account, I am sure your parents will be able to place you in a gifted education program."

"Yes, sir."

"You have a history of fighting," the judge continued. "I see you've been picked up frequently for getting into small scrapes. Yet at Darwin, your counselors have informed me that you get along well with everyone; however, they do mention moodiness, perhaps depression. You want to talk about that?

Michael shrugged.

"You will be required to continue counseling for a period of time. I want a report of your progress on a regular basis. I'll get one from your social worker, but I want to hear directly from you too, young man!" The judge smiled playfully.

Michael smiled too.

"All right, Mr. Bagley, I think I know what to do with you now." He pressed a button on his phone to summon his secretary. He reached for his robe and began to slip it on.

Steven opened the door and Sarah walked in first. She smiled and quickly sat in the large leather chair next to Michael's and took his hand. He gave her hand a gentle squeeze. Then Steven came in with Joe and several others, including the bailiff and the court reporter, at his heel. Michael was all needles and pins. Standing right there in the room with him was his father!

The judge peered over his glasses. "Mr. Simpson, meet your son Michael; Michael meet your father."

Michael squeezed Sarah's hand. He heard music. He felt the beginnings of a broad grin, but it quickly dissipated when Joe simply nodded politely in his direction. Crushed, he tried to remain upbeat.

"I've decided to render this decision in the confines of my chambers, as I have done in the past for cases involving minors," the judge began. "We may never understand what really happened that terrible day Jason Brown was shot; however, I do believe that, whatever happened, this young man had obviously reached a breaking point to have gone so far as to have obtained a gun, even if only for the purpose of threatening another individual. I am not convinced that, under normal circumstances, he is a risk to society nor do I believe he acted willful or intentionally with sound mind." The judge paused. The room was quiet.

"I have reviewed the bargaining agreement and I am in approval of all elements—for the most part." Steven and Sarah smiled. Michael beamed.

Joe appeared unmoved. "I am sentencing Michael Bagley to probation for a period of three years. I am ordering Michael Bagley to undergo psychiatric therapy for a period of one year, after which his mental condition will be reviewed and it will be determined if further treatment is necessary."

Although Steven had discussed this possibility with him, Michael could not hide the burn of embarrassment that spread across his cheeks.

"Furthermore, the young man is to enroll in school immediately. His progress is to be reported to his assigned social worker, on a regular basis, to be determined at a later date." The judge paused again and frowned at his hands. Then he sighed. His gaze met Michael's. "I will not enter a demand for child support payments as I am releasing this minor into the custody of his biological father, and *not* his mother."

The room erupted.

"Your Honor, I swear, I have turned my life around!" Sarah begged.

Steven approached the judge. "Your Honor, my client and his mother have a special bond, which I believe, if broken, will cause irreparable damage to my client—"

Joe stood and walked backward, eyes wide, mouth open.

"Silence everyone!" the judge ordered, banging his fist on his desk. "I know this is difficult to grasp, but I have been doing this for many years. As a judge and a prosecutor before, I think I know what is best for this child."

"Your Honor," Steven began. Joe looked at him as if he would kill him. "My client and his father just met today. May we request a warming-up period?"

"I do agree, Mr. Doyle, that there should be such a period. Therefore I am allowing the child to return home with his mother today. But he is to be delivered to his father in New York by a person other than his mother within seven days."

"Seven Days!" Sarah screamed. She sobbed as she clutched her son to her chest.

Michael tried to comfort her. He couldn't help, though, but notice the look of horror on Joe's face. The pain of rejection slowly turned into anger.

"No!" Michael shouted. "I won't go!"

"Young man," the judge warned. "You have no choice in this matter. If you violate one letter of this order, you will find yourself serving time in a state correctional facility."

Sarah wailed, "Your Honor, please don't do this to me, he is all I have, really!"

"Ms. Bagley, I do sympathize with you," the judge said softly. My intention is not to punish you. This is an opportunity for you to continue to build a life for yourself and Michael. I will be revisiting this case in one year, at which time these circumstances may change. All parties will return to the courtroom for a ruling on visitation in thirty days." He banged on his desk again and dismissed them.

As they spilled out into the hall, Joe pushed past the District Attorney in front of him and stormed down the long staircase. Steven rushed to catch up with him and spotted Sarah and Michael nearby, leaned against a wall for support.

"I'm so sorry," Steven panted.

"How could this happen?" Michael asked. "The judge must have seen the way that bastard looked at me!"

"I know you're upset—look, just go home. Go home and I'll call you, okay?"

Michael turned his face away.

Steven shook his head in despair and raced after Joe.

Chapter Seven

"He fucked this up royally," Joe cried. "I can kill him!"

"You know Steven's always been a saint. He's just trying to save people, like he always has." Chachi had been talking to Joe for hours now. It was 1:00 in the morning and he had a 4am wake-up call. Still, nothing came before his best friend. He'd stay up all night if he had to, as long as Joe needed him.

"I don't think I can forgive him for this one, Chachi. He should have stayed out of it."

"Steven was right, Joe. Sarah was going to come after you for help—however she could get it."

"What, was she gonna force me into her son's life? I don't think so. The most she would have gotten out of me was child support."

"Yeah, well, you think she would have gone about it quietly? No, she would have made a public mess of things. This way, at least it's not as bad as it could have been." Chachi yawned and shifted under the sheets. He hoped Joe's tirade wouldn't last much longer.

Joe moaned. "How on earth am I gonna break this to my wife, my children?"

"Quickly and delicately; If Lydia would stick with you when this shit first jumped off, after what you put her through, she's certainly not gonna bail on seventeen, eighteen years of marriage. She's a big girl. She'll get through it. You guys have too much invested in each other."

"Man," Joe reminisced, "that was a mess."

"*You* were a mess," Chachi pointed out. They both chuckled.

"And now it's started up all over again." Joe sighed.

Chachi remained quiet. Too clearly he recalled that evening he had the showdown with Sarah.

"Trust Lydia to work through it with you, Joe. You have to make her feel secure that Sarah will not be a factor in your marriage again."

"I know, I know," Joe conceded. "Look, I'd better let you go. It's late."

"Yeah. I've got to get up in a couple of hours. So what's the kid like?"

"I don't really know." Joe sighed. "I was barely able to look at him. Every time I tried, I'd see *her*."

"You've gotta tell Lydia and the kids soon. Tomorrow. Give them enough time to absorb it, to sort things out before he's ringing your doorbell."

* * * *

Steven volunteered to be the one to escort Michael to his father's house. It was the least he could do; he had screwed things up so badly.

Michael stared out the window of the plane and gave no indication that he noticed Steven put a soft drink on a pull-down table in front of him.

"Drink something, you'll feel better," Steven told him after taking a gulp of his whisky sour and setting it down.

Michael took the remainder of Steven's drink and poured it down his throat.

Eyes wide, Steven snatched it from his hand.

Michael rolled his eyes and leaned his forehead against the window. He drifted between restless sleep and quiet sobbing.

"You okay?" Steven asked after a while.

Michael nodded and sat up rigid in his seat. "How long before we land?"

"We've landed." Steven answered. He squeezed Michael's hand for support.

Michael had never even seen the inside of a limousine. For the moment he forgot his distress.

Steven got on the phone. He gestured for Michael to help himself. Michael opened the refrigerator door to an array of sandwiches and treats. Fresh-baked breads and pastries with spreads sat on trays on the marble countertops. He sampled a pastry.

Steven smiled. "Watch this." He showed Michael how many of the gadgets worked. Mike marveled at how the flip side of the television became a chalkboard for meetings. Then Steven showed him how to load up the video game and they played a couple of rounds of *Starboard*. Once Michael figured out how to operate the controls and learned the object of the game, Steven didn't have a chance.

"Feel better?"

"A little."

"Good," Steven said, putting the game-controllers away. "Because we're here."

Time stopped as Michael turned to look out the window. This couldn't be right. An immaculately paved walkway wound toward the house and split off, encircling a splendid fountain that spewed forth its sprays in beautifully synchronized patterns. They stood in front of the grand mansion, which sat high behind the fountain with so many windows Michael didn't dare count them. The backdrop was a forest of greenery and fragrant florals that hinted at more finery beyond the ornate gates where the eyes could not see.

"Pratt, this is Michael Bagley. He will be staying here for a while," Steven said.

"At your service sir." Pratt nodded. He hoisted Michael's single bag onto his shoulder.

Steven chuckled. "You see," he said into Michael's ear, "It's not going to be as bad as you thought."

The enormous doors had already begun to swing open.

Michael's heart skipped as he expected to see the man in the photograph standing there. Instead, another gentleman, dressed in a white shirt and black slacks greeted them.

"Hey, Sloan," Steven called out. He led Michael into the great hall.

"They *live* here?" Michael whispered.

"Sure."

"This is bananas!"

They walked between two Herculean staircases that wound in opposite directions to a higher level, and entered another room. This one was large as well, but cozy and kindly decorated with a feminine touch. Fresh flowers filled vases and a fireplace stood invitingly against a wall. A thick, thirsty rug sucked at their feet as they walked. They met a closed door. As Steven knocked softly, Michael's legs quivered.

The man in the photograph opened the door, slowly at first. He greeted Steven but his gaze was on Michael.

This is my father, Michael thought as he looked at him.

"Welcome," Joe said as he opened the door wider to reveal the remaining occupants of the room. A pretty lady around the age of his mother sat on the arm of an oversized chair. Her face was tear-stained and drawn and she twisted a wad of tissues in her hands. A teenage boy, who couldn't have been much older than Michael, stood next to her and stroked her arm. Across the room, a teenage girl about Michael's age, an even prettier replica of the lady, sat behind a huge desk and swiveled gaily from side to side. When she saw Michael, she instantly ceased swiveling and smiled happily.

"I'll just leave you guys alone for a moment," Steven offered as he attempted to back out of the room.

Michael grabbed Steven by the shirt, pulling him toward him. Surprised, Steven quickly exchanged glances with Joe who nodded for Steven to stay.

Joe extended his hand to Michael who slowly accepted it. "I want you to meet my family, uh—your family." Joe turned to look at the pretty lady who quickly looked away to avoid his gaze. "This is my wife, Lydia."

Lydia nodded in Michael's direction. Then she swung around so that her back was to them.

"This is my son, David." Joe waved his hand in David's direction.

Without even an attempt at politeness, David dropped his head to the floor.

Joe's color deepened. He snapped his wrist at Leah without introducing her.

She jumped to her feet and sashayed toward Michael, offering her hand. "I'm Leah," she said, her smile glittering in her face.

Releasing Steven's shirt, Michael took the hand she offered.

She grinned broadly. "We're practically twins!" she drawled.

Her mother rose from her seat and excused herself, promptly leaving the room through a side door.

Joe sighed heavily. “Enough, Leah,” he said softly.

She reluctantly pulled her hand from Michael’s.

Michael smiled. If no one else, he figured he was going to like her.

“Can you leave us alone, please?”

They waited until Leah, David and Steven had all left the room. “Have a seat,” Joe said to Michael when they were alone.

“I’d rather stand if you don’t mind,” Michael said quietly, his head bowed.

Joe jammed his hands in his pockets and paced. After a few moments, he said, “I wanted to meet with you before, well, you know, this whole thing with the family…” Michael looked up at him, his eyes hopeful. “But, well, as I’m sure you can attest, this has been extremely difficult, especially on my wife.”

Michael was unimpressed. They lived surrounded by opulence while he spent nearly all of his life in worse than poverty, and he was supposed to feel sorry for them?

“But, I hope you will be comfortable here, and patient, as we try to get to know one another.”

Michael looked straight ahead, in defiance, at a family painting that hung over another huge fireplace.

Joe followed Michael’s line of vision to the picture and rose. “Let me show you around a bit.” He gestured for Michael to follow him. He led Michael from one grand room to another, from verandas to sun porches, through indoor art galleries and a ballroom where parties were held.

Weary from the week’s events and just plain old tired of having to endure the excess, Michael stopped in his tracks as they were about to enter the main kitchen.

Joe turned. “You okay?”

“Yeah,” Michael breathed, “just tired.”

“Oh, I’m sorry,” Joe blushed. “Look at me! I’m going on and on. You can see this stuff anytime. You’ll be here for awhile.”

The reminder sent a streak of pain through Michael’s chest and he longed for Steven’s comforting presence. “Is Steven—”

"Yes, he's still here." Joe sighed with annoyance. "He's in my office. Come on, I'll show you to your room."

They mounted the winding staircase, which seemed to either begin or end at several places throughout the spacious mansion, and walked down a long hall. Michael's bag was already inside the room. The furniture gleamed and the mirrors and crystal decanters shone. Michael walked over to a set of glass doors and looked out. A magnificent swimming pool stretched below him. Beyond the pool were tennis and basketball courts. Under different circumstances he would have been jumping up and down on the king-sized bed with glee. Instead he stood brooding. He turned from the view and walked across the room to inspect the private bath. He loved bathing, a luxury he struggled to obtain every day. He should have been happy.

"Good enough?" Joe asked.

He must be joking, Michael thought. Instead, he said, "Yes."

"Good. I'll leave you to your thoughts. Steven will be up shortly," Joe said before he turned and left.

Michael sat on the bed and tried to compose himself. How could he have gone from living under a bridge to living in a mansion in just a few short months? Everything anyone could possibly want, materially, was in that house except love and affection, not for him. He unzipped his bag and began to unpack his meager belongings. Michael carefully hung his three prized shirts in the otherwise empty walk-in closet. They looked scant and lonely, the way he felt.

Steven knocked on his bedroom door, and let himself in. "Anyone home?" he asked.

"Hey," Michael smiled in relief.

Steven sat on the bed beside him. "You'll be fine," he reassured him.

Michael shook his head. "They don't seem too happy to have me here."

"It's gonna take a minute," Steven reminded him, "but they're good people, don't give up."

Michael sighed heavily.

"Look," Steven reached over to the bedside table and pulled the phone closer to the two of them. "This is my home phone number on speed dial," he said as he pointed to a designated button on the phone, "this is my work number, and this is my cell," he said. "Call me anytime you need me.

Michael drew his knees up. "What now?"

"Well, I've got to push off—"

Michael pouted.

"Now, don't start!" Steven warned.

"I'm cool," Michael whispered and buried his face in a nearby pillow.

"I'll be back to check on you everyday."

Michael lifted his face from the pillow. "Do you think I could call my mother?"

"Sure, it's your phone," Steven said, smiling. He chucked Michael under the chin. "Be good," he ordered and disappeared behind the door.

Chapter Eight

"Lydia and David were awful," Joe said.

"Well, Joe, what do you expect?" Chachi replied. He was running late for an early-morning appointment.

"I just don't know what I'm gonna do. I feel so disconnected from this kid. I think I'd feel something if he were really my son.... What do you think?"

"Who am I to say?" Chachi was struggling to clasp his Rolex while holding the phone between his ear and shoulder. A car was waiting for him; he hoped this call wouldn't be long.

Joe sighed. "Maybe I'm overreacting."

"Maybe not. Have him retested."

"How would I explain that?"

"What's to explain?"

"What do I say? 'Uh, Michael, we need to draw some more blood for some routine testing?' This kid is no dummy."

"Yep." Chachi had managed the rolex and was now shrugging into his jacket. "That's exactly what you say. Have Jake do it during a routine physical. He probably hasn't had a physical since he was born. It would make sense for you to set him up for one. He won't suspect a thing." He glanced at the advancing time on his watch. "At least you'd be sure. Not to say anything against Steven, but who knows what Sarah might have pulled to get those test results to go in her favor?"

"Okay. I'll do it. I'll talk to Jake."

* * * *

"I was hoping you'd come down for breakfast today."

Nearly a week had passed and Michael had spent nearly all of his time in his room.

Michael shrugged.

"You'll never feel comfortable around us if you don't come out of this room," Joe continued. "I was hoping that, by next weekend, you'd feel secure enough around us for me to invite more of the family over, you know, like my parents—and you have aunts, uncles, and cousins."

A panic swept over Michael.

"Okay…twenty minutes," Joe said. "Then I want you downstairs with the rest of us."

The breakfast room was adjacent to the kitchen and enclosed on three sides in glass. Outside, trees and flowers were being tended to by several members of the staff. Lilac trees and orange blossoms stood in breathtaking clusters. Michael paused a moment to take it in.

"Have a seat." Joe pulled out a chair next to him, jolting Michael from his trance.

David sat buttering a piece of toast and chatting with his mother, who sat next to him staring into her omelette.

Maxi, the head housekeeper, arrived. She was a heavy set, round-faced woman with smiling eyes. She sat a plate down in front of—now who was that?

"Hi, I'm Eric." Eric offered his hand to Michael for a handshake. He didn't smile either, but he seemed a lot more pleasant than David.

"Eric's here nearly as much as my own children," Joe joked.

"So what do you like to do?" Eric asked.

"I don't know." Michael shrugged. "What do you do around here?"

"You play ball?" Eric asked.

"Basketball," Michael answered.

"What about tennis?"

"Naw,"

"Golf?"

"Nope."

"Chess?"

Michael shook his head.

"I'll teach you," Eric offered.

"So, Michael," Joe said, "we're going to have to talk about your education."

Here it comes. He wouldn't be able to recall the last time he was in school if he had to.

David promptly stood up, took a swig of his skim milk, and excused himself. "I'll leave you geniuses to your limited conversation." He scoffed as he grabbed a newspaper from the table and left.

"You know you have to go to school," Joe went on, "so we'll work on getting that ball rolling."

Michael sulked as he nibbled on a piece of toast. Joe pushed his plate away and Maxi appeared on cue.

"Let's go play video games!" Eric exclaimed as he also pushed away from the breakfast table and bounded toward the recreation room. Michael had to move quickly to catch up.

"You didn't excuse yourselves…" Joe called uselessly after them.

"What games are you good at?" Eric asked as he settled into one of the cushiony game chairs in front of the big screen dedicated to the video gaming system.

"I played *Starboard*," Mike said, taking the seat next to him, "but I learn fast."

"Cool." Eric started up the gaming system. "That's the hottest game out." After explaining a few basic rules to Michael, they were laughing and going at it like they'd known one another for years. "Owww! You killed me!" Eric howled placing his hands on his forehead in disbelief. "Nobody beats me at *Starboard!* Nobody!"

Michael beamed proudly.

Michael turned to find Leah standing over him, leaning on the back of his chair.

"Leah's a big flirt," Eric said reading Michael's expression. "But she's harmless. As soon as Chachi gets back home, she'll be back up in his ass again."

"Shut up!" She slapped Eric's head.

"Here, do this for me," David said as he approached Leah, holding out his arm so that she could clasp the links on his cuffs.

"What are you getting all dowdied up for?" she asked.

"Marcy will be here in a moment. We're taking the boat out," David said stuffily before leaving the room.

"What's in his ass?" Michael asked Eric.

Eric laughed. "He's an asshole, yes; but he's really insecure, especially now with this whole thing involving you."

"I think I have more rights to be insecure than he does."

"Well, I don't know." Eric lifted a brow. "When Steven told Uncle Joe about you, he and Aunt Lydia fought viciously for three days. No one was talking to us, so me, Leah, and David decided to pay a visit to Steven to see if he could tell us anything."

"What'd he say?"

"He said you looked a lot like your mother and Uncle Joe. That got David mad right off."

Michael snorted. "That's not my fault!"

"Doesn't matter to David," Eric said with a shrug. "Then to add fuel to the fire, we found out you were Uncle Joe's namesake!" He leaned into Michael and whispered, "And that you have the ancestral trait like this." He pulled down his collar and showed Michael his birthmark. It was the familiar dollar sign, much like Michael's, only fainter and a bit larger.

"But you have it too!" Michael breathed in astonishment.

"Lots of us have it. David doesn't. To find out his illegitimate brother has the mark and the namesake too! David would have you burned at the stake if he could." No wonder David seemed to hate him so passionately.

* * * *

Eric and Michael were becoming great friends. On the other hand, David and Michael were becoming great enemies. David used every opportunity he got to let Michael know he was not welcome. They didn't last ten minutes in a room together without a heated argument over one thing or another.

Michael had received his regular plainly wrapped package from Sarah and had gone to his room to eagerly open it. He threw aside the bottle of pills Sarah sent him monthly and dug through the box filler past books and CDs from Pooch until, finally, he uncovered the carton of cigarettes. He had run out and was almost crazy for a smoke. He ripped open the package and pulled one of the slender stems from the pack. Then he searched the box for matches and, after striking one and placing the flame carefully to the cigarette, leaned back against the bed on the floor and inhaled deeply, savoring the nicotine rush. He turned to see Joe standing in his doorway. David stood close by, his arms folded across his chest, a smirk on his face.

"Give me those!" Joe ordered, advancing on him.

"No." Michael shook his head. The cigarette dangled from his mouth.

"Don't say *no* to me!" Joe bellowed, "Give me the goddamn cigarettes!"

Michael slowly handed Joe the pack. He tried to take one last pull off the one in his mouth before handing it over, but Joe almost hit him in the face, yanking it from him.

"All of them!" Joe demanded, holding his hand out.

Reluctantly, Michael handed him his entire precious carton of smokes. "I need them," he begged.

Joe ignored him and started toward the door.

David giggled softly in secret provocation.

"I'll quit!" Michael called desperately after them, "but I can't go cold-turkey! Just one cigarette—"

Joe spun around angrily and pointed the cigarette in Michael's face. "I guess I failed to relay the rules of this house to you," he said, his voice chilly. "There will be no smoking of anything, no drinking of alcohol, no drugs, no sex, no pornography, and no lies under my roof!"

Michael drew himself up. He looked wildly from Joe to David. A rash of obscenities crossed his mind. "You were spying on me!" he charged David. "Is there no privacy around here!"

Joe glared at David, who blinked innocently. "He was smoking! Anyone could smell it! Who has to spy?"

"Lucky for you, this is serious enough for me not to pursue that right now," Joe said to David, "but if I ever hear of you invading anyone's privacy in this house again, you'll wish you hadn't."

"I hate this place!" Michael shouted. "You don't care about me!"

"David, go to your room until I summon you." Joe shoved David gently.

"I'm sixteen years old, Dad!" David protested.

"Michael, I suggest you stay here and cool off." Joe took David by the arm and ushered him to the door.

"You've fucked with me for the last time, you punk!" Michael yelled after David.

Joe dropped David's arm and turned to Michael. "Don't you use that language in my house."

"You used it on me!"

"This is *my* house!" Joe shouted. He took in short breaths.

Michael stared angrily at David, "You've fucked with me for the last time," he repeated, red-faced and hyperventilating.

"Go to your room," Joe told David again. This time, David wasted no time getting out of there.

Joe walked over to Michael. "Don't you ever threaten a member of this household. If you ever put your hands on my son—" Regretfully, Joe snapped his mouth shut.

"I hate you!" Michael snarled. He needed to get out of there. The arrangement had become toxic and somebody had better do something…fast.

Chapter Nine

"I think Michael needs to be removed from the house." Joe sat in his office on the phone with Steven.

"You know what will happen to him if he leaves your custody," Steven reminded him. "He'll be incarcerated and God knows what will happen to him then."

"I can't help that," Joe replied. "He threatened David."

"I meant to talk to you about David, Joe. Michael's been complaining to me for days now about how David provokes him."

"Don't put this off on David!" Joe snapped. "They've both been at each other. I tried to play referee and Daddy and all that, but the game's over when the threats start flying."

"Well, they've been threatening each other. Kids do that. That doesn't mean—"

"This boy shot his father. Let's not forget that!"

"*You're* his father! Don't forget *that*!" Steven countered.

Joe sat breathing heavily into the phone.

Steven sighed. "Okay. Maybe he can stay with me for a few days."

"Well, that's a start," Joe muttered.

"Is the therapy working at all?" Steven asked in a calmer tone.

"I can't tell," Joe answered, "but I can't wait for it to kick in. I can't tolerate his threats. You should've seen his face, his eyes were venomous! David is scared to death."

"Give me a couple days to change some things around and I'll come get him until things cool down," Steven promised.

"Good."

"One thing though."

"Yeah?"

"Michael tells me some guy came to his room and drew blood from him. What was that for?"

Joe hesitated. "Um. I hired a private service. I'm having the paternity test redone."

"Why?" Steven shouted. "Don't you trust me?"

"Its not that," Joe insisted, "mistakes happen. I just want to be sure, that's all. If I've got to deal with this mess, I want to be sure it's my problem. I don't want just a mere blood test. I want DNA evidence!"

"He's not a fool, you know. He knows what you're doing. Although I can't say he isn't as anxious as you and David are to find out that he doesn't belong to this family.

Joe closed his eyes and inhaled through his nose. "I'm sorry, Steven. I don't want to hurt him, really. He's a nice kid, but I don't want him to hurt David either. I'm sorry this isn't working out. I know you did what you did out of the goodness of your heart, but its not working."

"It's okay." Steven sighed. "I've got to fly out for a couple of days to see a witness in the McKinner case. Once I return, I'll pick him up. Then we can talk about what's next."

"I'm getting the hell out of here tonight. If I don't somebody's gonna get hurt."

"Mike, please calm down," Sarah tried to console her son.

"I feel like they're setting me up, Ma. When I stay in my room, he makes me come out. When I come out, David's there to terrorize me. If he doesn't want me here, he should just let me go. I'll take my chances."

"He owes you this, and more!" Sarah spat. "How dare he! How *dare* he!"

Michael paused for breath. His hands were trembling. "Can you just come get me?" he whimpered.

"I don't have the money, honey, and I can't violate a court order. I talked to Steven; he's leaving for a short trip, but he promised me he'd take care of it. Just ignore David in the meantime."

"Ignore!"

"Please, honey, at least until I can speak to Joe and find out what is on his fuckin' mind!" Sarah sighed. "He hasn't accepted one of my calls since you've been there. Can you believe that? He has *my* son, and he won't even talk to me!"

"I'll just…I'm gonna have to leave, then."

"Don't leave, Michael, don't you dare do that! If the police pick you up, or anything happens, you're in more trouble than you started with! Just—just wait for Steven, okay? Do you have a direct line for Joe? I can start there."

* * * *

Michael continued to stay in his room, hoping Steven would arrive soon. Eric and Leah were his only welcome visitors. He had his bag packed and ready to go. Something would change today. The thought made him anxious and he paced back and forth across his bedroom floor.

Eric knocked on the door and stuck his head inside. "Can I come in?" he asked. "What's going on?" Eric looked at the duffle bag waiting near the door.

"I'm outta here, that's what."

"You *leaving*?" Eric asked, his brow creased. "Since when?"

"Steven should be here any time now. I just wanna be ready." He instinctively felt his pant pocket. "Shit! I need a cigarette!"

"So, where're you going?" Eric asked.

"Anywhere. I don't know. Maybe Steven'll let me crash with him for a while." His hand went again to his pocket to no avail. Michael moaned and stood up. "Aw man, I just wanna go *home*!"

"What's this?" Leah walked in and noticed Michael's packed bag. "You're leaving?" Michael didn't answer, but she ran to him and put her arms around him. "Oh, don't leave—you can't leave! It's gonna be okay!"

He managed a weak smile for her.

"A family meeting is what we need!" Eric proclaimed. "We can all sit down together and talk this out. Uncle Joe needs to know that David has issues!"

"Uncle Joe threatened to kill me over his precious David," Michael stated, his eyes blazing.

Leah sighed. "Well. We have to do something. Maybe if Eric and I talk to him. David's always been able to fool Daddy, but enough is enough!" She stuck her lower lip out. "You just got here, you can't leave!" she whined.

The phone rang. Michael ran to it.

"That little shit!" Sarah screeched. "He hung up on me!"

"Who?" Michael asked.

"I called the number you gave me and respectfully asked to speak to Joe, right? Why did that little bastard ask me how I got the number? Like it was any of his business!"

"Who, ma?"

"I oughta hop a plane right now and go beat the crap out of him! I see what you mean now, honey! I don't want you there anymore!"

"Ma, what are you talking about? Who hung up on you?"

"David! I asked to speak to Joe and he told me he couldn't take my call, and just hung up on me—"

Michael dropped the phone and headed for the door.

"Uh, Oh," Eric muttered. He and Leah scurried after him.

"What's going on?" Leah asked as they descended the staircase. Michael ignored the both of them.

"Look man, this is just ridiculous!" Eric put his hand on Michael's shoulder but, with a shake, Michael sent him sailing down several stairs before Eric was able to stop his fall by grabbing hold to the banister railing.

Michael searched rooms, kicking doors open, until he found David in Joe's study, reading an investment magazine. David spun around in surprise.

"You hung up on my mother, you little prick?" Michael growled.

"Wha....?"

Michael's fist made contact with David's jaw, knocking him backward out of his chair.

"Daaaad! Daaaad!" Leah shrieked.

Michael grabbed David by his shirt collar and punched him over and over again.

Eric made a fruitless attempt to separate them before Joe and Dominick came rushing from the adjoining office.

David's shirt was already splattered with the blood oozing from his nose and mouth when Joe reached them.

"Stop it!" Joe demanded. He wrapped his arm around Michael's neck and attempted to pull him away from David. He underestimated Michael's strength and all three of them went toppling forward.

Dominick wedged his body between the two boys to help separate them. It finally worked.

"What is your problem?" Joe yelled at Michael.

"Fuck you too!" Michael spat at him.

Joe touched his hand to his face and watched the wet stuff drip down his finger in disbelief. "He did not just spit on me..." he said, his eyes widening then shrinking as his face darkened.

"I hate all of you!" Michael shouted. His chest heaved, his eyes were red with anger. "You think you're gonna treat my mother like a piece of shit, you good-for-nothing, stuck up—"

Joe dived on top of Michael.

They tussled on the floor before Michael twisted from underneath his father. He sprang to his feet with the agility of youth, fist raised and ready.

Joe stood too, aghast with shock. "*How dare* you," he snarled, seething with anger.

Eric, Leah, and David huddled behind Dominick, watching helplessly.

"Oh, you're a man now?" Joe challenged Michael, his chest laboring. "You think you're man enough to take me, Michael? Cause if you think so, let me know, and I'll beat your ass like a man!"

"I swear," Michael panted, "you hit me, I'll kill you."

Joe slapped Michael's face with a force that sent him reeling.

Michael responded with a right hook, grazing Joe's chin. Stunned, Joe cradled his face. He's dealing with no ordinary boy.

Michael darted across the room and headed for the stairs as soon as Dominick was able to detain Joe.

Joe shook himself from Dominick's grip. Leah ran for the phone.

Michael raced for his bedroom, attempting to push the door closed behind him, but Joe was already at the threshold. Using his foot and shoulder, Joe pushed his way in, slamming and locking the door behind him.

Michael retreated to one side of the bed, Joe the other, out of breath, gazes locked.

Outside the door, Lydia and Dominick pleaded with Joe.

"So, whatcha think now, Michael?"

Michael's shoulder's sagged. "Just leave me alone!" he pleaded.

Joe lunged across the king-sized bed and grabbed him.

"What's wrong?" Joe asked, his face distorted and close, his breath coming fast. "Something wrong?"

Michael shook his head frantically.

"Oh, you've decided you don't wanna be a man now, huh? C'mon Mike, make up your mind! You're a man or a boy!"

Michael shut his eyes tight and lowered his head.

A key turned in the door.

Joe yelled, "*Don't come in here*!" He turned back to Michael. "I didn't hear you."

"I'm not a man," Michael whispered, humiliated. He just wanted it to stop. This dude had gone mad.

"Oh, now I hear you," Joe's eyes were shining. "You're a boy now. Good." He shoved the boy onto the bed and unbuckled his belt, removing it from his pants loops. "Now I'll just beat your ass like a boy."

Joe sat in his office and swiveled in his chair. He could hear the commotion outside his door. Lydia, crying, begged for him to come out.

Jake's voice trailed toward the staircase. More muffled voices, then Dominick was at the door making his appeal.

Joe knew he screwed up. He was upset with himself for losing control; but he was not crazy and he knew he had not done enough harm to cause Michael any permanent damage. The phone on his desk rang. He figured it was Chachi or maybe Sarah, or whoever. It didn't matter. He was going to handle this his way. It wasn't until Steven showed up, furiously banging on the door, that he decided to emerge.

"Come out you crazy mutherfucker! You coward!" Steven shouted.

Joe yanked the door open. Steven stared at Joe with rage-inflamed eyes. Joe leaned casually against the frame.

"You beat that little boy like *that*?" Steven yelled.

Joe waved a hand at Steven. "He'll be okay." He turned back into his office.

Steven stormed in behind him. "Okay? Are you crazy? That boy is up there hanging by a thread! You almost killed him!"

"Bullshit." Joe walked over to his desk and sat down. "If I was trying to kill him, he'd be dead."

"You think this is a game, don't you?" Steven bent over Joe's desk to meet his face.

"What's your *point*, Steven?"

"My *point*? I'll show you my point!"

Dominick and Jake had come in quietly. Steven had almost run the two of them down storming out of the office.

"Where are you going?" Dominick grabbed Steven's arm.

"I'm taking him out of here!"

"Don't you touch him!" Joe shouted. Steven turned to look at him. "He's my son, and I say don't touch him!"

Steven breathed deeply. "I'll file a motion in the morning to have this child snatched from you so fast it'll make you dizzy!"

"Do what you have to do," Joe warned. "But don't you touch him."

Steven spun around, but Jake blocked his path.

"Wait a minute!" Jake pleaded. "Joe, what's going on?"

Joe exhaled. "I know I lost it." He shot a hot glance in Steven's direction.

"But I've got it under control now."

"You need to see a doctor!" Steven charged.

"*I* need to see a doctor?" Joe flushed. "The boy spit on me! Spit! And he punched the fuck out of my face!" Joe turned his head to the side to display a bruised chin. "And yes, I beat his mother-fuckin' ass; and nobody is gonna come into my house and tell me how to raise my kids—not you," he pointed at Steven, "not the judge, not the police!"

"You're sick!" Steven shouted.

"Is he gonna be okay, Jake?" Joe asked as coolly as if he were asking about the weather.

"He's got a bloody nose and some cuts as well as some bruising. He'll be sore but he'll be okay," Jake said.

"Good." Though Joe smiled, his eyes did not. "See?" he said turning to Steven with a sneer. "Now get the *fuck* out of my house!"

Chapter Ten

Three days passed since Joe put Michael on his back. The house had become like a convent where everyone walked softly and peered at Joe suspiciously. Joe and Steven hadn't spoken since, and Joe refused to return anyone's calls.

In court as scheduled, Joe appealed to the judge to postpone a decision on visitation until the family could work through some issues.

"I think I should go back to work," Joe broke the silence at breakfast. He had taken a leave of absence from the production company he and Chachi owned and operated together when he learned that he would have to take custody of Michael.

Lydia looked up at him from her eggs. "Why now?"

"Well," Joe said with a sigh. "It'll give me something to do. Take my mind off things."

David and Leah exchanged uneasy glances.

"Look," Joe said, "I'm sorry this happened. I didn't want to hurt Michael like that. I lost it. I've admitted that. But I can't say that I wouldn't do it again under the same circumstances. Michael is a member of this family, like it or not, and you're going to learn to accept that," he pointed at David, "and so are you," he said to his wife, who nodded.

"He's not eating, sir." Maxi appeared in the doorway. "Doc told me to let him know if he didn't take food today. I thought I'd let you know too."

Joe wiped his mouth and dropped his napkin on his plate as he rose from the table.

Lydia pleaded, "Joe…"

"I'm not gonna hurt him," Joe exclaimed. "What do you think I am? I just want to see about him." He left the kitchen and climbed the stairs to Michael's room with Maxi close behind.

Michael lay on his side with his face buried in a pillow.

Joe pulled a chair up to his bed. "Michael," he called softly.

Michael's breathing picked up.

"Come on, I want to talk to you." Joe pulled at the pillow. "I'm not gonna hurt you." He pulled until Michael relinquished the pillow. "Hey." He put his hand out to touch his face. Michael recoiled.

You wanted him to fear you, Joe thought, *now he's afraid of you*. He understood how the boy felt. His own father was a strict disciplinarian and Joe was most often the target of his anger and disappointment. He grew up with an innate fear of finding himself the recipient of his wrath. He promised himself he would not be so hard on his own children. But every now and then, he was ashamed to say, he saw his father in himself. "I'm sorry," he whispered sincerely.

Michael turned his face away.

Joe shut his eyes tight. "We'll get through this, okay?" He clasped the boy's hand. "Michael, look at me."

Reluctantly, Michael turned to face him.

"I know you don't feel like it, but you have to eat." Joe wiped perspiration from Michael's brow. Michael winced with each touch. "Maxi tells me you haven't eaten." He reached for a bowl on a nearby nightstand. "Is this what you prepared for him, Maxi?"

"Yes, sir. That's a soup I made for him. Doc says not to give him anything too rich until he starts to eat regularly."

Joe picked up a spoon and dipped it into the soup. "Here, take a little," he urged, "just two spoonfuls and I'll leave you alone."

Michael buried his face in his arm.

Joe sighed. "Is he at least drinking something, Maxi?"

"I don't know sir. I haven't seen him drink anything. He's got to be going to the bathroom, though, or he'd be getting sick by now."

"Okay," Joe said and stood. "Mike, I'll leave this here," he returned the bowl of soup to the tray, "hopefully, you'll eat a little later. But if you don't, Michael, I'm not gonna let you lay here and try to kill yourself."

Maxi's brow crinkled with worry. "Doc said I should call him if he doesn't eat."

"Don't worry about that, Max," Joe said as Michael covered his head with his pillow. "I'll call him."

Joe's nights had become sleepless, throwing his whole schedule off. He'd come home from the office exhausted, fall asleep at about 8:00, only to wake up again around midnight. He'd walk through the house like a ghost, checking on the kids. He'd eat, read, listen to music, or look over work papers, anything to keep him occupied until sleep claimed him again at around 5 or 6 o'clock the next morning, an hour or two before he was scheduled to get up again. He still hadn't spoken to Steven. He finally broke down and called Chachi when he threatened to drop everything and come home. Chachi made him promise he'd get help for his violent outbursts. Actually, that wasn't a bad idea.

When Maxi called Joe at the office to alert him that Michael still had not touched his food, Joe called on Jake to help him make a last-ditch effort at putting an end to his hunger strike.

Jake met Joe at the house and they barged in on Michael with two nursing assistants and hospital equipment in tow. Mike sat up, mouth gaping at the sight of them.

"You see this, Michael?" Joe held a tube in his hand. "This is a feeding tube. This gets shoved down your throat and into your belly and we force food into your body with it." Michael swallowed hard. "This," Joe grabbed the nursing assistant's wrist to display a bag of clear liquid she was holding, "is an I.V. pouch. With it, we will force liquids into your system and this," he held up a smaller device, "is a catheter. This we poke into your—"

"Wait—wait!" Michael begged. "Okay! I-I'll eat!"

"I don't want to keep playing the bad guy," Joe said softly, "I'm *trying*, Michael."

Michael's mouth turned down as he rolled his eyes away.

Jake walked over and put his hand on Michael's shoulder. "Here, lay back. This won't hurt," he said nudging Michael backwards onto his pillow.

"I-I-I thought…"

"You're dehydrated," Jake explained. "I think you still need the I.V."

That was a week ago. Although Michael was getting stronger physically, he was becoming emotionally detached and depressed. Was it too late for them?

* * * *

Upstairs in his room, Michael stuffed the last of his paltry wardrobe into his old faithful duffle bag. He had known the day Joe beat him that he had to leave. Images of Jaye's bloody face kept looming into his head. He didn't need any more Jayes.

He waited patiently for just the right time. He overheard Maxi and Jory, head of house security, discussing weaknesses at the south gate. Apparently, one of their new apprentices had problems staying awake during the night watch.

He tip-toed down the stairs toward his exit. He made it to the breakfast room door and fumbled with the latch in the dark. The strap of his bag kept sliding down his arm so he set the bag on the floor.

"I'll hold that for you."

Startled, Michael swung around. The voice came from the breakfast table.

The silhouette stood and walked toward him. "Going somewhere?" Joe asked, his voice tranquil.

Michael's blood turned to ice. His new father was the only person he could ever remember being afraid of in his life. He watched the power he wielded with the courts, the police, his family, even his friends.

Joe's face shone in the moonlight. "There's no chance of reconciliation?" he asked softly, his dark eyes sad.

Michael looked down at his father's slippered feet and shook his head.

Joe sighed heavily. "I made a mistake, Michael," he said. "I think we've both learned some lessons, don't you? You're a part of this family, like it or not, and I want to keep it together. Now that you're here, we will never be the same again without you."

Michael shifted restlessly. He sucked in his bottom lip and looked away.

"Come on. I say we try again."

Michael gathered his nerve and looked Joe squarely in the face. Joe looked soft, yet regal standing in his robe with his hands in the pockets. The moon illuminated him with a celestial light. Mike wished it had been different. To be a part of a real family— "No. I can't," Michael said.

Joe looked away briefly. Michael picked up his bag.

"Let me at least have someone escort you to where you're going," Joe insisted. "Can you wait until daylight?"

Nothing.

"You know what will happen if you get picked up, don't you?" Joe asked.

A wave of panic swept across Michael's face.

"No, I'm not going to call the authorities," Joe assured him, "but as soon as they find out you're not here…" Still nothing. "Okay." Joe exhaled. "I'll let security know you'll be leaving." He undid the latch and pulled the sliding door open. "You know where I am if you need me."

Eric charged into the breakfast room where the family was mulling over the first meal of the day. "He's not there!" Lydia dropped her fork. "Michael's not in his room."

Leah gasped. David looked at his father. Joe continued with his breakfast, appearing neither shocked nor surprised.

"Oh my God, Joe!" Lydia exclaimed.

"He left before daylight this morning," Joe said, his voice composed.

"And you let him go?" his daughter cried.

"I couldn't keep him," Joe explained. "I hope that by letting him go, he'll come back on his own."

"What'll happen to him?" David asked.

"I don't know." Joe averted his gaze to maintain his composure. "They'll eventually pick him up and he'll probably go to a foster home."

"Or to jail!" Leah gasped. Joe's silence confirmed her statement. "Oh, Daddy, *no*!" she wailed.

"Joe, you need to fix this!" Lydia scolded him.

"Well, this is a turn of events!" he snapped. "Fine time for the family to become *supportive*!" He tossed his napkin angrily onto the table. "Excuse me," he mumbled and left them.

Joe called into the office and retracted his early return from family leave. Why couldn't they just go back to where they were before Michael appeared on their doorstep? He spent all that day and the next looking out of windows and grabbing the telephone.

Another night fell. In his study, he gazed at the phone. Taking several deep breaths, he dialed Steven's number. If his friend was mad at him before, he'd be furious after finding out that he let Michael run away.

"Steven?"

"Yeah,"

"Don't be angry when I ask you this. Have you heard from Michael?"

Silence. "How long has he been gone?"

"He left early yesterday morning. I thought maybe he'd have called someone by now."

"Not me. Maybe he called Sarah. Let me call her," he said. "I'll call you back."

Joe's tension mounted when he learned that Sarah had not heard from Michael either. Her calls to his cousin Pooch also turned up nothing.

She called Joe screaming and crying, blaming him for everything. He let her. But bad became worse when she informed him that she had called the police.

"Do you know what this means Sarah?" he asked her. "If he's caught, he's going to jail. Is that what you want?"

"It's no worse than the jail he's running from!"

He had Steven contact a private detective. They had to find Michael before the police did. Steven waited with him until detective Hardy showed up. Joe was surprised at how inattentive he had been. He had heard news reports where parents could describe what a missing kid was wearing from windbreaker to socks. He could not.

After the detective gathered all the information he could and had gone, Joe walked over to the window and looked out. What if something terrible had happened?

Steven touched Joe's hand.

"I'm sorry!" Joe blurted, as if Steven's touch had yanked the words from him. Steven was a dear friend simply trying to do what was best and he had made him pay for it.

"We'll find him," Steven said.

Sloan handed Joe a package. "This came for you, sir, while you were busy with the gentleman."

"Thank you, Sloan," he said eyeing it intently. "It says 'Lab Results' on the cover," he said to Steven.

"The DNA results," Steven said.

Joe ripped into the package and scanned the document. He was said to be, with 99.999% certainty, the father of Michael Bagley. He sank into a nearby chair.

"Hey," Steven consoled him, "We knew this already."

"You know what I've done?" he cried. "I've taken it all out on him. Everything I felt about Sarah, the guilt I had every time I looked at my wife and kids—I took it out on him! You were right, man, I'm a coward."

"I don't see a coward now." Steven smiled at him. "Look at me." He put his hand on Joe's shoulder. "I see a loving father. I see my best friend, my brother, and I knew he'd come back."

* * * *

Nearly a week and still no word from Michael. Between private detectives and the police, no one was able to turn up anything.

Joe's brother John, Eric's father, who was also his nearest neighbor, called one evening.

"What's up, brother?" John greeted him.

"Hey. How was your trip?"

"Profitable. I picked up three stations for the price of one."

"So I read," Joe responded. His brother was into radio and TV stations and was making a mint buying fledgling properties, reviving them, and re-selling them for big bucks.

"You okay?" John asked. "You sound weird. How're things working out with the new kid?"

"You've been talking to Eric."

"Eric hasn't told me anything," John assured him. "I'm your brother, remember? I can tell when something's wrong. I just took a shot in the dark, that's all."

"Well, we ran into a bump in the road, but we'll get there."

"That's to be expected," John said. "It's tough enough dealing with a kid you've known from birth. I can only imagine trying to get into the head of one already fourteen years old."

"Yeah."

"Hey, look," John said. "Mutton got out again. The Brightons called Meg and said she ripped up some of their hyacinths. We sent someone over, but she had moved on already." John's dog was notorious for wreaking havoc on the neighborhood landscape. If Mutton hadn't been respected as John Simpson's furry best friend, she'd have been shot ages ago.

"Why don't you keep that beast on a leash?" Joe frowned.

"If you see her around, call us, will you?"

"Sure."

"Oh, and good luck with the boy."

Night in and night out, Joe awakened and walked the house, sipping his cup of tea, brooding. One night, he slipped quietly into Michael's room. He saw no trace of him, as if he had never been there. He sat on the bed and picked up one of the pillows, squeezing it to his chest.

He picked up the phone and leafed through the caller identification system. Sarah Bagley, Gherri Wells, Sarah Bagley, Steven Doyle, Unknown, Melanie Bagley… He paused. Melanie Bagley. Joe dialed the number. Just as he was about to hang up, a sleepy female voice answered.

"I am so sorry to call your house at this time of night—"

"Who is this?" Melanie interrupted his apologies. She didn't appear to be very friendly.

"I'm sorry. I'm Joe Simpson." He paused. "Michael's father?"

"Oh." Melanie let out a long breath.

"Michael's been missing for a few days."

"We've heard."

"I was wondering if, maybe there's something we've missed that your son can fill in for us."

"Pooch," Melanie offered.

"Pooch." A ridiculous name that sounded ridiculous coming out of his mouth.

"He hasn't heard from him."

"Perhaps not, but there may be something he can provide that could help us…do you mind, please?" he asked.

"Well—it *is* late…"

"I'll try not to keep him too long."

"Hold on." Melanie put the phone down. A short while later, a young man's voice came in over the line.

"Hi, Pooch," Joe said awkwardly.

"Todd," Pooch corrected him.

"Todd. Yes. I'm Joe Simpson."

"I know."

"Todd, you haven't heard from your cousin, have you?"

"No," Pooch whispered quickly.

Joe exhaled sharply. "Would you tell me if you had?"

"I don't think so."

"I know what you're thinking and you're right," Joe said. "We had a terrible time and I'm ashamed of it. But I think we can work it out. If you know anything—"

"I already told Mr. Doyle about some of the types of places he likes to hide out."

"What about his friends? Is there anyone else he would contact?

"No."

They said nothing to one another for a while before Joe broke the silence. "We didn't make him feel very welcomed, but when he comes home, and I know he will, I want to know a little something about him to help us catch up. Can you help me, Todd?"

Pooch inhaled slowly. "Well… he comes off rough around the edges, but he's really not."

Joe recalled some of Michael's angry antics. He'd say he was rough more than around the edges.

"He talks a lot of smack to protect himself, you know, on the streets."

Joe listened intently.

"Smart as a whip too," Pooch continued. "Can't get him to stay in school worth a damn, but he helps me with my homework, and I'm in high school."

"I can tell." Joe smiled.

"On the street, they say he's got the punch of death." Pooch laughed. "You got a chance as long as you don't let him hit you."

"I can believe that too," Joe said, massaging his chin where Michael's punch had grazed him. "What are his favorite things?"

"He'll sit for hours watching a tree or a squirrel or the sky. He took care of every stray animal he met. He could barely feed himself. And he loves gardening. He'd put weeds in vases and give them to his mom, anything that had blooms. One time he brought her poison ivy. We were scratching for a week."

Joe laughed. "What did he ask for at Christmas?"

"He doesn't really do Christmas," Pooch answered. "He sort of disappears during the holidays. When he was younger, he asked for things. Like one year he wanted that train set with the train station and all the houses and stuff. He wanted a bicycle, and he loves anything musical, instruments, CDs, anything. After a while, he just stopped asking."

"You really know a lot about him, huh?"

"Michael is the most interesting person I know. I plan to write my college thesis on him. I've been video taping him since the beginning."

"No kidding." Joe sat up straight.

"Sure."

"You mean you have film of when he was a baby and everything?"

"Well, when he was a baby, I wasn't much more than a baby myself; but my mom had an ancient camera and she used to tape stuff all the time...before she became weird and stopped doing anything but go to church. I can make some copies for you if you want me to."

"Pooch…that would be wonderful!" The words caught in his throat.

"Then it's done."

"Pooch, thanks for everything," Joe said.

"Okay. I'll send you that stuff," Pooch promised before they hung up.

That night, Joe decided to take the medicine Jake prescribed to help him get to sleep.

* * * *

Another night found Joe sitting in his usual chair at the breakfast table in the dark, long after everyone else had retired. He sipped his nightly cup of tea and looked out the window at the sleeping flowers. They were beginning to shrivel in aniticipation of fall.

A flash of lightening illuminated the garden, followed by a crack of thunder. Joe wondered if Michael was someplace dry. Another flash lit up the sky and the sleeping flowers were rocked by the wind's momentum.

The next clap of thunder startled Joe. Uneasy, he flicked the light on. Sheets of rain fell heavily against the glass doors and windows that separated the breakfast room from its attached sun porch. Then he saw another flash of light, only this one was different from both the lightening and the moonlight. He moved to get a better look. A dog barked. His cell phone rang in his bathrobe pocket.

Who would be calling him at 2 o'clock in the morning?

"Hello Mr. Simpson, it's me, Jory."

"Oh, hi Jory." Joe relaxed. "I didn't know you were working the night shift."

"Yes, sir. We had to let the young man go that was covering the south gate, so I'm picking up the slack until we find someone reliable."

"That's thoughtful of you, Jory."

"That's me with the flashlight, sir. I saw your light on and figured you were up mulling around again. Didn't want you to be worried."

Joe smiled. Evidently, he was the gossip of the household staff. "I appreciate that, Jory."

"Looks like that damned dog's gotten onto the property again…your brother's dog."

"Yeah," Joe said. "He told me she was on the loose." Mutton barked furiously. "Can you put her in the garage when you catch her, Jory?"

"Sure thing sir...whoa!" Jory shouted. Mutton growled viciously.

"What happened, Jory?"

"The damn dog almost bit me! She's going after something…" Jory's voice faded in and out as if he were running. "I think she's after something under the porch, sir." In the background the Scottish Terrier barked then growled deep within her throat. "Probably a rabbit or something—don't you worry about it though, sir. I just wanted you to know it was me knocking around out here, not some intruder."

"Thanks Jory," Joe said absentmindedly as he hung up. He stood in the window and watched Jory's shadow grapple with Mutton's.

"Come on, dog! Come on!" Jory shouted. But Mutton would not be deterred and Joe became suspicious.

He trotted to his office and retrieved a small revolver he kept locked inside his desk drawer. When he returned, Jory had Mutton muzzled and leashed, dragging her away from the porch. Defiant, Mutton's feet sank deep into the mud. Man and dog were soaking wet. But Mutton kept trying to get at something under the porch. Joe instinctively unlatched the door and stepped out, revolver drawn.

"Everything okay, sir?" Jory asked, his eyes wide in surprise at the gun in Joe's hand, it's chrome brilliance reflecting in the moonlight.

"Let me have your flashlight, Jory."

Jory, struggling to maintain control over Mutton, tossed his flashlight onto the porch.

With his free hand, Joe picked it up, bent over the railing, and aimed it at the latticework. At first he thought he saw another dog huddled against the foundation of the house. He could barely make it out underneath the porch. Then he saw a shoe.

"Come out!" he demanded in a stern voice.

Jory reached for his own gun as the form crawled into view.

Joe clutched the revolver tightly and swallowed.

Michael pushed his hood off his head so that they could see his humiliated face.

A wave of euphoria swept through Joe. "What are you doing down there?" he asked when it had passed. Mutton leapt up and down anxiously, trying to get at the muddied stranger.

"I-I wanted to get out of the rain," Michael whispered.

Joe stared at him. "Take the dog away," he said to Jory who tugged at Mutton's leash. "Come, come," he beckoned Michael. "Wait here," he said when Michael made it to the porch. He ran inside and grabbed towels. He returned and helped Michael wipe down and take off his shoes before he stepped inside. They faced each other.

"I'm sorry," Michael whispered breaking the silence. "I'm sorry." He was shivering violently.

"Here," Joe said, blinking at hot tears as he tugged at Michael's jacket. "We'll talk after you've had a shower and something to eat."

"I'm sorry," Michael repeated.

"Step on this." Joe placed a towel at Michael's bared feet to protect

Lydia's prized white carpeting. He pointed. "Go into my office. You can use my shower." He wrapped another towel around Michael's waist as he stepped out of his mud-soaked jeans and underwear.

"I'm sorry," Michael said again, as if a broken record was lodged in his throat.

This time Joe gazed at him tenderly. "So am I." He grabbed Michael's face and quickly kissed his dirt-streaked cheek. It was the first time he had really even touched him. He nudged Michael in the direction of the shower and watched him walk shakily away. Then he jogged to the kitchen and freshened his nightly pot of tea, pouring two cups. He returned and set them on the coffee table in his study. He jogged up the steps to retrieve one of his robes from his bedroom closet, careful not to wake Lydia, but she raised her tousled head anyway and lifted her eye mask.

"What's going on?" she asked sleepily.

"Nothing." Ecstatic, he kissed the top of her head. "Go back to sleep. I'll be up soon." He reached the door of the study in time to catch Michael coming out of the shower, dripping wet, and clutching a towel. "Here." Joe took the towel and dried his hair.

Michael's gaze never left his father's face.

Joe finished drying his hair and let the towel drop to the floor as he wrapped him in his plush robe and led him to the sofa where he thrust the cup of tea in his hands. "Drink."

"I'm sorry," Michael said again, trembling. He winced as the hot tea spilled from his cup onto his convulsing hands.

Joe took the cup and set it on the table alongside his own. It wasn't until he grabbed both Michael's hands in his and said, "It's not your fault," that Michael let it go. Surprised at the surge of emotion, Joe rocked with him 'til daybreak, Michael clutching his robe.

Chapter Eleven

Mike was awakened by the clatter of dishes. "Darn it!" Maxi barked. She kissed the side of her hand that had been scalded by the chafing dish. "Well, good morning sleeping beauty!" She smiled when she saw him awake and watching her.

Michael looked around the room. Everything was different. He sat up and pulled the thick, fluffy comforter to his nose. It was snowy white and smelled of new jasmine. He inhaled the fragrance as he took in his new surroundings. This certainly wasn't the room he had when he left.

This room was much larger with white marbled paint and a creamy trim. The furniture was a beautifully stained white cedar and the posts on his bed reached high toward the ceiling. Sunshine poured in from sliding glass-doors that were opened to reveal an oval balcony. Fragrant wildflowers in brilliant colors posed from vases.

"I thought you'd sleep all day," Maxi said as she went about serving up honey-smoked ham with eggs scrambled in onions and sausage, French toast, and bananas foster, with orange juice, milk, tea and fresh fruit. "I had your clothes and your bag cleaned. I'll bring them up as soon as they get back."

"Thanks," he said, still unsure whether he had actually awakened yet. "But what's all this?"

"Brunch." She grinned. "You missed breakfast and lunch, but we're still a stretch from dinner, so I thought you could use a little something. You and your father must've had some night. Last time I checked, he was in there sleeping like a log too."

Last night. He thought he had dreamed it. He looked down at himself. He was still wearing the robe Joe had wrapped around him. He surveyed the fabulous array Maxi was placing on a bed tray in front of him. "Maxi! I can't eat all this."

"From looking at those bones you're clanking around in, I say you give it a try!" She laughed. "Call me if there's anything else you need," she said before she was gone.

Michael sank his teeth into a slice of buttery French toast dusted with powdered sugar. "Ummmm," he moaned. A breeze blew him kisses from the balcony making the window sheers dance. Summoned by the myriad of exotic scents carried on the wind, he instinctively rose, toast still in his hand. Stepping out onto the balcony, he gasped at the sprawling expanse of flowering bushes and trees, petals lazily drifting to the ground. A chorus of birds sang for a passing butterfly, whose wings caught the sun with a cheerful shimmer.

"I heard you liked flowers." Joe smiled. He stood behind Michael and took a bite of the toast Michael held in his hand; then he wrapped his arms around him from back to front. "This is the coveted garden room that only my best guests get to sleep in. Leah begged me for this room for two years. I had to get her approval, but I knew you'd be comfortable here with it being right over the garden."

Michael couldn't speak. A winding stone staircase led from his balcony onto the garden path. He imagined walks before bedtime in his own paradise. "I love it!" he whispered.

Chapter Twelve

The Simpson clan gathered for a formal dinner to introduce the new member of the family. Michael stood close to his father as they greeted Simpson after Simpson and butterflies did cartwheels in his belly. There was Gramps, Grandmother Sophie, Joe's brothers John, Simeon, and Lyndon, and his sister Heather with their spouses and tribes of children. There was Joe's uncle Burton (Bert), already tipsy when he arrived, his uncle Thaddeus, his aunts Margo and Shannon, and several cousins. All in all, about thirty-five people were present for dinner. Maxi and Lydia had prepared a spectacular meal, but Michael didn't taste any of it. He felt on display in the midst of them, eyes on his every move while he struggled just to remember what fork to use. They seemed nice enough, except for his grandmother, who barely even smiled when she lightly brushed her body against his in what was supposed to be a hug, and his aunt Heather, who had trouble hiding her disapproval. After all, he was the bastard child. Finally, the family grabbed their wraps and bid one another goodbye. Michael endured a wave of hugs and kisses and watched them drift toward the convoy of luxury vehicles that lined the circular driveway. The liquor had everyone in a spirited mood. Even his aunt Heather offered him a kiss before she tottered away in her stilettos. Joe and his brother John engaged in a shoulder-shoving match as they tried their strength. In the midst of the battle, Joe dropped his cell phone and Michael picked it up. Grandmother fussed at them to stop. Michael smiled at his father's playfulness.

Back in his room, Michael couldn't wait to draw a bath. He still lost his breath every time he saw the massive spa tub, separate sauna, shower, and powder rooms. He turned on the taps and watched the water gurgle into the tub. He walked over and selected a jar of jasmine-scented salts and poured a generous amount inside.

He went back to his bedroom undressing along the way. His father's cell phone fell to the floor. He had forgotten to give it back. It rang when he picked it up.

The caller didn't speak right away, obviously surprised that someone other than the phone's owner had answered. "This is a different voice. Are you Joe's assistant?"

"No, I'm his son." *Why was this voice familiar?*

"You must be Michael. I've heard so much about you. I'm Chachi, a friend of your father's."

"I've heard about you too. They talk so much about you around here, I thought I recognized your voice."

Chachi was silent a few seconds. "That's a very interesting remark," he said. "You must be a poet."

"I am." Michael blushed. He liked this friend of his father's.

"So am I," Chachi said. "We'll have to share sometime. Now tell me why you are answering your father's cell phone."

Michael had almost forgotten. "Oh," he laughed. "My dad and Uncle John got into a little tussle tonight."

"Friendly, I hope."

"Yeah, Dad dropped his phone in the process and I picked it up. I forgot to give it back. I'll run and get him."

"Don't bother," Chachi said. "It's not important. So your uncle John was over tonight?"

"Yeah, Dad had dinner for the family."

"Oh that's right! In your honor."

"I guess."

"So how do you like your new family in its entirety?"

Michael chuckled softly. "I guess they're all right."

"Come on. You can be straight with me," Chachi teased.

Michael only laughed.

"You are now surrounded by the insane," Chachi said, imitating a television announcer's voice. They both laughed. "I'm glad you found your way home," Chachi added in a more serious tone. "Joe's very fond of you."

"I guess."

"How are you and David getting along?"

"Better."

"That's Good." Chachi yawned. "Well, sir. I am about to retire," he said playfully faking a stuffy accent. Michael chuckled again. Then returning to his natural voice Chachi said, "I am pleased to have finally met your acquaintance, Michael."

"Likewise," he responded.

Michael emerged from the bath feeling relaxed and sleepy. Joe knocked on the door as he climbed in bed.

"Come in."

"So, what do you think?" Joe asked sitting next to Michael on the bed.

"It was nice. Everyone was great."

"Well, not everyone," Joe said, frowning. "But that's your family."

Michael nodded.

"I can see you're sleepy. I have one question for you. I didn't want to bring it up tonight in front of everyone. I didn't know how you'd react."

"What is it?"

Joe exhaled deeply. "What do you feel about taking my name?"

Michael knew it was coming, it made sense. But he couldn't help feeling like he was slowly abandoning his mother. He would be peeling off another layer of his old self. "How do you think my mother would feel about that?"

"I'll talk to her," Joe assured him, "but you are my son. You should have my name and hand it down to your children. Michael looked down at his hands.

"Think about it," Joe said patting him on the back and rising.

"I want to do it," Michael said quickly.

Joe smiled, satisfied. "Trust me. If your mother had my name at her disposal, she would have given it to you. He chucked Michael under the chin. "I'll get Steven started on the paperwork. Goodnight."

"Oh, Dad..."

Joe turned.

"Chachi called." Michael held his cell phone out to him.

Joe laughed. "I hadn't even noticed it was gone."

"You dropped it when you were playing with Uncle John."

"Thanks. So you got to talk to Chachi, huh?"

"Yeah, he sounds real cool."

"Yeah," Joe smiled as he sighed. "He's a lot of things. I guess cool is one of them." Joe gazed thoughtfully at the bed as if he had gone someplace else for the moment. "I'll see you in the morning," he said.

Michael stared up at the ceiling and recounted the day's events. Not many months before, he might have been trying to warm himself beneath a shabby cardboard box. "Today was a good day," he whispered as he drifted off to sleep.

He was awakened by Lydia in the middle of the night.

"What's wrong?" Mike asked.

"I need you to go see about your father. He's in the screening room."

Michael had never done more than peek into the screening room. He shot up, alarmed. "What's wrong?" he asked again.

Lydia turned and led him down the stairs to the screening room. She opened the door and let Michael walk in past her. The room was designed to seat up to fifty people. A huge cinematic movie screen nearly covered an entire wall. On the screen Michael watched Sarah coax his younger self to walk. He must have been less than a year old. "Come to mama," she cooed. The toddler Michael teetered from side to side before regaining his balance and taking his first steps towards his mother. "Good boy!" Sarah clapped. Toddler Michael clapped too, his fat hands coming together so forcefully his cheeks shook. His giggle bounced around the room via the aid of Joe's high technology surround sound system.

Joe sat in the middle of the room clutching other tapes Pooch had packed in the big box. The glow from the movie screen reflected off his tears in the darkened room. As Michael got closer to him, he saw pictures of himself, in his crib, wrapped tightly in blankets just coming home from the hospital, his first day of pre-school… Joe sobbed as Sarah picked up the toddler Michael and kissed him all over his chubby face.

"Dad?"

Joe's chest heaved as he sat and rocked an armful of unseen tapes.

"Dad?"

Toddler Michael threw his arms about his mother's neck and climbed onto her lap. Michael gently removed the tapes and pictures from his father's arms and set them on floor. Then he eased into the seat next to him.

Joe sobbed into his shoulder. "I missed it. I missed all of it. I'll never get it back," he cried. "I'll never get it back…"

"It's okay, Dad. We have now. We have tomorrow."

"I'll never get it back…" Joe sobbed.

Toddler Michael held his hand out to his mother and she kissed it. "I love you," she sang to her little boy. "Say: 'I love you,'" she instructed him.

"I love you," Michael whispered in his father's ear.

Chapter Thirteen

Michael reported to Joe's office and took a seat in one of the big, cushy chairs in front of the desk. "You lookin' for me?"

Joe paused his rummaging through papers and clasped his hands together. "Seems you far exceeded Dalton Academy's requirements. I'm going to have to hire a tutor 'til I can research a more challenging facility."

"That's cool," Michael said softly.

"So, what's going on?" Joe asked, picking up where he left off with the pile of papers on his desk. "Where did Joan leave those papers?" he murmured to himself.

"Nothing."

"We never discussed what your goals are. What are you interested in?" Joe asked leaning toward him.

Michael shrugged.

"Don't you have the slightest idea what you'd like to do with your life?"

Michael nearly shrugged again, but caught himself. "I don't know," he said. "My concern was surviving the day. I had no reason to think about the future."

"Until now," Joe added.

Lydia called for Joe's assistance from another room.

"Don't move," he told Michael as he stood up. "I'll be right back. We're not finished with this."

Michael sat alone, taking in the surroundings. He hadn't had a chance to get a good look at Joe's office. He walked around, reading the many awards and certificates. A smaller version of the same family portrait that hung in the library sat nobly on a shelf. He smiled at the thought of how much pain he had felt when he first saw it. He picked up a photo of Joe and his college buddies and was inspecting it when the phone rang. He looked at it and then toward the door, expecting Joe to come in any minute. When it was obvious his father would not return in time to answer the call, he rushed over to the desk, reaching the phone just in time.

"Joe Simpson's office." A familiar silence.

"Michael?"

Michael was surprised at the recognition.

"It's Chachi,"

"Oh!" Michael laughed. "How'd you know it was me?"

"Who wouldn't recognize that voice?" Chachi teased.

Michael laughed again.

"Are you taking over the business or something?"

"No!" Michael laughed. "He just stepped out. We were sitting here talking, that's all."

"How's everybody doing? How's Eric? I hear you guys are short of inseparable."

"We're cool."

"I hear you got into a little trouble recently."

Michael blushed. He and Eric had been busted a few days ago making out with girlfriends Sasha and Genie in the car in front of the house and had to endure Joe's 'safe sex' speech. "Does he tell you everything?" Michael asked, exasperated.

"Pretty much, but don't mind me, I'm not your father. I applaud any man that gets his freak on."

"We were on a double-date," Michael said, falling into conversation with Chachi like an old friend. "Dad held Eric responsible, which I didn't think was fair."

"Ah, a double-date!" Chachi sighed. "Reminds me of when Joe and I were younger."

"I can tell you're great friends. You must talk every day. If you're not calling him, he's calling you."

"We're closer than great friends. We're more like brothers…twins even. But we talk everyday because we're in business together. I'm on the road a lot lately, and we keep each other abreast of the goings-on."

Michael leaned forward to get a glimpse outside the office door to see if his father was coming "Speaking of business," he whispered, "what business exactly is my father in?"

"He's never talked to you about what he does?" Chachi asked.

"I guess it never came up. Steven told me that he's a major shareholder in the law practice he runs. I hear he dabbles in all kinds of stuff, I just don't know what."

"Why don't you just ask him directly?"

"Naw. Forget it if it's a big deal."

Chachi inhaled deeply. "Well, let's see. First of all, your father makes his money above table; nothing funky is going on. He does dabble in a lot, there's real estate, he has the law firm, he has shares in his brother's media business... But his real baby is a production company we started together. It houses Turn-a-bout Records, a dance academy, acting school, fitness center, and polishing school. We take undiscovered or washed-up talent—"

"Wait a minute!" Michael's heart skipped a beat. "Duke Spencer is with Turn-a-bout records!"

Chachi hesitated. "Yes, we have Duke signed—"

Michael nearly dropped the phone in his exuberance. When he righted it (after several tries), Chachi was laughing.

"I take it you're a Duke Spencer fan."

"Are you *kidding*?" Michael yelled into the phone. "I do not *believe* this! I've been a Duke Spencer fan for as long as I can remember!"

"That can't be too long, you're only fourteen."

"Fifteen!" Michael gushed. "And I can tell you *everything* about him!"

"Wow,"

"I mean, I know *every* song, I can tell you the year they came out, *everything*! You mean my father knows Duke Spencer and he didn't tell me?"

"That stuff's not important to your dad. He could care less about that super-star bullshit. He *made* Duke Spencer."

"But I *love* Duke!"

"You ever told Joe?"

Michael paused. "No, why would I?" he said. "But he can't miss that big-ass poster on my wall! So what are you like, his managers or something?"

"I produce him. Your father and I co-manage him. We have a lot more hot acts than just Duke Spencer. We have Jump-Start, Sure Thang, Fresh Linen—"

"Oh, my God! You don't even know how you just shook my world! Wait 'til I tell my cousin Pooch. He's gonna be psyched! You think I can meet him someday?"

"Sure. He's on tour overseas right now."

"Is that where you are?"

"Yeah. He's our biggest act, so I accompany him on tour, while Joe handles the business back home. He'll hit the States again in a year or two, maybe we can arrange for you to see a concert and meet him backstage."

"Oh, *shit*! I mean—I'm sorry," Mike added quickly. "I'm just so frantic! Why hasn't Eric or somebody mentioned it?"

"It's not a big deal to them anymore. You guys have been dealing with so much drama over there, I'm sure you had other things to focus on."

"I can't wait to meet him. What's he like?"

"He's an asshole."

"Really?" asked Michael, sobering. "All that stuff they write about him is true?"

"Pretty much."

"I thought the tabloids were full of lies."

"There's no need to lie about Duke. He makes enough news just doing what comes natural."

"Oh, Well. In any case, he's my idol. He can sing his *ass* off!"

"I'll tell him," Chachi said, laughing.

Joe returned, breathless. "I'm sorry Mike, I didn't know you'd still be waiting—who's on the phone?"

"Dad's back," Michael said. "Dad, you never told me you knew Duke Spencer!"

"That would be Chachi." Joe made a face and held his hand out for the phone.

Michael gushed, "I'm his biggest fan—"

Joe held his hand out, nodding with the phone to his ear. He paused to whisper to Michael. "We'll talk about it later," he said. "Let me talk some business with Chachi and I'll tell you everything you want to know."

Michael rushed to call Pooch the moment he discovered that their idol, their crowned prince of musical genius, was practically a friend of the family. He tossed around ideas, dreaming up the possibilities. He saw himself at all the Duke's concerts, writing number-one songs for him, casually lunching with him. It was a little far fetched, but it could happen. After all, his father was in control of Duke's career, made decisions about it everyday.

He dug underneath his bed for his coveted treasure chest of poetry and music Pooch sent to him a while ago.

He picked up a torn piece of cardboard with a song that he had yet to complete. He went over it again in his head; the tune came back to him easily. He grabbed his writing tablet and hopped back onto the bed, writing eagerly as new ideas sprang into his head. Then he picked up the phone and called Eric.

"This is good Mike!" Eric had rushed over, eager to see what Michael had for him. He, David and their friend Justin had been struggling to put together a group. Chachi said they weren't quite good enough. Eric was convinced that, with the right material, they could make an impressive showing. "This is beautiful." He held up a scrap of cardboard. "How does it go?"

Michael blushed and cleared his throat. Softly he began to sing a short verse:

Have I been misused?
I hadn't noticed
All I know is that your love keeps me focused
Your hunger feeds mine
And I know that this time
You'll stay with me tonight

Eric tried to follow him on his guitar. "One more time," he said.

Michael lent his voice to the tune once more. "Now you try it," he told Eric. Michael was surprised at the quality of Eric's voice. "I didn't know you could sing!"

"Me either," David said as he entered.

"Good, it's you." Eric motioned for David to sit. David sat cross-legged on the floor. "Here." Eric handed him the paper. "Let's try this together."

"Without Justin?"

"Sure. We just wanna learn the song."

It wasn't long before David and Eric had learned the song, their harmonies blending with the notes of Eric's guitar. Joe appeared in the doorway.

"You guys sound pretty good. That song is fantastic!"

"Michael wrote it!" Eric gushed. "Look at all this, Uncle Joe!" He held up a handful of papers and scraps.

Joe poured over the documents. "Did you write all this, Michael?" Blushing, Michael nodded. "This is wonderful," Joe continued. "All this time, I thought you had no real interest in anything. Is this what you do?"

Michael fidgeted uncomfortably. "Sure. I write all the time."

"Look at this." Joe removed a particular reading from the stack. "Do you know what we can do with this stuff?"

"You can help us," David said. "Chachi won't audition us without decent material, but he won't give us decent material until we've earned it. You can be our songwriter!"

"Yeah!" Eric exclaimed. "Uncle Joe, don't you think we're good enough to audition for Chachi now?"

"I always thought you were good enough. Sometimes, a bad song will eclipse a great talent. With Michael's material, you guys might get another chance."

* * * *

"I'm telling you Chachi, with Michael's material, they're ready. They blew my mind!" Joe said.

"Yeah, well, you're the *technical* guy. No offense, but I wouldn't bet the house on your choice of talent. Remember the 'Baby Dolls?" Chachi chuckled at Joe's mistake of signing the group in his absence in the early days of Spencer-Simpson. They lost a small fortune in the process.

Joe cringed. "You ever gonna forgive me for that?"

"I'm just saying…"

"I think I've learned a little bit over the years watching which ones rise and fall. I'm telling you, they could be the next talent we're looking for."

"I'll be the judge of that," Chachi said.

Joe had an idea. "I'm gonna have them make a tape and send it to you, then you'll see what I'm talking about."

"David's been bugging me about producing," Chachi said. "He wants to get behind the scenes. Here's his shot: tell him to shoot a music video with him and the boys showcasing their talents. If I see something, I'll think about it more seriously."

"David's not ready for that!"

"I expect it to be chintzy. But even from that I'll know whether he's got it or not. I've got to go now. Let's start with that. Tell em' to call me later if they want to talk more."

Chapter Fourteen

No sooner had one occasion passed before the Simpsons began planning the next. The lighted pumpkins and spider webs of Halloween were gone and, in its place were bountiful bouquets in warm orange, browns and gold. Fall leaves lined the banisters and drapes, and gleaming gold-dipped servingware adorned the Thanksgiving dinner table.

Steven stood in the drawing room having a brandy with Joe and Dominick. David and his uncle John were engrossed in a game of chess in the game room. Lydia and Joe's sister Heather worked in the kitchen. Only a few feet away, Eric, and Leah entertained a couple of their cousins while Michael stood gazing out the window. Finally, Pratt's long black limo wound around the drive.

Lydia and Heather had just appeared in time to see Sarah, far beyond lovely in black clinging velvet, enter the house with Michael and Pooch following closely, arm in arm. Pooch had to beg Melanie to let him come when he found out that Michael would not be home for the holidays. Sarah petitioned the courts for shared holidays. She had lost custody of Michael to Joe but she figured the judge would allow her one holiday. Joe didn't want to give in so he convinced Lydia to endure Sarah's presence for Thanksgiving.

"I'm glad you could come," Joe said, smiling good humoredly.

Lydia turned to go back to the kitchen.

"You must be Sarah," Heather said with a sneer. "You look lovely. I think I have that dress," she tilted her head and blinked at the ceiling. "Lara Dunne, right? Last season?"

"You're right." Sarah smiled sweetly. "I bought it off the discount rack. I thought it was a steal, for an old rag."

"Good thing I won't allow myself to be caught dead in the same dress twice." Heather issued a fake laugh. "Wouldn't it have been terrible if we had come to the same party looking just alike?"

Sarah smiled her winning smile. "Oh, I wouldn't worry about looking just like me in this dress if I were *you*," she drawled as she slithered past Heather's broken face. She took Michael's arm and followed him to the battlefield.

Dinner looked great, but Michael barely tasted any of it. He was too busy glaring at his mother. She sat with Steven at dinner and laughed too easily, smiled too brightly and asked too many empty questions. But Michael wasn't fooled. Her performance was not for Steven's enjoyment, but for Joe's.

Michael watched Sarah pull out her mirrored compact. Of course she could have excused herself and went to the powder room to freshen her face but why would she do that? She loved being the center of attention. She pretended to dab at her nose.

Joe's gaze wandered between his brother John, who was speaking to him, and her loveliness.

After dinner, Sarah sat in the family room flanked by Gramps, Uncle Bert, and Uncle Thaddeus. Grandmother stood with Lydia and the others watching Sarah's unbelievably bold maneuvers. Joe's face was damp with perspiration. Michael's was ablaze with fury.

"You are so silly!" Sarah hit Thaddeus to punctuate her last word. She crossed one shapely leg over the other, making sure to show more thigh than was appropriate.

Michael had enough. "Mom, you look tired. I'll ask Pratt to take you back to the hotel."

"I'm not tired." She smiled at him.

"You need your rest," he said gruffly, reaching for her hand.

"I'm not tired," she repeated, jerking her hand away, her smile strained.

"I insist."

"I'm a grown woman, Michael. I think I can keep up with my bedtime," she said, rising, in her 'don't mess with me right now' tone of voice.

Michael drew in a breath, squared his shoulder, and looked directly into his mother's almond-shaped eyes. "Mom," he said again, slowly, "you look *tired*. I'll ask *Pratt* to take you back to the hotel."

They stared each other down for a long moment. The room went dead silent. Joe made himself another drink.

"You're right, sweetheart," she said softly and placed her hand on his cheek. "Always thinking about mommie, aren't you? Bert, be a dear and grab my wrap." She winked and Bert leaped like a jack-rabbit. She turned to Lydia. Michael held his breath. He'd drag her kicking and screaming from that house if she dared say anything out of line. "Thanks for having me." She extended her hand to Lydia who took it hesitantly and shook it. "Dinner was wonderful. Goodbye kids," she sang out to Eric and the others. Leah dropped her head. David looked away, fuming. "Joe," she called. He turned sharply. She wouldn't dare. "May I have a word with you?"

Joe glanced at Lydia.

"In private," Sarah added. Michael started toward her, but Joe raised a hand to stop him. When they were in the foyer, Bert had returned with her wrap. She thanked him quickly, dismissing him with her eyes and gestured for Joe to help her with it. "I'm sorry if I embarrassed you," she began, "you know how I get when I drink. I can be too much for the average Joe—no pun intended." She chuckled.

"No harm done," he said, helping her into her wrap. "I hope," he added under his breath.

"The real reason I wanted to talk to you...I miss Michael. I want to know when we can work out a more equitable visitation schedule."

"I'm working on it."

"You're working on it!" she cried. "I thought he was *our* son!"

"We'll talk about it later," Joe said, lowering his voice.

"I want to discuss it before I leave," she whispered. "I'll be here 'til

Sunday. Won't you come by then and we can talk about it," she said, slipping a note into his hand. "Besides, I think we have some other things to rehash."

"Oh, no!" Joe shook his head, thrusting the note at her.

"What?" she asked, blinking innocently. "I just want to talk. Don't you want closure?"

"I *have* closure." Joe looked over his shoulder.

"Well, I don't! We never talked about what happened that night I disappeared. I never told you about how your friends tricked me—threatened me! I never would have left like that, I thought you—"

"Sarah, this is not the time or the place," he said through clenched teeth. "Besides, what does it matter now?"

"I'm tired of this!" she wailed. "I want to see my son more, and I want you to know what happened! I'm not asking for anything else. You can tell your wife that, contrary to popular belief, I am not after her husband! I just think we owe each other an explanation—or something!"

"All right, all right!" If he could only touch those long soft tendrils curling around her spectacular face, streaming down her back. "Anything, just—go now, all right?"

"What are you afraid of?" she asked, the lids of her large, brown eyes dipped coyly at half-mast. "You think I'll bite you or something?" Her lashes softly brushed her cheeks as she blinked.

He shifted under her gaze.

Michael stepped up to his rescue.

"There you are." She grabbed his face and kissed it all over like she used to. He was unresponsive. "You were totally correct, I *am* tired! Now, kiss Mommie and I'll be on my way." She held her cheek out to him, but he did not move. "You're angry," she said, pouting. "Oh, well," she sang, "I'm gone. I hope I don't get shot or hit by a bus, or I hope my plane doesn't crash," she called out to him over her shoulder as Joe held the door open for her. She stopped at the door and turned to Michael, her eyes sexy slits, her hand on her hip. "If so, you'll regret not kissing your mother goodbye." She turned and took Pratt's waiting arm. Joe closed the door behind her and looked at Michael.

"Whew," he said, chuckling softly. "She *is* a pistol!"

Michael didn't respond to him either. He stood glaring accusingly.

"What?" Joe asked, his eyes wide with bewilderment.

Michael turned and joined the rest of the family.

* * * *

Michael and Leah lay on the floor in the family room playing a game of Boggle and Lydia sat reading nearby when David burst into the room clutching his new video tape production to his chest.

"Where's Dad?" David gushed.

"What's that?" Lydia eyed the tape in his hand. He drew it back as if she might take it from him.

"I don't want anyone to see it before Dad does."

"Michael, call your father on his cell phone," Lydia said. "There's no harm in showing it before he sees it, is there?" she prodded. "Come on, I'm excited!"

David gave in and, after taking off his coat, began to set up for the screening. Michael grabbed the phone. He called Eric to come over first, then he dialed his father's cell number.

"Hello," a sultry voice answered. He heard fumbling as the phone must have been dropped. He heard his father say, "Don't ever do that!" Then the dial tone. Michael looked at it as if it were a monster.

"What's wrong, Michael?" Lydia asked. "Did you reach him?"

Michael shook his head.

"Try again in a few moments."

Michael slowly reached for the phone again, but it rang before he could pick it up.

His father's cell number was on the display.

"Hi, Puppy."

"I just called you."

"Did you?"

"Some woman answered the phone—"

"Let me speak to Lydia."

Michael's breath caught in his throat. With a look between stupefaction and anger, he handed Lydia the phone.

"Hi sweetie," she said. "Oh, nothing, David just wanted you home for his video debut…yes…okay, darling. We'll just show it again when you get home." She hung up. "He won't be home 'til late," she announced.

Dumbfounded, Michael quietly joined David and his sister on the sofa to watch the video tape. Leah screamed and David hooted as the group pranced around on-screen. Lydia clasped her hands in pride. Michael watched with a phony smile plastered on his face but his thoughts were racing. Home late, huh? His father had been coming home late the last couple of weekends. He tried to focus on the video, but the phone call haunted him and his stomach ached. "Hello." He replayed the greeting in his head. He'd know his mother's voice anywhere.

Chapter Fifteen

Christmas was coming! Lydia had professional decorators come in and deck the halls. Light-filled trees of varying sizes adorned every room. Fresh pine and balsam wreaths and garlands with berries and apple ornaments lined doors and windows.

Wow! Michael was finally getting a taste of what he had seen children on television enjoy. The delightfully yeasty-sweet scents of baked goods, fresh fruit baskets, and scented candles made him feel festive and secure.

Michael called Pooch to get Christmas gift ideas. For the first time in his life, he had money to buy presents. He asked about his mother.

"She's not there with you?" Pooch asked.

"No!" Michael exclaimed.

"I thought she said she was going to spend the weekend before Christmas there with you."

"Next weekend," he pointed out. They sat in thoughtful silence. "Did she leave a phone number with Auntie Mel?"

"I'll ask," Pooch said hastily. "Hold on."

Moments later, Michael dialed the number Pooch had given him. When the hotel front-desk clerk answered, his suspicions were confirmed. She was staying right there in town, only a few miles away, yet she hadn't even called to let him know it.

Michael felt a sense of complete disruption. He struggled to control the rage burning in his chest. His father was downstairs in his office with Dominick, but he had heard him tell Lydia that he had a late 'meeting.'

He hung up abruptly and paced the floor. *Stay out of it, Michael. It's none of your business.* But against his better judgment, he grabbed his coat and went out.

The hotel wouldn't give out her room number, so he lurked around the lobby, ducking and hiding, until he saw his father stroll in. Joe stepped on the elevator, but quite a few others crowded on with him, so Michael couldn't tell what floor he got off on. Moments later, the two of them stepped out laughing and gazing at one another. Shuddering, Michael stared in shocked silence.

Michael barely slept all night. He couldn't even look his stepmother in the face.

That very next morning, he called the hotel and left a note for his mother. 'Meet me in the hotel lobby at 10,' it said, 'I have a surprise for you.' When he hung up, his heart was racing. He could be in a lot of trouble if something went wrong.

At half-past 9, he had Pratt drop him off in the vicinity of the hotel and walked the rest of the way. He called the hotel from a nearby payphone and left another message. 'Sorry, I'm running a few minutes late. I'll be there before you know it. Wear something nice.' Then he went to the hotel and waited. Within minutes of the 10 o'clock hour, Sarah stepped off the elevator. She looked around the lobby. He hid near a large plant in his dark hat and shades.

Sarah looked at her watch a couple times before walking over to the front desk. "May I use your phone?" she asked.

Oh, no! She's going to call him! He was screwed! Perspiration broke out on his forehead. He'd have to confront her right then. He couldn't let her call his father. Then he got a stroke of luck.

"We happen to have a message for you, Ms. Bagley," the hotel clerk said.

Sarah smiled when she read it. "Thank you," she said sweetly and headed for the elevator.

Michael followed. He quickly slipped to the back. She didn't even glance at him. She got off on the penthouse floor. He trailed her, being careful to turn in the opposite direction. She turned a corner and he spun around, sprinting after her. He watched from behind a wall as she slipped her key card in the door and went inside.

He took a deep breath, took off his hat and glasses, and approached the door. He knocked with vigor. She flung open the door with such vitality that her body was thrown into him. She stumbled trying to avoid the collision.

"Expecting someone?" he asked in his low, velvety voice. His eyes burned with accusation.

Her brilliant pupils widened, then faded into a violent expression. She clutched her silk robe closed and turned away from him. Gliding over to the window, she lit a cigarette. The scent of nicotine made him long for a hit.

Sarah stared out the window and smoked in silence while he glared at her.

"How could you?" he admonished in a whisper.

"How could *I*?" she shot back. "This is none of your business!"

"You're sleeping with him?" he asked.

Brusquely, she turned so that her back was to him.

"No matter what you did, no matter who said what about you, I always gave you the benefit of the doubt!" he snarled. "You did what you had to do. That's what I made myself believe. You would never deliberately hurt anyone! How could you *do* this?"

"He loves *me*!" she screamed. Her eyes raced.

Instantly, the rage went out of him. She was losing it. "He's married, Ma! He has a *wife*!"

"He was mine! He was always mine!"

He reached out to hug her. Trembling, she pushed him away.

"He doesn't love her! He never did. She trapped him!" When she swung around, her robe floated after her. "He never would have married her otherwise, he told me so." She touched his face. "You always dreamed of having both your parents together. I lied to you all those years about Jaye being your father. I couldn't bear to tell you the truth then. I had no idea what fate had in store."

"Fate?" With a mirthless laugh, he fixed her with an accusing stare. "This is not *fate*, Mom. This is a deliberate attempt to break up a family."

"He loves me!"

"He will never leave his family."

"Aw," She waved her hand in the air. "His children are almost grown and that mouse of a wife—"

"You've *got* to stop this, Mom!"

"You stay out of this!" she pointed a finger of warning at him.

"I won't," he said softly. He turned to leave.

"Joe won't tolerate your meddling," she cautioned, but it was a shaky threat. Her trembling jaw told him that even she wasn't sure how Joe would react.

Michael kept walking.

"I'm warning you!" she said shrilly. "You will regret it if you ruin this for me!"

He stopped at the door. Then he turned and looked at her long and hard.

She shrunk back from his gaze. "What are you going to do?" she asked timidly.

He opened the door and walked out, closing it behind him just in time to hear glass breaking against it.

"I've gotta go," Joe said gulping down a cup of coffee.

Michael sat bolt upright.

"When are we going to spend some holiday time together?" Lydia asked in a tone that was careful not to ruffle any feathers. "I thought we'd do some shopping and have lunch together."

"Sounds good," Joe said. "But not today."

David asked, "Can I catch a ride, Dad? I don't wanna drive today. You going into the office?"

Joe kept his eyes on his plate. "No...I have an appointment. I'll give you a ride, though."

"How 'bout me?" Michael asked. "Can I get a ride? I'm meeting mom for shopping and dinner."

Joe looked like he'd turned to stone. Michael's words hung in the air between them.

"But...you can't," Joe began.

"Why?" Michael cocked his head. *Because my mother's your appointment.*

Lydia glanced warily at him. "Joe?"

"U-Um," Joe stuttered, and unbuttoned his collar.

"Are you all right?" Lydia asked, rising.

Michael looked at him coldly.

"No—yes, I'm fine..." Joe took short, deep breaths. "I, uh...we'd better get going then..."

At the door Joe grabbed Michael's shirt-tail. "I'll meet you in the car," he said to David.

Michael folded his well-toned arms across his chest and waited.

Joe closed his eyes. "How long have you known?"

* * * *

Michael was fully dressed, having breakfast and awaiting a call from his mother. "I start the weekend with Mom today," he reminded Joe and Lydia.

Joe's genial smile turned to one strained with anxiety.

"You'll stay the night?" Lydia asked.

"I think so," Michael said, picking up a slice of her toast and biting it. "In any case, I'll be home by tomorrow night."

"Good, because we trim the tree," she said, a merry glint in her eyes.

In the background the phone rang. "Probably Mom," he said. "I'll see you guys later."

Sarah wanted to postpone her visitation with Michael, insisting that she was ill.

"Mom, it's Christmas. Don't you want to spend some time together?"

"I used to have to send a search party after you during the holidays. It's never been your cup of tea. I just have a little business to take care of this morning. I swear, I'll call you this evening and we can get together then."

"What business, Ma? The whole purpose for you coming to town was so that we could spend time together."

"Did you say anything to your father?" she asked.

"No!" Guilt surged into his chest.

"You sure?"

"No, Mom. I haven't said anything to Dad."

"Then why didn't he come?" she asked herself distractedly. "Is he there?"

Michael sighed, exasperated. "Mom..."

"I just want to talk to him for a second, just a second."

Mid-protest, Joe walked up and stood at his shoulder. He fixed his father with an icy stare and handed him the phone.

"Sarah," was all Joe managed to say before she pelted him with a tirade that even Michael was able to hear. Michael and Joe exchanged meaningful expressions, while Joe listened regretfully. "I'll be there in an hour," Joe said before hanging up. "I swear," he said to Michael. "Nothing happened between us but conversation."

Michael gazed at his shoes.

"Let me talk to your mother before you go to her. I'll be right back." Joe headed for the stairs to get dressed. He turned back. "I'm so sorry."

Joe returned two hours later. Michael sat in the game room challenging himself to *Starboard* while he waited. Joe sat next to him and removed his gloves. Michael paused the game, but Joe avoided his eyes.

"I'm sorry," Joe said again when he could look at him. "I don't— I don't know what happened. I know it sounds flimsy."

"How is she?" Michael asked softly. Joe shook his head and blinked at the floor.

Michael reached for his jacket and eased it on.

"Pratt is waiting for you." Joe's voice was anguished. "She's gonna need you."

Chapter Sixteen

Christmas Eve was magical. Eric and his family and a few friends were over for dinner. Afterward, they drank eggnog and sang carols while Leah played the piano. They wrapped presents and peeked at the decorative boxes under the tree like little kids. Michael celebrated with a note of sadness. He spent the last couple days letting his mother cry bitterly on his shoulder. He said a prayer and tried to push the image out of his mind and join the festivities. After all, it was his first Christmas with a real family all his own.

They got to bed late and Michael was still very much asleep when Leah pulled the covers off him. "C'mon," she said, jumping up and down. "Time to open presents!" She bolted down the stairs and he groggily sat up.

When he made it down, the house had already given way to pandemonium. Wrapping paper was everywhere. Everyone spoke at once and handed or received gifts. Lydia laughed loudly at a hat she presented

Joe with, which he wore cocked humorously on the side of his head.

Eric held a box out to Michael as he approached. "Open it!" He grinned.

Michael opened gift after gift. It seemed everyone tried to make up for lost time. Later, they sat talking quietly, drinking eggnog, and surveying the mess.

"I have something special for you," Joe said as he stood to accept several large, long boxes Lydia and David pushed toward him. He walked over and sat next to Michael on the floor. "I've been studying those tapes Pooch sent to me." He swallowed. "It's hard for me, not having been there when you needed me most. I missed so much." He took a deep breath.

Michael blinked back his own rising emotions.

"I thought about the birthdays and Christmases I missed. What would I have given you? What would you have asked for?" He reached for the first box and opened it. It contained other brightly wrapped items. "Lydia helped me to pick out some things I might have gotten you had I had the chance."

Inside was a yellow squeeze toy with mirrors. Everyone laughed between sniffles.

"That's cute," Michael said, smiling. He shook it and squeezed it a few times, making a face and laughing at each kookey sound it made.

"Wait, there's more," Joe said, handing him the second gift, an activity center just right for a two-year-old. It had musical notes and bells and whistles….

The third box contained a plush toy, a teddy bear. And so it went. With each presentation, Michael uncovered a toy appropriate for each age he would have been for each Christmas Joe missed. He uncovered poseable wrestling and comic-book figures, a tricycle, a train set complete with the train station and surrounding village, a basketball and hoop, a baseball and gloves, a hand-held video game, a scooter, a skateboard, a bicycle (he was weeping openly now), in-line skates, keyboard, and a leather bomber jacket. Fifteen gifts in all. When he was done, there wasn't a dry eye in the room.

"Thank you, Dad."

Joe reached out and wiped away a tear. "My pleasure."

They embraced, holding on to each other tightly.

"I don't know where I'll put them all, but I'll keep them forever."

Joe stood up and accepted a tissue from his wife before exiting the room. Lydia sat down next to Michael in his place.

"Thank you, Lydia," he said softly.

"No, thank *you*, sweetheart." She kissed his lips. "I know everything," she whispered.

Michael's gaze met hers in secret understanding.

"You helped me get back what is most important in my life and I know how hard it was for you to make that decision." Michael looked away tearfully. Lydia continued, "I will *never* forget it. I was being so stupid, hoping it would go away."

Eric and David exchanged puzzled looks.

"I'm glad things...worked out." He smiled. "I just hope you'll be there for *my* stupid moments."

Lydia closed her hand over his. "They are bound to come, and yes, I plan on being there."

* * * *

Chachi stepped out of the shower and dried himself. When he was done, he let the towel fall to the floor and strolled, naked, into the bedroom portion of the suite where Renee, his longtime girlfriend, waited patiently on the bed. But he didn't go to her. He walked over to the humidor Joe sent him for Christmas, filled with the best Cuban cigars, and selected one. He rarely smoked cigars, but he liked to offer them to his guests and, from time to time, he liked to hold them in his mouth, tasting the sweetness. He saw her in the mirror across from him, watching. He didn't look a day older than when they graduated from college. He'd cut his hair shorter and oftentimes let a 5'oclock shadow age his face, but then he'd smile the smile of boyish charm...

He felt her gaze upon him and fought back a snicker. He was dreadful with women and collected them like famous autographs—the more beautiful, the better. He was drawn by beauty, hence his relationship with Renee. Although a real beauty, she was a hanger-on, and he hadn't been able to shake her since college. But she was good in bed and a slave to him, so he tolerated her. She wanted him badly and he knew it. Course, he wanted her too, but he liked to tease her. He'd make her wait a while longer.

He was oversexed as it was, admittedly a bit of a sex-guzzler. It would get so crazy sometimes on the road with all the parties that he'd have sex everyday for weeks, sometimes with two and three at a time. But he was getting older and growing tired of it. His mother asked him every phone call about when he planned to marry. She liked Renee and was gunning for a hook-up between them.

He poured himself a drink and turned to her. She sat up in anticipation. As he approached her, she leaned back and let the straps of her gown fall away and brought her knees up to receive him.

She was writhing like a snake and screaming when they climaxed. Her lips searched frantically for his as she pulled him closer. He shrugged out of her grasp, rolled over and lit a cigarette.

"I love you," she whispered in his ear.

He found the remote control and turned on the television.

"That's it?" she asked.

He said nothing.

"Chachi!"

"I have work to do," he said. He got up and removed a stack of disks from a suitcase. He returned and loaded one of them into the bed-side disk player. A group of four pretty women pranced across the screen singing. He watched them, emotionless, and jotted notes on a pad. Before the disk played to completion, he ejected it and inserted another in its place. A young male stud sang his heart out.

"I like him," Renee offered.

"Of course you do," Chachi said dryly and ejected the disk.

She snuggled up against him.

"Okay, let's see what you got," he mumbled as he popped the last disk in. He smiled at David holding a microphone, introducing the newly formed group, Simpson & Sybak.

"Oh, look at David!" Renee said groggily.

David spoke, “This is my cousin Eric Simpson, my friend Justin Sybak and I am proud to introduce our new writer, my once-estranged little brother Michael—

“Younger brother,” Michael corrected him off camera. When Michael didn’t step into focus, David made a face. Eric and Justin both pulled at him until, unwillingly, he came into view.

Chachi sat up. “So that’s Michael,” he said under his breath.

“Where?” Renee asked, rousing herself.

“There,” Chachi said, pointing. “I would have never guessed it.”

“Oh, he is so adorable!” Renee sat up. “He does favor Joe. Unfortunately, he looks a lot like that bitch Sarah too.”

Chachi leaned back and put out his cigarette. “Come on, guys lets see what you got.”

The boys blended their vocals. Chachi wasn’t impressed, but he lifted a brow and began to bob to the beat. With the first note something went off in his head. A slow-forming smile softened his face. He knew a hit when he heard one.

After the third song, his pupils became dilated and his heart raced. He was a master at sniffing out talent. People had credited him with the Duke Spencer superstardom, but what they didn’t understand was that Duke Spencer was born, not made. Chachi was the marketing genius who groomed and presented the star to the world. But Duke’s material was growing stale in a business where youth reigned supreme. He needed a fresh sound, and now he was facing another opportunity—it was like lightening striking twice. Great voices came a dime a dozen, but the music was the lasting connection.

“Wow, they’re really good!” Renee marveled.

“No, they suck,” Chachi muttered, his eyes glazing over.

“Uh, oh. I’ve seen that look before…” Renee frowned. “If they suck, why are you looking like you just struck gold?”

Chachi picked up the phone and dialed Joe’s cell number.

“What in God’s name would make you call me at this *hour*?” Joe grumbled.

“I got around to viewing the boys’ performance.”

"Really?"

"I'm looking at it."

"So, do we have ourselves a few stars or not? What do you think?"

"I think I'm coming home."

Chapter Seventeen

Chachi was coming home. Joe and Lydia were hosting a smashing party to celebrate. He had been gone nearly a year and his friends couldn't wait to see him. The guest list was getting out of control until Joe insisted they limit it to 250 people. They would turn the guesthouse into a lavish setting for a spring reception.

Simpson & Sybak rehearsed relentlessly every day after the New Year, as this event would mark their maiden performance in front of a real crowd. Lydia hired two world-renown chefs and caterers and set about the task of sampling foods and selecting a menu as well as designing the invitation and assigning seating.

Gorgeous people milled about drinking champagne and discussing business. Lydia rented an elaborate stage where the boys were to perform, but at the moment, a twenty-one piece band played. Michael stood in a corner, as far out of view as possible and took in the fabulousness of it all. Stars were everywhere, talking and laughing with his family like old friends. He recognized top recording artists and movie stars.

Eric found him drooling at the beautiful Slomeek, lead singer of the group HotLine.

"Here you are!" he blew air out of his cheeks. "We've been looking all over for you! We have to rehearse. We need you to check our harmony. Chachi's plane finally landed. He'll be here within the hour!"

"How much more rehearsal do you need? If you sing another note, you're going to be croaking like a frog up there." They were all nervous wrecks. "That's Slomeek over there." He nudged Eric.

"I know," Eric said.

"How much time do we have?"

"I don't know. It's not clear whether he's coming straight here or if he'll stop off at home. He only lives a few miles away."

"Well, you go and rehearse. You don't need me to check your vocals. I'm staying right here. I don't want to miss a thing."

Eric hurried away and Michael stayed, soaking in the sights. A tray of h'orderves floated by and he grabbed a couple. He eyed an approaching tray of champagne. Dare he? His father would have his head if he were caught. He snatched up a glass a moment before it was out of reach.

Chachi was very late. Eric kept appearing and re-appearing with messages from Joe. Their performance was postponed. They couldn't go on until the guest of honor arrived. That was all fine with Michael. He had more than enough to keep him entertained in that corner.

Shortly after midnight, a commotion erupted at the entryway. Michael looked in its direction, but all he could see were people rushing the entrance. Joe rose and stretched his neck for a better view. His cell phone rang and, upon answering it, he broke out into a wide grin and started in the direction of the upheaval.

Eric appeared by Michael's side. "I think that's him!" he said, bouncing on his heels.

The throng moved together. A host of suited men wore headpieces and held out their arms to keep the crowd at bay. Michael stood on his toes and squinted through the flash of cameral bulbs.

"Oh, my God…" he grabbed Eric's arm. How was he going to thank Lydia and Joe for this surprise? Joe said he didn't know if he could pull it off, but he would try to get his musical icon to make an appearance. "Oh shit, shit, shit!" Michael bounced up and down like he had to go to the bathroom.

"Chachi!" Eric screamed and ran to him, joining Leah and David as they leapt upon him.

Michael felt the room move under his feet and his mouth went dry. *Chachi*? He placed his hand on the wall to steady himself. Chachi looked in his direction and smiled, but Michael had seen that smile before. Dumbstruck, he could not believe it had escaped him for so long. He was looking into the face of Duke Spencer.

The crowd swelled as they hugged, kissed, and clawed at him. Joe must have held him a full five minutes before he let him go. Chachi beamed with sociable delight as he reached out to touch his friends.

Michael remained frozen. An array of emotions swept through him; shock: he could not believe that the star he had idolized for as long as he could remember, the man whose face was on nearly his entire CD collection upstairs, was standing only a few feet away from him! Fear: what would he say if they asked him to speak? Anger: they had all been lying to him. Sure, he hadn't asked the question straight out: was Duke Spencer and Chachi the same person? But they all knew how he felt about both. They let him make a fool of himself.

The room became a blur of garbled voices and big grins. Eric turned and gestured in Michael's direction. Michael couldn't move.

"Come on over, meet Chachi!" Eric grabbed him by the arm before he knew it and was pulling him toward the crowd, which had started to slowly disperse. Michael stood speechless and staring amidst a bevy of snickers and chuckles. His family seemed to think it quite funny, the joke they played on him.

"Mike," Chachi smiled, "we finally meet."

Their voices seemed to move far away. He slightly felt Joe's hand on his shoulder as his father rattled off words Michael could no longer understand. Leah's high-pitched voice piped in next but was equally unintelligible.

"You okay?" He heard Chachi ask, his youthful face lined with concern.

Michael spun around and ran, leaving them all gaping after him.

In his room, he paced the floor and tried to catch his breath. He pinched his own arm. Could this be happening? How on earth had he not noticed that something did not add up? All this time he'd been on the phone with Chachi, telling him how big a fan he was of Duke Spencer's, how much he loved his music, how totally cool he thought he was, and all the time, he had been saying these things to Duke himself. He felt so stupid. He sat down on the bed and looked at the telephone. Pooch would never believe it.

Gay music and party voices drifted upstairs to his room. He took off his jacket and tossed it onto a chair. He won't be there when Simpson & Sybak performed tonight.

"I'm sorry."

Startled, he looked up in time to see Chachi slip into the room and close the door behind him. His mouth fell open and the breath went out of him.

"Don't blame them. I asked them not to tell you."

"Why?" Michael tried to ask, but instead, it came out more like a shallow exhale.

"I thought we had established a nice little friendship," Chachi explained, his lips turned up sheepishly as he made imaginary circles on the armoire with his finger. He stopped making the circles and looked squarely at Michael. "You liked me for who I was and that was cool. I get so tired of the whole groupie-fan thing; it would have changed everything if I had told you." He eyed a life sized, framed publicity photo of himself that Michael had mounted on the wall. "Not bad," he said.

Michael looked from the photo to the man and still could not believe it. Not much airbrushing was required to enhance his good looks. He was a big man, taller in person, maybe six-foot-three or four. His body was well cut, a reward for years of performing onstage. He had strong, defined thighs, a nice, broad chest and a wash-board of a belly in-between. He was dressed more conservatively than in the photo, but when he turned and smiled, it was as if the sun came out.

"Can you forgive me?" Chachi pouted playfully.

Michael looked down at his hands, still trembling.

"Come on, Mike. Come back to the party. I came all this way to hear your songs. Joe tells me you have a box full of 'em."

Michael shook his head vigorously. He had yet to find his speaking voice.

"Come on!" Chachi walked over and slapped him on the back, sounding more like the Chachi he had spoken to on the phone many times. "You've got to be ready for anything in life. Always ready! You never know what life brings. Now come on," he nudged him, "enough of this."

Michael took a deep breath and wiped perspiration from his face. He reached for his jacket and struggled to his feet, then walked, in a daze, to the door.

"Michael,"

Michael turned to look at him, now leaning against the bedpost.

"You haven't said one word to me yet. Not one word."

Michael swallowed hard and cleared his throat. Up until then he had been behaving like a smitten schoolgirl. Who was Chachi or Duke or whatever he called himself, but a man like any other? He drew another deep breath and parted his lips, determined to say his piece and end this nonsense. He opened his mouth and heard himself say, in a barely audible whisper, "Hi."

The rest of that night blew past like a windstorm. "They sucked, didn't they?" Mike murmured to Chachi after Eric and the others were out of earshot.

"Yeah," Chachi breathed through his perpetual smile, "but *you* didn't." One eyebrow lifted mischievously higher than the other. "Just imagine what can happen when your songs are the basis of a good performance—a *great* performance!"

* * * *

He didn't see much of Chachi the following weeks. His father was constantly on his way out the door to attend one gathering or another in his friend's honor. Still Michael jumped out of his skin when the doorbell rang, hoping he'd get another look-see.

Pooch, who thought he was the luckiest guy in the world, made him promise to soak up every move he made and tell him about it. That was an easy task, since he hadn't been able to stop thinking about him since.

He caught a glimpse of him one evening picking Joe up for dinner. Michael was just returning from a date with Sasha when he heard voices in the library. He peered around the partially opened door and watched the three of them—Dominick, Chachi, and his father—in playful banter. They were laughing and joking like teenagers. They looked rich in their long, dark, tailored coats and broad shoulders. Michael forgot he was in the act of peeping and almost gasped aloud when Chachi turned, winked at him, and turned back. Stunned and embarrassed, he raced to his room.

Another week passed without any sightings, then, one evening as he lay on his bed writing music, his father knocked on his door and yelled that there was pizza downstairs. He was met with a flurry of laughter and conversation. The whole lot of them, his father, Steven, Dominick, Jake and his wife, Uncle John, Lydia, David, Eric, and Leah sat around the family room drinking beer and soda and ripping at huge rounds of pizza. Chachi sat in an armchair in the corner with a beer in one hand and the most beautiful woman Michael had ever seen, besides his mother, on his lap. He grabbed a slice of pizza and a soda and quietly slipped into a chair across from Chachi and his girlfriend, where he could get an eyeful and not be noticed.

Chachi looked like an oversized teenager in his sweat pants, sneakers, and t-shirt that had "Suck me" emblazoned across the front. His eyes, the light golden-brown of a wolf's with flirty lashes made a soft contrast against his fair skin. He had a full, shapely mouth that liked to smile. In fact, it seemed he was always smiling. Happiness radiated about him and he was quick to laugh. He couldn't hear what Chachi and the beautiful lady said to one another, but she squirmed on his lap. Chachi responded by running his less-visible hand up her thigh until it disappeared underneath her skirt and she erupted into a bundle of giggles. She playfully slapped him and he jerked his smiling face away from her. They played that way for a while then, disinterested, he ejected her from his knee and she sashayed away as if she expected it, only to be replaced by Leah who gleefully let herself fall onto his lap. Excusing himself, Chachi walked over to the bar to get another beer.

Michael followed his every move, his slow deliberate steps, how he twisted off the cap with his teeth, then returned to his seat...except he passed up his seat and headed straight for him! Oh, no! Chachi pulled up a chair directly in front of Michael's and sat so close to him that, had Michael not had his knees drawn up to his chest with his feet in the chair, they'd be touching.

"Close your mouth," Chachi said smoothly, his eyes still on his beer.

Michael struggled to draw breath.

Chachi took a swig from the bottle and looked him in the eyes. Michael was captivated by those amber jewels. "This is the last opportunity you get to stare at me like a freak, so go ahead," Chachi said.

Michael flushed. All this time he thought his stalking and spying had gone unnoticed. He looked away, his heart beating rapidly.

"Don't turn away now," Chachi teased. He lightly gripped Michael's chin and brought his face back to him.

Michael jerked it away from him, frowning.

"You've spent the whole evening watching me," Chachi said again, softly, his head tilted slightly, the corner of his mouth threatening a wry smile. "I can't come to my buddy's home anymore without you staring at me. Now I understand what this means to you and I appreciate you being a fan, so go ahead, stare. But after tonight…no more."

What arrogance.

"Come on, this is your chance."

Michael glared at him. He had a mind to tell him to go fuck himself.

Chachi leaned closer and turned his head from side to side for proper inspection.

"Hold it there," Michael said.

Chachi, a bit surprised, froze in position.

"Now turn your head slowly to the side..."

Chachi smiled slightly and turned his head per Michael's instruction.

"Good, now hold it right there." Michael leaned in close and peered into his face. He pretended to inspect every inch of him, taking in his eyes, the shape of his ears, the mole on his neck. Chachi couldn't hold it in any more and burst into laughter. Michael laughed with him.

"I knew I liked you the first day I spoke to you." Chachi grinned at him.

"I almost told you to go fuck yourself." Michael grinned back.

Chachi laughed. "I just miss that guy I used to talk to all the time. I almost can't believe that was you. You were so talkative and fun and now you're sneaking behind doors and hiding in chairs, you haven't said more than ten words since we've met."

A fierce blush burned its way up Michael's neck. "I'm sorry. I'll try not to do it again."

"What are you guys up to?" The beautiful lady wedged herself between them and sat on the arm of Michael's chair.

"You met Michael, Renee."

"Yessss!" she drawled. "How are you, sweetie?" She held her hand out and he took it. "You are adorable!" He felt like a puppy. "Why, if you were only a few years older, somebody," she jabbed Chachi in the side, "would have a run for his money."

Chachi bristled. "Who's running after who?" he scoffed and rolled his eyes.

Michael's gaze journeyed from her shapely legs up to her doe-brown eyes before blushing his approval. This girl was a knockout.

"Don't mind him, he's just jealous." She motioned toward Chachi. "We're gonna have to become fast friends," she whispered, leaning close to Michael. "That way, you can keep an eye on him for me."

"He's good at that," Chachi mumbled.

* * * *

It was still cool out, so Joe hosted his weekend get-together for the crew indoors. Everyone was in high spirits, having already indulged in the bubbly. It seemed they all had a need to talk louder than one another to the point of nearly shouting. Though no one but the crew was formally 'invited' to these events, Joe didn't mind when the kids would stop through and maybe hang out for a moment or two. Michael and Eric used this excuse to slip in and out to steal champagne.

Joe was in a stellar good mood, as he had been since Chachi came home. He was doubled over in laughter, holding onto Steven, at a comment made by Jake. Dominick sat absorbed in a game of Chess with David. Lydia and Renee had retreated upstairs over an hour ago. Chachi sat in his favorite chair, sharing the laughs from a distance.

Sasha and Genie stopped by unexpected. Michael stiffened as Pratt showed them into the room. "What are you doing here?" he whispered angrily to Sasha. He had no plans with her and was happily satisfied with crashing his father's party.

"I wanted to meet Duke Spencer! Eric told me he'd be here. I used to drive by his house all the time but I could never get a glimpse. Please don't be mad!"

"Okay," he said, sighing. "But don't do anything funky like scream or say you're his biggest fan and stuff like that. He secretly hates it."

"Okay," she agreed.

Chachi stood as she approached.

Sasha squealed.

Chachi smiled courteously. "You must be—"

"Sasha!"

"Sasha," he repeated. "Is this your girlfriend?" he asked Michael, who looked at him with dismay.

"Yes," she answered feebly for him, and with a little less enthusiasm than he expected. He shook off a wave of jealousy when she dreamily looked up at Chachi and declared, "I swear, I'm your biggest fan! You are even more beautiful in person!"

"Thank you. You're adorable. Nice meeting you." Chachi had to wrestle his hand from her grip.

Michael took her elbow and nearly dragged her from the room. He could hear Genie greeting Chachi in a more sensible manner behind him.

"Why'd you do that? You made a fool out of yourself!" he scolded her once they reached the door.

"I'm sorry, it just came out. He's my favorite! Remember, I told you."

"I know, but it's different now. I mean, he's…family."

"I know!" She exhaled dreamily.

"Anyway, you should have called first. My father's having a private party."

"Ooooh, can I stay?"

"I said *private party,* Sasha."

"You let me stay at one of his parties before."

"I know. But now that Chachi's here, they're a little protective of his privacy."

"I swear I won't stare or babble. I won't say anything else to him, I swear!"

"I *can't*, Sasha, really!" he said a bit rougher than he intended. Her shoulders drooped. "Look, I'll call you tonight before bed," he promised as Genie joined them at the door. He opened it to escort them out.

"Eric's a bit wasted, isn't he?" Genie asked, her brow furrowed.

"Yeah. I'd better get back in there."

After they were gone, Michael headed for Eric. Lurking around the bar, Eric winked across the room at Michael.

Michael paused to apologize to Chachi. "I'm sorry about that, I wasn't expecting her."

"It's okay. I'm used to it. Besides, she's very pretty."

"Yeah," he muttered and continued on, his gaze on Eric struggling to slip a bottle of champagne under his shirt.

"I think you've had enough," he said as he tugged at the bottle.

"Hey!" Eric slurred. "What's up? You started this!"

"I know, but it's over. You don't know when to quit. You're gonna get us both caught!"

As the evening wore on Eric, having consumed too much champagne, laughed uncontrollably without provocation. He stumbled clumsily and staggered in spite of Michael's attempt to hold him steady and get him to leave the room before they could be found out. When he fell awkwardly over an ottoman that wasn't even in his way, Joe looked at him curiously.

"*What* is your problem?"

Eric laughed stupidly in response. Chachi, sitting nearby, came to his rescue.

"He's okay, Joe. I'm just having a little fun with him."

Joe glared at them, but slowly returned his attentions to his friends.

"Come here." Chachi beckoned Eric, who tried to steady himself as he approached. He giggled as he bent low enough for Chachi to speak into his ear. "I suggest you go ask Maxi for a cup of strong black coffee and take your silly ass in another room and sit down before your uncle discovers you've been dippin' in the broth."

Eric put his hand over his mouth to stifle a chuckle but he found his way out of the room.

Michael wasn't surprised when he, too, was beckoned. He knelt on the floor next to Chachi's chair. He'd rather take a lecture from Chachi than his father any day.

"You know, Joe thinks Eric has a strong influence over you," Chachi began, "because he's older than you are, he thinks a lot of the stuff you guys are getting into—the girls, the booze—is because Eric has introduced you to these things. But you and I know otherwise."

Michael looked at him precariously.

"Your cousin adores you. You're the most fun that's happened to him. He has been given the responsibility to look after you, but there is no looking after *you*. Eric can't handle some of the things you do for fun."

Michael looked down at the floor. Chachi was right. They couldn't have consumed more than two bottles of champagne and Eric was about ready to pass out. He, on the other hand, could barely feel the effects and he drank more than half the lot.

"You have a responsibility to look after *him*, Michael."

"I know." Michael nodded, shamefully.

"Do you know what would happen to him if Joe caught him in this state?"

Michael nodded again.

"I sent him off to get a hold of himself. He usually listens to me, so let's hope he does that."

Michael nodded again. He was so ashamed of himself.

"Don't look like that, I'm not gettin' in your shit," Chachi consoled him. "I just want you to know that it's not in his character to do these things. He's doing them because you are. You're family, and you have to look out for him."

Michael hoped Eric would be okay. If he started throwing up or anything, they'd be in trouble.

"Your girlfriend was very pretty," Chachi said.

"So you said."

"Why'd you put her out?"

"I didn't put her out!" How did this man seem to always know?

"Well, she looked like she wanted to stay."

"Not with *me*." Michael sulked, recalling the way Sasha had looked at Chachi.

"Aw, that means nothing," Chachi said, reading his mind again. "*You* should know that."

Michael blushed.

Chachi laughed at his discomfort. "When are you gonna get some of that music together for me?"

"It's upstairs."

"Maybe later we can go over some, huh?"

"Sure." A surge of warmth rose in his belly. He was going to get to showcase his work for Duke Spencer! He smiled to himself and swung his legs around, leaning against the back of Chachi's chair, dreaming of the possibilities.

Dominick pulled his own chair next to Chachi's, cutting Michael off, and he was soon forgotten. He sat on the floor behind that chair most of the evening, unbeknownst to his father and friends. David had finally been sent off, the girls remained upstairs, and the fellas were left to their own devices.

He got an earful that night and learned a lot about the crew. He was surprised to learn that his father and Steven were best friends as were Dominick and Chachi before they all met. He learned about their college days, and the trouble they got into. His ears perked up when they began to recall their sexual conquests, reliving their glory days of orgies and deviant sexual experiences. The conversation got deeper the drunker they became. Michael half expected his mother's name to pop up. However, when Joe mentioned the name Norris Bradford, Chachi quickly changed the subject. Michael sat up straight. This was a new development.

Then Joe brought up that Dukakis Sr. was in town and the group sobered.

"He just asked me to make sure I let you know, that's all." Joe sighed.

"So what," Chachi said, his tone flat.

"Dude, you're an old-ass man. What does your father have to do?"

"Nothing."

"He wants to meet us for lunch." Joe explained. "I for one haven't seen him in a while."

"Then *you* meet him!"

"Chachi—"

"Joe, face it. We just don't get along. It happens sometimes. He's my father and I give him props for that, but that's as far as it goes. We won't be going to ballgames. We never have and we never will. Now drop it."

"I feel so sorry for him," Joe mumbled. After a long silence, he made a last appeal. "Will you at least call him? He's been trying to reach you all week."

"I'll *call* him."

"Well," Dominick stretched his long arms and yawned, "guess I'll be moving along. I've got some calls to make in the morning myself."

Slowly, the rest of them followed until Joe and Chachi were left alone.

"I wasn't trying to run everybody off," Joe muttered.

Chachi snorted. "Who cares?"

They fell silent again.

"Wanna play some pool?" Joe asked.

"Naw. I'm gonna see what kind of songwriting skills your baby boy has."

"Michael? I'm sure he's upstairs with those earphones on." Joe rose with a deep yawn. "Go on up, I'm sure he hasn't turned in yet."

"Okay. I'll let myself out," Chachi said to Joe's departing back. Then he got up in the chair on his knees and looked down over the back of it at the top of Michael's head. "You ready, Mr. Eavesdropper?"

An hour later, they sat grooving to the sounds of Michael's keyboard.

"I like that," Chachi said, sounding genuinely impressed. "I didn't know you had all this talent, boy!"

Michael grinned. They sat on his bed surrounded by papers with songs he had written since he was ten. Eric lay sprawled on the other end, passed out.

"I'm gonna have these archived and indexed," Chachi said, gathering the irregular sheets together. "This is too valuable to keep in a shoebox. You've gotta be careful with these."

Michael shrugged. "I got 'em in my head." He played song after song on the keyboard he got for Christmas. "You know, not too long ago, my cousin Pooch and I sat on his bed like this," he looked across the room at his Duke Spencer poster, "looking at that exact poster and talking about making music.

Chachi smiled. He glanced over at a sleeping Eric.

"He's out cold." Michael chuckled.

"I'd better go." Chachi rose. He turned to Michael. "What?"

"How do you *do* that?" Michael asked.

"I could tell you wanted to ask me something."

"I know, but *how?*"

Chachi shrugged.

"I hope I'm not crossing a line," Michael began, "but—what's with you and your father?"

Chachi studied him carefully as though his features might tell him something. "Why do you think I'd discuss my father with you?"

Michael turned his face to hide his embarrassment. "I don't know—I just thought—I just—you seemed so angry when Dad mentioned him tonight. I thought since I kinda went through the same thing with my Dad..."

After what seemed like an eternity, Chachi spoke, his face as blank as a wall, "Your relationship problems with your father are nothing like mine.

I only discuss my personal affairs with my very close and trustworthy friends, Michael." He opened the door. "Maybe someday I'll tell you about him."

Chapter Eighteen

Both Eric and David were to graduate high school the same week. In the midst of preparations, the group spent hours in rehearsals and training. Joe and Chachi explained to Michael all about royalties and copyrights, much of which he already knew. He could stand to make millions from the little songs he penned in his loneliest hours.

As the new songwriter, he began to spend a lot of time with the behind-the-scenes guys: the control room operators and engineers, the producers and musicians and, of course, Chachi. Their friendship flourished. Michael was no longer shy and insecure in his presence, though he remained in awe of him every time he sang a note or danced a step.

His days had become so saturated with music that he often forgot to eat. His only communication with his mother and Pooch had been via voice mail. Sasha was on her fifth ultimatum about their relationship.

They worked late into the evening, debating which songs to include on the group's first CD and which would go to Duke. Michael did voice work as they tried out various ways to sing the same songs. He was exhausted when Chachi finally threw in the towel and offered to take him home.

When they pulled in front of the house, the lights were still on in Joe's study. Chachi turned off the ignition when Michael showed no signs of movement.

"I had fun," Michael said finally.

Chachi smiled and opened his sunroof. A million stars littered the navy sky.

Michael gazed wistfully at the lighted window. "He's waiting up for me."

"Does that bother you?"

Michael hesitated. "I don't know how I feel about the way he smothers me. I've gone from being almost invisible to being scrutinized."

"He adores you," Chachi said.

"I adore him too. It's just different. It's tough sometimes."

Chachi hunkered down and lit a cigarette. "Your father isn't as tough as he seems," he said, blowing smoke through the roof of the car.

"Oh, no? He ever hit you across the head?" Michael asked in half jest.

"I'm telling you. He's easy to crack." Chachi hesitated as Michael took the cigarette from his fingers and pulled on it long and hard, savoring the nicotine.

"Oh, Lord! It's been so long since I've tasted a good cigarette!"

Chachi half-lifted a brow and shook his head. "Your father is a control freak," he said after a short pause. "His father was a control freak, and his father's father was the same. For people like them, you have to give the pretense that you'll give them what they want. Joe is a sucker for his kids."

"Hasn't worked for me." Michael chuckled.

"You're too much like him. You'd rather wrestle him for control. You have to learn to be a kid and let him make the decisions. Then you appeal to him for change, you know, a little adjustment here and there. He just likes to feel he's got it handled."

"I'll try that," Michael promised.

Chachi took the cigarette from Michael and took a long draw from it. They smoked in silence for a few minutes, gazing at the sky. Chachi broke out his flask and took a sip from it.

"He never asked me whether I did it or not," Michael whispered.

"Did what?" Chachi squinted at him.

"Shot my stepfather on purpose."

Chachi breathed deeply and took another drink from the flask. "*Did* you?" he asked quietly.

Michael took the flask from him before answering. "I don't know." He looked directly into Chachi's face. "I wanted to. I *hated* him. He tried to take the gun from me and it went off. But I-I-I could have squeezed the trigger…I'm not sure." He passed a hand dazedly over his face.

"Why does it matter now?"

"He's paralyzed, probably for life. I could have killed him. I'd like to know if I'm a potential murderer."

Chachi lay back as far as his seat would go and turned to Michael. "We're all potential murderers, Michael. Most of us may never get around to actually committing a murder, but we're all capable of it. I believe that something so terrible compelled you to want to kill this man and somehow, someway, whether you did it or fate had a hand in it, you were rescued from him."

In that moment under the starry sky, hearing those words, looking into those bourbon eyes, Michael felt a door open inside him. "I never thought of that."

"I would bet my fortune that you wouldn't hurt a fly unless you had to. Now if you had to, you'd kill the President. That's if you *had* to. We have a lot in common, you and me."

Michael sniffed. He hadn't realized he was crying until Chachi used his thumb to wipe away an escaped tear. "I'm sorry." He laughed nervously.

"It's okay. Sometimes you just gotta hit the rinse cycle."

Michael understood what drew everyone to Chachi.

"I couldn't imagine that you ever cry," Michael said.

"Oh, sure. You're not a man if you can't cry. You're not even human if you can't cry." Chachi rolled his left shoulder as if something was bothering it, a gesture Michael noticed before. "You know, I hated my father growing up too. He did something I never forgave him for. He spent every day afterwards trying to make up for it but," he sighed, "I just couldn't forgive him."

Astonished, Michael's dark eyes probed Chachi's face. He wasn't expecting him to open up so soon.

"What did he do?"

Chachi smiled, but it was laced with the pain of bad memories. "He abducted me. Kidnapped me from my birth mother."

Michael sat very still, afraid that he'd lose the moment if he moved.

Chachi stared into the dashboard as if he saw something there. The moonlight shone on his face and gave it a softness and innocence. Michael reached over and squeeze his arm for support.

"I was only five." Chachi's voice wavered. He closed his eyes and slid further down into his seat. "I can still smell the breeze on the water. I can feel the hot sun on my skin. The sun would get so hot…" he looked down at his hands. "I remember everything." He reached for the flask.

"Here." Michael nearly turned it up to Chachi's mouth for him. "He just snatched you off the street?"

Chachi inhaled deeply. "No…it wasn't that simple. There's more to it. A lot more."

"Like what?"

Joe opened the front door and stood in the doorway.

"You'd better go," Chachi said glancing at his watch. "I had no idea we were here so long."

It just seemed like the wrong time to leave. Michael felt such a connection. He wasn't alone in his tortured childhood, his longing for his mother, his hatred for his now ex father-figure.

"Thanks for trusting me," Michael said.

Chachi smiled as if the painful memory had never existed. "See ya tomorrow!"

Chapter Nineteen

Spring took a bow and summer made its entrance when they put the finishing touches on the group's CD. During one of their weekly meetings, Chachi announced that he would be taking a few of his protégé's, including Simpson & Sybak, with him on a nationally televised concert appearance. This was the stuff they could never learn in class. Michael begged to tag along.

He rode with the band to the stadium. There was about twelve of them altogether. Chachi and his entourage had taken a separate car.

At the stadium, they had several checkpoints to get through. The venue was much smaller than the one where he and Pooch had first seen Duke Spencer live. Still, the room was prickly with electricity even though the doors wouldn't open to the public for hours.

From sound to lighting, the area was crawling with technical people. They all took seats and watched the band do run-throughs. After a couple of hours of that torture, they were all given a cold lunch delivered by a nearby deli and ushered into waiting cars. They made the rounds for the next five hours to various local radio and television stations where they watched Duke, surrounded by an outlandishly large entourage of staff and bodyguards, answer the same questions over and over. With his fresh, boyish smile and easy laugh, he engaged the interviewer and answered each question with new enthusiasm as if it had not been posed to him a hundred times before.

Back at the stadium, Chachi received final touchups in his dressing room. Three people were simultaneously adjusting hair, makeup, and costume.

Enthusiasm bled up from the tips of Michael's toes. Chachi was no longer Chachi, but had transformed into Duke Spencer—the same Duke Spencer he revered on stage, on CD covers, and on wall posters. There wasn't so much a different look as much as there was a different attitude about him. Chachi gazed thoughtfully into an enormous wall-sized lighted mirror, examining every detail of the results of his transformation. He didn't flinch when they came in, but continued his scrutiny as they quietly and dutifully lined up along a side wall, well out of the way.

"Ten minutes!" a stage hand shouted.

Chachi took one last look at his reflection and sighed his readiness. Another knock at the door and Michael was pleasantly surprised to see his father hurry inside.

"Dad!" he gushed before he could catch himself; they had been instructed to keep quiet.

"Hey, Puppy!" Joe grinned and hugged him in spite of their guide's, Norma's, furrowed brow. "You taking it all in?"

Michael nodded happily.

Joe acknowledged the rest of them with hugs, a pinch on the cheek or a rustle of the hair before turning to Chachi.

"Ready, babe?" he asked, picking up Chachi's headset and placing it on his own head.

"I am now." Chachi sighed with relief.

"I'm sorry; I had an out of town meeting and missed my plane."

The roar of the crowd filled the dressing room, and they were no short distance from the arena. Duke rose as if in response to it and, as if on cue, the door to the dressing room opened and a sea of people—staff, bodyguards, and some members of the press who had received exclusive access—greeted him and parted, making a path for him. He walked with long, stately strides. When he reached the stage entrance, he halted. His stylist began to fuss with his hair and he irritably shoved her hand away while his makeup artists stole a quick dab at a few beads of perspiration that collected at his brow.

Michael grinned with anticipation.

"You're really getting into this," Eric said, smiling.

They were barely seated when the show began. Michael thought he'd burst with pride when Duke danced over to their section and purposefully put the microphone to his face for a sing-a-long.

"Come up, come up!" Duke urged him, but Michael couldn't move.

Eric ribbed him angrily in the side. "I can't believe you!" he screamed over the crowd.

They filed backstage after the show and were pushed and shoved by throngs of people who joined them as they made for his dressing room. They took their places along the wall and watched as a bunch of lucky fans, media contest winners and groupies, pressed him for autographs.

After signing his name many, many times and hugging and kissing strangers who cried, begged, and declared their love, Chachi finally waved. A staffer immediately began to hand out pre-autographed photos to the disappointed fans who failed to get a personal signing.

Duke's shoulders sagged in exhaustion as soon as they were gone.

"We still got press," Joe reminded him.

"I know," he said. He turned to the group of them. "Ready for this?" He grinned. A scattering of laughter ran through the group. Chachi turned to Michael and frowned playfully. "Scaredy-cat."

Smiling apologetically, Michael said, "You should have warned me."

"I told you to always be ready."

"I know," Michael admitted. "But to *sing*?"

Then, the press was allowed in and he was Duke again, answering the same questions with feigned interest and not even blinking in the rash of flashing bulbs that engulfed him.

* * * *

"We won't be leaving until morning. What do you want to do today?" Joe asked.

"Let's go swimming," Justin suggested.

David frowned.

"What do you wanna do?" Joe turned to David.

David shrugged. "Probably nothing," he muttered.

"There's an amusement park nearby," songstress Donna Clark piped in. "I saw the signs as we were driving to the stadium."

"I did too!" Eric sat up, grinning. "Hey Mike, you wanna go to the amusement park?"

"I've never been to one. That sounds great."

"You've never been to an amusement park!" Joe gasped. "Then that's settled. We're taking Michael to his first amusement park. You guys be ready in an hour."

"What about Chachi?" Michael asked. "Should we leave him a message? He may still be asleep."

Joe lifted a brow. "So? What do we need him for?"

They rode the tour bus the forty miles to the amusement park. They played cards, sang songs and told jokes. The boys flew paper airplanes back and forth and everyone shouted over one another. Joe sat at the front of the bus with the chaperones he commissioned to accompany them, including Norma and several of the bodyguards. Michael could have gone all day just kicking it on the bus with the group, until he saw the colorful flags bearing the amusement park's emblem. He grew as agitated as a five-year-old as they all cheered the way into the parking lot.

They waited impatiently as Joe paid for the tickets and doled out spending money before bursting through the gates and into the park like pre-schoolers.

Joe called after them, "We're meeting back here, in this spot at the front gate for lunch at noon!"

They split off into smaller groups and for three hours rode rides, played games, ate pizza and other junk foods, and drank lemonade. Michael wanted to ride everything. He had missed so much of this stuff growing up and he wanted to catch up on it all that day. Each ride made him want to undertake a more daring experience. David spent most of his time at the gaming section and Eric, getting pretty close to Donna Clark, seemed to be more interested in just taking in the scenery and munching on goodies with his new 'girlfriend.'

Justin and Toby of De-generation rode with Michael most of the time, but when they reached the Daredevil, the park's newest and most adventurous ride, even they had to decline and leave Michael to his madness. Michael didn't want to ride alone, and didn't want to sit with some stranger, so he succumbed to their pleas for lunch.

No one knew exactly why they had to meet for lunch; they had been cramming their mouths with junk all morning. Even as they waited, Michael finished off a double-decker ice cream cone. Slowly, each member of their group joined together at the front gate with their own stories of who won what prize and who screamed like a baby on what rides. Finally, Joe approached with Norma, Tank, and—Chachi!

"Hey!" Eric called out as he ran the few short steps to meet them. Chachi threw an arm around his neck as they walked up and joined the rest of the group.

Chachi wore navy blue designer jeans, a crisp white shirt, a navy blue cap and dark shades. People turned and looked at them with uncertainty.

In spite of a lack of hunger, they ate, feasting on chicken, pizza, burgers, fries, hot dogs, and a variety of drinks and deserts. The bright sunshine and warm breeze of early summer made them flighty and playful. Slowly they began to disperse to different areas of the park.

"We'll meet back at the front gate one hour before closing!" Joe yelled. Eric and Donna rose, holding hands.

"What's up?" Michael asked. Wasn't it enough that Eric spent practically the entire morning with her? "Where're you guys going?"

"Just around…" Eric shuffled his feet. "Wanna come?" he asked half-heartedly.

Michael shook his head and slumped in his seat.

Joe smiled at Michael's disappointment. "Eric's a little older than you, Michael. He's at the age where he will start to get serious about girls. He might be drifting away from you a lot in the coming days."

Michael shrugged and sighed.

Chachi laughed. "I thought she was after *you,* Michael. You mean you let Eric slip in there under your nose?"

"He never notices stuff like that," David said with a wave of his hand in Michael's direction. "That girl did everything but straddle him and he didn't notice."

"Donna?" Michael asked, eyes bulging. She was friendly toward him, and he talked with her a lot, but there was never any suggestion… He wasn't interested in her anyway.

"Eric tries to be a player and juggle three and four at a time." Joe clucked disapprovingly. "Michael's a gentleman."

David snorted. "Oh, like twenty girls a day don't call the house for him, too!"

"Still. I've only seen him actually have a relationship with Sasha." Joe glanced in Michael's direction.

"Sasha who?" Michael's lip curled with disgust. As he devoted himself to his music, he had grown tired of Sasha's constant badgering him for more time alone.

"You're too young for all this seriousness anyway," Joe scolded. "You need to have fun. I think you're pretty smart to hold these girls at arm's length."

"Is that why I'm sitting here *alone*?" Michael asked, "with you, Chachi, and with—" he flashed his gaze in David's direction, "—him?"

"What's wrong with that?" Joe demanded as David and Chachi snickered behind slices of pizza. "What's wrong with hanging out with your old man, or Chachi, or your brother?"

Michael rolled his eyes and sat up. "Okay. Then, will you ride the Daredevil with me?"

"Uhhh." Joe looked from David to Chachi. "David'll go with you."

"No I won't!" David shouted.

Shielding his eyes from the sun, Joe turned in the direction of the ominous steel demon. Its victims could be heard screaming even from where they sat. "I don't think so, son…" he said, eyeing the 'Daredevil'. "But we can do something else. Let's play some games or something."

Sighing, Michael rose from the table. "Okay, let's play."

They won so many stuffed animals they had to give them away to children at the park. Joe did agree to go on a less daunting ride called the people-shooter, but after it was over, he declared that he was done with riding for the day. He left to take in a burlesque show with Tank and Chachi.

As evening settled in, a tired Michael found a bench and sat alone waiting for the hour before closing so that he could meet up with the group at the front gate as instructed. The Daredevil soared under the stars. He was not expecting Chachi to sit next to him.

"Hey there, lonely boy," Chachi said.

"Hey."

"What are you doing here by yourself? Still pining over Eric?"

"I'm not pining over Eric!"

"Then what're you sitting by yourself for?"

Michael played with his fingers. "I'm just waiting for the time to go," he murmured.

They sat quietly a few moments.

"I was surprised to see you here," Michael said.

"I woke up and found out that everybody had left me." Chachi frowned. "Joe left me a note. I wasn't too keen on romping around an amusement park, but…"

Michael chuckled. "Must've been some party last night."

Chachi grinned.

"So, you got my message."

"*Your* message? I thought Joe left that message."

Michael blushed.

When Chachi leaned forward and peered into Michael's face, his smile was magic. "Thanks," he said, "for thinking about me."

Michael's heart swelled inside his chest.

"It's almost time to head out," Chachi said, rising.

Michael's mouth turned down at the corners. "Ride the Daredevil with me first?" he asked, his eyes beseeching.

Chachi shook his head. "Sorry. I don't do rides."

"Please Chachi—"

"Ride it by yourself!"

"I don't *want* to ride it by myself. I don't *want* to ride with a stranger. Please?"

Chachi looked over at the snaking giant and shook his head again. "I don't know, Michael. I get sick on those things."

"When was the last time you'd been on one?"

"I don't know!" Chachi threw his hands up in exasperation. "I'm thirty-six years old!"

"*Please?* It'll be fun!"

"Nope. Come on, let's go."

"I can't believe you're scared of a kiddie-ride. Maybe Dad, but not you!"

Chachi narrowed his golden-brown eyes at him. He contemplated the steel monster. "And what do I get if I ride?"

"You name it."

"Come on."

They headed toward the ride, Michael bouncing in front, Chachi trudging regretfully behind with Tank, who had been lurking nearby, walking at a safe distance. They picked up David and Justin, and later Donna and Eric on the way. As Michael and Chachi waited in line, Eric spotted Joe and Norma and gestured for them to join them. As they approached the front of the line, their friends and family began to cheer in support.

Chachi moaned as the ride slowed to a halt and dizzy patrons stumbled out. "I am out of my fuckin' mind!"

Michael clutched his arm until they were seated and strapped in. A park assistant checked each seat before take-off. Then they were off, slowly at first, climbing higher and higher, then picking up speed. Mike shouted and waved at his family and friends so many miles below him.

"This isn't so bad." Chachi pushed up from his slumping position, and waved at the crowd below; which meant he wasn't prepared for the plunge that followed. They dropped one hundred feet at about sixty miles per hour before being yanked along a mad series of circular tracks, twisted through a maze of tunnels, twirled three hundred sixty degrees, pulled back up into the heavens, and again dropped for a repeat performance—in reverse.

Michael fought the force of speed by placing his fingers in his ears to block the screaming wind. *Wait a minute. That's not the wind.*

Chachi pressed his head into Michael's shoulder and screamed like his little sister. Had it not been for the safety restraints, he'd have been on the floor.

Laughing, Michael tried to help him by throwing both arms around him. Finally, they slowed. "You all right?" Michael asked, still chuckling and holding on to him.

Chachi's face was pale and damp. His eyes had that unseeing look and his chest heaved with an effort to breath.

"You all right, sir?" The teen-aged attendant rushed to activate the safety restraint release.

Chachi shoved the safety mechanism away from him, but stood up too quickly and fell backward into the seat. He tried again to stand but stepped out on the wrong side of the car, in spite of attempts to guide him, and fell across Michael's lap.

Joe, Tank, and Frank had come over to help out.

A crowd gathered. "That's Duke Spencer!" someone yelled.

"Oh, shit," Joe muttered.

The crowd pressed in on them. Spectators pulled out their instant cameras, snapping pictures as Chachi struggled to walk with Tank single-handedly holding him up in a one-arm embrace. In spite of Frank and Joe pushing the crowd away and Dennis and Norma trying to pry open a path, an over-zealous fan rushed Chachi and raised her camera just in time to receive the contents of his stomach.

Between the pushing, shoving, screaming, shouting, and camera bulbs flashing, even Michael became disoriented and felt Frank's strong arm around him. Without adequate air and already severely shaken up, Chachi had all but collapsed against Tank and park security had to assist them in making it to the tour bus.

Safely inside, Michael noticed he had been scratched several places. His shirt was ripped and he had blood on his scalp where his hair had been torn out. He was nobody, why'd they attack him? He looked pitifully at Chachi, whose skin now had a horrible pallor. Now was not the time to make apologies. They began the long ride back to the hotel.

Every gaze was on Chachi. He sat with his head propped against the window, his hand over his eyes. Michael dared not speak.

"He'll be all right," Joe said into the silence.

Forever the clown, Eric broke the quiet. "Well! That was fun."

The air on the bus became peppered with nervous giggles. Chachi raised his head and glared at them but his shapely lips hinted at a smile, so they dared to laugh a bit harder.

Michael leapt from his seat onto the seat next to Chachi. "I'm so sorry," he said. "I should have never made you go."

"You didn't *make* me go," Chachi said, speaking out the side of his mouth.

Eric asked innocently, "Hey, Chachi. Did you check your pants?" The bus erupted into fits.

Chachi chuckled. "That's okay Eric. I *got* you."

David added, "I didn't know you could scream that loud dude, I heard you all the way where I stood! You shouldn't have any problems hittin' your notes."

"All right, that's enough," Joe said, but he was laughing too.

Mike turned to Chachi. "I'm sorry."

"That's okay. I'm glad I did it."

"Why? Because you faced your fear of rides?"

"No." Chachi flashed a mischievous grin. "Because you *owe* me."

Chapter Twenty

"Two hours to freshen up, pack, and get back on this bus!" Joe shouted as they spilled out. "I mean it! Pack your things and leave your luggage in front of the door of your room. The hotel will take it from there. Don't test me now! One of the biggest lessons I teach my artists when we travel is how to get home by yourself from anywhere in the world—the hard way!"

They scrambled off the bus.

"You riding back with us, Chachi?" Eric called out as Chachi, flanked by his guards, sauntered to the hotel entrance.

"Hell naw!" Chachi called back. "I don't ride tour buses, I'm a star!" Still smarting from the teasing he took on the bus, he flipped them off with his middle finger.

But just before they pulled off, Chachi and his gang showed up and the bus cheered. The kids were disappointed when he sat next to Joe at the front of the bus and went over business issues, his ear to his cell phone.

They made a middle-of-the-night pit stop. When Chachi boarded the bus again, he headed for the back laden with junk food, cigarettes, and alcohol. The party was on. Tank, Chachi, Frank, and Dennis passed alcohol and cigarettes, played music and 'talked shit.' Joe and Norma tried to sleep up front.

Eric and Michael picked up their game of sneaking alcohol, but Chachi was on to them and warned them to keep their paws off.

"Your father ain't holding *me* responsible," Chachi said, his eyes bright with the stimulation of gin.

As dawn broke through night, the back of the bus rocked. In spite of Chachi's efforts to stave off the pillaging of his stash, the noise on the bus gave evidence that the grownups weren't the only ones getting high.

"What is this?" Joe yelled, standing over them in time to see Michael toss a lit cigarette in Tank's direction. They all jumped, disturbed as Tank's massive form dove out of his seat with the quickness of a cheetah, but they dared not laugh.

"You feeding the kids drugs, Chachi?" Joe said with an air of authority sufficient to quell the best high. The boys groaned and tried to appear as sober as possible to prevent too severe of an attack on Chachi.

"I ain't feeding them shit!" Chachi retorted, spurned on by the alcohol. "If they're getting it, they're stealing it. I told 'em to keep their hands off. They're gonna do what they're gonna do. That's on them!"

"No, that's on *you!*" Joe shouted. "*You* are their manager! *You* are their role model, hell—you're David's *godfather!* Frank, Dennis, and Tank are supposed to be *protecting* them; what kind of example is this?"

"Look, Joe," Chachi held up his hands, "I am not the one to baby-sit your kids, and I am not a chaperone. I was supposed to be on a plane, remember? I had a tough show and a long day and I'm trying to unwind.

It's 4 o'clock in the morning and these kids should be asleep. If you and Norma want to sit ya'll asses in the front of the bus and sleep while the kids are back here doing God knows what... I'm sorry, I ain't watching no kids!"

"I don't believe you said that!"

"Well…"

"These kids' parents have entrusted them to us!"

"I am an artist." Chachi slapped his chest. "I will teach them everything I know and steer them away from trouble when I can, but I ain't a father-figure. You know that. And I ain't no mother-figure. That's what Norma is here for."

"You need your ass kicked," Joe fumed, his brow-line inverted in anger. "I know you have a fucked-up view of the world, but I always thought I could trust you with the kids."

"What are you trying to *say*?" Chachi shouted, his shoulders squared.

"They are drinking and smoking in your face, and instead of you guys preventing it, you are aiding and abetting—

"Joe! I am *not* doing it!" Chachi amplified even more. "I am not babysitting no kids! This is what they do every time they get a chance, behind your back!"

Michael and Eric cringed.

"Now, if you're that concerned about it," Chachi raged on, "then bring your mother-fuckin' ass back here with 'em!" A unanimous gasp traveled the bus. "Or take the lil' mother-fuckers up there with you! But *don't* say another word to me about it!"

Joe and Chachi stared one another down coldly. Then Joe glanced from Eric to Michael to David before angrily retreating to his seat. They rode on in silence.

"I knew I should've kept my first-class ticket and went home on the plane," Chachi mumbled to Tank, who nodded quietly.

Eric cleared his throat. "We didn't mean to—"

"Shut *up*!" Chachi snapped.

They were silent again.

"Boy, Dad can sure suck the life out of a party," Michael said under his breath, hoping to pacify Chachi; after all, they were old enough to know better.

Chachi looked at him with smoldering brown eyes, then produced and lit a cigarette. "Your father can suck my dick," he said, gaze fixed straight ahead.

Chapter Twenty-One

Michael turned sixteen without fanfare. He got gifts in the mail and phone calls from Pooch, Gherri, and Sarah, and had a quiet dinner at home. After a few months of camping, sailing and a trip to Europe, they dove into work hoping to release the new CD by fall.

The single hadn't done as well as expected in spite of the group opening for Duke on several shows and the release of a slammin' music video. They had to admit that Chachi had done all he could. They just didn't have "it". At least Michael met a fresh-faced, pretty girl named Illian, a video dancer. High-spirited and effervescent, Illian seemed to want nothing from him but a good laugh and a good time. She was a refreshing change from Sasha.

While Eric delved deeper into a relationship with Donna and Chachi and Joe busied themselves trying to salvage Simpson & Sybak, Michael spent his spare time with Illian, who knew all the night spots and had the best weed-man in town.

A botched CD meant the group goes on hiatus for re-assessment, which left David and Eric free to explore higher education. David, eager to be free of parental control, packed up quickly and, with Joe and Lydia tagging along to help him get settled, flew off to the same film school to which Joe had just last year sent Pooch.

The following weekend, Eric also packed to leave. Michael offered to help him, despite his black mood. The little white pills his mother sent him in his care packages helped less and less. He hadn't heard from her in weeks and no one had seen her, nor had she responded to the CD sample he sent her. Pooch called less and less and Michael got his voice messaging-system more and more, and now Eric was leaving him, no doubt he'd come back a different person after the college experience.

"Hey. I'll tell you a secret." Eric beamed, as Michael helped him drag his luggage down the stairs to the car. "I gave Donna a ring!"

Michael gasped, mouth open, eyes wide. "A ring!"

"Not *that* kind of ring. Just a token, you know, a promise."

"A promise to what?"

"A promise to promise. I like her a lot, Mike. Actually…" Eric blew out a breath. Michael held his. "I love her."

Michael exhaled and collapsed on the stair. "Eric..."

"I think she's the one. I know we're too young and it's too soon. I'm thinking maybe in a few years we might get married."

Michael stared at the ceiling.

"You'll be my best man," Eric continued. "Don't tell anyone, okay?"

Michael looked at him, long and hard. Eric glowed. How could Michael be a true friend and begrudge him that just because *he* felt like crap. "That's cool," he said finally.

Eric held out his hand and Michael let him pull him to his feet.

"It's about time!" Eric's father said when they made it to the door.

A light rain fell. They all stood under umbrellas and watched Eric and his father help the driver load the luggage into the trunk of the car. Eric's mother sat dabbing at her eyes in the front seat. Joe smiled proudly; he had more to do with the way Eric turned out than either of his absentee parents.

They exchanged final goodbyes. Joe put his arm around Michael and squeezed as the car carrying his best friend snaked away.

Back in his room, Michael's sadness threatened to consume him. He needed music, and he needed it *loud*. So he turned it on and up. Sitting cross-legged on his bed, he placed his hands over his face. He had to call somebody, get out of the house—something. He thought about Sasha, but she had been so cross with him lately. He called Pooch and got voice mail.

He called his mother. No answer. He called his auntie Mel, but she swore she hadn't seen nor heard from his mother in about a month. He kept dialing 'til finally, he dialed the number that he wanted to dial in the first place.

"Hey, what's the matter?" Chachi asked.

"You busy?"

"I'm home today looking over some contracts. What's wrong?"

"Can I come over?"

A pregnant silence.

"Sure," Chachi said. "Have Pratt drive you. See you in ten?"

"Okay."

If Michael thought his father's mansion was a vision of opulence, Chachi had the keys to a kingdom. His sprawling estate sat on many acres of well-tended land adorned with enormous evergreen trees, towering statues, and fountains. The décor was a reflection of his personality, bold but not gaudy, colorful and fun. He used lots of creams and whites and threw in shocking colors such as purples, blues, greens, and yellows. Ornate lighted sconces and candleholders lined the walls.

Michael immediately felt better when he saw Chachi leaning over the banister at the top of the staircase clad in his bathrobe.

"Come on up," he said, his smile wide.

"Nice," Michael said as he reached the top. Cloaked in Chachi's high spirits, his dark cloud had no choice but to dissipate.

"Thank you. I'll give you a tour later." Chachi led him into a room with music blaring. An enormous roll-neck chaise, large enough to seat three adults, sat against a wall. Two matching settees and richly carved tables were scattered throughout. A bar with two stools stood in a corner and a big-screen television surrounded by amplifiers, receivers, and other equipment revealed the source of the loud music. Chachi went over to turn the music down. "This is my own little space," he said.

"I love it!" Michael looked around. *Little space?*

"My bedroom's over there." He pointed to an adjoining room flanked by large columns. "I have one bathroom here and two in the bedroom. My workout room is back there, my office is next to it, and this is my sitting room."

"Wow."

"Come over here and sit down." Chachi led him to the cushy chaise. "Tell me all about it."

Expelling all the air from his lungs, Michael said, "He's marrying Donna."

Chachi rolled his eyes.

"You knew?" Michael asked.

"He told me. But I blew that off. He's way too young. He won't do anything that stupid. Not now."

"They could run off and elope."

"The men in your family are too controlled to do *anything* on a whim."

Michael sighed. "I just feel like he's different now. We don't spend any time together anymore."

"He's in *love*."

"What's your point?"

Chachi laughed and walked over to the bar. He poured two glasses of wine. "I feel you. I never understood what happens to people. They get all googley-eyed and fucked up in the head because, what, you run into a fine chick?"

"There must be something else."

Chachi shrugged and handed him a glass. "Beats me. You're still young. You'll probably find out soon enough. Me, if I haven't fallen yet, I probably ain't fallin'." He sipped his wine.

Michael shrugged. "I doubt if it's in the cards for me either. Do you have cognac?" Michael asked, handing back the wine.

"Cognac? What do you think this is, a bar?"

Michael groaned.

"I'm not kidding Michael, I'm already foul for giving wine to a minor and you want cognac?"

"Come on, Chachi, are you done lecturing?"

"No!"

"'Cause I *really* need this."

Chachi took the wine glass and set it on the bar. He reached for a fresh glass and a bottle of cognac and poured a half-inch.

"That's all?" Michael whined. He took the bottle out of Chachi's hand and poured the glass half full. "If anybody asks, I haven't seen you," he promised. He sat back on the chaise and reached for a pack of cigarettes that sat on a side table. "You got a light?"

"You insist on securing my place in hell, don't you," Chachi said before producing a cigarette lighter and placing the flame against Michael's cigarette.

Michael laughed. "Thanks. See, you made me laugh."

Chachi looked away briefly.

Lounging on the chaise, wide-legged, Michael blew puffs of smoke into the air. He picked up the glass of cognac and drank it in one long swig, then continued puffing on his cigarette, looking thoughtfully at the ceiling. "So you think it's all bullshit?" he asked, taking another pull of the cigarette, "Eric and Donna, I mean."

"I don't think they'll do anything for a few years and by then, Eric will have met all kinds of ass up at school."

Michael smirked, satisfied.

"What else Michael, there must be something else bothering you."

Michael's smile collapsed. He handed the cigarette to Chachi, who put it out in an astray on the table next to him. "I haven't heard from my mother in a month."

"No shit?" Chachi straightened. "That could be serious. Did you mention it to Joe?"

Michael shook his head. The last thing he needed was to have his father go rescuing his mother and screwing everything up with Lydia.

"You talk to Steven? I believe they stayed in touch."

"No, but that's a thought," Michael said softly. "I'll call him." Michael reached into his pocket and pulled out a rolled joint. "Can I borrow your lighter again?"

"Now what!"

"It's just a joint, Chachi, relax!" He laughed, accepting the lighter. Michael pulled on the joint and closed his eyes.

"Where'd you get the drugs?"

"Illian," Mike responded, handing him the joint.

"Illian? What kind of name is that?" Chachi asked, taking a turn at the joint.

Michael blew smoke at him. "You know her; she danced on the video shoot."

"The chick you were laying all over?"

"Laying all over?"

"With the pink and blue hair?"

Michael laughed again. "Yeah, that's her." The smile faded and a shadow passed over his face.

"You've had enough of this," Chachi said, taking the joint from his hand.

"Tell me something nice," Michael said, reclining. "Tell me about your childhood, about the sun and the water. Or tell me one of those stories about you and Dad in college."

"All right," Chachi said, lying next to him and crossing his wrists behind his head. "Lets see..." He gazed skyward. "Okay I got one. Did I ever tell you about the time we put dye in Steven's talc?"

"No way," Michael said, already snickering.

"We learned about this substance from Jake's medical book. I forget what it was, but some guy in his chemistry class concocted a powder for us that, when wet, would turn black."

Michael laughed fitfully.

"Anyway, one day, Dominick and I decided to play a trick on Steve. He was such a goody-two-shoes, we could barely stand him in college! He had a ritual, probably still does, where he has to sprinkle this talc on his private parts after showering right?"

"Right," Michael managed through his laughter.

"We used to tease him about it. So we got this powder and mixed it with his talc."

"Weren't you afraid it could hurt him, like, burn his skin or something?"

"Who thinks of stuff like that when you're playing a prank? Anyway, he took his shower and sprinkled his little talc in his pants—"

"And what?"

"Well, nothing happened right away. But that evening, he went into the bathroom to shower and screamed." They both laughed. "We we're cracking up. He just grabbed his clothes and ran to the emergency room."

"That's terrible!" Michael said, laughing so uncontrollably he had tears in his eyes. "What happened then?" he asked when he could finally compose himself.

"They gave him some kind of ointment. They had no clue what it was. Luckily, it wore off in a few days. Joe told him we did it." Chachi's lip twisted into a wry smile. "We never should have let him in on it."

"I bet Steven tried to kick your ass!"

"Steven? Naw. He could've gotten us expelled, but he was a good sport. He thought it was funny."

Michael sighed. "You know how to brighten my spirits." Michael pushed up on one elbow and leaned over Chachi, kissing him ever so slightly on the lips.

Chachi jumped. "What was that?" he demanded.

"Just a kiss. No big deal." Michael reached over Chachi for the lighter and cigarette he never got to finish.

Chachi caught his arm mid-air. "You just kissed me!"

"What's wrong with that?" Michael gazed innocently at him.

"What's *wrong* with it?"

"It was just a kiss." Michael chuckled. "It didn't mean anything other than thank you or—whatever. It's just an expression."

"Of what?"

Michael giggled. "You remind me of Pooch." He smiled. "He hates when I get what he calls 'touchy-feely'. I'm sorry. I didn't mean to offend you." His eyes were innocent again.

Chachi released the breath he was holding. "No offense, I was just taken off guard. I certainly wasn't expecting that. Pooch is right, you shouldn't make that a habit." Chachi did the roll-of-the-shoulder thing.

"My mom taught me to kiss."

"Your *mom*? That's a little weird, don't you think?"

"To some people," Michael said, "but she and I know we don't mean anything by it other than that we love each other."

"You shouldn't kiss your mother the way you'd kiss, say Sasha."

"Why not? Who makes the rules?" Michael scowled. "It's just another way of communicating."

"So your mom would get a nice peck on the cheek..."

Michael shook his head, then leaned in and pressed another kiss to Chachi's lips, this one bolder and more generous, mouth parted, tongue…

"All right, don't do that again!" Chachi stood up and backed away from him.

Michael bit his bottom lip to hold his laughter. "I was just showing you how I kiss my mom."

"You kiss your *mom* like *that*?"

"My mom taught me everything I know about kissing." He sat up and drew his knees into his chest. He could have been talking about baseball. "When I was six, she stuck her tongue in my mouth." Chachi's mouth gaped open. "I thought it was the grossest thing. She was showing me how she kissed her boyfriend. I had been spying on them and I asked her about it."

Chachi was in a rare state of speechlessness and made no attempt to respond when Michael paused for his reaction.

"She was so beautiful. Still is. I have to admit my mother used to turn me on when I was little."

Chachi scratched his head. "Most guys start off with a crush on their mothers. They don't tongue em' though."

"Nothing more ever happened." Michael frowned. "I mean, she's my *mother* for god's sake; Give me a break!"

"Thank God for that," Chachi muttered. "No offense. I just think it's inappropriate to suck face with you mother, that's all."

"I don't *care* what you think!" Michael said, his tone cold. Then his face softened. "I'm sorry. I do care. I didn't mean to weird you out. I just feel like I can be myself around you."

"And who is that?" Chachi joked.

Michael cocked his head. A smile played on his lips. "You'll just have to find out."

"I'll tell you what," Chachi said. "The next time you wanna kiss me, try this." He pulled Michael's head close and planted a firm kiss on his forehead.

Michael laughed. "Deal."

"Good. Now get up. There's someone I want you to meet."

The old man leaned into a bowl, inside of which he mixed a concoction that was obviously very dear to his heart, for after a sip of the white liquid that dripped from the spoon, his head emerged from the bowl with a smile of satisfaction and his dark eyes were warm with remembrance. He didn't hear them come in and turned with a start when Chachi spoke.

"Papi, I want you to meet Joe's son, Michael. Michael, this is my Uncle Papi."

Chachi's Uncle Papi. After more than a year, to finally meet Papi, such a monumental part of Chachi's life. He reached for Papi's hand in greeting, but the aging fellow dropped his spoon and grabbed hold of him, hugging him tightly to his breasts. He smelled of fresh coconut. A peace enveloped Michael as he wrapped his arms tight around the waist of an old man he'd just met. From Chachi's stories, he had imagined Papi to be squat and small with ruddy cheeks like Santa Claus, perpetually sporting a starched, white apron around his belly.

Instead, he looked upon a man of great stature, despite his age. At 70, his shoulders did not droop in spite of his seamed face. His bright, black eyes reflected his delight. His hands were big and strong, and probably knew many an occasion where he might have mishandled things, yet they were gentle as he brought them to Michael's face and raised his chin.

"Finally we meet," he said, his smile never fading.

Michael repressed a mild shiver. Papi. The grandfather of Michael's dreams. He knew then he'd be seeing a lot of that place where Papi was. And it was no small matter that Chachi would be there too.

Chapter Twenty-Two

For his seventeenth birthday, Lydia, once again, displayed her creative stuff and presented Michael with a blow-out surprise birthday party. She turned one of the party rooms into a dazzling dance hall with disco lights glittering overhead and live disc jockeys who welcomed guests with the latest music. Joe flew in any of Michael's friends and family who would come. Among them were Gherri and Pooch, Pooch's sisters Lorna and Marie and, of course, Eric, David, and Justin all came in from school.

"Where's Chauncey?" Michael asked them. He was disappointed to learn that his friend was still doing time in the joint for a lifetime of mistakes.

Joe unveiled his gift to his son: a brand new Porsche truck, 'stankin-red' as Michael called it, with gleaming chrome molding and rich navy blue leather seats.

Sarah finally called and informed him that her birthday 'package' was on its way. He lit into her immediately about her absence. How could she not even call him? She was his mother, for god's sake.

"Everything is not about you, Michael!" she shrieked. "I need this time for myself!"

He didn't want to fight with her on his birthday. "When will I see you, Mom?"

She hesitated. "I'll try to send for you soon," she said quietly.

At least she called.

The party was in full swing and so was Michael's spirits. Despite Joe's efforts to thwart Eric's repeated spiking of the punch bowl, everyone's head was buzzing. Illian slipped Michael a few birthday joints, but he didn't dare light those in his father's house. The question of the day was whether they were going to get a glimpse of the famous Duke Spencer.

"Is he coming?" his friends would ask.

Michael periodically slipped away to check the driveway or peek in his father's study.

"Everything okay?" Joe asked.

"Sure. I'm having a ball!"

In the midst of 'getting down dirty' with a pretty girl from the neighborhood, Michael looked over his shoulder and saw Chachi standing with Joe in the doorway. They had been sharing a laugh, watching the kids have fun. Michael gestured for him to step inside. Still smiling, he vigorously shook his head and eased back further into the shadows.

Michael slipped away to join them. "You made it!"

"Happy Birthday."

"Thanks." Michael stood grinning like an idiot.

"I saw those wheels, baby! You're ballin' now!" Chachi slapped Michael's shoulder.

"Wait'll you see what Chachi bought you," Joe said, cutting his eyes in Chachi's direction. "I think he tried to upstage me."

"No way!" Michael gaped at Chachi. *What could he have possibly bought to upstage a Porsche?*

Chachi smiled and rolled his eyes. "Nobody's upstaging you, Joe." He jerked his head in a gesture to get Michael to follow him. "Come on, I'll show you."

Outside, what would become the object of his affection caught the moon with a shimmer.

"It's beautiful!" Michael breathed as he ran his hands along the glistening headlights. A black Ducati motorcycle. He raised quizzical eyes at Chachi.

"I know it's generous. Your dad wants to kill me, but when I saw it, I knew it was you."

Michael was speechless. "Whoa..."

Chachi laughed. "I'm glad you like it."

They stood together, surveying the bike reverently for a long moment.

"Come meet my friends," Michael said, excitement in his eyes.

Chachi sighed. "Not today, okay?"

"Why? You don't wanna meet my friends?"

"Of course I do, just not all at one time. I'm not feeling it today."

Michael smiled his understanding.

"I'm sorry," Chachi said.

"No, no. I understand. Another time, huh?"

Chachi nodded.

The noise from the party room grew louder.

"I think they're summoning you," Chachi said.

Michael nodded, then reached up and, using both his hands, pulled Chachi's face to him and kissed him on the forehead. "That's the way you like it, right?"

Chachi chuckled, shaking his head. "I'll see you later."

* * * *

"I bet this is gonna be good." Michael sat perched on a stool in the kitchen with Papi, helping him roll out a buttery pastry dough for his highly acclaimed dumplings. Papi would later stuff the dough with seasoned, cooked pork, stewed apples, and onions.

"Chachi's always loved these," Papi said. "When he was a boy, we couldn't get him to eat certain things unless I cooked them for him." Papi laughed proudly. "My sister was so jealous." A look of nostalgia passed over his face.

"You miss home, don't you?" Michael said softly.

Papi stopped rolling the dough and looked up at a corner of the room as if there were a window to the past there. He nodded almost imperceptibly. "Yeah."

"Why don't you go back?" Michael asked, though he would hate to even think about Papi leaving.

"I'll never leave Chachi. I'll be here until he decides to go too."

Michael's breath caught. Chachi had a big career here. Might he one day return to his home? "Has he ever talked about going back?"

Papi began to work hurriedly now. "We've talked about it. He gets tired of his pace and thinks about making the trip, getting some r&r for a few years, retiring eventually. His mother would be delighted." Papi's head jerked as he glanced at the panel of buttons, some lit in a vibrant, fiery red, others not.

"What's that?" Michael asked. That house had lighted buttons everywhere, near every door, on every telephone…

"Chachi's home," Papi said, returning to his work.

"How can you tell?"

"You see that?" Papi pointed to the first button on the panel. "That's his button. Number one. It just lit up. That's mine, there, number two. The rest belong to the household staff. Whenever we come or go, we try to light or release our button. This lets us know at a glance who's in and who's not."

They finished the dough, cut it into squares, filled them, and put them into the oven. Later, Papi would add them to a delicious gravy simmered with his special blend of herbs and spices.

"What happened to Chachi?" Michael asked after a while.

"He probably went straight to his room."

"Without even saying hello?"

"He does that sometimes. Hard day, maybe. He'll surface after he's had a nap. Hey, you wanna help me make the sauce?"

"In a minute."

Michael left the kitchen and moved carefully down the hall and through several rooms before climbing the ornate staircase to Chachi's bedroom. The door was closed. He knocked. It crossed his mind that, with the size of the room and its many adjoining rooms, perhaps Chachi might not be able to hear him, so he opened the door and quietly stepped inside.

He was met with soft music. The song playing was a ballad from the album, one that he and Chachi co-wrote. He blushed briefly. "Chachi?" he called out softly. Something thudded to the floor. "Chachi?" He quickened his pace.

They hadn't even made it to the bed. With a squeal, the young lady grabbed her blouse and tried to cover her naked breasts. Chachi sat on the edge of the sofa, unabashedly naked, and met Michael's stare of disbelief with one of his own.

Michael stood stupidly looking back into Chachi's stunned face. It was pointless to try to explain. Nothing could erase the shame. He hurried past Papi and his dumplings, got onto his motor bike, and rode home like the wind.

Before the call came in, he had already decided to do something about his behavior. No more touching or kissing, no matter how innocently. Chachi made clear that it made him uncomfortable. He would fix it. Whatever he had to do, he would not have Chachi look at him that way again.

He picked up the phone on the first ring. Might as well get it over with. "I was waitin' on your call," he croaked, mouth dry, voice barely above a whisper.

"What the hell were you doing in my room?"

"I-I knocked..." It was useless, but he couldn't let him think he was some kind of psychopath.

"There's a bell."

"I know—I forgot."

"So you just barged in?"

"I thought I heard something. A thump or a thud, I thought you were hurt!"

Chachi took a long, deep breath. Michael braced himself.

"I don't want to have to go to your father and tell him we might have a problem," Chachi threatened in a low, urgent tone. "I like you too much to have to take it there, but I will if you don't stop snooping and lurking around me like that. You're freakin' me out."

Michael bit his lip hard. The nerve! He had a retort on the tip of his tongue, but promised himself to let Chachi say all he had to say.

"I don't ever want to see you in my room uninvited," Chachi continued, "and do not show up at my house without notice."

Michael was beginning to feel criminal. He parted his lips to respond but the phone went dead in his ear. He was shaking with the pain of humiliation. Was he that bad? Hadn't they become special friends?

"I won't bother you again," he said into the telephone to no one on the other end.

Chapter Twenty-Three

The temperature took a dip with his spirits and Michael waded through fall in depression. He began to spend more time with his family, trying to get through it. Perhaps Chachi was right. Maybe he *was* unstable. Why else would his life be such an emotional roller coaster? Joe tried to get him to talk about it. Leah spent more of her time in his room, blowing her nails dry and chatting about her boyfriends, her hair, her makeup. She'd occasionally throw Sasha's name into the conversation. Little did she know, Sasha was the furthest thought from his mind.

His stepmother took him aside one afternoon, placed her hand over his, and asked him straight out. "Honey, are you in love?"

"No!" He'd said, recoiling and wrenching his hand from hers.

Lydia blinked with surprise.

"No," he said again, a bit more composed.

"Oh." She smiled nervously. "I just thought…"

"I'm okay," he mumbled.

"*Something* must be wrong."

"I don't wanna talk about it."

"All right," she conceded, "but if you ever need to talk, I told you, I'll always be here."

A week before Thanksgiving, Sarah called. She would be arriving in town in a couple of days and wanted to see Michael. He perked up and even started laughing again. Eric and David came home from school. He felt alive again, in spite of that little nagging ache in the base of his gut…

Sarah asked to meet him at a restaurant. She was only stopping through to see him and didn't want to bother booking a hotel room. Michael realized how deeply hurt his mother was by his father's rejection and felt a pang of guilt for his part in it.

He scanned the restaurant and would not have recognized his mother had she not lifted her arm to attract his attention. He stood aghast, rooted to the floor, unsure at first whether it was her. She waved again and he moved toward her. He hadn't seen her in well over a year, almost two. She had changed a lot, and not for the better. "Mom, what's going on?"

She was thin, thinner than the average thin person. Her skeleton threatened to break through her skin. Her eyes were moist and red-rimmed. Her hair fell in frizzy tufts onto her shoulders. She wore a brown knit hat that had no relationship to her outfit, a long, blue, ankle-length, formless dress. There was no resemblance to the stylish Sarah Bagley.

She put out her cigarette and immediately lit another. She held it out to him, but he did not take it, nor did he take his gaze away from her face. She put it between her own lips and puffed. A long silence played out between them.

"Mom, what's happening? What have you done to yourself?"

Sarah exhaled cigarette smoke and looked away.

"Mom," Michael pleaded, "Look at me! Talk to me!" His beautiful dark eyes were filled with tears.

Sarah began to laugh hysterically.

Michael jumped to his feet, his hand clutching his shirt in the area over his heart.

"Do you need help, sir?" the Maitre'd appeared out of nowhere.

Michael looked around slowly. They were a spectacle. People were standing and craning their necks to see.

"No, no...we're fine," he said. "Come on, Mom, we're leaving."

"No!" Sarah abruptly recovered from her laughing spell.

"Mom, you need help. Let me help you."

Sara drew back suddenly. "Don't look at me like that! I don't need your help!"

Michael's bottom lip quivered. He felt alone and helpless in such a public place under critical scrutiny. No one told him what to do in case your mother went nuts in a trendy, high-society restaurant.

"You're so thin..." he whispered.

"Don't you judge me, you little snot!" Her pupils darted quickly from side to side.

"Please, Mom. I'll take you home with me. Dad'll know what to do."

"No!" she yelled so loudly he had to raise his hands to calm her. "I won't step foot in that house again as long as I live!"

"Okay, okay."

"I don't care if I never see Joe Simpson again! And you! Look at you! You're just like them now," she snarled, "with your hoity-toity clothes and your hoity-toity friends and your hoity-toity little music, running around with the likes of that scumbag!" Her hand flew to her head. She held it there, pressed to the side of her face.

"Is it the headaches? Are they worse?"

Sarah sat holding her breath. Michael waited. Slowly, her hand fell to her lap. "I'm sorry, darling," she whispered hoarsely. "I wish I had been a better mother for you. I wish I was stronger."

"We'll get help; we'll check everything out. I'll be with you every step of the way."

Sarah lowered her eyes.

"I'll come home," he decided. "I'll pack right now!"

She looked up at him, her eyes hopeful. Then she shook her head. "No, honey," she said, her voice thick with sadness. "As badly as it hurts to let you go, I always knew you belonged with your father. He gave you a chance at something else and now look at you!" She beamed.

Michael blinked at the sudden change. He had to do something. Quick.

"May I get you something else?" The waiter stood above them, eyeing Sarah's glass of wine precariously.

She blushed and ran her fingers through her dry, brittle hair. Michael watched in frustration as she batted her eyes and flashed yellowing teeth at him.

"Where is your bathroom?" he asked shakily. He followed the waiter's pointing hand to the men's room. Once inside, he pulled out his cell phone and tracked down his father. If they had to take her kicking and screaming, she would get help.

Joe told Michael to stall her; he'd be there in twenty minutes.

Michael exhaled in relief, clipped his phone to his belt, and said a prayer. He splashed his face with cold water and smoothed out his clothes. Then he strolled back into the restaurant. He didn't want Sarah to suspect anything.

He stopped abruptly. His heart sank. An ugly brown hat lay in a pool of wine, the only sign that Sarah had even been there.

* * * *

On the eve of the New Year, Joe celebrated with his family and very close friends in the warm glow of the fireplace in the comfort of his family room, drinking champagne and toasting good times. Michael sat in his usual corner and nursed the one glass of champagne his father allowed him. He spent much of the last few weeks avoiding Chachi. Michael had completely stopped calling him, would find any excuse to leave the house whenever Chachi came by, discontinued his visits to Papi (most regretfully), and would quickly change direction if he happened to approach him in the halls at the center. He even suggested that they pause work in the studio for a while, citing burnout. Professional to the bone, Chachi never stopped greeting Michael when he'd run into him and he'd give him that 'don't be silly' look when he noticed his attempts to avoid him. Now as he sat watching Chachi, seated on the edge of his chair, crouched over a chess board with Steven, his brow crinkled in that funny way, he missed the way things were with him, with Eric, with everyone.

Everything seemed to be changing so quickly. He felt guilty about his depression. He had absolutely no reason to be. He had a wonderful family. He smiled at Eric, who was giving Jake, Lydia, and Renee his best rendition of country line dancing. With his thumbs tucked in his belt loops and his feet kicking out from side to side, he had them in stitches. Good old Eric.

His mother was receiving much-needed treatment at a recovery facility for her drug and alcohol abuse. Joe had been relentless in finding her and convincing her to get help.

"All right everybody, all right!" Joe clapped his hands. "It's the moment of truth!" Only seconds away from the stroke of midnight, the party people rushed to fill their glasses and huddled together in the center of the room.

"HAPPY NEW YEAR!" they shouted in unison at the stroke of midnight and broke into a rowdy chorus of Auld Lang Syn. Glasses clinked together, arms locked in embraces, kisses were passed around freely.

Eric approached Michael with his arms outstretched.

Michael stood up to meet his embrace.

"Happy new year, buddy," Eric whispered and Michael held on to him. He felt like he was holding the old Eric to him, preventing him from getting away and becoming someone else, someone's husband, someone's father…

But others wanted to share the first fruits of the New Year and he let Eric go to hug and kiss his parents and the many others that would expect it.

"Happy new year."

He turned to see Chachi and hesitated before nodding.

Chachi stood without speaking for a short while. Michael felt uneasy under his gaze. Michael had grown quite good at reading him, and vice versa. Chachi was deciding their fate.

"I owe you an apology," Chachi said, his hands steepled under his chin, brows raised in a graceful arc.

Michael became interested in the ceiling.

"You're still mad at me!" Chachi shouted in an effort to speak over the new wave of cheers that had erupted in the room.

Michael looked away.

"Look. If you don't want to accept my apology, that's fine. But let's be big about it. We have work to do. I know you've been avoiding me, but lets put that aside and finish this album. After that, you don't have to write another song for me."

Eat shit and die! Michael screamed in his head, but his mouth uttered a simple, "Fine."

"Good." Chachi smiled. Then he sighed and shook his head. "It wasn't you, Michael, it was me. These bells are going off in my head. I don't know what it is about you..."

Joy crept into Michael's gut but he kept the excitement at bay. "What's different now?"

"Nothing." His lips threatened to smile. "Besides the danger of Papi flogging me for the public's amusement, nothing. Except that I miss you, nothing. I miss having you around and talking to you on the phone."

Michael looked away to avoid breaking into a gleeful grin. The noise in the room rose exponentially, causing Chachi to move closer to him. "You never should have stopped calling Papi, though."

"I know. I'm sorry. I just didn't understand what happened."

"He was so pissed at me." Chachi laughed. "*What did you do*!" he mimicked Papi's voice, sending Michael into chuckles. "*Don't stop people from visiting me just because you're crazy*!"

"You sound just like him!" Michael marveled.

Chachi opened his mouth to speak again, then snapped it shut.

He's going to grovel now, Michael thought.

Renee slithered between them. "Happy New Year, handsome," she said to Michael. She planted a big kiss on Chachi's lips, ending it with a flick of her tongue. "Happy New Year to you too, big boy," she whispered provocatively and winked.

Michael disliked Renee. No, that was putting it mildly; he despised her. His feelings were irrational and totally unjustified. The woman had done nothing but compliment and flirt with him and she was wonderful eye-candy. He couldn't put his finger on why she annoyed the hell out of him.

"Where's my New Year's kiss?" she said to Michael in her imitation baby-voice.

Michael's irritation must have shown, for Chachi interjected, "I'll book the studio next week." He grabbed Renee by an arm and drug her away. She frowned and eyed his hand on her arm with drunken disapproval. "I'll call you with exact times; you'll be there?"

Michael nodded slowly and glared at Renee for her timing. Her brow was still crinkled with confusion as Chachi whisked her away. And he had all those choice words fixed in his mouth to say.

Chapter Twenty-Four

It was good to be with Papi again. Although Chachi seemed to have totally gotten over the incident, Michael made sure his visits were reasonable in length, stayed close to Papi and tried to visit during times when Chachi would not be home, like when he was traveling, as he was on this day. Michael spent the day kicking back with his heels up watching television with the wonderful old man. He had already gained three pounds just eating Papi's great meals.

"Hungry?" Papi asked after they had finished watching a riotous comedy, during which they laughed incessantly.

"Oh, no Papi; I'm getting too fat as it is. You're gonna have me in the gym eight hours a day!"

"Nonsense!" Papi snorted. "I'll just run to market and get a few things. I'll be making my famous shrimp scampi: colossal shrimp in a sweet butter wine sauce sprinkled with toasted bread crumbs over a bed of garlic mashed potatoes."

"Ummm," Michael closed his eyes. Just the thought of Papi's comfort food made him feel warm and sleepy. "Okay, I'll have just a taste," he said as he stretched out across the cushiony sofa and grabbed a pillow for his head. "Can I take a nap?"

"You nap," Papi ordered as if it were his idea. "I'll shop and run some errands. I'll be back in a few hours—don't you run off now."

Michael was awakened by a cold jab to the forehead and peered through a haze to see Chachi looking down at him, his eyes glittering with mischief, holding a bottle of champagne.

"I-I'm sorry," Michael began. He had planned to be gone long before Chachi got home. Chachi wasn't due back until tomorrow. He must still be dreaming. "You're back already?"

"Yeah," Chachi said, smiling brilliantly. "Things went really well."

"Oh." Michael sat up, rubbing his eyes. He wasn't dreaming.

"We just sealed a deal to open offices in two more cities," Chachi gushed. "We stand to double the return we've seen on the center."

"Oh," Michael said again. "Congratulations." He tried to match Chachi's enthusiasm but he could not understand why people with more money than they could ever spend continued to pursue money. "Where's Papi?"

Chachi frowned. "I'm sure Papi went to bed over an hour ago. He's usually all tucked in by 7 o'clock."

Michael gasped. "7 o'clock! What time is it?"

"Eight-thirty."

"I must have been asleep for hours!"

"You must have been tired." Chachi held the bottle of champagne out to him. "Wanna celebrate?"

"Looks like you've celebrated enough," Michael commented, chuckling softly at the twinkle in Chachi's eyes.

"I'm not drunk! Joe and I had a couple of shots on the plane. That's all. Come on." He tossed his head in the direction of the staircase.

Michael followed him to the kitchen where Chachi retrieved a tray from the refrigerator. "Papi told me to make sure you got this." He placed the tray of shrimp in the microwave and 'nuked' it for a few moments. "It's a no-no in this house to reheat seafood this way, but—come on."

They climbed the massive double staircase to his private quarters. Michael hesitated at the entrance.

"Come on," Chachi urged, doing his jerk of the head thing again.

As usual, Chachi had the music blasting. His luggage, thrown across a sofa chair in the TV area, lay half opened with its contents spilling out. Chachi walked up the three-tier steps and plopped down on his enormous bed, one leg underneath him. Michael did the same on the side opposite him. He smiled nervously as Chachi set the tray of shrimp down on a bedside table and retrieved two glasses from an overhead cabinet. Chachi popped the cork like a pro and filled the glasses.

"Cheers," he said, handing Michael one.

"Cheers," Michael repeated. They drank the entire first glass without speaking. Then Chachi poured them both another.

"So things went well, huh?"

Chachi's eyes brightened. "Oh, man! This is such a sweet deal! This is what we've been working for all along. I'm sick of performing but I love the business. I truly want to retire and work behind the scenes."

"Chachi, you can't retire yet!"

"I can and I will," Chachi said, draining his glass.

"But I wrote all this new stuff! How are you just gonna quit on me?"

"People will be clamoring for your songs," Chachi said, gesturing with his glass, champagne sloshing dangerously near the rim. "I'm too old for this game. I just don't have to do it anymore, period. I mean, I'll do guest appearances and collaborations from time to time, but I told Joe I want out."

The tipsier Chachi became, Michael knew there'd be no convincing him. They continued to talk about the music business and shared a few laughs about some of the people in it.

I haven't seen Renee around lately." Popping a shrimp in his mouth, Michael tried to sound nonchalant.

"She's been visiting her mother," Chachi said with equal lack of concern.

"What does she do?"

"Who?" Chachi frowned, searching for his train of thought. He obviously had more than a couple shots on the plane.

"Renee. What does she do for a living?"

Chachi laughed. "Live," he replied.

"No, really."

"I'm serious!" Chachi laughed again. "She's associated somehow with her father's businesses but in actuality, Renee's lazy-ass doesn't do a damn thing all day but look good." He drained his glass again and fell backward onto the bed.

"You think you guys might get serious one day?"

Chachi looked at Michael, his head tilted curiously. "Why?"

"Just asking. You've been together a long time, right? You know she's looking for a ring. That's what Lydia said."

Chachi yawned. "She's been looking for a ring since she's had a finger."

"You don't ever plan to get married?"

"I don't *plan* on it."

"Maybe she doesn't know that."

Chachi sat up, swaying slightly. "Who are you, her marriage advocate?" He chuckled. "Seriously though, I'm just not the marrying kind. I make it clear that I don't want to marry, I don't want children, and I'm not down with mon-ogo-mous relationships." He frowned. "I just wanna have a good time. If you're not down with that, move on. I like to stay open, I like to play, I like new expe-ri-ences." He paused and mouthed the word again, as if checking its correctness. "I like people that can keep it light, not heavy."

"Like Norris?" It slipped out so unexpectantly, he surprised himself. But it was too late to take it back. He thought he'd be pelted with another burst of Chachi's anger.

Instead, Chachi cocked his head and eyed Michael from underneath half-closed lids. "You've been dying to ask me about him, haven't you?"

Michael exhaled with relief. Chachi hated people prying into his private life, yet he hadn't thrown him out on his head. "Not really. It was just conversation."

"Good, 'cause it's none of your business." He opened a side desk drawer and removed a silver box. Then he scooted backward on the bed until he was able to rest his back against the headboard. Michael mimicked him. Chachi opened the box and removed its contents: some cigarette paper and a bag of weed. As Chachi worked at rolling a joint, Michael removed a sheet of the wafer-thin paper and used his fingers to pinch an ample amount of the gray-green stuff from the box. "Be careful, that's potent," Chachi warned him.

Michael smiled at his luck. Obviously, Chachi had given up on playing 'watch maid.' Once they were done, they lit up and leaned back, eyes closed, allowing the mellow feeling to wash over them. From a control panel near the bed, Chachi switched from the rollicking, hard-hitting music to a soft, soothing ballad. Michael moaned with pleasure. The soft music, champagne, and weed made him feel divine.

"Watch this." Chachi activated another gadget near the bed.

Michael's jaw dropped as a circular ceiling over the bed slid open.

"Holy shit!" he gasped. Clear, dark skies twinkling with stars lay above them. The large skylight was filled with many triangular panes that would open with the push of another button, allowing the fresh balmy night breeze to caress their bodies. The alcohol and weed made the experience surreal.

"Man, that's tight." Michael sighed with content.

"Yeah, when I can't sleep at night, I just open this window and let the night rock me to sleep. And the rain…I like to fall asleep to the rain beating against the panes."

"Fuckin' fantastic," Michael whispered as sleep crept over him.

"Yeah…" Chachi yawned and turned on his side with his back to Michael. The sound of soft breathing said he had fallen asleep.

It seemed to hit Michael all at once, the champagne, the smoke, the melodious jazz piece that played softly from hidden speakers. In the base of his brain Michael warned himself of the perils of falling asleep. With only an hour or so before curfew, he tried to rouse himself, but the sweet sounds of the saxophone engulfed him, relaxing him so that he couldn't lift his limbs. The champagne built a small fire that burned in the pit of his stomach. *Just five more minutes*, he told himself before surrendering.

He thought he was dreaming that he lay next to Chachi, thought he had dreamed the whole thing. Thought he was still asleep in the TV room, on the bountiful sofa, and within moments, Papi would return with his ingredients for the Shrimp Scampi and Chachi still wasn't due back from his trip until tomorrow—except for the chill…

The night air had grown colder. Michael snuggled closer to the warmth next to him. Chachi instinctively turned to face him, eyes still closed. Half asleep, Michael examined the face, the creamy skin, the soft, brown lashes lining his handsome eyes. Even sleeping, he seemed to be about to start or finish a smile.

Chachi surprised him when he opened his eyes and actually did smile. Before Michael could gather his wits about him and decide this was not a dream, he felt himself being touched, his hair being stroked. He intended to back away, but instead he moved forward, and rested his head on Chachi's chest. He absorbed the warmth of Chachi's embrace and no longer felt the chill of the breeze. He felt soft lips move across his brow experimentally and screamed at himself to get up but he was dead weight in Chachi's arms. He lifted his face and was met with a kiss on the mouth that started small, but suddenly became a heated, frenzied exchange of pent-up passion and longing. He felt oddly disembodied. He felt good.

This is weird, he thought as he explored the new territory. A kiss. Just a kiss. It won't go beyond that...

He didn't know how long he had been asleep and at first, didn't know where he was. The room was filled with crushing darkness. Soft music still played. The breeze overhead had become even colder. Shivering, he moved to sit up and felt the pang of discomfort in his loins. Surprised at his bare skin, he shot bolt upright.

"Oh, shit," he breathed, "Oh, shit…"

He exploded out of bed searching frantically for his clothes and dressed silently. He fumbled with his car keys; his hands shook. He whipped his head around. Chachi had not moved.

"Oh, shit..." He looked at the clock on the bedside table. He was already hours past his curfew. Hung over, head pounding, stomach turning, he was stiff, sore, and in pain, and if his father took his wrath out on him on top of everything else—well, he might as well just kill himself.

He made his exit by tip toe. Jory's shift ended at 2. He had twenty minutes. If he could get to Jory in time, he might convince him to let him scale the garden wall to his bedroom balcony. Hopefully, his dad was fast asleep. Hopefully.

Papi nearly collided with Michael barreling down the stairs. "Where have you been?" Papi asked. "Do you know what time it is?"

Michael's lips moved without sound.

"Something wrong?" Papi moved closer.

Michael blinked rapidly holding onto the railing to steady himself.

"Are you drunk?" Papi's dark eyes narrowed with suspicion. "You stay put 'til I call Joe. I don't want you driving home this late by yourself. Maybe you should just stay until morning..."

Michael pushed past Papi and charged down the stairs, and out the door.

He had been an avid climber since he was three; still, he fell twice before making it to the top of the wall. He landed with a thud on the other side. He raced up the balcony stairs and picked the lock to gain entrance to his bedroom.

The phone was already ringing. Michael seemed able to tell when he called. It was as if the phone rang differently. The ringing stopped. He held his breath. Seconds later, it started up again.

"Jesus!" he cried, then slammed his hand over his mouth. He wished Chachi would just go away! But it could be Papi calling to make sure he made it home okay. He must have frightened him to death! And if it *was* Papi and he didn't pick up, Papi might call his father… He dove onto the bed and grabbed the receiver.

The familiar short silence, then: "Michael?"

Michael felt as though the air had been sucked out of the room. "Yeah?"

"You okay?" Chachi asked softly.

"Yeah."

"I mean…really…"

"Yeah."

"Sure?"

Go to hell! "I'm okay."

"I'm sorry you missed curfew. I'll talk to Joe. I'll make something up. I'll tell him that—"

"No, please don't!"

"I was just gonna say—"

"Don't say anything! I'll handle him."

"You sure?"

"I'm sure." Michael wanted desperately to hang up the phone.

"Okay. You left suddenly, and I just wanted to make sure you were all right."

"I'm fine, but I have to go before my father comes in." That should get him off the hook.

"All right. I guess we should…talk later?"

Michael closed his eyes, disgusted. "Yeah."

Chachi said, "Call me if you need to talk," before hanging up. The nerve.

Michael stood with his eyes closed and took deep breaths. He had stepped into a self-created nightmare. Now that he got what he must have thought he wanted, he wanted to puke, to kill himself.

He lay on the bed, his knees drawn in, and hugged his pillow to his chest. He could still feel him, smell him, hear the song that played, in his head. He squeezed his eyes shut.

"You'd better have a *really* good explanation for coming in my house at this time of night, baby, and you get just one crack at it!"

Michael hadn't heard Joe come in. He moaned into his pillow, clenching it. He thought his brain would snap.

"Sit up!" Joe shouted.

Michael struggled to sit up. He kept his eyes downcast.

"How *dare* you openly disobey me!" Joe yelled, furious. "Look at me!"

Hesitantly, Michael raised his gaze to meet his father's. It didn't matter what he did to him now. He just wanted it over quickly.

"I'm disappointed in you, Michael, and I'm waiting for an explana—what's wrong with you?"

Michael averted his face. *Think of something. Quickly.*

Joe lifted Michael's chin. "What happened to you?"

Michael weighed his options. He could keep the secret and live in its darkness forever, or he could purge it and not only ruin Chachi's life, but destroy the wonderful friendship he had with his father. Their friends would be forced to take sides. Either way, he could never look Chachi in the face again. "I'm sick."

"Sick? What's wrong?" Joe felt his forehead and massaged his neck, looking for swollen glands.

"I don't know…I just…I feel sick in my stomach…and my head hurts, and I…It must be the flu or something…"

"I'm gonna call Jake." Joe reached for the phone.

"Dad, please. You know I hate doctors."

"But this is Jake, Michael."

"I know. I just don't like it!" Michael moaned and lay back on the bed. "I'll be okay if I could just stay home and rest today."

"You have lessons you've neglected, and there's a deadline on the album. You're needed in the studio."

"I can't."

Joe sighed. "Okay. I mean, if you're sick, you're sick. We'll just have to work around you. I'll have Maxi keep an eye on you." Then he pointed a finger at Michael. "And you're gonna schedule an appointment with Jake for a full check up. You've gone too long without a thorough physical."

"Sure,"

"Next time, you call me if you're sick and can't make it home!"

Once he was alone, Michael drew a hot bath. He poured nearly a whole bottle of his favorite scented oil in it. He dumped bubble bath in with it and settled inside. Up to his neck in foam, he leaned back against the cool porcelain and let his tears fall. Confused and ashamed, he thought about the consequences. If his father found out, he'd blow a gasket *after* he killed Chachi. He imagined the look on the faces of his friends and family. Pooch, Eric, David—they'd think he was—gay. Was he gay? He shook his head. And Papi. What would poor Papi think?

He could just hear what his aunt Melanie would have to say. It was a sin against God, and he would burn in hell for it. He grabbed a bar of soap and began to rub it all over his body. Then he grabbed a loofah and scrubbed, painfully scraping at his skin until he could no longer feel those hands…

His father's voice out in the hall awakened him. He must have slept all day. He didn't recall getting out of the tub, but there he lay in just his pajama bottoms snuggled between fresh linen. An untouched bowl of soup and a glass of orange juice sat on a tray nearby. Maxi. She must have helped him into bed. He'd have to remember to lock his door.

"Hello, sleepy head. Feel better?" His father came in wearing a designer suit that said he had meetings today.

"A little." Michael squinted through eyes swollen tight.

"You look worse." Joe cupped Michaels chin. "Your face is swollen."

"Oh, my!" Lydia gasped as she slipped into the room and joined Joe at Michael's bedside.

"I say we call a doctor now," Joe said. They were looking down at him as if he were a specimen of science.

"Dad, no! I'm okay, really!"

"You look terrible, honey," Lydia agreed, her brow crinkled.

"I look worse than I feel! Please?"

"Jesus Christ, what happened to you?" Eric arrived with David at his heels.

Michael grabbed his pillow and placed it over his head.

"What's wrong with him?" David asked.

"The flu, probably," Joe said.

"The flu?" Eric grimaced. "That looks like more than the flu."

"He looks like he's been beat up," David observed.

"Did you check for fever?" Lydia asked Joe.

Leah walked in. "What's going on?"

"Your brother has the flu," her mother replied.

Leah quickly backed out of the room. "Oh, God! I certainly don't need to catch *that*!"

"Get out! Go! please!" Michael begged. He sat up, annoyed. "I know you're concerned, but please get the hell out of my room before you give me a stroke!"

Joe and Lydia exchanged worried glances.

"All right," Joe said. "But tomorrow, if you don't look any better than this, Jake'll be here."

Michael breathed a sigh of relief when they had all gone.

All night long, he had sex with Chachi in his head. The next morning, he looked and felt as though he had never slept.

"I'm calling Jake," Joe said with such finality that there was no talking him out of it.

Jake arrived in less than an hour. He examined Michael closely, looking into his eyes, peering down his throat, and listening to his heart beat inside his chest. "You seem to be fine," he said with furrowed brows. "What did you say your symptoms were again?"

Michael glanced at him warily. After all, he *was* a doctor. He could probably see right through him. He cleared his throat and stuck to his story. "A headache…and my stomach's been upset."

"Hmmm."

"Think it could just be some bad food?" Joe asked.

"Could be," Jake said thoughtfully.

"But it's not the flu, huh?" Joe pressed.

"I doubt it," Jake said, coming to life and snapping his doctor's bag closed. "Even absent a fever, you can usually see some sign of the immune system's response to a virus." Jake peered interestedly at Michael's face and let his gaze run down the length of his body. "Let me talk to Michael alone for a minute."

Shit! Michael kept his eyes cast downward, away from Jake's probing stare.

"What's really going on?" Jake asked once Joe had gone.

"Um...I don't know what you mean."

"Is this just an attempt to get out of working or studying for a while, or do you really feel ill? I know you're not used to this pace."

Whew! He was on the wrong trail! Michael felt safe enough to look him in the eye. "No. I really do feel sick."

"Had you been drinking?"

Michael looked away.

"Okay," Jake said after a long silence. He sighed and stood up. "Maybe it's just a hangover and rest is all you need. If you're not better in a couple of days, I'll have you come in for a thorough look-see."

Michael nodded. At least it bought him another couple of days of alone time without his family breathing down his neck. He had another restless night.

* * * *

"Who is it?" Michael called from beneath his comforter.

"It's me," Maxi replied through the door, "with lunch. I'm surprised you haven't wasted away in that bed. You haven't touched food in days."

"I'm not hungry."

"Boy, if you don't open this door, I'm gonna take it off its hinges. You haven't seen old Maxi at her best; besides, I've got—" she stopped, hesitating before continuing, "—your favorite here. Homemade chicken noodle soup."

That's not my favorite. Maxi knew all his favorite foods, why would she say that?

"Michael!" Maxi snapped.

Puzzled, Michael got up and unlocked the door. He'd just dump the soup in the toilet. He turned to walk back to the bed and froze in his tracks when he heard the door open, shut, and lock behind him. Turning slowly, his blood ran cold. There Chachi stood holding the bowl of soup. They had tricked him.

"Oh, Mike…"

Michael quickly turned his back. If he had just died right there, it would have been fine with him.

"I'm so sorry! My God, I never intended…"

Michael's eyes welled up at the remorse in Chachi's voice.

"I made a mistake! Boy, did I make a mistake! It's all my fault! I don't want you to feel responsible for this in any way," Chachi choked out. "I will talk to your father…I will tell him everything…no matter what happens."

"No!" Michael turned, his eyes blazing. "Don't you dare!"

Chachi's voice softened. "Look at you. You're a mess. You need to talk to someone."

"Please don't tell him," Michael pleaded. "Please don't, I've been enough trouble."

"Trouble?" Chachi walked over to put a supportive hand on his shoulder, but Michael shrank away. Chachi drew his hand back. "I'm sorry," he said again. "Look, if anyone's in trouble, it's me, but I can handle it. I don't want you to keep any secrets for me."

"Not for *you*," Michael said. "I just don't want anyone to know." A stubborn tear escaped down his cheek inspite is attempts to stay dry.

Chachi exhaled loudly in frustration and walked over to the phone.

"Don't!" Michael shouted.

"Calm down. I'm not calling anyone."

Chachi dialed and waited, then mumbled something into the phone as he bent to write a number using a pen and pad on the nightstand. "Here." Hanging up, he handed Michael the slip of paper. When Michael didn't move, Chachi walked over and stuffed it into his hand. "If you don't want to talk to someone you know, call this number. Someone's there twenty-four hours a day. They can help you."

Michael looked at the number and crumpled it.

"Promise you'll call."

He said nothing.

"Promise, or I'll have to—"

"I'll call." He turned to look Chachi, finally, in the face. "I promise."

* * * *

Oddly, he felt better after seeing Chachi. It wasn't the humiliating experience he thought it would be...well, it was in the beginning. He wanted him to leave while he was there. Don't touch him. Don't talk to him. But after he had gone, he wanted him to come back. Did that qualify as insanity?

He didn't know what he felt anymore. He had always had trouble with drawing lines between friendship, love, and sex. He couldn't tell what he wanted from Chachi, but he wanted something...

He sat up in bed during another sleepless night and gazed at the life-sized portrait of Duke Spencer on the wall. The brandy-colored eyes were looking right at him and he had to look away before looking back again. Those perfect teeth in that perfect smile drew him in and he began to relive the forbidden moments.

The same song began to play in his head and he closed his eyes. He could smell the pungent weed they smoked and taste on his lips the sweet champagne they sipped. Chachi's laughter rang in his ears. His handsome face loomed into view. Michael recalled everything, every touch, every kiss, Chachi's hands in his hair, his breath on his face, his voice tender… Then he recalled his own passion, his heated response, his fingers being pried away from the bedposts and kissed. Chachi's voice in his ear: "Do you want me to stop?" His own voice, passionate: "No!"

He shook away the vision and sprang out of bed. He paced the floor again, periodically glancing at the telephone. Maybe he *should* talk to someone. It couldn't hurt, could it? He certainly wouldn't get any sleep. Each time he tried, his thoughts intruded, strangling him.

He went to the nightstand and picked up the crumpled paper from the drawer. After dialing the number and hanging up three times, he finally held the phone to his ear long enough for a kind female voice to answer. The voice on the other end was so sympathetic he began to cry.

"How are you?" she asked. "Do you want to talk about something?"

Michael sniffed into the phone.

"It's okay. It's okay to cry. Did someone hurt you?"

"Yes. I mean, no. This is so stupid!"

"It's okay." The voice quieted, giving him time to pull himself together. "Can you tell me what happened? You don't have to give me names or anything, unless you want to."

Michael shifted nervously. "It wasn't like that."

"What do you mean?"

"I mean, it was consensual...I think."

"Sex?"

She said it so casually and without shame.

"Yes." His cheeks were hot even though he knew she couldn't see him.

"I see. May I ask how old you are?"

"Seventeen,"

The voice grew softer. "There is no such thing as consensual sex with a minor, sweetie. You don't have to be ashamed. This wasn't your fault." Perhaps it was the change in the tone of her voice or maybe just the weariness that had been eating away at him every second that made him resentful of her implication.

"It wasn't like that!"

"Your perpetrator's strength comes from your silence," she said. Michael stiffened. "The secret is power over you."

"It's not like that," he said again, but less forcefully this time. He was so tired. He hadn't slept, really slept, for days.

"What is it like?"

He sighed and swallowed, gathering his thoughts. How could he explain? "Like I said, he didn't…force me…or anything."

"Doesn't matter. You obviously feel horrible about it. Is he an adult?"

The conversation was taking the wrong turn. He just wanted to talk to someone, express his feelings—get it out so that he could move past it. He didn't want it to become an investigation. A manhunt.

"Yes," he said in a small voice.

"Is he a friend or family member?"

Michael stiffened again. He began to feel a need to protect Chachi.

"He's my father's best friend…"

"You're also dealing with a breach of trust," the voice said without so much as a gasp at Michael's confession. She must have a similar conversation many times a day. "I know it's difficult, but you have to think about yourself. Did he threaten you?"

"No!"

"Okay, it's all right."

"Look, I made a mistake," he said. "I shouldn't have called."

"It's normal to be afraid to talk about it."

"I'm not afraid. I just don't want to get him into trouble."

"What he did was wrong. Don't protect him. Do you feel ashamed?"

Michael began to cry again. How did this person know so much about what he was feeling? "Yes," he whispered tearfully.

"It's common to feel that way. I can help you. Is there someone close to you that we can talk to? Someone you trust?"

"We?"

"If you find it too difficult, I can intervene. Otherwise, I can accompany you, by phone, if you want, while you talk to someone you trust."

"No!" Anger brewed inside of him. She knew nothing about Chachi, how dare she judge him. He visualized Chachi's face when he came to see him, the regret and sadness in his eyes. "I-I really need to go now. I need to think about this some more."

"I understand," the kind voice said. "Can I count on you to call back?"

"I don't know."

"If you feel like you need to talk?"

"Maybe."

"Okay. Someone's always here. My name is Patti, if you want to ask for me by name."

"Thanks, Patti."

"Is there anything else I can do before I go?"

"Yeah, there is," Michael said, "will you pray with me?"

The voice hesitated. "Sure, if that will make you feel better."

He closed his eyes and prayed. He asked God for forgiveness and guidance for himself and for Chachi. He asked for peace. Then he breathed a sigh of relief and a wave of sleepiness flooded him. Until then, he hadn't even been able to pray. "Thank you," he whispered gratefully.

"Anytime. Now remember, call back anytime you want."

"I will. I promise."

He curled up to his first night of restful sleep in a week.

* * * *

He felt so much better the next morning. The day dawned beautifully with a clear periwinkle sky. As he lay in bed and watched it, his heart softened. He replayed the scene in his mind for the one-hundredth time and it didn't seem so terrible.

He desired Chachi and it frightened him. Yes, he idolized his art, his voice, his star power, and it may have started out as just that, but it had become something else. He pretended not to know why he loved being with him so much, watched for his coming, waited for his call. He made sure he was in places Chachi was expected to be and visited often the people he was closest to. He divorced himself from those desires and took up with Illian and then others to convince himself that it wasn't true. The possibility that he wasn't a 'normal' boy sat heavily in his spirit.

In the shower he imagined his father's reaction. He might be understanding, but he wouldn't understand. No, he had to make sure no one found out.

He headed for the kitchen and met the unmistakable smells of strong coffee, yeasty fresh bread, and smoky bacon.

"Well, I'll be!" Maxi grinned widely. "He lives!"

Joe looked up from his morning paper, surprised.

"Hey, Puppy. Feeling better?"

"Much," Michael said grabbing a strip of bacon with one hand and a slice of French toast with the other.

"Looks like you made a full recovery." Joe smiled.

Michael shrugged and began stuffing his mouth.

His father watched, mildly amused. "You're all dressed; you going in to the studio today?

Michael stopped chewing long enough to speak. "I don't know. I figured I'll hang around the house this weekend and start over Monday." Michael continued eating, making up for lost time with scrambled eggs, more bacon, and oatmeal.

Joe eyed him curiously. "Are you sure you're all right?"

"I'm fine," Michael said with his mouth full.

"Don't do that." Joe frowned and rose to go. "I'm going in early today; you sure you're okay? Because you know, you can talk to me about anything."

Michael stopped chewing. *Yeah, right.* "I know, Dad."

He spent the weekend at home sleeping, eating, and wandering the gardens. As he walked, the branch of a lilac tree bent to brush his cheek. Leaning against its trunk, he closed his eyes and let the breeze dust his face with its sweet scent. He held a white rose to his nose and thought about Chachi. He'd never felt so embraced as when he was in Chachi's arms. He'd never been so kissed, so made love to…

After a weekend of reflection, Michael felt ready to get back to life. David and Eric were home for the summer and he needed to finish some songs with Chachi and catch up on homework.

* * * *

Chachi stuck his head outside his office door and called to his secretary. "I'm getting ready to leave. I'm done today. No more phone calls. Call me on the cell if, and only if, the place is burning down—"

Michael emerged from his hiding place and trotted boldly past the two of them into Chachi's office, and took a seat.

Chachi followed him inside and closed the door. He sat down at his desk and fixed Michael with a fierce glare.

"I'm not crazy," Michael ventured to say after he'd had enough of the long silence. "Really, I'm not." He could hear Chachi breathing. "I just came to apologize. Honestly."

"About what?"

"I feel silly acting the way I did. I was just…confused. I'm feeling better now."

Chachi inhale deeply. "Good." He stood and leaned on his desk, one hand on one hip, signaling an end to the conversation.

Michael remained seated. "You said I could talk to you if I needed to talk."

Chachi blinked and his icy demeanor melted, leaving lines of fatigue. He looked off to the side.

"You're the only person I can talk to about this."

"No. I'm not. I told you—"

"I called that number."

Chachi stiffened.

"I couldn't talk to them," Michael added. The strong lines of Chachi's jaw softened. "I don't feel like that."

Chachi sighed and sat down. "What do you want to talk about?"

Michael cleared his throat and stood. He stuttered slightly, to his fury. "That night…what did you feel? I mean, what did it mean to you? Why'd you—do it?"

"I didn't mean to hurt you..." Chachi paused, thinking. He shook his head as if to clear it. "Look, I can't have this conversation with you."

"Why?"

"Because I *can't*!" he shouted and turned away.

"But you're the only one I have to talk to."

Chachi groaned. "Okay, talk."

Michael weighed his words carefully before letting them go. "I just want you to know that I wasn't angry with you. I told myself I was, but after I thought about it, after I really gave it some thought, it was clear to me that you weren't the issue at all. I was."

"Why would you say that?" Chachi surveyed him with interest.

Michael swallowed. "I know I drove you to it."

Chachi began shaking his head.

"No, no, hear me out. This is hard for me." He swallowed again. "I wanted you. I always have. You knew it. You ran from me just like you're doing now." He took a breath to give himself the courage to continue. "I guess I wanted to know what it would be like—with you. And when I finally did it—at first I thought...this is awful—but then…" He tried again. "I guess I was so upset because, I expected it to 'fix me.' I expected it to fill some void, whatever it was I was looking for from you." He felt increasingly like he was babbling and began to perspire. "I figured if I did it—you know, I'd hate it. It would be awful and I'd be over you. I'd be disgusted with myself and disgusted with you, and I'd be over you. But it didn't happen like that."

Chachi gave him a sidelong glance.

Michael pressed on. If he didn't say it then, he'd never get to say it. "I tried to pretend that I was so pissed off at you, but," he sighed before continuing, "I was angry because—I liked it."

Chachi closed his eyes and shook his head wearily.

"I did. I liked it." His words hit a wall of silence.

Chachi walked over to the big picture window and looked out over Times Square. "What do you want me to do, Michael?"

"Nothing. I just wanted you to know. I just needed to say it."

"Okay. You've said it."

Michael walked over to stand behind him. "I overreacted and I just don't want that to change our friendship."

Chachi said nothing.

"I want us to still see each other," Michael said.

"No!" Chachi spun around, his brilliant eyes suddenly sharp.

"Tell me you don't feel anything for me," Michael gushed in his breathy, provocatively low voice.

"I don't. It was just sex. It was a mistake. I'm sorry. And now you should go."

"Okay." Michael allowed himself a smile. He knew Chachi well enough now to know that he was lying. "Just promise me again you won't say anything to my father."

"I said I wouldn't."

"Okay. Well…see you around?"

"Bye," Chachi said without turning around. Michael was wise enough to be satisfied with that.

Chapter Twenty-Five

Michael flopped down onto the sofa chair with a sigh of exasperation.

Joe looked up from his papers. "What's wrong?" Joe peered through reading glasses that rested abstractly on the edge of his nose.

"Nothing." Michael sighed again and settled deeper into the sofa.

"Okay." Joe removed his glasses and folded his hands. "I have five minutes, tops, then I have to get these papers out. Now, what's wrong?"

Oh, it would have been great if he could unload on his father, on anyone! Keeping secrets like the one he lugged around was a tough business.

"What's that?" he asked, pointing to the stack of papers under Joe's folded hands. He couldn't very well tell his father what was *really* bothering him.

Joe's previously lackluster eyes lit up. "We're going public!" He grinned and began sorting through the papers again, placing his signature here and there.

"Why?" It wasn't a question born of ignorance; Michael knew why companies chose to go public. He also knew that his father had more money than he could ever spend, even if he went on a shopping spree for big-ticket items every day of his life. Why didn't he just retire and enjoy the fruits of his hard work? Keeping stockholders happy was a constant tap dance.

"Why not?" Joe frowned. "This deal is gonna take us over the top, Michael."

"You say that after every deal."

"I know, I know," Joe waved away Michael's astuteness. "But this is my baby, so this is a big deal! There's this sick cycle that the rich get caught up in. The more money we make the more afraid we are that it's not enough. You tell yourself 'just one more hundred million and I'll take a rest,' but it's never enough!"

"But it *is*," Michael said.

"It is, but then it isn't," Joe said, ending the subject with a shrug. "Speaking of which..." He shuffled papers. "Your stock is certainly upward-bound. Did Dominick tell you how much you'd be worth if Duke sells the units we know he will?" He searched his desk. How did he ever find anything?

"Whatever." Michael shrugged, indifferent. "It's only paper."

Joe half-lifted a brow. "You certainly don't sound like a son of mine."

Michael sighed again.

"What's wrong?" Joe inclined his head.

"I don't know." Michael exhaled. "Nothing and everything."

"Well, let me finish up here. Give me two minutes to finish signing these papers so I can ship them over to Chachi, then you can have me all to yourself."

A light went on in Michael's head. "You're sending those over to

Chachi?"

"Yeah. I have a messenger waiting. Steven has to file these by 5:00."

Eureka! This was an omen if he ever saw one! "I'll take them to him." Michael leapt to his feet.

Joe frowned. "I don't know, honey. These are highly sensitive documents. Chachi has specific instructions on how to execute them. If one page gets out of place or goes missing—

"Dad. I'm not six years old!" Michael snorted. "I think I can handle some silly papers. Come on. I don't have anything else to do." He added as an afterthought, "I want to see Papi anyway."

Joe chewed on his bottom lip. "All right." He began to write a note to Chachi.

"What—are you giving me a *note!*" Michael asked, horrified.

"It's important that he gets this right," Joe insisted. "He needs to sign here." Joe pointed to an area designated for signature on the document. It had a little red arrow stuck to it that said 'sign here'. "And here, and on all these pages in the spaces required."

"So, you don't think he can *read* the little arrows?"

Joe darted coal-black eyes at him. "Yeah, but then he needs to initial here and here." He shuffled through the documents quickly. "Then he needs to read all of this—"

"I got it, I got it!" Michael reached impatiently for the bundle.

"Wait!" Joe clutched them to his chest like precious gems. "You're taking this too lightly! Maybe I ought to just go with the messenger..."

Tread gently. His window of opportunity was slipping. "I heard everything you said. There are 129 pages." He eased the stack of papers from his father's grip. "And you want him to sign here, here, here, here." He went through the documents slowly and carefully out of respect for their 'importance.' "And on all these pages. Then he needs to initial there and there, as well as there, there and there and read all this...fill this section out with his personal information." Michael knew his gift of mind retention would come in handy one day. "Sign here and here...."

"All right," Joe conceded. "I see that Chachi could use your help." He placed the papers gently into a large envelope and handed them to Michael.

"Be careful with these."

"I will."

"Pratt is out. Have Sloan drive you."

"I will."

On the drive over, Michael couldn't help smiling smugly to himself. He chuckled, anticipating the look on Chachi's face. And he couldn't do anything about it 'cause he came bearing precious documents.

The massive entry doors opened the moment they pulled up. Joanie, a young girl working with Chachi's publicist, and Briggs, his personal assistant, both rushed out to meet him.

"I'll take that," Joanie smiled, anxiously reaching for the package. "Mr. Spencer is waiting for these."

"*I* got this," Michael said and held the papers away from them. They drew back in unison. He walked coolly to the entryway.

Chachi called from upstairs, "Hurry up, Joanie, time is running out!"

Michael mounted the staircase. He felt eyes on him, Briggs, Joanie, and other members of the staff. As he reached the top, Joanie dashed past him, nearly colliding with Chachi as he emerged from his room.

"He wouldn't give them to me, Mr. Spencer!" she blurted out, sounding like a spoiled child.

Chachi's puzzled gaze left Joanie's face and landed on Michael's. To Michael's surprise, his eyes didn't go wide, nor did he scream and yell or demand an explanation. In fact, a slight smile curved the finely cut lips.

"Dad thought I could be useful," Michael said, handing the package over.

"Oh?" Chachi asked with equal calm.

"Yeah. There's a lot to read and a lot to sign. With my memory and—well, you know." Michael saw yearning in the depths of Chachi's eyes and blushed. "Dad thought I could help you get it done," he said softly, blinking at him through generous lashes, "in time."

Chachi's eyes narrowed but his smile widened. He was too seasoned to fall for these games; still, he dismissed the others and led Michael to his room.

They had to cross his bedroom to get to his office space. Passing, Michael glanced quickly in the direction of the bed. Flashbacks raced through his mind...

Chachi's office was bigger than Joe's, of course; Chachi did everything bigger. He sat at the oversized desk and eased the documents out of the envelope.

Michael snickered at the way they were all handling those sheets of paper with kid gloves.

Joe's unfinished note fell out. Chachi picked it up and read with knitted brows.

"Here." Michael stood behind him and reached across him for the papers so that Chachi's head was between both his arms. "He wants you to sign here, and here…" He leaned in close to Chachi's ear and turned each page. As Chachi signed and initialed, Michael moved in closer so that his hair could brush Chachi's face. "And then you need to sign here…"

"Why are you doing this, Michael?"

The question was asked in such a sad, awful tone. He was sure he had detected pleasure in Chachi's face upon seeing him, but now it didn't seem so.

Michael pulled up a chair next to Chachi and sat down. He took a deep breath and covered one of Chachi's hands with his own, or at least he tried to. "I'm sorry. I saw a chance to see you and I took it. I don't wanna lose you, Chachi. I don't wanna lose what we had. I got scared and fucked it up, but it wasn't because of you! It was me! I didn't understand what I was feeling. I was afraid of what it meant, but I'm not anymore."

Chachi sat motionless and contemplated Michael's hand on his. "I'm trying Michael," he said quietly. "I'm trying to do the right thing. Let me for once in my life do the right thing."

"The right thing for who?"

"The right thing for both of us!"

Michael held his gaze. "I know what I want," he said.

Chachi turned to him. "And what about me? Do you know what could happen to me?"

Michael had to look away then. It was selfish, what he was asking, still…

"And don't give me that crap about no one having to know. How long do you think we could keep this? Eventually, everything gets out."

"I'll be eighteen soon."

"You're seventeen now. Seventeen is not eighteen and eighteen is not twenty-one!" Then he sighed and his shoulders slumped. "I'm twenty years your senior, Michael, and your father is my *best* friend." He turned back to the task at hand and tried to re-focus.

Michael sat quietly, pondering his next words. "All I know is that for the first time in my life, I care for someone. Really. And if that's wrong then, I'll just have to have my heaven right here on earth and have hell to pay for it later."

"You have no idea the problems we'll have. I will lose everything. As hard as I've worked, you think I want to leave the game like that?"

Michael dropped his gaze. He sat with his head down a long time. He could feel Chachi's eyes on him. "I can't say we won't be found out."

"We will."

Michael sighed. "All I can say is that I'll never abandon us, no matter what my father or anyone else has to say about it." He gripped Chachi's arm. "Please don't abandon *me* now."

Michael waited as Chachi pretended to sift through the documents. In a last-ditch effort, Michael leaned into him and kissed him on the cheek, a soft, lingering, sensuous kiss that he hoped conveyed all he was feeling.

Chachi slowly turned his head so that their lips met and Michael felt the fight go out of him. He wrapped his arms around Chachi's neck and squeezed.

Chachi smiled, then quickly pulled away and returned his attentions to the papers. "Now what else do I need to do here?"

"Sign every page here where you see the little red arrows, and he wants you to read all this…" Michael flipped through the pages with composure, but his heart was dancing.

"I assume Joe and Steven read it. What does it say in a nutshell?" Chachi scanned the pages.

Reading over his shoulders with the gift of speed, Michael summarized its contents. "Here it's talking about recourse in the case that one party fails to uphold its obligation…" He continued to absorb the document as Chachi did his best to keep up. "And here it's talking about rights and responsibilities…and here it outlines conflicts of interest…."

Chachi looked over the document another five minutes after they were done, initialing where necessary, then tossed the pen onto the desk. "Done!" he announced, smiling at Michael. Michael returned the smile and Chachi picked up the phone to call Joe. "I'm done." Chachi listened and nodded. "I'm sending them straight to Steven by messenger." He placed them carefully back in the envelope. "Yeah, he was *very* helpful," he said, smiling at his conspirator. "It's a little scary," Chachi sighed and glanced at Michael. "But I'm all good." He continued to listen while he toyed with the pen on his desk. "Me too. Hold on, I'll ask." He looked over at Michael. "Are you on your way back?"

Michael blinked.

"He's gonna stay a while."

Chapter Twenty-Six

The days Michael spent with Chachi were the happiest of his life. They spent loads of time together, in the studio making music, out to lunch or dinner under the guise of business meetings, and on the phone late at night talking about—anything. Michael poured so much of his thoughts and his time into Chachi that he barely noticed Eric or the rest of his friends or his family for that matter. He'd come in late from studio sessions with Chachi, wait for his late-night call, talk until the early morning hours and get up only hours later for a quick breakfast before dashing out the door to see him again.

"I guess whatever had him so down has got him back up," Joe mumbled to Lydia as the family sat around the breakfast table and watched Michael gulp down a bagel and orange juice before muffling his goodbyes through a mouth full of food and gliding out the front door.

The time they spent in the studio wasn't just a smokescreen. They worked so well as a team the music poured out of them. They couldn't believe how good they were together. The hits sprang up like weeds. They'd have enough to put out two—maybe three CDs in the next year. Embroiled in a flaming affair, they could keep neither hands nor eyes off each other.

He even got a note from his mother one sunny Saturday morning, as if things could get any better. Sarah wrote that, though she wasn't yet ready for company, she was doing very well and she missed him very much. She knew he was receiving the best of care and she read everything written about his songwriting career. She told him she was proud of him. He recognized her handwriting with her steady, decorative strokes. There wasn't one out-of-the-way word or bizarre thought that would hint at any psychosis. Michael was thrilled.

If one situation gnawed at him, it was Renee. He couldn't explain it. She seemed nice enough, but he didn't like her at all. There was something about her—or was it perhaps his own guilt? After all, she was Chachi's honorary long-standing girlfriend. He couldn't tell whether she was on to them, but strangely, she began to pop up more often, fawning over him with her artificial sweetness. He knew many challenges would come to test their unconventional relationship, and he knew Renee would be one of them.

One evening Chachi lay naked, a silk sheet draped loosely across him, and gazed up at the darkening sky, a picturesque scene of millions of twinkling stars and a crescent moon so unbelievably golden, it could have been a prized painting rather than the view from the skylight overhead. The season had taken a chilly turn, so in spite of the sticky sweat that clung to his body and the heat still emanating from it, the skylight remained closed.

Michael stirred and Chachi turned to watch him sleep. He reached out and placed a hand to cup his cheek and smiled as Michael, still wrapped in dreams, smiled at his touch. In two hours, his alarm clock should spring to life with the reminder that their time was up. Curfew had arrived. Time for the boy to go home.

It sickened him to think, really think about what he was doing. He could have practically anyone in the world he wanted; yet he lay next to a child. His best friend's son, at that, and they were sneaking around as if they were *both* children—scheming, hiding…

On one hand it was exciting and new. It brought back the thrill he loved, when he was younger, of living on the edge. His father, if he had done anything for him, had blessed him with the genes of seemingly eternal youth. But, Michael made him feel young *inside*. Work was becoming less important. The business was his life up until now. Now what he enjoyed most was being with his young lover.

He ran his fingers through Michael's thick, baby soft hair and heard him moan softly. He could forget most of the time that he wasn't of age. Michael had a grown-up sense about him and wisdom beyond his years.

What he found most difficult was dealing with Joe. Chachi was becoming increasingly uncomfortable around his friend, barely able to look him in the eye. Lately, Joe had been particularly interested in Michael's secrecy and long absences. He even casually joked about how Chachi now sees Michael more than he does, making flip comments such as, "Tell my son I said hello when you see him," or "So, has Michael gotten any taller since I saw him last?"

It required all of Chachi's acting skills to laugh off-handedly at these jibes when he was, in fact, churning inside. If only Joe knew.

Then there was Papi, the only other person, besides Joe, who could give Chachi the eye and cause him remorse. Chachi was able to skirt around conversations about Michael with Joe, but Papi wasn't fooled. He endured many lectures during which Papi urged him to reconsider before it was too late.

"He's gonna get hurt, Chachi, really hurt! And Joe will never forgive you!"

In his heart of hearts, he knew the old man was right. He couldn't recall him ever being wrong, and oftentimes by the end of their exchange, he'd resign himself to somehow ending it all. But then he'd see Michael…

Things were becoming risky. The relationship was changing and Chachi didn't know how to slow it down. "We have to tell Joe, Michael."

They were having take-out pizza and sitting on the floor playing scrabble, Michael's favorite, when Chachi decided to bring it up once more.

"Tell him what?" Michael asked.

"You know what."

Michael put the finishing touches on a word Chachi had never seen before.

"That's not a word!" Chachi exclaimed, though he wasn't sure.

"Of course it is," Michael said patiently. "Look it up."

"Well, that's a gazillion points." Chachi sighed and pushed the game board away, upsetting the pieces before Michael could catch them. Michael began to pack the game away. "I wanna talk about this, Mike."

Michael said nothing for a while.

Chachi watched him until he'd placed the last game piece inside its box.

"Fine, Chachi, *tell* him."

"Seriously?"

Michael looked at him as if he had grown a fish head. "No, fool! You know we can't tell him—not yet anyway. I thought we said *I* was going to tell him. When I was ready."

"You'll never be ready." Chachi got up from the floor and sank into an armchair. "In the meantime, he knows something."

"He does not."

"He feels it. I know him." Chachi gazed past Michael. "He doesn't know what it is yet that's nagging at him, but he knows it's something."

"You're paranoid." Michael flicked his wrist and moved to get up with the game box. Chachi's hand shot out and grabbed Michael's arm a little rougher than intended. The box fell to the floor sending game pieces scattering out of reach.

"I'm sorry," Chachi said to Michael's flushed face. "I didn't meant to do that, but don't blow me off like that. Don't wave me away when I'm talking to you. I'm serious about this, it's—spooking me!"

Michael inhaled deeply and sat down on the arm of Chachi's chair. He stared at the floor.

Chachi stared at Michael.

"You think if you tell him, it will be easier than this?" Michael asked softly. "You think he'd understand? I mean, what *do* you think, Chachi?"

"He'd try to kill me."

"You're goddamn right. He'll try to kill us both."

"But I *know* him, Michael." Chachi reached for his hand and held it. "He'll get over it…eventually. At some point. Maybe."

"You're not sounding so sure."

"But I know for a fact that if he finds out some other way, if he hears it from some nosey spy or reads about it in the paper or—God forbid, catches us in some uncompromising position, it's all over. He'll make sure we don't see each other again before you turn twenty-one and our friendship will be destroyed forever. Forever! Can you live with that? Because, I can't risk that!"

"No, but…" Michael frowned.

"Trust me on this one, baby. You have to if you want a remote chance of us ever seeing one another again."

"This is too heavy, man." Michael ran his hands through his coal-black locks in despair.

"I know. But I feel it in my gut. Something's about to jump off and we want to control how and when it goes down."

"I know you think you know him, but I know another side. He's harder on me, Chachi. I can't just walk up to him and go, 'Hey Dad—'"

"I won't let him hurt you."

Michael sighed and slid down next to Chachi where he could lay his head on his chest. Chachi played in his hair.

"I know you're scared, Chachi. You're always asking me to trust you, but trust me sometime. I will tell him soon. I promise! But this is not the right time."

Chachi nudged Michael away from him.

Undaunted, Michael demanded, “Promise you won’t tell him ‘til we both agree.”

Chachi rubbed his face with his hand.

“Promise!” Michael insisted.

After a few moments, Chachi nodded, but he couldn’t look Michael in the eyes when he did it.

* * * *

Joe had been badgering Michael about going away to college, perhaps a military academy of higher learning where he could also have private lessons for gifted students in the math and sciences, but Michael didn’t think any college had anything to offer him. He was breezing through his current lessons and Joe changed private professors three times to challenge him.

It had become at least a weekly battle between him and his father, usually on Sunday, his day off from the center. To escape this last fight, he rode his bike to Chachi’s where he found Papi supervising Sunday dinner and Chachi unwinding in the video room watching television, a rare treat.

“Whatcha watching?” he asked, dropping his weight onto the sofa next to him.

Chachi was still in his bathrobe, his favorite at-home attire next to his pajama bottoms. “Shhhhh.” Chachi lifted a hand half in greeting, half to quiet him. On the television was a show chronicling Duke Spencer’s life. “They are so wrong!” Chachi complained. “They said I was a shy kid, bullied in school. Me! Bullied by kids in school!” He paused to take in a bit more of the program. The narrator spoke in a newscaster’s voice. A picture of Chachi’s childhood home appeared on screen, an Antebellum beauty surrounded by a sprawling expanse of trees and grass. “They said I seduced my science teacher for a grade when I was fourteen—well, I *did* do that.” He paused again, focused on the screen.

A guy about Chachi’s age sat on a stool with a wistful smile on his face and recalled the days when they would play together—basketball, baseball, even the guitar sometimes.

"And who the hell is that!" Chachi bellowed. "I sure the fuck didn't play with him! I don't even know who the fuck that is!"

Michael couldn't hold his laughter anymore. He laughed until tears sprang to his eyes.

"Liars," Chachi growled. "I ought to sue the bastards. They only did that shit 'cause I wouldn't support the program. I'm tired of them diggin' up the same old shit! The same old questions!"

"Wouldn't you want to support the program so that you control what they say?" Michael massaged his shoulders, still laughing.

"You can't control what they say. Besides, as long as I've been in this business, you'd think they'd have had enough on me, all they're gonna get anyway." He used the remote control to switch the channel. "Enough of that."

Michael bent so that his lips were close to Chachi's ear. "Who could get enough of you?" He leaned over to kiss him on the cheek.

Chachi drew him in for a longer one. "You come here to start trouble?" he whispered.

"Ummm hmmm..." Michael kicked off his shoes. It was bound to happen, so of course it did. They were in one of those uncompromising positions Chachi spoke of so fearfully when a guest arrived. Had to be a friend to have shown up unannounced. Still, if Chachi's keen ears hadn't perked up just in time...

Chachi hastily put on his robe and slipped out the room, closing the door behind him.

Michael felt a sense of alarm, but didn't know why. He moved to the door and pressed his ear against it.

He heard Chachi say, "Oh, really? Kind of early for a drink, isn't it?"

Then he thought he heard a voice say, "Something wrong?" But it was muffled and he couldn't make it out.

Chachi said, "You know I don't like surprises, why didn't you call?"

"I have to call now?" The voice said.

Clearly a man's voice...or was it? They had moved too far away for him to make out anything else. After a while, he heard Chachi's footsteps approaching. "No problem. I'll call you," he said.

Michael ran to the sofa, grabbed a magazine, and began to leaf through it, but more than an hour had passed and Chachi was showered and fully dressed when Michael saw him again.

Mike flipped impatiently through the television channels, jerking the remote toward the TV.

Chachi burst in. He began tidying up, straightening the palms, the throw, the magazines. He never cleaned. He paid people to do that. Besides, Michael, in his compulsive orderliness, had already done that. "What happened?" Michael asked softly.

Chachi pretended not to hear.

"Chachi?" Realizing the fruitlessness of his inquiry, Michael went silent and continued his channel surfing while watching Chachi out of the corners of his eyes. How dare he have the nerve to be angry at him—for what! Because he had an un-invited guest to barge in on them? Thinking about it made his face hot. "Must have been one of your bitches," he mumbled.

Chachi picked up a snack bowl and slammed it down onto the table, then turned a fiery glare on Michael.

"Who was it?" he asked again and held his breath.

With an almost fiendish smirk that made Michael's skin prickle, Chachi answered, "Your father."

Part Two
Age of Consent

Chapter Twenty-Seven

"Let's grab some lunch," Joe offered. They had been in meetings all day hammering out details regarding an upcoming tour. Chachi welcomed the respite. He hadn't been on his best game. He couldn't focus on anything of late, with Michael on his mind.

During the ride to the restaurant, Chachi couldn't help but notice how talkative and spirited Joe was. He went on and on about one subject or another, laughed a lot and, even though he was driving, he'd pause to give Chachi a buddy-punch in the shoulder from time to time. Chachi sunk deeper into his seat, his long legs cramped in the small Bentley, and stared out the window.

Joe said, "I don't see the point in your company, get out of my car."

"Come on, Joe. I'm here. I just got a lot on the brain."

"What's wrong with you?"

Chachi looked up just as they pulled in front of La Chez's. "Oh, look—we're here." He quickly escaped the confines of the car and Joe's interrogation.

They were escorted to a private area enclosed by heavy drapes. They ate at La Chez's pretty often so the restaurant staff was prepared with the usual impeccable service.

They waited while the waiter popped the cork with deft expertise and poured the bubbly before quietly slipping away.

"What's wrong with you?" Joe asked again.

Chachi tried to look bewildered. "Nothing. What, a man can't have a thoughtful moment?"

"You haven't been 'thoughtful' in the twenty years I've known you."

"Then it's about time, right?" Chachi grinned unconvincingly and took a sip of champagne.

Joe shrugged and began to talk again as Chachi's thoughts once more drifted away.

Last night Michael had finally given words to what they both knew they were feeling. At first Chachi thought for sure he was losing his mind. He could no longer focus in meetings, and couldn't sleep at night. He found himself wondering all the time what Michael might be doing. He was tinged with jealousy when others admired Michael, afraid that he'd suddenly realize how ridiculous they were together, a teenage boy with a man twenty years his senior. He half expected him to run off at any moment for a young, pubescent schoolgirl (or worse, school boy). Such thoughts were becoming more frequent and he was just beginning to feel new alarm when Joe pricked him on the hand with a fork.

"Ow!"

"Jesus Christ, Chachi. Where *are* you?"

"Are you out of your fuckin' mind? You stabbed me!" Chachi rubbed the spot on his hand and pouted like a baby.

Joe laughed. "I barely touched you!"

"You did! Look!" He held out his hand to show the faint redness, probably more from his rubbing the hand than anything else.

Joe was unimpressed. "I'm trying to talk to you here! If you wanted to be alone, you should've said so. I hadn't planned on lunching with a goddamned zombie!"

Chachi rubbed his hands across his face. "You're right," he said.

"I mean, you haven't said two words."

"I got stuff on my mind."

"You've always been able to talk to me before. What's eating you?"

Chachi shook his head. "It's not that serious. Just something I'm trying to figure out."

"Well, come out with it," Joe urged, helping himself to warm, soft bread and whipped butter. "There's nothing we haven't been able to solve together."

Chachi's heart warmed for his friend, but guilt sprang to the surface and spread like veins through his system, glazing his eyes with tears. He looked away briefly so that Joe wouldn't notice.

"What were you saying?" he asked as a diversion.

"I was saying..." Joe swallowed. "I feel like I'm in the twilight zone.

Nobody's behaving the way they should. Sarah's in a mental institution, for God's sake. You're out to lunch most of the time lately, and— did you know Steven had a girlfriend?"

"No!" Recovered, Chachi gaped at him.

"Another lawyer. Lydia and I saw them out at dinner last weekend. Then, Michael's slinking around, ducking and dodging."

Chachi stopped breathing.

"I know he's seeing somebody," Joe's eyes glittered. "I'm sure of it. Lydia and I think he's in *love*." Joe grinned. "He hasn't said anything to me yet, but he's walking on air. I tried to get the goods out of Eric but," Joe frowned, puzzled, "close as they are, he seemed pretty clueless himself." He took another bite of the bread as the menus were set down before them.

"Care to hear our specials?" the waiter inquired.

Joe waved him away, and it was just as well because Chachi couldn't answer. His throat had suddenly dried up. He reached for the glass of water and immediately wished he hadn't. His hand began trembling so that droplets spilled all over the starched tablecloth.

Joe watched but kept talking as he reached for a napkin to wipe up the mess. "Papi has to be in league with him. I'm sure of it." Joe shrugged. "Oh, well. Maybe he'll come out with it in time. I think he thinks we meddle too much." He chuckled.

Chachi sat glued to his seat. There was something surreal about that moment. For months he'd been tortured with keeping the secret, trying to figure out a way to have the discussion with Joe, desperately trying to persuade Michael that the time had come, and now here was Joe, opening the door for him. Was it a sign?

Suddenly he wasn't ready for it. He wanted to cherish the last of this perfect friendship.

"I'm glad he has Papi, though," Joe said with an internal sigh of fondness. "I'm sure Michael thinks I'm a prude, especially with the way I react anytime I see him romantically involved with, well anyone. I know he's a young man, but to me, he's still my baby. Never mind the fact that he's been fuckin' grown women since he was thirteen, a thought which makes me sick."

Well, that sealed it. Chachi felt his tongue swell in the dry cottony heat of his mouth. Joe's voice faded from hearing, sounding cartoonish as it ebbed away. A panic rose in Chachi's chest. His consciousness ebbed. He felt dazed and detached. It was the wrong time, he shouldn't tell him.

"Joe…"

"And what does he do there anyway?" Joe continued.

"Wha-What?"

"Michael. What does he do there all day with Papi? He's not stashing some girl there, is he?" A shadow passed over Joe's face. "Chachi, you wouldn't let Michael bring girls to the house, would you?"

Chachi swallowed hard. Joe's words choked him, making it quite difficult, not that he deserved it to be anything but. "No," he said hoarsely.

"'Cause, I forbid it. You know that, right?"

Chachi nodded, but couldn't look at him.

"I don't allow it in my house. Nobody's fucking in my house, but me and my wife." He laughed.

"Joe…"

"What is it, Chachi? Spit it out boy!" He smiled playfully.

The waiter returned with their usual appetizers and Joe helped himself. "May I take your orders now, sirs?"

Joe ordered a steak, medium, and a cocktail.

Chachi passed. His jaw stuck and he couldn't spit it out. He wished he were someplace else. Just take Michael and go. But then he'd be kidnapping him and he could definitely kiss his friendship with Joe and everyone else goodbye. He couldn't believe he was entertaining such thoughts. He'd gone nuts.

Joe looked up from his calamari. His eyes began to narrow. "You know something," he charged, pointing his fork accusingly at Chachi who simply shook his head tiredly. "You do!" Joe leaned toward him, smiling cleverly. "You know something and you're gonna tell me."

Chachi exhaled exaggeratedly and looked down at his hands. How could he break this man's heart?

"Michael swore you to secrecy, didn't he?" Joe grinned. "Well, you're my best friend!" Joe slapped the table with his hand, sending champagne and water rocking like tidal waves in their goblets. "We don't have secrets from each other, remember?"

Tears sprang to Chachi's eyes and his hands flew to cover his face.

"Chachi?"

Chachi began to sob into his palms soundlessly. His shoulders jerked and his body trembled.

Joe fell back into his seat, shocked. He looked around nervously. "Chachi, what is it? Tell me what it is!"

"I can't Joe," Chachi muttered behind his hands, "I can't…"

"Did somebody—die?"

Chachi shook his head.

"Is someone sick, is your mother...?"

Chachi shook is head again.

"Then it can't be that bad. Whatever it is, it can be fixed. We'll fix it. Tell me what it is."

Good old Joe. There wasn't a better friend. Joe would do anything for him—anything, and he'd do anything for Joe. How could he do this to Joe? How could he do this to their friendship? How could he not...

"Joe, I've done something."

Joe reached out and pulled Chachi's hands away from his face and held on to them. He spoke in the same tone he used to comfort his children. "Whatever it is it can be fixed," he repeated.

"You're gonna be so angry with me." Chachi freed a hand to dry his tears with a napkin.

The waiter returned with Joe's steak. "Anything else I can do for you, sirs—is everything all right?"

"We're okay; we just need to be alone," Joe said. "Can you make sure we're not disturbed? I'll summon you if I need you." Joe turned back to Chachi. "What happened?"

His stomach knotted, Chachi cleared his throat and blew out his breath. Might as well get it over with. "I've…been seeing someone…behind your back…"

Joe shuddered. "Sarah?"

Chachi grimaced.

"Just a wild guess." Joe said.

Chachi made no move to enlighten him and they sat watching each other, the tension like being on the edge of a precipice.

"Not my *daughter...*" Joe said, his words laced with warning. Leah has had a lifetime crush on her godfather.

"Of course not!" Chachi shot at him, then looked away with shame.

"Well," Joe sighed with relief, "as long as you're not fucking my wife, my mother, or my daughter—"

"Joe, Michael has been coming to the house to see *me*."

Joe stared blankly. "Why?"

"I've been wanting to tell you for a long time. I just didn't know how."

Chachi stopped speaking. Joe's expression was too sedate for what he was telling him. The thought that he and Michael would get together in *that way* was so far removed from his mind, he hadn't allowed himself even to hear what Chachi was saying. Another, more direct approach was necessary. "Joe, I love Michael."

Took him still another second or two, but then Joe's face began to register a change, growing dark with realization, then sharpening and draining of all color. "You what?" he croaked.

"I swear to God, I didn't want this to happen, I tried to stop it; I did! I did everything I—"

"Tell me you're kidding." Joe had become a deep shade of red, his jaws set, his eyes red pin-pricks in his head.

Chachi's mouth opened and shut like a beached fish. He had never been on the receiving end of Joe's fury before. It was as frightening as he'd heard.

"Tell me it's not true."

"Joe..." his mind raced for a cure. "It's not how you think."

Joe looked around the room wildly. "This is insane," he said, his face crumpled miserably. "This is crazy...it can't be happening..."

"I wanted to tell you," Chachi's eyes were pleading. "I tried."

Joe's head snapped around android-like and he glared at Chachi with a look that should have turned him to stone.

Chachi shrank back.

"How long?" Joe mouthed the words.

"I don't know, a few months maybe."

"*Months*?" Joe repeated and laughed, a hollow, foreign sound that made Chachi's arm hairs bristle.

"I don't know how to explain myself, but let me try—"

"Months!" Joe shouted. The soft murmur of voices outside the protective curtain halted.

Soon after, their waiter appeared. "Everything okay, sirs?"

"We won't be dining today." Joe dropped a credit card on the table. "Settle the bill and bring my car around, please."

Chachi turned to the waiter and smiled. "Can you make sure we have like, *total* privacy?"

The waiter looked from Joe's distraught face to Chachi's tear-stained one and nodded before scampering away.

"Oh, God," Joe moaned and bent forward, his arm across his middle. "You haven't—"

Chachi groaned.

"You haven't—touched him, have you?" Joe's eyes widened. "You haven't, have you?" His hands were shaking.

Chachi could only gaze remorsefully at those hands.

"You son of a bitch," Joe said in a soft voice. "You sick son of a bitch, you've been fucking my baby, Chachi? *My* baby?"

Chachi lowered his head onto the table and sobbed.

"He's a child, Chachi, a kid. He idolizes you! Of all the people you could have had, you had to go and—" Joe glanced around him as if looking for a weapon. He drew back his arm and surprised Chachi with a punch to the jaw. A dish crashed to the floor. People stirred outside the curtain.

Chachi leapt to his feet, glad for the cover of curtains. "Okay," he said, his hand cradling his swelling face. "I deserved that." His lip bled. He wiped at it with a table napkin.

"You deserve more than that!" Joe said, rising. "You're a *rapist*, you know that, don't you Chachi? A child molester!" Inflated with rage his chest labored. "Why'd it have to be my—" his voice broke as he cried.

"Oh, Christ," Chachi whispered.

The restaurant's manager, who knew them both well, eased the curtain aside, a look of apology on his face.

Chachi waved him away. "It's okay, we're leaving," he said hastily. When the man disappeared, Chachi walked over to Joe and wrapped his arms around him.

"How could you do this to me?" Joe sobbed and held on to Chachi. "How could you do this to Michael?"

"I know what I've done is inexcusable, but please, please believe me that I would never *plan* to do anything that I thought would hurt you or Michael. I didn't want this, Joe, honestly I didn't. But, I love him—"

Joe pushed him violently. "You love him?" He sneered. "You *love* him? Mutherfucka, you've never loved anything in you life!"

"That's not true!"

"Nothing! You may have fooled some of us into thinking that, but then look at what you've done to me! If you could do this to me, who you're supposed to love like a brother, you've got to be incapable of love!"

The waiter returned with the check, blinking with discomfort. Joe scribbled his name on the receipt. Then he ripped out his wallet, stuffed the card inside, and threw loose bills on the table.

"Joe, stop!" Chachi pleaded. "You have every right to be angry, but—"

"But what?" Joe shouted. "But what?" His tears began to flow again. "You were my brother!" He cried and banged his fist against his heart. "You broke my heart..." He swung around.

Chachi reached out to stop him, but was met with a crushing blow to the chest that sent him falling backward across the table. Anything left standing on it went crashing to the floor with him.

The manager reappeared, wringing his hands.

"Where's my car!" Joe growled at him.

"It's waiting."

Joe stormed toward the private exit.

Chachi struggled to his feet and charged after him.

"I'm sorry, just send the bill to me," he said as he dashed by, charging through the door after Joe. A blast of air freeze-dried his tears.

"No problem, sir," the manager panted, working hard to keep up with them, "but shall I call someone?"

"Where're my keys!" Joe bellowed, searching his pockets frantically.

"In the car, sir."

"Did anyone recognize us?" Chachi whispered while Joe fumbled around in the car, disoriented.

"I'm afraid everyone could hear you, but I don't think anyone knows who you are."

"Good. Can your staff be trusted?"

"Yes."

"Hold on." Chachi sprinted to the car just as Joe was shifting it in reverse. "Joe, you can't go like this!" He held on to the door handle. "I can't let you drive in this condition!"

"Try to stop me, fucker!" Joe hit the accelerator, nearly taking Chachi's hand off.

"Where are you going!" Chachi called after him, but a sinking feeling in the pit of his stomach came in answer.

"Can I help?" the manager asked again.

Chachi pulled out his wallet and handed over all the money he had. "I need to borrow your car."

Michael had been having a good day. He rose at dawn and had a spirited jog around the grounds. After that, he spent all morning in his room bathing, listening to music, and just pampering himself. He and Eric were hooking up to do some very early Christmas shopping. They hadn't been spending much time together and he was looking forward to it. Still wearing a towel, he leaned over his dressing table, face nearly touching the mirror, and began the dangerous task of trimming his brows.

"Ouch!"

Eric barged in. Startled, Michael nearly stuck himself in the eye.

"My bad," Eric apologized. "What ya doing?"

"Blinding myself, thanks to you."

"Man, you're gonna put your eye out one of these days."

Michael grunted.

"For real, though. You're only butchering them, anyway. Leave 'em alone!"

"There," Michael said after he was done. "Looks better, doesn't it?"

"You groom yourself more than any woman I know."

Michael opened his mouth just as the phone rang. As always, he knew it was Chachi. Odd time for him to call. Chachi had meetings all day. He suppressed a wave of panic and answered on the second ring. "Hey you," he said discreetly.

"Are you dressed?"

An odd question. The urgency in Chachi's voice was not mistaken.

"Not yet, why?"

"Do me a favor."

Michael could sense Chachi's struggle to sound calm.

"Sure."

"I need you to do exactly as I say and not ask questions. There's no time."

Michael felt his face grow hot. His palms began to sweat. "What's wrong?"

"Put some clothes on, anything quick—a robe, some sweats—and step outside for a few minutes."

"What?"

"Just five minutes. Stay hidden. Make sure no one sees you. After about five-ten minutes, you can come back inside."

"You're nuts!" Michael laughed, hoping it was a joke. But Chachi wasn't a prankster.

"I'm not kidding and I don't have time for you to question me. Do it, now!"

"Why? I—It's cold outside!"

"Put a fuckin' coat on!"

Michael felt a bit of cold down his backbone. "Chachi, what's going on?"

Eric rose at the mention of Chachi's name. "What's going on?"

"Just do it, baby," Chachi plead. "There's no time to explain, but I'm on my way."

"Here?"

"What's going on?" Eric repeated.

Chachi asked, "Is someone there?"

"Eric."

"Shit. Well, tell him to get lost. If Joe sees him, he'll question him and he won't be able to lie to Joe."

Michael's body went rigid. What did his father have to do with this? He clutched the phone to his ear. "Joe?" he rasped. "What's this got to do with Dad?"

Michael could hear the anguish in Chachi's sigh. "I told him. I wasn't planning on it, it just came out. I don't know if it was the right time. You were right. He's pissy mad."

"You told him about *us*?" Michael whispered.

"I'm sorry…"

"Oh, God!"

"What happened?" Eric demanded. He was standing directly next to Michael now. "Jesus, Michael, what?"

He'll kill me, Michael said to himself. His eyes glazed over with fear and he gripped the phone so tightly his hands were like ice.

"If you can avoid the first few minutes of his anger, he can get control of it. Just stave him off a few minutes and I'll be there. That's why I want you to leave the house, now go!"

"He's coming…here?"

"Yeah." Chachi sounded tired and impatient. "He went ballistic when I told him. He punched me and trashed the restaurant…"

Michael dropped his towel.

"What is it?" Eric pressed.

Michael looked at him helplessly. "Sweet Jesus—"

"There's no time for you to fall apart!" Chachi said. "Grab a coat and get out of the house. He'll be there in a minute.

Michael gasped.

"But I'm right behind him, baby."

Michael stood rooted to the floor, hyperventilating into the phone.

"*Now*!" Chachi bellowed.

Michael slammed the receiver into its cradle.

Eric held his breath for the worst.

"I need your help," Michael said, shivering.

"What?" Eric replied, hands palm-up and at-the-ready.

"I'm in trouble. Dad's on his way here to kill me."

Eric almost laughed with relief, except Michael still looked as if he was going to faint.

"Tell me what to do."

"I need clothes," Michael said, grabbing his jogging pants off a chair and pulling them on. "Can you grab a shirt for me?"

"Where're we going?" Eric asked. He had already made it to Michael's closet, grabbed a white shirt, and thrust it into Michael's arms.

It was the word "we" that made Michael stop and look at his cousin, eyes wet with affection. Without even knowing the nature of the trouble, Eric was willing to go wherever he had to go. Michael moaned and grabbed his cousin by the shoulders pulling him to his chest. He held on to him like a magnet.

Eric wrapped his arms around Michael. "Mike, it's okay."

They both jumped when the entry door slammed. Even upstairs Michael could feel its vibration.

They stared at each other, wide-eyed, as Joe's footsteps crashed against the stairs.

Eric pushed Michael. "Run!"

Michael's feet would not move. He stood planted, fixed, still clutching the shirt in his arms.

Joe kicked the door in.

Eric threw himself flat against the nearest wall.

Michael remained rooted, petrified.

Joe stood in the doorway, his shoulders sagging, his face wet with tears. Lydia, David and Leah quickly appeared behind Joe and some of the staff milled slowly past them, hoping to get a glimpse.

"What's happening?" Lydia asked, drying her hands on a towel.

No one spoke.

When Joe found his voice, it was deep and husky. "You faggot!" he growled.

The room gasped. Michael shut his eyes tight. This had to be a nightmare, if he could just wake up.

"Joe!" Lydia exclaimed through her shock.

"How could you?" Joe slowly advanced toward Michael.

"Joe, stop!" Lydia screamed.

"Daddy, please!" Leah cried.

"You hate me, don't you?" Joe asked, still inching his way forward.

Michael shook, still planted in his spot.

"All this time, I believed you'd forgiven me, that you'd come to be a part of this family, that you loved us, the way we love you; but you had this planned all along, hadn't you?"

Michael, eyes still closed, shook his head vigorously. With his mouth, he formed the words 'no' over and over again.

"And you won't stop, will you, until you have destroyed every relationship I have with *anyone*—"

"Joe you can't mean that!" Lydia cried.

"Will you!" Joe boomed, causing all of them to jump.

A sob escaped Michael's throat.

"Will you!" he said again, this time grabbing Michael by the shoulders and shaking him.

"Joe, Stop!" Lydia yelled as Leah, cowering behind David, screamed.

The entry door slammed a second time. Chachi leapt up the stairs and pushed past David and Leah, nearly knocking them both to the floor.

"Let him go, Joe. This is between me and you."

Joe stood, eyes glaring, nostrils flaring. He eyed Chachi with such contempt Lydia began to cry.

"Take your hands off him," Chachi warned.

Joe released Michael and turned on Chachi, his eyes so reddened, his face so distorted with anger, Leah screamed and ran at the sight of him. "You dare step foot in my home, you perverted son-of-a-bitch—"

"Please," Lydia whimpered. "Please."

Joe struck Chachi, delivering a clean jab to the chin. The room erupted in a chorus of cries.

Chachi staggered backward slightly before regaining his footing. "Fine," he said, gently massaging his bruised chin. "I deserve that too. Just don't you touch him." He stuck a finger in his mouth and pulled it out, frowning at the blood on it. "And I'm putting you on notice that I'm not taking any more of your sucker-punches either!"

"Oh yeah?" Joe mocked him, his mouth twisted in a sadistic grin. "What ya gonna do, Chachi? Huh? You gonna spank me? You gonna bend me over too?"

The room gasped again.

"Joe, that's uncalled for," Lydia said.

"Or am I too old for you?" Joe continued.

Chachi held up one hand and shook his head, his other hand making a sweeping motion at his throat.

"Is that it, you swine...you child molester…you fuckin' *pedophile*!"

Chachi lunged for him. They fell to the floor in a violent struggle. Lydia shot a frantic glance of disbelief at Michael, who sank to the floor in despair.

"Stop! Stop!" Lydia squealed, clawing at Chachi as he writhed on top of Joe. "This is lunacy! You're best friends! Stop, Chachi, stop!"

They disentangled themselves and sprang to their feet, chests heaving.

She grabbed them both by an arm. "We can get through this, we can! Just don't fight! I've never seen you guys like this!" She paused. "You *love* each other! We'll get through this!"

Chachi and Joe faced each other with fists clenched. Lydia stood between them.

"Get out!" Joe bellowed. "Get your ass out of my house and don't you come back!"

Chachi turned toward Michael.

Michael rolled his head listlessly in Chachi's direction.

"Don't look at him like that!" Joe pushed Chachi in the chest, looking frantically from one to the other.

Michael shook his head slowly. Joe stormed over to Michael's telephone. "And don't think about calling!" He snatched the cord out of the wall. He spotted Michael's cell phone charging on its base and confiscated it too, stuffing it in his pocket.

"Joe, you're acting like a child! Stop it!" Lydia screamed.

"Get out!"

Chachi backed away slowly toward the door. Eric and David parted.

"Just go, Chachi," Lydia said softly. "Michael will be all right."

Chachi's gaze met hers full on, as if just noticing her presence. He touched her hair lightly and disappeared down the stairs.

The room seemed to exhale. Joe's anger dissipated with Chachi's exit. He placed his hands over his face and cried.

"Come on, darling." Lydia took him by the arm and led him from the room. "It's all right."

She gave Michael a sympathetic glance before closing the door behind her.

Eric, Michael, and David shared the pained silence left in their wake.

"You're the devil," David said to Michael after a long while.

"Shut up!" Eric snarled.

Michael was mortified. Things couldn't get any worse.

"I told him not to let you stay here," David went on, "but he wouldn't listen. Now look where it's got him, where it's got all of us!"

"I said shut your fat fuckin' mouth!" Eric took a step toward him, fist balled.

David took the same step backward. He watched Eric with his lip curled in distate. "What does it take for you, Eric? You think he's your little friend? You idiot! Don't you see? He hates all of us. He sucked us in, but Dad's right. He had this planned all along. There's no telling what else he's got cooked." With one last glare in Michael's direction, David turned and left the room.

Eric watched as Michael struggled from his place on the floor and fell onto the bed.

"You all right?" Eric asked. He walked over and touched his shoulder. "You want me to stay?"

Michael shook his head.

"You want me to call Pooch?"

Michael shook his head again.

"Tell me what to do."

"Just leave me alone," Michael said.

"You won't do anything foolish, will you?"

"Just go! Please!" Michael sobbed.

Eric exhaled loudly. "Call me if you need me."

"I don't believe he did this to me!" Joe's emotion had run the gamut.

"Joe, take the focus off yourself for a moment," Lydia said. "Can you imagine what Michael must be going through?"

Joe had a good cry and now his rage had returned. He paced across his bedroom floor. Lydia sat on the bed, one leg underneath her, dress still damp from where he had lain his head in her lap and wept. "Chachi has totally overstepped his boundaries. He's gotten away with everything he's done wrong in his life, but not this time!"

"I don't think he forced Michael to do anything, Joe. You know how crazy Michael is about Chachi."

"He's a kid! God knows how old he was when he started fucking him! Jesus!"

"I know."

"Then you know he's committed rape!"

Lydia sighed. "Law aside, the fact still remains that your son loves your best friend. You'll have to tread lightly from here on. What you do about this can alienate him from you."

"He'll get over it," Joe mumbled.

"I don't think he's really gotten over anything he's been through. I think he's just storing all this inside him and forging ahead. He's a ticking time bomb. But Joe, I haven't seen him happier than in the last several months."

"What kind of parent are you?" Joe turned on her. "What if this had happened to David!"

"That's not fair!" She winced. "Michael is not David!"

"His being smart doesn't mean he's wise. He is not equipped to make decisions like this or handle this kind of responsibility at his age!"

"But he *has* done it, Joe. All of his life!"

"We weren't there to protect him, then."

"We weren't there to help him, either. But he survived."

Joe stared at her like she had sprouted a beard. "Lydia, I'm surprised at you!"

"I just don't think we can write him off as some gullible kid who didn't know what was happening to him. We have to listen to him!"

Joe exhaled long and hard. Again, his anger began to dissolve into tears. "And Chachi?"

Lydia shook her head sorrowfully. "Did you see how he looked at Michael, Joe? Did you see how they looked at each other?

Joe moaned and walked over to their bedroom window.

"Joe, open your eyes. I know it's hard to face, but they *love* each other. There is no way Chachi would do something like this unless something powerful was compelling him."

Joe closed his eyes. He wished he could go to bed and wake up again, start the day over, have it turn out different. "Is that an excuse? What kind of father would I be if I turned my head?"

Lydia walked over to him and hugged him from behind. "You'll do what is in your heart. I just want you to step away from your sense of betrayal, your anger, so that you can make clear decisions."

He turned to her and cupped her face in his hands.

She smiled.

Joe dropped his head. "I said awful things to Michael," he whispered. "I called him a—"

"Oh, Joe…"

"He'll never forgive me."

"You were angry. He'll come to realize that in time."

"I should apologize." Joe moved to go, but Lydia caught him by the arm.

"Not now. Michael won't be ready. Let some time pass. But I don't think you should leave things like this between you and Chachi."

Joe's eyes sparked with fight. "And I should say what to that cradle-robber?"

"He's your best friend, no matter how you slice it. He's wrong. There is no doubt about that. But he loves you. Whatever he did—it wasn't out of malice. Just listen to what he has to say. You owe yourself that!"

The spark in Joe's eyes died again. "This is so fucked up…"

"We'll get through it." She began to massage his shoulders as he dropped gratefully into a chair. "Weaker families have survived more. We have too much love between us to let even this rip us apart. We're talking about two people that love each other. Love is love—you get who you get. We won't understand all of life's mysteries. You think you can put the anger aside and deal with this sensibly?"

Joe nodded, but he wasn't so sure.

"You go see Chachi. I'll talk to Michael."

Chachi selected items of clothing and handed them to the maid who folded and packed them as Papi looked on. Dominic stood at a nearby window smoking a cigarette.

The air tensed and Chachi turned to see Joe. "Leave us alone for a minute, please," Chachi said.

The maid filed past. Dominic placed a hand on Joe's shoulder affectionately and Papi lay a hand on his face as they passed.

"You're leaving," Joe said after they were gone.

"For a little while. I need to think."

Joe nodded and hung his head. "Probably best," he said to his shoes. He stood quietly as Chachi loaded clothes into a suitcase.

"Why'd you come?" Chachi asked after a while.

"I don't know, exactly. I just wanna understand."

Chachi shrugged. "I don't know what else to say. I can't justify anything."

They were quiet again. The silence seemed so loud.

"I'm sorry I let it happen." Chachi sighed. "I'm sorry I hid it from you. I didn't intend to hurt you or anyone, I don't know, I don't know any more than anyone."

"What the fuck does that mean?"

"I don't know."

Joe found a nearby chair and sat, solemnly watching, until Chachi pressed the last of his underwear in the over-stuffed suitcase and forced it closed. "You know, as his father, I can't look the other way."

"I'm not asking you to," Chachi answered, eyeing him curiously.

"I can't say what will happen."

Chachi did not respond.

"When you come back, you might...have to answer...to the authorities."

"So what are you saying?" Chachi asked conversationally, but the muscles in his neck stuck out like cords. "That I shouldn't come home?"

"I'm just saying, what kind of father would I be if—"

"This is my home," Chachi said evenly. "I'm going away for a while, a few days, to think. Then I'll be back. No one drives me from my home." He picked up the suitcase and walked it to the door, dropping it with a loud thud. "You do what you have to do." Chachi picked up an already packed carryon bag and slung it alongside his luggage at the door.

"What about the business?"

"What about it?" Chachi stopped and looked at Joe.

"We're partners. What are we going to do about that? Are we going to be able to work together after this?"

Chachi chuckled in frustration. Shaking his head.

"I don't know..." Joe continued.

"Whatever, Joe."

"What do you expect me to do?"

"At this point, Joe, I really don't care!"

"Well, that's the problem, isn't it Chachi? You don't care about much!"

Chachi's eyes flashed gold. "Don't you dare say that! I love Michael! I was wrong, I succumbed to my emotions, but it's not like I snatched him off your knee and drug him down a dark alley!"

"Don't you get it? I don't think you realize the magnitude—"

"Oh, I realize that what I've done is wrong, he's too young, I got that. But if it happened four years, ten years from now—would you feel any different? No! Because this is about you, not him!"

"That's a lie!"

"I betrayed *you*, right? How could we do this to *you*, right?"

"Yes! I feel betrayed!" Veins pushed against Joe's neck. "How do you expect me to take finding out that my best friend's been fuckin' my *son*, no less, behind my back!"

"Okay." Chachi held his hands up. "I've apologized. I've tried to explain it but I can't. Obviously, you need something else from me. I can't give it to you."

"You know Michael's never been strong emotionally," Joe said more softly. "He is not capable of handling this."

"He has been the happiest of his life with me, and you know it!"

"That doesn't justify anything!"

"Whatever."

"Besides, I don't want to be the one to bring it up but I think you need to ask yourself why, Chachi. I don't think you wanna face the true motive behind your actions."

"Don't go there..."

"I have my son to think about."

"Then think about him! But don't bring that shit up again. We're talking a hundred years ago!"

Joe quieted and watched Chachi toss things around.

"Where are you going?"

"Whereever I end up, probably to my mother's."

"When do you leave?"

"As soon as my pilot arrives. I'm taking the Learjet."

"Need me to drive you?"

"No."

Joe fell silent again. After a while he sighed and rose to go. "I don't want you to contact him, Chachi."

Chachi gasped. "I can't leave without saying goodbye. He'll misunderstand."

"I'll worry about that."

"You want him to think I abandoned him? You think then he'll be angry enough to forget about me, huh?"

Joe stood up, his cold, dark eyes smoldering. "You *will* abandon him and he *will* forget about you. You'd better hope he does. Because you touch him again, you're going to jail *if* I don't kill you."

Chachi glared at him and turned away.

"We still haven't discussed the business," Joe pressed. "What am I to say? We have obligations."

Chachi spun around. "Joe, take the business and all your obligations and stick em' up your ass."

Michael sat on the bed, knees drawn up, staring toward his window. He was amazed at how beautiful the day was. The sun shone so brightly he had to blink against it. Leaves painted a myriad of dazzling fall reds and tangerines floated gracefully from the trees at perfect intervals, barely kissing the ground as they landed. He was feeling so dark he expected the skies to be overcast.

"Michael?"

He turned his head toward Lydia.

"I just came to see if you were all right."

He shook his head and turned his gaze back to the window.

She sat next to him and pressed her lip to his ear. "You've done nothing wrong! You hear me?" She cupped his chin with her hand and turned him to face her. "You did nothing wrong."

"David's right," he said. "Whatever sin I was conceived—"

"You hush," she cooed. "You can't blame yourself for the foolish choices we adults make."

"But isn't it odd how I ended up here—"

"That's enough. I don't want to hear any more of that gibberish! David has no idea what he's talking about. He's acting out just like we all tend to do."

"You have to admit, a lot changed when I came."

"You're damned right, it did!" She pursed her lips defiantly. It almost made Michael smile in spite of his depression. "Before you came, we waddled around in our pretend-perfect lives, with our money and our servants, avoiding each other, avoiding our issues, avoiding real life! You came along and shook the picture. I had to look at my husband and make him accountable for cheating on me because, suddenly, the evidence was staring me in the face. He had to look at me and decide if he loved me enough. Suddenly, David had to share things, his space, his parents, his heart. Leah had someone who noticed her, who spent time with her. You became a brother to her. Eric found a friend. You made us *feel* things, Michael. Good or bad, that's better than feeling nothing at all."

"I didn't mean for this to happen. I didn't even know what I felt until, I mean, I never even had any attraction to men—"

"Who knows who they are at seventeen-eighteen years old?" Lydia smiled. "Some of us, old as we are, are still trying to find ourselves."

"I wanted to kill myself."

"Why, because you fell in love?"

His head jerked to face her. To hear it spoken aloud in a way that didn't sound filthy or wrong...

"I told you it would happen one day," she said, holding his hand. "And I told you I'd be here for you when it did."

He let himself fall apart, sobbing until limp, his head in her lap. Afterward, he lay quiet so long, she thought he had fallen asleep. "I hate the way everyone looked at me," he whispered.

"Well," she said, "you have to admit, it *is* shocking."

"They think I'm some kind of freak. Especially *him*."

"*Him* is your father, and he loves you very much," she said softly. "He was shocked. He felt betrayed. He said things he didn't mean."

"He called me a faggot."

"I know. It's an awful word. He regrets it already."

Michael sat up, his face puffy from so many tears. "And what do *you* think?"

She smiled and placed her hand over his. "Who you sleep with doesn't make you who you are. I *do* think you're in a bit over your head, but Chachi loves you. I saw that in the way he looked at you today. I've never seen him look at anyone like that. I believe he'll be careful. He'll look out for you. You understand though, that your father is right." Michael lowered his eyes. "A thirty eight-year-old man has no business with a teenage anything. Your father has a responsibility to protect you and every right to feel the way he does."

Michael looked away. Silly laws were just that. Who's to say who should fall in love with whom and at what age?

"On the other hand," she continued, "we all know how much good it does to tell a teenager to stay away from a first love. Look at my face."

Slowly, he turned to meet her gaze.

"I would never condone a relationship like this. You're too young. It would be irresponsible. Still, I know those words fall on deaf ears. But I do want you to hear this: Whatever you do, whatever you decide, your father and I will always be here for you. Don't doubt it for a second. He's flawed, Michael, like every other human being on this earth. He gets angry and says things he doesn't really mean. He has to continue working on that. But no one loves you like he does. Do you hear?"

Michael nodded.

"Good." She exhaled. "Maybe by the time Chachi gets back, we'll all have settled down enough to discuss this with clear heads."

"Get back from where?" Michael sat up, alarmed.

"Oh…he thought if he went away for a few days, it would be the best thing—"

"Went away! He's leaving?"

"I'm sure he'll be back honey—"

Michael sprang from the bed and began rummaging for clothes. "When? When is he leaving?"

"Well, your father just called me before I came in to see you. He had gone to see Chachi and said he was packing for a trip. He might already be gone."

In a panic, Michael grabbed a sweatshirt from his dresser drawer and began pulling it over his head.

Lydia wrung her hands. "I'm sure he'll be back, darling!"

"That asshole! I don't believe this. He was gonna say nothing to me?"

"I'm sure he would have called if he could."

Michael froze with just his head sticking out of the sweatshirt. He looked over at the phone cord sticking out of the wall and recalled Joe stuffing the cell phone in his pocket. "I hate him!" he growled as he grabbed a pair of sneakers and sprinted out the door.

He ignored the surprise on Chachi's and Papi's faces when he stormed in. "You *leaving* me?"

"No, I'm not leaving *you*, Michael. I just thought I'd let things cool off a few days."

"And when were you gonna tell me?"

Chachi removed from Papi's hand a letter, already twisted and curling at the edges from sweat. Michael glanced at the envelope briefly and tossed it aside without opening it. "A letter, Chachi?"

"I wanted to call. I almost asked Eric to take his cell phone to you, but I didn't want to involve him, and I didn't want things to get worse than they already are. I'll be back in a few days—"

"I can't believe you're running away!"

"I'm not running away!"

"You know how he is and you're leaving me with him!"

Chachi rolled his shoulder as if testing it. "He hasn't hurt you, Michael, has he?" Michael didn't answer. "He won't."

"I won't stay with them! They're disgusted with me! You saw how they looked at me! Take me with you—"

"I can't."

"Why!"

"You know why!"

"I won't stay here!"

Papi reached his hand out but Michael pulled away.

"It's okay, Papi. Leave us alone," Chachi said. They waited until Papi had gone. "No hug? No kiss?"

"I'm not kidding, Chachi."

Chachi set his bag on the floor and took both Michael's hands. "You've gotta trust me on this."

"Trust you. Trust you. That's what you say! But that's the reason we're in this mess!"

Chachi's mouth sagged open then snapped shut. "Doesn't it always work out?"

"I don't care!"

"Michael, listen. I'm telling you, I know your father. He'll be much more receptive in a few days when he's had a chance to calm down."

"At first you said a few hours, now its a few days. Yeah, you know him so well," Michael sneered, "you didn't seem to know him so well today."

"I admit I lost control of the situation. I didn't really know what to expect," Chachi said half to himself, "still, he came by to see me afterwards; that was a good sign."

"Take me with you!"

"I—*can't*!"

"You're a fuckin' coward! I can't believe you're gonna just leave because he wants you to!"

"Who says I'm leaving because he wants—"

"*Shut up*!" Michael screamed. "You don't care about me! You're only concerned about losing your precious friendship! Makes me wonder if you're fuckin' him too, you fuckin' liar—*Ah*!" He brought his hand to his face where Chachi struck him with enough force to make him see stars in daylight.

Chachi was so stricken he couldn't move. They glowered at one another.

"I think you should go home now," Chachi said, his voice strained.

Panicked, Michael threw himself at Chachi's feet and wrapped his arms around his legs. "No. I can't let you go."

"You've got to be kidding." Chachi sounded as if he would laugh.

"You're not going unless you're taking me with you."

Chachi removed his cell phone from a clip on his belt.

Joe picked up on the first ring.

"Come get your son."

"I'm right here." Joe stepped into the room and snapped the phone shut. His cold, black eyes were hard and fixed on Michael's face.

Michael looked up at him with dismay. He wanted to kill Lydia.

Joe's voice was icy. "Let go of his leg. You look like a fool."

"No." He held on tighter.

"Come on, Mike," Chachi pleaded, "You're not as crazy as you'd like people to think."

Michael held on. Maybe Chachi's pilot would leave him. Maybe he'd see how much he needed him and decide to stay. Maybe anything.

"Michael, get up!" Joe shouted. Michael loosened his grip a bit out of fear, but he did not let go.

"I'm giving you one more chance."

Joe lunged forward at the same time that Chachi moved into his path to protect Michael. Michael stood swiftly, glaring at them.

"Mike..." Chachi said with a moan.

Joe sighed. "Come on," he extended a hand. "You can leave your car here, I'll drive—"

Michael raced from the room.

Chapter Twenty-Eight

Michael stayed in his room for days. He no longer found any interest outside his door—not much inside either. Chachi's leaving was a profound statement and it killed something inside him. Joe insisted Michael join them at the table for meals, rather than pine away in his room. Michael finished breakfast and asked to be excused.

Joe's cell phone rang, nestled in the pocket of his robe. He fumbled to remove it, quickly scanning the display. His face colored. "Hello?"

Michael froze on the stairs on his way up to his room. He wasn't sure if there was a response from the other end, but the fear in his father's voice was unmistaken.

"Chachi?" Joe's chair crashed to the floor. "Chachi, where are you!"

Michael stood still and listened to his father's frantic cries from the breakfast room. His hand gripped the stair railing. He felt doom in the air as thick as old musk.

"What is it?" Lydia cried. Joe didn't answer. Michael could feel him listening.

"Where are you! Chachi?" Joe waited. "Oh, God."

"What? What happened to Chachi?" Lydia shrieked.

"Something's wrong," Joe said. "Lydia, get Papi on the phone. See if you can find out where Chachi went. David, call the police."

"What can I do?" Leah squeaked.

"See if you can get Dominic on the phone. Chachi may have told him something—Maxi!"

"I'm right here sir!"

"Pack me a bag. I don't know for how long."

Michael walked up the remainder of the stairs and paused on the landing to watch the bustle below, his heart drawn into his chest like a fist.

"Dominic doesn't know where he is," Leah reported.

"Papi said he called yesterday, but he can't seem to find the number now," his wife called from the study.

"Call the phone company, they should be able to trace it."

Each minute seemed an hour. Dominic must have been hiding in the bushes. He was there in the blink of an eye to pace the floor with Joe.

"Dad, its detective Sanborn," David said, holding the phone out to him. Joe pressed it to his ear, stone-faced.

Chachi had been staying at a hotel in St. Tropes. Once detective Sanborn was able to locate his whereabouts, he promptly notified the hotel staff, who found him lifeless and not breathing. Joe had his bag packed and was headed for the door. He would take a private plane to join Chachi at the hospital. Dominic and some of the others would follow later. After final kisses and consoling goodbyes, Joe's eyes met Michael's. He had remained on the landing, leaning against the railing, watching the spectacle below.

"I'll call you as soon as I know something," Joe said.

Michael stared at him blankly.

"He'll be all right," Joe said with tears in his eyes.

Dashing into his room, Michael closed the door and pressed his back against it, panting as if he had run a mile. He thought he could be angry enough to forget that he loved him…even hate him. But he found out he wouldn't be getting off that easy.

* * * *

It was a morbid thought, but looking at Chachi, Joe realized he was getting a glimpse of what he would look like if he were dead. With nearly all of life's color gone from his skin, its pallor was dry and chalky. His muscles were rigid, an effect of the poison the doctors believed he ingested. On one side of his face was an ugly, dark bruise sustained in the fall he suffered before losing consciousness. Joe ran a finger along the tubes that feebly connected him to life. Two down his nose, one for each nostril, and a big one down his throat. Another ran past the I.V. needle in his arm and disappeared beneath the covers.

Poison. The first thing the paramedics noticed was that he had been eating. They recognized the fish immediately as one of the poisonous. It was considered a delicacy in certain parts of the world, where some seemed to get a sick thrill at the potential hazard of eating it. If not correctly prepared by the most qualified of chefs, ingesting it could be fatal.

Even considering Chachi's adventurousness, Joe couldn't fathom his flirting with death in such a manner. If the stakes were a billion dollars, he wouldn't bet one red cent on his intentionally taking or even risking his own life, no matter what. Still, nothing made sense, and only days ago, he would have never believed Chachi was capable of the acts he admittedly committed with Michael.

He put his hand on Chachi's cheek. It was cold to the touch. His lips were dark and cracked and there was a dried substance in the corners. Joe tried to wipe it away. He leaned his ear close to see if he could hear him breathe. He watched the rise and fall of his chest, the work of the loud apparatus beside the bed.

A nurse, probably in her fifties, with an old face and girlish figure, poked her head in. “There’s a phone call for you, Mr. Simpson.”

Joe squeezed Chachi’s cold hand and followed her down a dim, eerie corridor into an artificially bright office and picked up the phone lying on the desk.

“How’s he doing?”

“Jake! You need to get here. He’s hanging by a thread.” Joe glanced out the corner of his eyes to see if the nurse was within earshot. “He needs to be moved right away. I don’t think they have what it takes to save him here.”

“I’ve been in contact with the doctor on his case. They’re trying to flush this poison from his system and from what I can tell, they’re doing everything they can right now. I don’t think it’s a good idea to move him yet. He hasn’t stabilized.”

“But you should see it here. There’s hardly a skeletal staff!”

“A friend of mine is on his way. He’s seen cases like this before. I haven’t. I don’t know anything about this poison. But I’ll be there as quickly as I can, no later than tomorrow.”

“Okay,” Joe said, feeling a bit better.

“I’m also making sure we’ll be ready here. As soon as he stabilizes, we’re flying him out.”

“Good.” Joe heard his voice crack and felt the sudden urge to cry.

“Ring me right away if anything changes,” Jake said.

Chachi’s family and friends descended on the little resort like a flock of anxious birds. Doctor Leonard Phelps, Jake’s friend and associate, sprang into action the moment he arrived. He mobilized his team of two assistants and they went to work, pulling all kinds of solutions from a huge trunk they brought with them. They changed IV bottles, adjusted tubing and replaced certain machines with monstrous contraptions they had flown in. By the time Jake arrived late that night, a hint of color had returned to Chachi’s skin and he was breathing on his own.

It had been a while since Joe had seen Chachi’s parents, so when the senior Spencer opened the door, the likeness to his son hit him unexpectantly and he fell into him with grief.

"Oh, God…" Spencer moaned and Joe realized he feared the worst. Chachi's mother elicited a sharp cry from the corner of the room.

"No, no…" Joe said quickly, wiping his eyes on his sleeve. "He's not…"

"We just checked in," Spencer said. He nodded towards his wife. Joe noticed she sat in a wheelchair. Chachi hadn't told him. "We were on our way to the hospital. How is he doing? Don't spare us anything."

Joe glanced at Mother Spencer. Her hands clutched the arms of the chair, causing her knuckles to protrude like little stumps. The tale-tell signs of illness covered her face like a mask: the dull skin and severe weight-loss.

"He's got some of his color back," Joe said.

"Is he conscious?" Spencer asked.

Joe lowered his eyes. The elder Spencer was too quick for him. He could sniff out a lie before it was completed.

"Is he…breathing on his own?" Spencer pressed.

Joe swallowed hard. "He is now."

Mother Spencer began to cry.

"Listen," Joe added, "Jake feels good about his prospects. This doctor-friend of his has turned things around quickly. Chachi's very healthy. It's a good sign that he's breathing on his own now. He wasn't doing that yesterday. If his kidneys hold up—"

"What happened?" Spencer breathed. His eyes, a total replica of his son's, were both sad and frightened.

Joe sighed and took a seat on a nearby sofa. "We had a fight," he said softly, not looking up. "A big one…and Chachi and I agreed it would be best if he went away for a while."

Mother Spencer glanced at her husband whose face hardened.

Joe sighed. "The next thing I knew, he was trying to call me on his cell phone. He couldn't tell me what was wrong before he collapsed. I had to trace him down and get help for him."

Mother Spencer opened her mouth to speak but her husband silenced her with a wave of his hand.

Joe looked up at him. He knew exactly what he was thinking, he thought it himself many times, but it was just not in Chachi to try to kill himself. Still, there were so many unanswered questions.

"I just don't know," Joe answered Spencer's questioning face in barely a whisper.

"What on earth could you two have fought about that would make it even a possibility that he might try to hurt himself?" Spencer asked.

Joe's chest tightened. "I think he should be the one to tell you that."

Spencer blinked. "I want to know," he said, determined.

Joe inhaled deeply. "He confessed he'd been sleeping with my youngest son…for months."

Mother Spencer gasped.

Spencer's face flushed with shame. "But he can't be more than—"

"Barely seventeen now, but who knows when they started."

Spencer groaned.

"We fought. I told him to leave, that I never wanted to see him around my family again. I said I'd have him arrested."

Chachi's father sat in a chaise across from Joe and stroked his forehead.

Mother Spencer cried softly.

"I'm so sorry," Spencer muttered. He spent much of his life apologizing and cleaning up after a son he's never been able to manage.

"Hey," Joe leaned forward to touch his hand. "It's not your fault. God knows I love Chachi with all my heart. I have no idea what I'm gonna do."

They sat quietly a while before Spencer spoke again.

"Do you think he really tried to—"

"Kill himself? I don't buy it for a second.

Mother Spencer piped in. "What if this was someone else's doing? What if that chef wanted to kill him…I mean, he is a star. There're all kinds of crazy people out there!"

Joe and Spencer exchanged looks.

"I'm sure the police will look into that," Spencer said.

Mother Spencer clutched her chest. "So you believe…"

"No," Spencer said quickly, shaking his head. "My heart tells me it really was an accident. Besides, he brought too much clothing. He had planned on being here for a while.

"How's your son?" Mrs. Spencer asked softly. Joe had nearly forgotten about Michael.

"He's not speaking to me. He's very angry right now."

"I don't know what Chachi was thinking!" she exclaimed. "If there's anything we can do to help…"

Joe smiled weakly. He wished he knew what that was.

"We'd better get going over to the hospital." Spencer stood. "You'd better get some sleep," he said to Joe, sounding like his son. "You look like shit."

* * * *

Within a week, Chachi had stabilized but failed to regain consciousness. Jake had him flown back to the States where he could receive the best care.

Joe folded the newspaper he had been reading and stretched his legs. He'd kept a near constant vigil at Chachi's bedside, showing up at the hospital early morning, as if he was reporting for work, and not leaving 'til late evening. He'd take breaks for lunch and snacks, sometimes dropping in at home for a nap, but for the most part, he conducted his business and managed his affairs from the hospital.

"I'm leaving now, darling," Renee announced as she sashayed into the room carrying a cup of coffee she had gone to get for him. "Dom said he'd be here in another hour. How long do you plan to stay?"

Joe lifted one shoulder. "Visiting hours will be over soon. I guess I'll stay 'til then."

"I'll be back then. I'm staying the night."

Joe smiled and watched her empty too many little packets of cream and then sugar into his coffee. That was the way Chachi took his coffee, milky and sweet. Joe liked his black, but Renee, ingrained with the ever-growing quest to please Chachi, hadn't bothered to ask Joe how he liked his coffee when she offered to get him some. Instinctively, she prepared it the way she prepared everything in her life—the way Chachi liked it.

As she bent over the cup, Joe took in her long brown hair swung to one side as it partially framed her right breast, bulging out of her tightly fitted blouse. Her waist was as tiny as a girl's. Her ample hips and buttocks stuck out past full, lovely legs, slightly spread apart as she bent over.

What Chachi's problem was, he'd never understood. Why he'd need anything more than this vision of loveliness, who'd take a bullet to the head for him, was beyond Joe's comprehension. Sure, Renee was overbearing and possessive at times and a conniving snake-in-the-grass to boot, but hell, nobody's perfect. Yet from the day he'd met her, Chachi maintained enough lovers to run a brothel. Renee waited him out patiently, certain that one day, once he'd sown his wild oats, he'd be all hers. She was still waiting.

He realized she had been holding the cup out to him. "Oh, thanks baby." In the last few weeks, he saw a side of her, a loving, caring, nurturing side of her, that wasn't often displayed. Between the two of them, Chachi was never alone.

"Let Dominic take over. I'm sure you have things to do," she said.

"Yeah. I'll probably break for a few when he gets here." Joe took tiny sips of the scalding liquid and moaned with pleasure.

"Okay, well…" She eyed Chachi's still form, a half smile playing on her lips.

"Go!" he insisted. "I'll let you know if anything changes." That had been their parting line all week.

After she had gone, Joe pulled a chair up to Chachi's bed. They had his hair cut the day before. Joe placed his hand on his head. "Hey dude," he whispered into his ear. "I miss you, man. It's been long enough. Come back. Don't leave me like this…before we work things out." He used his finger to trace the lines of his face, his eyes, his nose, his mouth, before letting his hand drop with a sigh of heaviness.

"What happened?" Joe asked for the hundredth time. "How did things turn so badly, so quickly? Michael is like the walking dead. You're… If you had just come to me! Now, I don't know what to do." Joe laid his head on Chachi's chest, feeling it rise and fall softly. "I love you with all my heart and I miss you, brother. Don't leave like this."

After a while Joe began to doze. His head sprang up. Chachi's breathing had changed. Slowly turning, he met Chachi's gaze and nearly lost his bowels. Chachi's caramel-brown pupils moved ever so slightly. Joe held his breath. He should do something, scream, call for a nurse. He sat trapped in his seat like stone, staring at him, praying, willing him to move again. Prove that he had come back to life. Slowly, Chachi blinked and Joe whooped with glee.

"Hey! You're back!" he shouted. He leaned over Chachi with both his hands on the sides of his face. "I'm so glad to see you! You had me scared!"

Three nurses rushed into the room. One tugged at Joe to move away from the bed. "Please, Mr. Simpson, I need to take his vitals."

Joe stepped back. He sank against the wall for support and watched them work.

"Well, well," the nurse said, "you *do* have the prettiest eyes!"

Joe grinned. If the nurse was talking to him, he must have indeed awakened. "Have you called the doctor?" Joe asked through labored breathing.

"My assistant is doing that now."

Jake was just as elated to see Chachi open his eyes. They stood over him, he and Joe together, grinning. Chachi didn't appear to register any of this attention. His eyes moved from them to various objects in the room, expressionless.

"How do you feel buddy?" Jake smoothed his hair as he spoke in soft tones. "Don't you worry. I'm taking care of you."

"He hasn't tried to speak," Joe said after a terrible thought struck him. "What if he can't?"

"Give him time, Joe," Jake answered, still gazing at Chachi. "I can see it in his eyes that he's aware. These things take time."

"I've got to call Lydia and Renee. Did you call his parents?"

"Not yet. I don't want them rushing out here. Jake turned to Joe. "Joe, I'm gonna have to ask you to leave."

"No."

"I've got a ton of tests to run. I've got to do it while he's awake."

"I won't be in the way. I'll wait outside."

Jake peered at Joe over his glasses.

"Okay," Joe sighed. "But give me one minute with him."

"I can't."

"One minute, Jake, I swear! If he goes back under, I may not get another chance."

Jake's eyes narrowed. "Okay." He stepped aside. "Sixty seconds."

Joe leaned over Chachi and pressed his lips to his forehead for at least fifteen of his sixty seconds. "I've been with you from day one and I'll never leave," he whispered.

Chachi's eyes rolled slowly to meet Joe's gaze. A blink produced a drop of moisture.

"Chachi?" He thought he saw a glimpse of tenderness in Chachi's eyes before the light went out and they grew cold again, leaving nothing between them but shadow.

* * * *

Michael decided to take his father's advice and go away to school, anything to keep busy. Joe had already picked out a private program. He'd hand picked everything down to Michael's room-mate, a wiry kid with spectacles and brassy hair that stood in spirals all over his head. Michael flew through the four month course and passed all his classes with the highest marks. He had to deal with stuffy professors and even stuffier students, but he didn't care. His only purpose was to be away from the house, from the business, from his father, from David, from Chachi. Better still, a class trip would take them to South Beach for an end-of-term celebration.

Illian flew down the second weekend to meet him. It was a comfort seeing someone from home. She floated about without ambition, like most of the too rich and too famous, constantly in search of either herself or the answer to life. She obviously hadn't found it in school, she dropped out in her second year of high school. She would often take small jobs acting, modeling, or dancing to fool her parents into thinking she was actually doing something with her life.

Chachi's recovery had been slow, but in four months time, he was almost new again. Almost.

Michael hadn't gone to see Chachi when they flew him home to the local hospital, nor when he was released to in-home care and rehabilitation. He couldn't bring himself to. Eric told him Renee moved in to supervise his care. Perhaps that was the way it was meant to be after all. Still, as soon as he was well enough, Chachi began to call. Some nights, Michael would play his messages over and over, yet he could not reply.

Soon after his recovery, Chachi's mother fell ill. According to Eric, Chachi's three day visit to his mother became three weeks more. Renee again rushed to his side and Michael was left to his imagination. She would make the most of the opportunity now that he was out of the way. Certainly, Chachi hadn't been celibate all this time, and neither had he. He had Illian to fill his lonely hours. Chachi would have Renee.

Illian sat on the bed across from him in just her panties and rolled a fat blunt. Michael watched her brown curls dangle in her face as she bent her head low.

She finished her task and lit up, taking a long pull and sinking into her pillow before handing it to Michael. "So, we're not doing as well as we thought we would, huh?" she said underneath a cloud of smoke.

"I'm fine."

"Oh, come on, I thought we were friends."

He could confide in her. She had yet to reveal anything he'd ever told her in confidence. "Really," he said, "at least I think I am. I can't say I don't still love him. But I survived before him, I'll survive after him."

"Whatever." Illian sat up for her turn at the joint, before falling back onto the pillows and closing her eyes.

"I'm serious."

"Of course you are, boy-toy."

"Illian…"

"You don't fool me, even if you fool yourself. But don't worry; you have plenty of time to sabotage those nupticals."

"What nupticals?"

"You haven't heard?" her eyes sprang open.

Michael vaulted to the floor, horrified. Certainly his father would have said something. "When! Where did you hear this?"

"Down boy!" Illian said, sitting up. "Don't get your dick all in a pretzel. I don't know that invitations are out. For pete's sake, they don't get married until, what, August or September?"

Chachi didn't even *like* Renee. There had to be some mistake. Michael stuck his finger in his ear to relieve it of an annoying ring.

"Your cell phone, silly." Illian giggled.

That sealed it. He was done with Illian and her dope. The moment he heard Eric's voice he was flooded with homesickness.

"It's gonna be in the press soon, so I wanted to call ahead," Eric said.

"What now?" Michael groaned. He was getting a headache.

"Chachi lost his step-mother."

Michael gasped. For a moment, he forgot to breathe. Chachi was very close to his adoptive mom.

Michael shook his head to get his brain to work. "How is he?"

"I've never seen him so bad. He's taking it pretty hard."

"God…"

"She was sick. But she had gotten better. He had just come home from seeing her last weekend when it happened."

Michael ached to help. There was nothing Chachi spoke of with more affection than his mother. All the love he denied his father he lavished on her, and then some.

"When are the services?"

"We don't know anything yet. Think you'll come?"

Michael hesitated. With Chachi already in emotional distress... "I'll have to think about it."

Eric sighed.

"Eric, wait!"

"Yeah?"

"What do you know about Chachi and Renee getting married?"

Eric's silence was all the confirmation Michael needed.

"Son of a bitch..."

"Mike, I would've said something had Uncle Joe not made me keep quiet. Besides, it's not official—"

"You call me all the way up here to tell me his mother died; you didn't think I should know that too?"

"I wanted to tell you, but, like I said, Uncle Joe—"

"It's no longer important."

"You know it's just a farce! He's only doing it because you won't see him and to appease Uncle Joe."

"He told you this?"

"Well, no, but he told Uncle Joe—"

"Oh, they're on speaking terms now?"

"Well—"

"So it was me, just me in everybody's way. With Michael out of the way, Joe and Chachi can remain friends. With Michael out of the way, Chachi and Renee can get married. My father gets exactly what he wants."

Eric sighed. "If you want him, go get him."

"I don't want him. Not anymore. I'm tired."

"So you're not coming for the funeral?"

Michael pressed the ball of his hand against his forehead. "No," he said finally. "Give Chachi my condolences. I'll send him a card or something."

"You're so angry, Michael, that you would miss something so important to Chachi?"

"Not angry, just beaten. It's time to let go. Renee is where she should be. My showing up at the services would only make him uncomfortable."

"So what are you going to do?"

Michael looked over at Illian who had begun to doze, her shapely leg draped across his lap. "I'm going to the beach."

* * * *

Why were funerals on dreary days? Here he was in sunny Florida, yet the sky was overcast, obscuring his view of the beach. Gulls squawked, sounding eerily human and melancholy as they swooped across the water. The first drops of rain began to fall. It was as if Chachi's sadness and grief was reaching out to him, shading everything he laid eyes on an ugly gray.

He stood in front of the window in pajamas with the drapes pulled back, debating. It helped him to think when he looked out at nature. He had decided not to attend the funeral. He sent flowers and a card instead. Joe had agreed that his presence would only complicate matters.

But he woke up restless, cagey, feeling as if he was missing something important, something he was supposed to do. Knowing that, at that very moment, Chachi was preparing to go through another painful event without him made him feel sad and useless.

"You're going, aren't you?" Illian's tone confirmed rather than asked. She had been laying very still, her head sandwiched between two pillows, her voice muffled and far away. He thought she was asleep.

He turned to her but said nothing.

"I think you should go," she said, sitting up with effort.

Michael walked over and sat down beside her. He began to massage her temples.

"So what, it didn't work out. You still care about him and he cares about you. If it were you in the same situation, he'd be there. He fought you for a ticket to your graduation because it is an important accomplishment in your life. You weren't there for him when he was sick and it's been eating at you; anyone can see that. You have to go for your own peace of mind."

"I don't even have a flight out. They've been flying family in from all over. My dad wouldn't even be able to send for me on such late notice."

"What? You too good to fly commercial now?"

"I fly commercial all the time!" he shot back. "What are you talking about?"

She picked up the phone on the nightstand and held the receiver out to him.

"I can't get a flight out now! Not in time to be home by afternoon."

Illian leaned close to him. "Boy, you are Michael Joseph Simpson's son. You'd better start acting like it."

* * * *

Chachi's parents lived in a sprawling mansion, rich with historic detailing, in the beautiful New Orleans. With his uncle Papi's island flavor and his step-mother's Cajun flair, Chachi could not avoid the gift of gourmet. As Michael's car sped past lush trees and quaint swamps, he couldn't help but imagine Chachi as a boy, playing among the vegetation.

Michael hated funerals. There was something so gripping and final about death that it caused him tremendous anxiety. Since he was a small child, he was constantly afraid his mother would die. He thought about her now.

Every room, and there were plenty of them, was stylish and comfortable. He tried to imagine Chachi, as a kid, running across the polished floors. It was easier to conjure the image of him in the islands with one pant leg rolled up to his knee, grinning underneath a straw hat, even then, positioned fashionably on his head. That was the image captured by his favorite childhood photo of Chachi. Papi had shown it to him first, and the same photo now sat on a mantel at his mother's house. Chachi must have been about four then. Papi said the photo had been taken shortly before Chachi was taken away.

"You must be Michael."

Michael's breath caught at the sight of Jasper Dukakis Spencer, Senior up close. He seemed very tall, perhaps even an inch taller than Chachi, or maybe he only appeared to be larger and more ominous because his face lacked the familiar warmth of Chachi's frequent smile.

"Yes," he said softly.

"I'm Jasper's father."

"I guessed."

From Michael's head to his toe, Spencer's eyes wandered, his face creased with both puzzlement and disapproval.

Michael knew what the father was thinking. He wanted to turn away. Fixated, his gaze remained on that face that was so familiar to him. A slightly older version of Chachi watched him with eyes that did not recognize him. "I'm sorry about your wife."

Spencer's face pleated with the pain of remembrance. "Thank you. She would have wanted to meet you." He resumed his inspection and

Michael shifted uncomfortably. "You're very young," the father observed in an appraising tone. "Just how old are you, again?"

Michael didn't like his tone and didn't think it was any of his business.

Lydia interrupted just in time. "So you've met!" she said, beaming.

"Yes," the father drawled. Michael couldn't tell whether it was a good yes or a bad yes.

"He's asking for you, honey," Lydia said to Michael.

He exchanged a look of surprise with the father then blushed.

"He's upstairs in the third room to your right."

Michael was glad to get out of there. He mumbled something and moved quickly toward the stairs. Even as he reached the landing, he felt those eyes…

Chachi was seated in the middle of a large bed, legs folded underneath him. An eye dangled from the head of a teddy bear he held in his arm and he flicked it over and over again with his finger.

"That yours?" he poked the teddy bear.

Chachi smiled. "She gave this to me when I first got here. I was missing my mother something fierce…my birth mother," he added unnecessarily, "and she convinced my brother to let me have it. It was the only way I could sleep. He paused and sniffed. "The moment I met her, I trusted her."

With his thumb, Michael reached out and caught a tear as it escaped and fell from the corner of Chachi's eye.

"She took care of me and loved me even though my being here caused her pain."

"Of course she did," Michael said softly.

Chachi placed a hand over Michael's. "Thanks for coming."

"I had to," Michael said. "Especially after—"

"Don't mention it."

Michael stood and walked around the room, surveying the lavish furnishings. "Was this your room?"

"Once. They turned it into another guestroom after I left. My mother knew I wasn't coming back."

They endured a short, awkward silence.

"I didn't hurt you at the gravesite, did I?" Chachi asked.

Michael thought of the way Chachi gripped him around the neck and sobbed at the funeral. It took two men to free him. He recalled Renee's jealous stare and smiled. "No harm done," Michael said. "You're gonna be okay, right?"

"I'll live. I'm glad you're here, though."

Michael shifted. "Um…I can't stay…"

Chachi didn't try to hide his disappointment.

"My plane leaves in two hours. I grabbed a round-trip, same day. It was last minute. I was debating whether I should even come."

"You just got here!"

"I know, but I left Illian up there alone. I told her I'd be right back. I just had to come see about you. I didn't want to…fail you again."

A hint of protest flashed across Chachi's face and disappeared. "I understand," he said quietly.

"I've gotta go."

Chachi only nodded.

"Call me if you need anything," Michael said, backing away.

Chachi smiled sadly.

Michael urged his feet to move him out the door and down the staircase. He hugged his sister standing at the foot of the stairs chatting with another girl and waved at David across the room. He spotted his father standing with Dominic and Jake and made his way over to them.

"Michael!" Joe exclaimed. "You're not leaving already!"

"I bought a same-day round trip. I left Illian alone. I told her I'd be back."

"But I thought…"

"I'll be home in two weeks. I promise."

"Oh, well." He put his arm around Michael. "At least we got to see you for ten minutes."

Michael hugged Joe, Jake and Dominic. He slipped up behind his stepmother and kissed her cheek.

"Hey, where are you going?" she called behind him.

He waved to her as he headed for the exit. "Back to Florida. I'll call you."

Eric fell into step beside him. “How much longer?”

“Two weeks at the most,” Michael said. “You should come down and join me these last two weeks.”

“Naw. There’s too much going on here.”

“Umph.” Michael grunted.

“It’ll be time for our annual camping expedition by the time you get back, you know. I’m already prepared.”

“That’s right. I almost forgot.” Michael felt eyes on him and looked up to see Chachi leaning over the banister looking down at them. He waved and Michael waved back, but the odd sense of being watched persisted.

“You take it easy,” Eric said. “See you when you get back.”

Michael scanned the room and found the source of his disquiet. Spencer Senior stood in a corner alone with a drink in his hand, watching them intently. It was like seeing a phantom of Chachi with another spirit. He shivered lightly. “Yeah,” he said, returning the stare. “See you when I get back.”

* * * *

“I’ve made a decision,” Renee announced defiantly. “I’m wearing white.”

Chachi grunted his response and re-dedicated his attention to the center’s quarterly earnings statement.

She shot around to his side with her hands on her hips. “Why shouldn’t I wear white? I’m a first-time bride! You’re a first-time groom! So what, I’m not twenty-one and we live together!”

“Wear what you want,” he said without looking up.

“Well…” she said, “I *do* want to be socially correct. I should wear cream, or maybe off-white.”

“Who said you couldn’t wear a white dress?” He had taken to wearing reading glasses when going over financial reports.

“No one exactly; well, Monte did look a little scandalized when I insisted—”

"That's ridiculous," he said, looking directly at her for the first time during their conversation. "Who the fuck is Monte to say what you should wear? All he needs to do is make the fuckin' dress."

"Designers know these things. I mean, we *are* living together."

Chachi sighed at the reminder. Losing his mother was the hardest thing he had to endure in his life. During that time, his family and friends overwhelmed him with love and care. He didn't recall one waking moment when he didn't find Joe at his side. But it was Renee who surprised him. Throughout both his and his mother's illnesses, she had taken over his affairs as if she were his wife, barely leaving his side. She talked Papi into allowing her to move in 'temporarily' so that she could help tend to him. When he'd become deeply depressed she'd climb into bed next to him in the middle of the night and soothed him back to sleep.

"You're right, who cares." She smiled as if she knew his thoughts.

He was grateful for the way she took care of him. So when she asked him to marry her, he swallowed his usual response and agreed. Not one day passed when he didn't think about Michael, but Michael hadn't visited him, not once, not even when he was in the depths of despair.

"Are you ready for a fitting?"

Chachi snorted. "I don't want to be fitted until I've picked up some more weight," he said, stealing a glance at her from underneath lowered lids.

"All right, Chachi," she held out her arm for him to fasten her bracelet, "but we're running out of time."

He didn't want to be married, but he couldn't tell Renee that now. Not after all she'd done for him, even after she found out about his affair with Michael.

"I wasn't surprised," she had said with a cool indifference when he tried to talk to her about it. "It's over now."

But it wasn't over. Much was left unresolved and he couldn't get Michael to talk to him so that they could put it to bed. As angry as he was that Michael hadn't come to him when he needed him most, he knew how much the boy loved him and no one could tell him different. Not even Michael.

"What are you gonna do today?" Renee asked as she slipped on her coat.

"I don't know," he answered, tossing the financial reports aside and crossing his ankles on top of a nearby cocktail table.

Renee glided over to him and bent down so that her face was within inches of his. She kissed him softly on the lips and slid her hand seductively between his legs, up his thigh, and cupped his crotch. "It's been a long time; you up to it?" she purred.

He gave her a quick smile but as he looked into the beautiful face of the woman he would pledge to have and to hold forever, he could not help but wonder if she noticed that, underneath her hand, he was totally unaffected by her touch.

Chapter Twenty-Nine

The sun emerged, a welcoming ball in the sky. Glad to be home, Michael basked in his parents' spirit-renewing gardens and thought-cleansing fountains. In spite of everything, he missed his family and was pleased that things were settling back to normal. He had a call from his mother (though they spoke briefly), and he hadn't spent more than a few moments a day (okay, and maybe an hour each night) thinking about Chachi. Compared to the state he was in the last time he'd been home, that was progress.

The real test would come later that evening. With the weather in full cooperation, his father was breaking out the grill for his regular 'cook out with the crew' and the grill-master would certainly be there with his lovely (though venomous) bride-to-be.

Michael sat in his favorite glider and watched two birds battle over a crumb. It was still early morning and he was in his pajamas. Maxie would start breakfast in about an hour and the sounds of the house awakening would have destroyed the moment, so he took advantage of it while he could. One of the birds became suddenly vicious, pecking furiously at the other.

"Hey!" Michael yelled and kicked in the direction of the two, startling them into flight.

"Talking to yourself now?"

He hadn't heard his father walk up. "Oh, hi Dad," he said, watching the birds that were now specks in the sky.

Joe sat next to him and they watched as other birds replaced the combatants, flying from tree to tree. "I missed you, son. I'm glad you're home."

Michael smiled. He'd made his father suffer enough. He laid his head on Joe's shoulder. "I missed you too."

"I never really apologized—"

"It's me who should apologize. I just…I'm sorry."

"Well," Joe wrapped an arm around him, "at least you're better. You're so much better."

Michael closed his eyes. It had been a while since he'd been in his father's arms like that.

"You ready for tonight?" Joe asked after a short silence.

"I can handle it."

"Sure? 'Cause you don't have to stay."

Michael sat up. "Maybe this will be the closure that I need, to see them together. I think I'll always feel something for him, but I'll be fine. I was fine when he showed up at graduation. I'm excited about moving on." He smiled.

Joe hugged him close. "I'm glad," he said into Michael's hair. "Well," he stood, "I stopped in to say good morning and you were gone. I came looking for you, but I knew I wouldn't have to look far. You gonna hang out here?"

"Yeah." Michael inhaled the scent of new morning infused with lilac and jasmime. "It's a beautiful day."

Dusk fell in blankety softness. If Chachi was surprised to see Michael, it didn't register on his face. He smiled warmly in his direction, gave a wave and moved on. Renee strutted in behind him, wearing a sexy chiffon number and pretended not to see Michael at all. All of Joe's friends were there, including his brother. David and Eric were also home for the summer. The scene, the laughter, the teasing, moved Michael. He hadn't realized just how much he'd missed them.

After a while, Michael moved out onto the gazebo. Eric was back to his old tricks of spiking the punch and Michael was on his third wonderful glass.

Chachi beamed with sociable delight, smiling good-humoredly and laughing in the right places. Still there was just a little something not right. He seemed kinder to Renee, allowing her to kiss and cuddle him, chuckling softly at something she whispered in his ear. Michael watched with a mix of sadness and reconciliation. He drained the rest of his punch and walked over to the side rail to look out over the gardens. A soft, fragrant breeze tickled his face and his belly flipped with the mixture of fulfillment and loss.

He sighed heavily, turning to go back inside, and his knees buckled. Chachi stood in front of him leaning casually against the rail across from him. Michael blinked, not sure whether he was seeing an image of the man or the man himself.

"I thought I spotted you in here." Chachi's face glowed in the combination of lantern light and moonlight. "I'm not disturbing you, am I?"

Michael shook his head and moved silently next to him.

"It's a beautiful night." Chachi sighed.

"Yeah," Michael croaked. He cleared his throat and tried again. "I love it out here this time of year."

Chachi smiled and turned his head toward him. The soft lighting made his face look fluid, almost as if he were a reflection in water. Michael was always surprised at how handsome he was and tensed to suppress a reaction bubbling to his surface.

Chachi touched his hand. "Wanna take a walk?"

Shivering from his touch, Michael's mouth fell open and he knew his face must have looked crazy, for Chachi quickly added, "You don't have to."

"N-no," he stammered. "That'll be…fine."

"After you." Chachi bowed slightly and gestured animatedly with his hand so that Michael led the way down the path through the garden.

The mingling of floral scents with the strength of Chachi's presence made him woozy. From time to time, Chachi would touch a flower or tap on the trunk of a tree. The silence between them rose like an erected structure. Once they could no longer hear voices clearly behind them, they stopped. Michael turned to find him watching. When he could bear it no longer, he looked away.

"I just wanted…" Chachi's voice broke the silence smoothly, like a whisper, "to finally end this."

"To say goodbye?" Michael asked weakly, his belly in knots.

"Not goodbye," Chachi said, his head tilted quizzically. "More like closure. I just want you to answer one question before—"

"You marry her?" The thought gave him courage as wisps of anger rose in him. He looked squarely at Chachi.

Chachi took a long time before he nodded. Michael turned his back, afraid he'd cry.

The rustling of the wind and grasshoppers at play dotted the ensuing silence. Michael could feel him staring at his back. He heard a voice drifting on the breeze, laughter in the distance, and wished he were back with his family, guffawing at Eric's antics, helping himself to his father's slightly burnt bratwurst…

"Why didn't you come to me when I needed you, after I nearly died?"

Michael felt as though he'd turned to stone. It was a question he'd proposed to himself over and over and knew Chachi would inevitably ask. Every reason he'd previously thought sufficient seemed empty and frivolous and was certainly not suitable fare with which to face Chachi's disappointed, accusatory gaze. He swallowed a lump in his throat and stood stock still, unable to speak or even turn around. Chachi stood just as still behind him, waiting.

The faint sound of laughter rose again and the sting of tears threatened. Michael blinked them back and when his vision cleared, he saw that Chachi had soundlessly moved and now stood in front of him.

"You owe me an explanation…if only that."

Michael nodded and took deep breaths, willing his speech. "I…" His heart thudded against his chest and he paused again until it subsided. "I was so angry…" he said faintly.

Chachi's brow furrowed. "You were *that* angry, Michael?"

The lines of pain in Chachi's face made him feel sick and he had to avert his eyes. He tried to anchor himself. His anguish was real, however silly it seemed to anyone else, it was real to him and he had a right to be angry. He replayed the events in his head and touched a hot button. Fury rose like bile in the back of his throat as he recalled the despair of abandonment and shame he felt that day. He thought he'd dealt with those feelings.

"You left me!" The growl of his own voice shocked him and Chachi too, whose brow shot up in surprise.

"I was coming back! I told you that—"

"*You* decided when it was right to tell *my* father about *my* choice, Chachi!"

Chachi parted his lips to reply then clamped them shut.

"It was the biggest decision of my life and you just fuckin' blurted it out in a restaurant!" Rocked with rage, he began shaking uncontrollably.

"*Michael*," Chachi said. He grabbed him by the shoulders and stooped slightly to look into his face.

Michael focused on a button on Chachi's shirt, third one down. He didn't want to hear what he knew he would say. He didn't want to hear how he knew what was best for him, how leaving town would buy them time until his father calmed down. He had left him there, alone, ashamed and defenseless.

"Michael, *please*…"

Michael closed his eyes then opened them slowly, raising his face to meet Chachi's.

"I am so, so sorry," Chachi said.

Michael blinked, surprised.

"I am so sorry I left you like that. I was so bent on doing what I thought was right, but I didn't stop to think about what was happening to *you.*" Chachi released his grip on Michael's shoulders and walked a short distance away, stopping with his back to him.

How those simple words relieved him. I'm sorry. All the anger and sadness began to drain away, seeping through the pores of his body out into the open air. The tension of holding it all in crept toward his limbs and out of his extremities. All this time, it was all he needed. An apology.

"Chachi," he said softly. Chachi's head moved slightly, but he didn't turn around. Michael touched him tentatively. "I'm sorry too. I'm sorry I didn't come. I wanted to—" He wiped tears from his face and walked over to flick the head of a hibiscus hanging lazily from a bush. "I was in so much pain, I couldn't feel anything. I wanted to come, but then, I heard about you and Renee..."

Chachi swung around.

Michael went on. "It was like my heart…exploded. It just blew apart. I understood then how easy it must have been for my mother to lose her mind, 'cause I lost all resemblance of sanity or reason. There was no question anymore of whether I should go to you or not—what was I gonna do? Both you and I were already dead."

"Mike..." Chachi touched his face.

Michael leaned in so that he could rest his cheek in Chachi's palm. Then he took Chachi's hand and looked up into his face. He smiled slowly and the emotional thaw began. He felt as though he was healing miraculously inside. He gripped the hand tighter.

"Mike..." Chachi said again and bent to find his lips. Michael pressed in hard, happy to taste him again, hungry for the way his love made him feel. He reached up to embrace him, his arms squeezing Chachi's neck. He was sure he'd fall if he let go, his legs had turned to jelly.

Finally, gripping Michael's head in both his hands, Chachi looked into his eyes.

Michael held his breath. "You can't marry her," he whispered.

Chachi nodded and rested his forehead against Michael's.

"I'm so sorry for her," Michael said. "I really am, but you just can't." This might be the last chance they would get and he was taking it. This time, he felt strong enough to take on Renee, his father, and whomever else didn't like it.

"I know." Chachi breathed.

They held each other with foreheads pressed together, rocking in the soft breeze, and listening to the sounds of summer night.

"What now?" Michael asked after a while.

Chachi sighed. "Give me a few days, okay?"

Michael nodded. He understood the enormity of what Chachi had to do and knew he had to give him time. This time he would trust him. "You'll call me?" he murmured, drowsy with the sweetness of love returned.

"Of course. You'll wait for me this time?"

Michael laughed and kissed his chin. "'Course."

"Forgive me?" Chachi asked, nudging his ear.

"I *do*." Michael looked up at Chachi with an expression that posed the same question.

"I never held it against you, really," Chachi responded. When they kissed Michael felt as though he were swallowing fireworks.

"I love you," Chachi whispered breathlessly into his scented hair.

Michael groped at the muscular currents underneath Chachi's shirt. "God help me…"

Chachi wasn't surprised to see Joe when he emerged from the darkness of the trees. "Hey," he said softly.

"Hey," Joe said, busying himself with clearing the grill.

"I'm, uh, gonna grab Renee and go. Sorry I missed most of the party."

When Joe looked at him, his eyes were cold. "Where were you?" he asked.

"I'll talk to you later, okay?"

Joe averted his gaze in response.

Chachi turned and walked into the house. Renee ran to him.

"Where have you been—wait, where are we going? We're leaving now?" She protested as he pulled her to the door.

The night wasn't over yet.

"Meet me at the door," Chachi said into his cell phone and hung up.

Within moments Joe admitted him into the darkened house. "Let's use my office," he said quietly and they moved through the shadows like ghosts.

Chachi closed the door behind them and the two men stood facing one another, each waiting for the other to start. After a long time, Chachi walked over to the desk and crossed his arms, his back to Joe. "I have to find a way to tell Renee I can't marry her." He turned to face Joe.

"Chachi, the wedding is in two months! Another few weeks, invitations will be out."

"Better now than then."

Joe sighed heavily. "Tens of thousands have been spent—"

"I'll pay for everything," Chachi snapped. "You know that's not an issue."

"The embarrassment…"

Chachi dropped his head. That part, he couldn't remedy with money or influence. The tabloids would be all over it and Renee would be humiliated. And after all she'd done for him. "I'm sorry Joe, it just can't be helped."

"Can't be helped," Joe repeated.

"It's not like I haven't thought about it over and over again. I knew I should have done this months ago."

"*Months* ago, huh?"

"I'm sick about it, really. Believe it or not, I love Renee—in my own way."

"In your own way…"

"Of course, it's cliché-ish, but I'm just not *in love* with her—will you stop repeating everything I say!"

"Sorry." Joe blinked. "So that little walk in the garden with my son had nothing to do with this decision?"

Chachi drew in his breath and blew it out slowly, his lip curled in a suppressed smile. He was impressed with the ease and calm with which Joe segued into the real discussion. "I'd say it had *something* to do with the *final* decision."

Joe snorted and sank into a chair.

"You know it's not right for me to marry her," Chachi said, walking over to him. "You know I was doing it for all the wrong reasons. You could have stopped me!"

"Oh no, don't pin this on me!" Joe raised a finger at him.

"Remember your marriage to Lydia?"

"That was different."

"She got knocked up and your parents were willing to let you throw your happiness away just so you could do what 'seemed' right. I physically threw my body across that altar to save you!"

Joe smiled. "That was different," he said again, unable to contain his humor.

Chachi grinned. Then they were both laughing.

"Still," Chachi said, wiping his eyes. "I felt in my heart that you were making a mistake and I did what I thought I had to do."

"My father nearly had you arrested. He was sure you were on drugs!"

They laughed again.

"Little good it did in the end—and thank God too," Joe said, returning to seriousness. "We've been married nearly twenty years now."

"That's not the point." Chachi paced the floor, stopping in front of Joe. "You know I should have never agreed to marry Renee. You know I wasn't thinking straight. I was acting out of gratitude."

"And you're just realizing this?" Joe smirked. He walked over to the bar to pour a fresh drink. "Maybe, just maybe, I thought marriage would be good for you." He held up the bottle, but Chachi shook his head. "You're nothing if you're not a man of your word, and if you commit to anything or anyone, I knew you'd stick with it." Joe sipped the strong liquid and spun around. "Maybe I *wanted* you to marry her."

"To keep me from Michael? You would sacrifice me like that?"

Joe smiled and gazed into his drink. "I don't know, Chachi," he said softly. "It's a tough position for a father to be in. My best friend or my son..." He looked apologetically into Chachi's face. "You understand, don't you?"

Chachi placed a hand on Joe's shoulder. "I do," he said, giving the shoulder a gentle squeeze. "And I know you can't understand how I feel."

"You're a grown man," Joe said, his voice eerily calm. "You can disregard what you feel."

"I did, Joe. I did for a long time, and this is going to sound terrible, but I don't *want* to anymore." Chachi paused to let his words sink in.

Joe simply sighed and moved to sit on the corner of his desk.

Chachi followed and put an arm around him, his hand cupping the back of Joe's neck to hold his face close. "You're my best friend. I don't want to lose you," Chachi whispered.

Joe closed his eyes tightly and opened them again.

"He's still so young, Chachi, and he's so, I don't know, he's just not ready for a relationship with a grown man—especially you!"

"He's already in it. Separating us didn't make matters easier, did it?"

Joe threw his hands up and stood to pace a bit. Chachi watched him walk and think. He knew better than to speak now, the battle was nearly won. All he had to do was let Joe lead now. When Joe stopped, Chachi knew he had resolved the issue within himself.

"How will you handle this at work?"

"No different than before," Chachi said. "We saw each other for months. It didn't affect our working relationship. Nobody knew anything. Not even you."

Joe's eyes narrowed at the last remark. "You don't plan to go public—"

"No, no. That would be career suicide!"

"It's bound to get out sooner or later."

"I'll bank on later and prepare to deal with it then. I've got eight publicists. They oughta be good for something."

"I don't want him to get hurt," Joe said after a brief silence.

"You can't protect him from that."

Joe sighed. He rubbed his hands through his hair. "This could be a phase for him, you know. He could wake up one morning and decide it's not what he wants anymore. He's young and you're his first. There will be others—"

"You can't protect me either, Joe."

They both smiled.

"We'll be crucified in the press if it gets out," Joe said.

Chachi shrugged.

"But that's the least of your worries," Joe continued. "Renee is gonna come after you with heavy artillery."

"I know."

"This is going to *crush* her, Chachi."

"I know," Chachi sighed.

"Have you said anything to her?"

"Not yet."

Joe inhaled deeply and let it out in a long, slow breath. "She's gonna blame Michael."

"I'll worry about her—"

"No. I'll worry about her," Joe warned. "If she targets my baby, I'm gonna have a problem with both of you."

"I don't think you give Michael enough credit—"

"This isn't Michael's fight. He's in the crossfire," Joe snapped. "He's still a kid, he has no business going at it with an adult."

"Understood," Chachi said softly.

"You'll look out for him too," Joe said in a tone that left no room for an option. "He lives in my house, he follows my rules and that means you do too."

Chachi opened his mouth to speak, but Joe rode right over him.

"That means he doesn't miss curfew, do drugs, smoke or drink. I don't even wanna think about that other stuff—"

"Whoa!" Chachi held his hand up. "I realize I have a responsibility here, but I am not trying to be his father. I told you that before. He's gonna do what he's gonna do. I can only try to make sure he's smart about his choices. I can't control what he does when he's not with me. I'm walking a fine line here."

Joe pursed his lips and eyed Chachi, arms across his chest. "We'll see."

"So are we okay now?" Chachi asked, his eyes wide in his youthful face.

Joe laughed.

"What's funny?"

"Nothing."

"I'm not expecting your blessing here," Chachi continued. "I just...want to make sure we're okay."

"I guess," Joe said finally, "as long as you don't start calling me Dad."

Chachi grinned.

"Deal."

Michael had been restlessly pacing in his room. A car had arrived. The guard's gates were only a half-mile from his bedroom window and he could see the headlights of cars that were admitted to the grounds. At this time of night, it had to be Chachi.

Their voices echoed as his father opened the door. He had been crouching on the landing at the top of the stairs. He saw Joe lead the way into his office in the study and close the door.

He crept down to listen, his ear pressed against the wood, but he couldn't hear a sound. Damn that house for being so solidly built! But then again, the quiet meant they weren't screaming at each other. He scurried back up the stairs to wait. He'd just have to tough it out.

He didn't realize he'd dozed until his cell phone rang. He was jolted at first. Shaking the fog from his head, he dashed from the chair he had been curled up in and lunged for the phone still clipped to his jeans. "Give it to me straight," he said breathlessly.

"I think it went fine."

Michael's tension was released in a burst of air. "He wasn't mad?"

Chachi paused. "I don't think so. He didn't give us his blessing, but he was pliable."

Michael plopped onto the floor with relief. "That's better than nothing," he said, breathing easier. "Now what?"

"Now comes the hard part," Chachi said. Still, Michael could tell he was smiling.

"That wasn't the hard part?"

"Renee vs. Joe? Between those two, I'd take on Joe any day."

Michael groaned and nibbled his bottom lip, his nerves creeping up on him again.

"You think I should talk to my dad?"

"If it will make you feel better, I'm sure he'd like that."

"Okay. When will I see you?"

Michael felt Chachi smile again.

"We'll see."

He walked slowly down the stairs. The light was still on in the study. It spilled out underneath the door. He stood there to collect himself, taking several deep breaths. Then he whispered a prayer and eased the door open.

Joe had made a fire in the hearth and was gazing into it. He looked up and smiled when Michael came in.

"You built a fire in June?"

Joe laughed. "Helps me think. Come here." He held his hand out for Michael to join him.

"So Chachi was here," Michael said after a few moments of watching the fire dance and cackle.

Joe nodded. "Sure was," he looked at Michael sideways. "You sure about this?"

"Dad, I've never been surer."

Joe frowned and Michael knew he had to suppress the urge to correct his grammar.

"Well," Joe said softly. "Who am I to say? I'm just your father."

Michael opened his mouth to protest but stopped when he saw the playful twinkle in his eyes.

"I know about the phone call to the rape crisis center.," Joe said softly.

Michael's mouth fell open. That seemed so long ago. He had forgotten about that.

"Now that I think back," Joe continued, "that was the reason you became so depressed. That was the reason you couldn't get out of bed."

Michael's mouth worked wordlessly before he was able to get his words out. "That was a long time ago—"

"You were so traumatized, you called strangers for help. What happened between then and now? What makes it okay?

"He *made* me make that call. I was confused, I admit it. But I'm not anymore. It wasn't Chachi that had me so messed up, it was…not knowing who I was anymore, not knowing how you'd think of me."

Joe studied Michael a long time, his gaze thoughtful. "You're a young man now. I'll have to trust you to make your own decisions. You're not like other boys your age."

"Thanks—I think," Michael said with mock sarcasm.

"Don't get me wrong," Joe said, stretching his arms and legs against sleep. "I trust *you*, it's that other son-of-a-bitch—"

Michael so rarely heard his father curse, he gasped. Then he laughed. "That son of a bitch is your best friend!"

"Oh, yeah, that's right." Joe chuckled. He exhaled through his nose and followed with another good stretch. "Which means I know him about as well as he knows me." He turned to Michael, lines of concern etched in his face. "He's too much for you, Michael. Chachi has his own issues to deal with."

"We all have issues."

Joe thought for a long time. Michael watched him, waiting.

"I think it's way past time for us to have…the talk."

"The talk?"

Joe nodded.

Michael frowned, puzzled. Then his eyes widened at the uncomfortable prospect of discussing sex with his father. "I thought we *had* the talk!"

"That was small potatoes. That was when I thought the worst would be catching you in the back seat of a car flipping some teenage girl. This is different."

"I think it's too late for 'the talk,' Dad."

"You're young, you're fresh, you're beautiful. He's enamored with you—right now. But you'll never be able to satisfy him."

Michael felt instantly hot and quickly looked down at the floor. "Dad…"

"I'm serious," Joe said, his face flushed. "I'll admit he's toned it down a *lot* since he met you, though at the time, I didn't know *you* were the reason," he added dryly. "But in a good week, Chachi would sleep with a woman every day, Michael. I've not seen him commit to anyone. Not once."

Michael sucked in air to calm his wildly beating heart. He glared at his father from underneath full, dark lashes.

"Renee was okay with that," Joe said. "Are you?"

Michael stared hard into the fire. He had considered it. He knew Chachi had seen other women. When the affair was hot and new, they were together all the time. He remembered how taxing, mentally and physically, the relationship was. Unless Chachi slowed *way* down, he couldn't handle him. "Would you say that he loved any of those women?" he asked his father.

"No. He might have cared more for one versus another, but love? No. Not even Renee."

"Do you think he loves me?" Michael held his breath.

This time, Joe did take a moment to mull it over. "If not, he's come as close as he ever has," he said quietly, "but I think he does."

Michael released the breath he had been holding and felt his heart smile. "Okay then."

"An open relationship is only as strong as those *in* the relationship," Joe said.

"Let's just say I'm not worried," Michael said smugly. "He's only holding on to those women as a security blanket, but not for long."

"Okay," Joe bent close. "That's out of the way; now how do you plan to protect yourself?"

Michael felt a new blush creep over his face.

"Come on! I know all about protection, Dad!"

Joe sighed. "I guess I thought your time with Dr. Morton—"

"Cured me?" Michael added, his lips curled with sarcasm.

"Well, I had hoped—"

"Don't be ridiculous, Dad."

"Okay."

They fell quiet.

"What do you even know about Chachi, besides the fact that he sings and he's a good friend of your father's?"

"What!" Michael laughed. His father must be kidding. "Of course I know him. Maybe not as well as you do."

"*What* do you know about him? Tell me something besides what I just mentioned," Joe challenged.

Michael shrugged. He had been sleeping with the man for months. They shared intimate thoughts. Of course he knew him. He just couldn't think of one thing in particular.

"Chachi is very good at disguising himself," Joe said quietly. "He only reveals what he wants people to see."

"Are you trying to scare me? Is there something I should know?"

"No. I'm not trying to scare you."

Joe paused. Michael waited.

"Did you know," Joe said, hesitatantly, "that his uncle raped him repeatedly when he was a child? They don't know for how long, but doctors guessed it was from the ages of about three and five."

Time stopped for Michael. He felt his hands and feet go numb. There it was, the missing piece. "That's why his father snatched him."

"That's why his father snatched him."

"That's terrible!" He felt sick to his stomach for Chachi. "He never said anything."

"He doesn't really remember it. He swears his father is lying. All he knows is that his father kidnapped him and his mother didn't come after him. He's angry with them both."

Michael wiped the sweat from his hands on his pajamas. "Who do you believe?"

"There's no reason for Mr. Spencer to lie. I know it's the truth. It makes perfect sense."

Michael took a moment to let it sink in. He looked up at his father with furrowed brows. "Why are you telling me this?"

"Well," Joe cleared his throat but his voice still came out croaky.

"Sometimes, people that have suffered abuse—"

"No!" Michael barked.

"I'm not saying that—"

"You are, and it's not true." Michael's eyes blazed with fury. "He's thirty eight years old, I'm sure he's not still acting on something that happened when he was a toddler!"

Joe sat still, his eyes on the floor, his lips drawn tightly together. "I just thought you should know," he said quietly.

Michael nodded and took in a lungful of air, letting it out slowly. Chachi loved him. He wasn't some kind of sicko preying on young boys. "Thanks." He rose quickly and bent to give Joe a peck of a kiss on the cheek.

Joe surprised him with an embrace and they smiled at each other. "I'm here if you need me," Joe said, tracing his son's face with a finger.

"I know."

Michael sat on the edge of the bed and jostled his leg impatiently, waiting for the phone to ring. He'd phoned Chachi twice and both times, his calls went straight to voice mail. He was anxious to see him now that they were free. No more hiding and pretending, well, not for family and friends, and that's all that mattered. He couldn't wait to know what it would be like to look at him and not have to repress the smile that grew inside him, not have to refrain from throwing his arms around him.

It was still dark, but morning would be breaking the night soon. Chachi hadn't said that he would come, but Michael couldn't shake the overwhelming feeling that he would. He learned to not only trust the unspoken connection they had, but had come to rely on it. He had, only moments ago, heard his father's footsteps fade in the direction of the bedroom he shared with his wife, but Michael couldn't turn in, not yet. His heart knew that his lover was somewhere close.

He picked up the receiver, looked at it questioningly, and replaced it, the sound snapping the stillness of the night. He started. There was another sound, or was there? He held his breath, listening. Amazing how loud quiet could be when he really listened. His heart beat in his ears and he released his breath slowly, willing his heart to slow down so that he could hear above it. Turning slowly, he smiled, nearly crying out in delight.

Chachi had come in through the balcony door. He looked fresh and irresistible in a bright white T-shirt and starched designer jeans, watching Michael intently. His big brown eyes were soft, his gaze lingering with an odd look of amusement. Michael thought his chest would split down the middle if he didn't touch him, so he leapt across his king-sized bed and fell on him in just two strides.

"Ow! God, Michael, how much do you *weigh*!" Chachi said, before Michael could still his lips, covering them with firm kisses. Their first kiss of freedom. "Shhhh!" Chachi warned, a finger pressed against Michael's lips, but his brown eyes danced and they both shook with muffled laughter. "Joe's still awake. The light is on in his bath."

"How did you get past security?" Michael gushed.

"I never left."

Michael threw himself against him, nearly climbing his body with passion.

"Glad to see me?" Chachi teased.

Michael laid his head on Chachi's chest and gripped him close.

Chachi rocked with him, kissing the top of his head and stroking his back. After a long time, when they could once again breathe normally, he pushed him at arm's length to look into his face. "Hey, you."

Michael thought he'd go to pieces again. "Hey, yourself," he whispered and touched his face.

"How'd it go?" Chachi asked. Michael blushed and nodded.

"I can't stay long. I had to see you."

"I tried to call you…"

"Shhh..."

They stood together, savoring the few moments, softly stroking one another.

"When can I *really* see you?"

Chachi laughed softly. "Soon," he said, kissing him gently. "But listen," the light in his eyes dimmed with seriousness. "Not until after I've dealt with Renee. She's done a lot for me and I owe her at least that."

"Sure. "So when?"

Chachi cupped Michael's face with his hands. "I'll call you," he whispered.

Michael lifted himself up on his toes for another kiss, this one light and sensuous. He gazed into Chachi's eyes and with a trick of his hand, Chachi reached behind his ear and presented him with a lily stolen from the garden.

Michael laughed. "That old trick! Where did you learn to do that?" He took the flower and brought it to his nose.

"To bed." Chachi tapped him lightly on the rear and spun him in the direction of the bed.

"I can't sleep now—"

"Sure you can. Come on."

Still grasping his hand, Michael let himself be nudged toward the bed. He slid underneath the coverlet.

Chachi smoothed the light, silky covering about him and fluffed the pillows like a caring father, then lay down beside him on top of the coverlet. He slipped one arm around him and peered into the deep, dark depths of his eyes. "Sleep."

Michael's lids fluttered in quick succession like butterfly wings. He moaned softly with both pleasure and exhaustion. "I'm so happy," he murmured.

Chachi kissed his forehead until his lashes dipped a bit further over his eyes.

"I didn't think I'd ever feel this way again." Michael moved further into the crook of Chachi's arm and felt the brush of sleep as Chachi stroked his hair. "This time, I'm never letting you go."

"You sleep now," Chachi said into his hair.

Michael wrapped an arm about his waist and squeezed. He smelled of fresh linen and verbena. Unsure as to whether God had anything to do with this incredible good fortune, Michael thanked him anyway and prepared to let sleep take him when he heard a thump in the hall outside his bedroom door. If Chachi were caught in his room…. He shot up in alarm and was surprised to see sunshine streaming inside. His arms were empty and the balcony's French doors were closed. Had he dreamed it all? For a disappointing moment, Michael was sure that he had. Then he looked down at the lily in his clenched fist, crushed and discolored, but still fragrant and alive with the memory of him.

Chapter Thirty

Chachi sat in a chair by the window and watched as Renee shifted slightly underneath the covers. She stirred again and Chachi narrowed his eyes in her direction. He had already turned away the breakfast tray twice.

"Renee..."

She sighed, stretched sleepily, and sat up, whipping the covers away. "Good morning, darling!" She slipped out of bed, making certain to show as much thigh as possible, and called down for breakfast. Then she walked over and kissed his face.

"Renee…"

She ignored him and sashayed into the shower, emerging minutes later flushed and refreshed, head and body wrapped in pink, embroidered towels of Egyptian cotton.

"Renee…"

"I know," she said softly.

He frowned, confused.

"I know you went to see Michael last night," she said, moving to sit on his knee.

"I did *not.*"

"But Lydia told me—"

"I went to see *Joe*. I saw Michael in the process."

She exhaled sharply and clasped his hand with hers. "Look, you know how I feel. I understand, if you have to—I mean—I'd prefer it wasn't with *him*, but, I understand there's something about him you can't seem to—"

"Renee!" Chachi twisted so that he could look into her face.

"Don't look shocked! You've never been faithful to me! You've never been faithful to anyone. I never expected it."

"This isn't about being faithful, Renee. Marriage requires more than that."

The maid bringing breakfast interrupted them. Renee waved it away. They waited until the maid had gone. "Our marriage will be whatever we decide it will be," she said. "It's about understanding and supporting each other, staying within whatever rules we make for ourselves. It's a commitment, Chachi!"

He stared at her.

"I'm not asking you to commit to anything more than you are able to give," she added quickly.

He sighed and put an arm around her. "You have always been there for me and I love you for it," he said softly. "But," he felt her go rigid and held her tighter. "It wouldn't be right for us to marry and you know it. You deserve more than this."

"Chachi, please! It's not a problem. Come on, I love you! Whatever, whoever you are, I love you; just don't do this to me! I've spent all this time planning this wedding! I spent all my life waiting for this…"

"I'll take care of everything Renee, I swear."

"I don't need you to take *care* of *everything*!" She leapt to her feet, her chest heaving. "I need you to, for once, honor a commitment!"

"I will," he said quietly. "But my commitment lies elsewhere." He stood up.

"Chachi." Tears glistened on her cheeks, but she tried to smile through them. "What—I mean—Michael is beautiful. He's young and smart and sexy; still, he's just a *boy*. What can a boy offer you, honestly?" She attempted to laugh.

He gave her the deadpan look, struggling to hold back choice words.

She went on, "I mean, sure he's a good time right now, and I'm not depriving you of that, but, how long can it last?" Her tone softened. "You need someone to take care of you, to look after you. Someone who understands you and understands your business. I can do that! I've always done it."

"I pay people to do that."

"It's not the same thing!"

"Renee, don't make this a circus. I have made my decision at whatever cost. I'm sorry, but I have to do this."

She sniffed at the floor. "Can you honestly say that you love him?"

The room went perfectly still. Only the faint voices of staff moving outside the door could be heard.

"Yes," he said hoarsely. "Yes."

"Oh, my God," she muttered and came apart. He sighed and wrapped his arms around her. "I'm so tired of you hurting me, Chachi, I'm so tired of it!" She sobbed.

"I'm so sorry," he whispered.

"All I've ever done was love you!" she wailed, "but I've not received anything in return—nothing! Except—"

"It's not you, Renee. It's never been you. I—love you," he said haltingly, "in my own way, but I could never give you what you need."

"But you do!"

"No, I don't. You know it and I know it, and one day, *we* won't be enough anymore."

They stood holding each other without speaking. His shirt was wet with her tears. She fingered the buttons on it.

"I want us to stay friends," he said into her ear. "You are *really* important to me. Nobody can change that."

She nodded and closed her eyes tight.

"I'll have Lydia help you pack."

She drew back. "Pack! You're asking me to leave *now*!"

"Don't you think it's best?"

"But I can't!" She looked around wildly.

"I'm going," he said, turning to leave, "to give you some time."

She knew what that meant. Be gone when I get back.

* * * *

"Enough!" Michael lay breathless and pushed Chachi's heavy form off of him.

"And that coming from an eighteen-year-old strapping stud in top form?" Chachi said, grabbing a handful of Michael's hair and using it to jerk his head back to kiss his neck. "You smell so good."

They lay, wrapped in each other's arms, and watched the sky. Fall was underway, but the weather was still balmy, so Chachi had the sky-light open.

Michael broke the stillness, "You heard from Renee?"

"She calls from time to time."

"She's not angry with you anymore?" Michael felt the warmth of Chachi's breath as he exhaled long and slow.

"Oddly, she never seemed angry to begin with, just disappointed." He released Michael and turned to lay on his back, one arm behind his head. "I know Renee is cooking up something. I just don't know what."

"Why won't she just let go!"

"Don't waste your time thinking about that," Chachi whispered. "We're together and that's what matters."

"I love you." Michael pressed his body hard against him. "Make love to me again—"

The phone, rang. They exchanged glances before Chachi grabbed the receiver. "Hello," he said anxiously, the soft lines of his face going rigid. "What are you calling me on this line for?" He listened for a bit, rolling his eyes to the ceiling. "I got your messages. I was gonna call you when I got time—" His brow creased with impatience. "Well I haven't *found* the time!" he bellowed, causing Michael to frown. "Look," Chachi said after another short pause. "One phone call is enough, okay? I told you, if I can make it, I'll make it. I got a lot of shit going on—what do you want from me?" He pinched the bridge of his nose as he waited through the caller's response. "All right, All right, whatever! I'll call you back, but I'm in the middle of something right now." Another pause. "I said I'll call you!" Still another pause. "Whatever!" He said and hung up the phone.

"Holy Christ!" Michael said slowly. "*You're* rude! Who the hell was that?"

Chachi yanked at the covers and lay down with his back to Michael. "My father."

Chapter Thirty-One

Dancing on air, the fall leaves made pirouettes of brown, red, and gold swirls before landing in soft mounds on the ledges of windows and doorways, carpeting the earth. Michael rose early. He had agreed to meet Eric and some of the fellas at the center for a game of basketball while the weather still permitted them to use the outdoor courts. He crept downstairs to the breakfast room. Maxi was up and already in full swing (he swore she never slept) and began pouring a glass of orange juice the instant she spotted him.

"Hungry?" she asked, handing him the glass.

The strong, citrusy scent of orange reached him before he could bring the glass to his mouth. "Nah, just some toast."

Lydia approached, fresh and pretty in a floral, silk chemise with matching robe.

"You're up early." Michael smiled. "Where's Dad?"

"He's sleeping in." She poured milk from a pitcher into a ready-made bowl of cereal. Maxi drifted to Lydia's side and began pouring coffee. "It's rare that he gets to do that, even on weekends. So, what's on your agenda today?"

"Basketball. I'm meeting the fellas. Then lunch with Chachi and it's back to the studio this evening. New songs."

"Hmmm," she said and bit into a slice of buttered toast.

They ate quietly, but Michael could feel an energy about her. What was she doing up so early anyway?

"Did you hear Renee was back?" She asked, peering at him out of the corners of her dark eyes.

The forkful of waffle he had just put in his mouth fell back onto his plate. He gaped. "Why?"

"Well, she hadn't intended on *staying* gone," she said slowly. "I suppose she feels like she can handle things now."

"Handle things…"

"You know, seeing you and Chachi together. That's still really hard for her."

Michael pushed his plate away. A bird landed on the window ledge. He watched it in utter despair.

"Don't look so horrible. We all know where Chachi's affections lay. I've told Renee time and again, if she keeps playing these little games, her efforts will blow up right in her face." She reached out and put a hand over Michael's. "All you have to do is not push him toward her. That's the only way he'll get there."

"You've seen her?"

"Not yet. She called last night. I'm supposed to meet her for lunch today."

"That's why you came down early."

Lydia sighed and gently lay her fork on the table. "I heard you go down. I wanted to talk to you before Joe got up."

"Does he know?"

"It's *nothing*, honey! She left for a while and she came back. Nothing changes." She leaned close to him. "She *wants* to upset you. She *wants* you to be suspicious. But Chachi hasn't wanted her in more than, what, nearly twenty years now…he's not gonna suddenly realize he needs Renee."

"He nearly married her."

"*Nearly*. And we all know what *that* was about."

Michael sighed deeply. He was just sick of the turmoil. He rubbed the spot above his temple. "How can you be friends with somebody like that?" he asked, his eyes dark with worry.

Lydia leaned toward him. "You stole *her* boyfriend, remember? It's silly, but she's doing what comes naturally to her." Lydia sighed. Renee wants what she wants, and there's hell to pay if she doesn't get it."

"Chachi know?"

"I'm sure he does. They stayed in touch, you know that, right?"

"Sure."

"So I'm sure he knows by now."

Michael ran a hand through his hair. "He didn't mention it."

"Probably wasn't worth mentioning." She waved her hand in dismissal. "I'm sure he will mention it in passing."

He shook his head, but the pain at the base of his skull held fast. "I guess." His eyes met hers. "If it's nothing worth mentioning, why did you get up early to tell me, when you could catch me alone?"

Lydia did that purse-of-the-lips thing that gave her that pouty youthfulness. "I just didn't want you to bump into her and be surprised, that's all. She'd just *love* that reaction. Anyway," she said rising as she drained her cup of coffee, "you enjoy your day and think nothing about it, sweetie." She kissed his forehead and smiled encouragingly.

"Thanks…for letting me know." He tried to smile back. 'Enjoy your day,' she'd said. Now how the hell was he supposed to do that?

Michael parked in front of the center, turning the car over to valet, and strolled down the carpeted halls, nodding at reception and security on the way to Chachi's office. His cell phone rang.

"Mike," Chachi said. He sounded calm, even pleasant. "We still on for lunch?"

"Sure, I was just on my way up."

"I'm not in the office," Chachi said hastily.

"I thought we said we'd meet here."

"Something came up."

Michael's heart congealed in his chest.

"I had an unexpected budget meeting outside the office."

The breath Michael held captive left him in relief.

"I tried to call you," Chachi said.

He had been playing ball. He'd left his phone in his locker. "What do you want me to do?" Michael asked.

"Meet me at Pazo's.

"Everything all right?"

"Yeah, why?"

Michael hesitated. The unease in Chachi's voice was unmistakable. "Nothing."

"Okay," Chachi continued, "fifteen minutes."

"We still in the studio tonight?"

Chachi grunted. "I forgot..."

"Oh, yeah, well, we'll talk about it—later." They endured a short silence where they both seemed to want to say something else. "I love you," Michael whispered, his mouth close to the phone. He was certain he heard Chachi's breath draw in sharply, still his voice came back smooth and controlled.

"I love you too, baby."

He had known an hour before that Chachi wasn't coming. More than embarrassed, he sat drinking cola (he couldn't even get a damned drink), trying to look perplexed about where his guest might be. He knew. He had known from the beginning, he just couldn't face it.

He had underestimated her. Whatever she had, it was enough to make Chachi lie to him. He had been with her, Michael heard it in his voice. He was probably fucking her right now.

He signaled the waiter. "May I have the check?"

"Don't worry, sir. It's all been taken care of."

"What?"

"Your check. We've taken care of it."

Michael frowned. "How?"

"I don't know, sir. I was just told that your check was taken care of, whatever you wanted."

"Fucking asshole," he muttered.

"Excuse me?"

"Oh, no, not you," he added quickly. *Chachi sent me to Pazo's just to get me out of the way*. "Shit!" He couldn't wait to hear what Sir Duke had to say this time.

He skipped the rest of his schedule at the center and drove home to change into something more comfortable, 'cause when he found this mutherfucka, they were gonna have to whip each other's asses. He may have underestimated Renee, but Chachi underestimated *him*. They were probably holed up in a hotel somewhere, but he'd find them.

Papi opened the door for him before he could knock. Michael hesitated at the threshold. "She here?"

"No," Papi answered, shaking his graying head.

He climbed the stairs to Chachi's suite. All that greeted Michael now was a deafening absence of sound.

Chachi sat at his dressing table, motionless except for his breathing. His eyes were downcast and he twirled a crystal sphere in his hands. He took a deep, cleansing breath and turned to Michael. "Come here," he said softly. "I've been waiting for you." He took Michael's hand and led him over to the bed, then sat.

Michael chose to stand. "You lied to me," he began. You sent me to Pazo's knowing you wouldn't meet me there."

"I'm sorry."

"Why?"

"I didn't want you…to see her."

"Renee?"

Chachi nodded.

"Why didn't you tell me she was back?"

"I was going to. She asked me to meet her and I started not to. I told her I didn't want to start this all over again."

Michael's voice came out barely a whisper. "But you did meet her."

"Yes. And when I saw her—" Chachi closed his eyes.

"Tell me. Just tell me."

He held out a hand for Michael.

Michael didn't want to hold hands. He wanted it straight. "Just tell me, Chachi."

"Not until you give me your hand."

Frustrated, Michael wiped his sweaty hands on his pants and placed the right one inside Chachi's, instantly regretting it. He might need that hand to punch his lights out. "All right then."

"Promise me that no matter what, you'll hear me out."

Michael rolled his eyes and shifted impatiently.

"Promise."

"All right."

Chachi wet his lips and took a breath before he began. "I love you more than I love life and I want you to know—"

"I don't wanna hear that bullshit! Now just tell me what the fuck is going on!"

"But I want you to know this!" He squeezed Michael's hand until he was quiet. "This changes nothing between us—"

His patience exploded. "Jesus Christ, Chachi! What!"

"All right." Chachi held Michael's hand to his lips, kissed it, and rested his cheek upon it. "She's pregnant."

Comprehension struck him like a sledgehammer, buckling his knees. He dropped, stunned into mental chaos. "Wh-what?"

"Michael, I'm sorry—"

"Wha…how?"

Chachi screwed up his face.

Michael stared at him, dumbfounded. "But…" the white fog began to transform into red anger, giving him his tongue back. "I thought you were using protection!"

"I was…I…" Chachi ran his free hand through his freshly cropped hair. "I don't know how this happened…I mean, I do but, it was…during the time when we were engaged. I thought you and I were over…maybe I got careless…I don't know…"

"She could be lying!" Michael grasped desperately for some sliver of hope. "Maybe someone else—"

"She'd have told me earlier if she were going to lie. She knew I'd pressure her for an abortion, so she stayed away until she was good and pregnant."

"She's…like—"

"Very pregnant. Delivering in…maybe a few months."

"*Fuck*!" Michael shouted and banged the fist of his free hand on the bed. "*Fuck*! *Fuck*! *Fuck*!"

"Michael please. Don't let her do this to us…"

Michael struggled to breathe. That evil bitch! She was somewhere laughing her ass off. The image of her holding his baby loomed into view and something snapped in his head.

"You stupid *dick*, you ruined everything!" he screamed and pounded Chachi with his free hand. He punched him every place he could while Chachi blocked his punches. He could have used that right hand, but Chachi held on to it like a vice. "I hate you and that bitch…" He collapsed into Chachi's arms. "Let me go," he said icily.

"No. Not like this."

"Let me go, Chachi…or I swear…"

"You swear, what?"

"Let me go."

"You have to promise."

"I won't promise you shit. I don't owe you nothin'."

"Just this, Michael: All I'm asking is that you think about this. I didn't believe that you and I would ever get back together again. I didn't even think it would be the right thing for us to do!"

"And now?" Michael glowered at him. Every breath hurt.

"I don't even care. All I know is that I love you. I wasn't trying to have kids, and I don't know if Renee pulled some funky move or I just fell off, but the point is, it happened and a baby is coming. I can't do this right without you."

"That's crap!" Michael sobbed.

"I mean it. I need you. It seems that just when we get things going our way, something—"

"No not 'something,' Chachi, *you*! You figure out a way to screw it up!"

"What did I do wrong this time, Michael?"

"You slept with her! You were going to marry her!"

Chachi held Michael's hand to his lips and closed his eyes for a long moment. "She took care of me when I needed her. I was already confused and sad, it just made sense at the time. You didn't want me anymore. I needed something..."

"Her?"

"Would you feel better if it were someone else?"

"Yes...no, but..."

"Before *you* it was her. Renee was the only constant in my love life." He pulled Michael close. "It was what I *thought* was a love life. I didn't know love until I met you, Michael. Only you. Always you. I don't care what happened before you and I won't care what happens after. All I care about is us, right here, right now. *We* are up to you."

Michael focused on a spot on the wall. "I need to go home."

"I know." Chachi sighed. "I'll let you go." But he held on another full minute before he spoke again. "Just do me this one other thing."

"What?" Michael whispered.

"Whatever you decide, promise me you'll come back and tell me to my face."

"Why? So you can dissuade me?"

"I won't try to dissuade you. Whatever you decide, I'll accept."

"All right. I'll come. Now let me go." He nearly fell backward when Chachi released his hand. He also felt a sudden sense of aloneness, a detachment from a part of himself. Trembling, he turned blindly and left.

He couldn't believe it was happening again. Here was another crossroad with Chachi. He was sure Renee did something underhanded, like poked holes in his condom. Still, a baby was coming. He couldn't handle that. Not with her. Maybe this was just another one of the signs he'd been ignoring. As electric as he and Chachi were together, it had to be wrong. Why else would they constantly find themselves in this same place? He swore he'd let nothing come between them again. He'd love to see Renee's face if he decided to stay with Chachi. She was certainly banking on his leaving him. But when the baby came, what then? This baby would be the focus of Chachi's attention and affection. He might *think* he didn't want it… Maybe he should do the self-less thing and just let them go on and be a family. He was still young.

The sun had set and he was all cried out. Time he stopped being the victim and took control. He would make a decision.

He rose and smoothed the wrinkles from his clothes. He only had a few hours before curfew. He promised Chachi he'd tell him to his face.

Chachi was asleep when he returned. He lay in the same spot on the bed with the lights out and a pillow clutched close to his face. Michael didn't have to touch him, his eyes sprang open before he could approach. Chachi sat up and drew his knees up, looking fifteen years younger. He searched Michael's eyes for their future.

"I…" Michael began but found it harder than he thought it'd be. "I just can't…I can't…"

Chachi covered his face with his hands.

Michael closed his eyes. "I can't live without you." It was not what he had practiced in his head.

Chachi grabbed him and hugged him tight, cutting off his breath. "Thank you, thank you, thank you…" Chachi moaned into his ear.

They comforted one another for over an hour before they lay still.

"She's gonna be a pain in the ass." Michael said in the darkness.

"She'll be *my* pain in the ass. I don't want her *near* you and I'll tell her that. You let me know if she says anything—"

"I can handle her."

They lay quiet again.

Michael asked, "Deep down, are you a *little* excited?"

"Scared. I can't imagine being anyone's father."

"You'll be a great father."

Michael nestled his head in the space between Chachi's neck and shoulders. They lay, clasping and unclasping hands.

"What's the future gonna be like for us, Chachi? Do you ever think about it?"

"All the time."

"What's there?"

"Just you. Beyond that, I couldn't care less."

Chapter Thirty-Two

In several weeks, the baby would be born, bringing with it changes to all of their lives. This frightened Michael to death.

He was fortunate not to have run into Renee for a few weeks after the bombshell of her pregnancy was deployed. He wouldn't have been able to handle it. Chachi must have been quite persuasive when he warned her to stay away from him.

His luck ran out a week later when Lydia informed him that she wanted to throw Renee a baby shower at the house.

"I wanted to check with you first. After all, this is your home too. I don't want you to feel uncomfortable."

"Don't worry. Just tell me when and I'll make myself scarce."

As fate would have it, he got sick on the day of the shower and as badly as he wanted to be away from that production, he could barely get out of bed.

He awakened in a cold sweat. Famished, he rose and stood beside the bed. The room swam around him, threatening to send him to the toilet. What a time to get the flu.

Michael opened the door and stuck his head out. No apparent signs of life. Perhaps he could quietly get to the kitchen for food before anyone spotted him. Going down the stairs was a trip—no pun intended, but he made it safely.

Maxi stocked orange juice in individual serving containers. He gratefully grabbed one and gulped it down. Now for solids. He opened the snack cabinet: cakes, donuts, cookies, potato chips—ah, crackers! He stuffed them into the pocket of his pajamas and twisted the cap off a second container of juice. Voices drew near. The tinkle of his stepmother's laughter grew as her footsteps approached.

Renee stopped short of the threshold, her mouth agape.

Michael turned toward her, the container of orange juice still halfway to his face.

It took her only a second to recover, then her lips melded into a grin of triumph. "Well, well," she drawled.

"Did you need something, honey?" Lydia rushed to his side. "You shouldn't be up."

"I was hungry," he mumbled. He had to avert his gaze from the sneer on Renee's face and the swell of her belly.

"Well, that's a good sign," Lydia said, flashing a glance of warning at Renee. "But you should have called someone." She felt his forehead with the back of her hand, searching for fever.

"That orange juice certainly won't help," Renee said, gliding in with her hand on her belly. "When the baby makes me nauseous, a glass of ginger ale works." She stroked her bulging middle.

Michael glared at her with contempt.

Her beautiful brown eyes flashed with a merry glint. "We're going to name him after his daddy, did you hear?" she said sweetly. "Oh!" she exclaimed suddenly, stopping to grasp the counter's edge. "He kicked! Wanna touch?"

"Renee, stop!" Lydia grabbed Michael's arm. "Come, sweetie, let me help you back to bed."

His belly lurched. In one disgusting spray, he showered everyone and everything within a foot of him with bile and vomit.

Renee screamed, hands outstretched, dripping. "You *idiot*! You nasty *idiot*!" she shrieked. The kitchen filled quickly with the rest of the party stragglers: his father, a couple of ladies he didn't recognize and, of course, Chachi.

"I'm sorry…I…" His stomach bottomed out, his head felt light, and his knees wobbled. Joe grabbed armfuls of kitchen towels from the linen closet and threw bundles to the ladies attending Renee. He stuffed a bunch of them in Lydia's arms and grabbed Michael.

"I'm really—I'm really sorry…"

Joe held a towel to Michael's mouth. "Is she okay?" he asked the nameless lady who was now softly patting the dry part of Renee's shoulder with her hand.

"She needs to get out of these clothes," the lady responded.

"She can put on my robe," he said. "Take them to my room," he instructed one of the servants who had rushed in after them.

"Are you okay?" he asked Lydia.

"I'm fine. Just get Michael back to bed."

"You…" His father narrowed his eyes at him. "Back to bed!"

"I've got him," Chachi said.

Michael looked up, surprised. Renee wailed in the distance. But Chachi was here—with him.

Chachi lifted Michael's arm and anchored it across his shoulder, placing his other arm about Michael's waist. Their eyes met full on.

Michael half walked, half rode the staircase under Chachi's arm and it felt like riding the crest of a wave, glowing light fixtures and blurred paintings whirling by. He felt his fever returning, and not all of it was the result of the flu.

* * * *

Despite his small victories in his on-going battle with Renee, the truth was, each passing day was a conquest for her. Every day of her pregnancy, he was conquered all over again, stabbed just underneath the heart and thrown into a dark prison where the future was unknown.

Chachi gave him all the attention he could between Renee's demands and midnight false alarms. He had already taken leave from work. Still, dividing his time between Renee and Michael and trying to meet the needs of both left him looking drained.

Renee began having pre-labor contractions and Chachi agreed to her invitation to move in with her those last two weeks…just in case.

One afternoon they were curled up on a sofa in Chachi's bedroom, looking at television, but not really watching it. Chachi's red-line kept ringing. Each time, he'd raise his head just enough to look at the display and each time, Michael's head was lifted out of its comforting daze.

Irritated, Michael scoffed. "Why don't you just answer it?"

"I don't want to."

"Who is it anyway?"

"My dad."

Michael let the matter go and drifted off peacefully. The ringing started up again. "Maybe it's important."

"It's not."

"How do you know?"

"I know."

Finally, the phone stopped.

Michael heaved a sigh. "Don't you think you should just deal with whatever it is, Chachi?"

"Stay out of it."

"I'm just saying, how do you bring a son into the world and raise him, when you can't even communicate with your own father?"

"We're not having this conversation."

"All right, I'm out of it." Michael squeezed his hand.

Chachi squeezed back.

The phone started up again, but this time, Chachi didn't bother to check the display. When his cell phone started, he snatced it up. "Hey, what's up?" His voice was laced with panic. "You sure?"

Michael watched his eyes blink and shift, his tension mounting.

"Are you in pain now?" Chachi asked.

Michael sighed.

"I'll be right there," Chachi said before hanging up the phone. "She's in labor," he announced.

"Again?" Michael sneered.

Chachi narrowed his eyes at him. "This could be the real thing."

"So, I guess you'll be moving in today instead of Saturday."

"There's no time," he said, pulling on his shoes. "I'll call you if something happens." He disappeared inside his dressing room and came out with a baseball jacket and cap. "Stay as long as you like." He bent to kiss Michael on the mouth. The table phone started ringing again. "Ignore that!" he called back without turning his head.

With Chachi's warmth gone, Michael felt cold. He pulled a throw over himself and raised his knees to his chest.

Papi stopped in and asked if he needed anything. He was going out. "Stay as long as you like," he said, echoing Chachi.

He must have dozed. When the phone rang again, he sprang up and answered without thinking. "Hello?"

"What the heck are you pulling! Jasper?" Dukakis Spencer's voice shocked him.

"No—he's…not in…"

"He was there a moment ago, Papi told me."

"He left. The baby might be coming."

"Oh…"

Silence.

"Is this…Michael?"

"Yes, sir. Good to speak to you again."

"Call me Dukakis, please."

Michael didn't see how that would be much easier.

"We had dinner plans," Dukakis said.

"Oh…I didn't know…"

"He probably had no intention of showing up anyway."

Michael shifted uncomfortably at the bitterness in his voice. "I'm sorry." It was all he could think to say since the man was probably right.

"Guess I came all this way for nothing. Sorry to bother you."

"All this way?"

"I'm at the gate. They won't give me clearance. Papi left the grounds."

Chachi hadn't provided permanent clearance for his own father? Shame on him!

"I'll arrange clearance," he offered.

"What's the point?" Dukakis sighed.

"I'm hungry," Michael said, surprising himself. What was he thinking? "No point in letting good reservations go to waste."

"I'm afraid the reservations have expired," Dukakis said.

"We can go someplace else. I'll eat anything."

Another long silence seemed to ebb and flow. Shamelessly, Michael waited.

"All right."

Michael called security and approved clearance. Then he went out into the hall, climbed over the railing, sat on the landing at the top of the staircase, and waited. He wanted a clear view when the maid opened the door.

Michael grinned when he saw him. That first glimpse still caught him off guard. It was like a trick of the mind. He shook it off quickly and put on a serious face as he knew Mr. Spencer would, no doubt, be wearing one.

Spencer said something inaudible to the maid and they both looked up the staircase to see Michael sitting cross-legged on the landing between the railing and the wall. The maid dismissed herself as if he did that everyday.

"Hello," Michael called down.

"You'll hurt yourself."

"I'm fine."

Spencer stared at him.

"I'll get my shoes," Michael said and leapt with athletic prowess over the railing, away from the beam of those eyes.

They rode in a new, sporty BMW, not shabby by any means, but certainly not the stuff of billionaire fathers. They took the scenic route and drove idly, quietly taking in the view, neither of them talking. Soon they pulled in front of Dante'-Anna's.

Finishing touches were hastily being made to a table for them. The waiter opened wine and poured some into Spencer's glass. When he moved to fill Michael's glass, Spencer raised his hand.

"It's only wine. I can drink wine."

"Not on my watch. Do you want a soda or something?"

"Water's fine." Michael scowled and picked up the goblet for a sip. Great. Another father.

"So why'd you come?" Spencer asked after drinking from his glass and nodding. Only then did the waiter retreat.

"I was hungry."

"Besides that."

"I wanted to meet you. I didn't get a chance to meet your wife before she passed."

Silence swelled between them. Michael fidgeted under Spencer's penetrating gaze.

"Why'd *you* come?" Michael buttered a roll.

"You seemed hungry." Spencer smiled for the first time that evening.

Michael laughed. At least he had a sense of humor.

Spencer had the salmon and Michael ordered a seafood pizza. It tasted nothing like pizza, but was actually pretty good.

"You're pretty young, aren't you?" Spencer asked halfway through the meal.

"I'm eighteen. I guess that's pretty young for some people."

They ate the remainder of the meal in relative quiet.

Spencer drained his glass and wiped his mouth on his napkin. "So, she's in labor now, huh?"

Michael rolled his eyes exaggeratedly. "Probably not. It's only about the tenth false alarm in a week."

"She's pretty much ready to go though, isn't she?"

Michael sighed. "I guess."

"And how will the new baby fit?"

"I guess we'll see," Michael said. He waited, not sure how to ask his burning question. "Why is he so angry with you?"

Spencer's smile dissipated. He swallowed hard and scanned the room.

"I've heard bits and pieces of the story from my father and Papi."

Spencer opened his mouth, then closed it, then opened it again. "I'm not sure he's angry with *me*," he said finally.

"You're kidding, right?"

"No." Spencer frowned at his hands. Beads of perspiration formed on his angular nose.

"Then, he treats you like shit because…"

Again, Spencer's mouth moved without sound. His gaze shot up to meet Michael's briefly, before dropping to survey the remains on the table as if he'd find the answer there.

Michael felt for him, but could not let up. "You've got to have a clue."

"I don't think he's angry with me, he's just—directing his anger *towards* me because it's safe."

"Who told you that? Some shrink?"

Spencer's eyes blazed at him. "Yes," he hissed.

"Figures. Looks pretty much to me like he's angry at you, pal," Michael said, taking another sip of water.

A crimson blush moved up Spencer's collar until it colored his face.

"So, if he's not angry with you, who is he angry with?"

"His—" Spencer inhaled sharply.

"Attacker? You sure about that?"

Spencer locked gazes with Michael.

Michael shrugged. "I'm not sure he remembers an attacker," he said softly.

"He has to," Spencer said quietly.

Michael shook his head. "It took me a while to figure it out. I thought he just didn't want to talk about it. But when my father said he thought he blocked the whole thing out... No—you're the only attacker in his version of the story."

Spencer's mouth hung. "But...he has to—"

"No one was in that room but you, him, and *the attacker*."

"So?"

"He thinks you made it up to get the heat off—"

"That's asinine!" Spencer cried but his eyes darted through memories, his breath coming in soft pants.

"Why won't you just apologize?"

"What?" Spencer's focus tore away from his thoughts back to Michael.

"Apologize," Michael said casually, "for what you've done."

"Because I haven't done anything besides rescue my son from a child molester!" Spencer said through clenched teeth.

"That's not how he sees it."

"It doesn't matter how he sees it! That's how it was!"

"*All* that matters is how he sees it."

Spencer fell silent, his hazel eyes drifting to a corner of the ceiling.

"My father and I had a time of it when I first came to live with him," Michael explained. "I had so much rage, he had so much guilt; still, there seemed to be no cause that I should be angry with him. But I was. I always felt he should have known I was out there, somehow. I knew *he* was. I dreamed of him rescuing me. When fate brought us together and I saw how lavish his children had been living, how they were healthy and happy…I was enraged."

"That must have been difficult."

"I ate trash and lay outside in the dead of winter without a decent coat."

"Where was your mother?"

Michael paused. He could never have blamed her for his past, though she very well could have been considered the most to blame. "My mother had just as much trouble, in a sense. She was trapped. She couldn't help me." He sighed. "Anyway." Michael shook the past from his mind. "The idea is that your parents can be counted on to protect you. No matter what. Yet you snatched him from the comforts of all that he knew and loved, practically from his mother's lap, and thrust him into a world he wasn't even old enough to have learned about in school yet…a foreign country."

"You make it sound so—malicious! I was protecting him! Don't you understand that?" Spencer skin had taken on the red, blotchy hue of distress.

"*I* understand. But it didn't happen to *me*. I'm sure he would understand if—"

"*If*?"

Michael hesitated. As Spencer's breathing stabilized, he continued, "If he could just get past the anger." He sat back and waited.

Their waiter brought the check and Spencer handed over his credit card without even looking at it. "What do I do?" he asked after a while.

"I think you know," Michael said softly.

Spencer exhaled a lungful of air. "But I can't even get him to answer my phone calls, let alone try to have a conversation with him! I doubt I'll see this baby before he goes to college. The first photo I see of him will probably be in the press."

"It's not that bad."

Spencer's aloof façade crumbled under the weight of their conversation. Lines became etched in the space above his brows.

"I'll help if I have to," Michael said, even as he cringed at the thought of Chachi's reaction once he found out he even played a part in this. "But whatever you do, let it wait until after the baby is born."

Spencer nodded, his gaze fixed on the table.

Michael watched him for a while. "I should be going," he said quietly.

Spencer looked up as if surprised he had spoken, but he smiled—the first smile of genuine warmth, not humor. "How did you get to be so smart?" he asked.

Michael winked, but the lids of his dark eyes drooped at half-mast. "Life."

* * * *

Spending his days (and nights) with Renee in the discomfort of the very last stages of pregnancy was worse than even he had imagined. Only a few weeks before, she had maintained that healthy mother's glow. But in the last week, her body had disproportionately expanded on all sides, her face puffed out like a blowfish along with her fingers and toes, and dark, dry patches appeared on her body. She was miserable and she made it known to everyone who came into contact with her. Had it not been for his joy in anticipation of the birth of his first child, he'd have lost his patience many times over and sent her into labor the unconventional way.

For the first time Chachi felt a little sad about his relationship with his father. Something about having his own child made him want to talk to him, ask him questions.

He sat at breakfast alone, leafing through newspapers and magazines left by his staff. He nearly missed it. One newspaper was folded back to a page and dog-eared to mark the spot. In the picture, he and Michael were having dinner in a place totally unfamiliar to him. It wasn't a good photo, but Michael's thick, gorgeous hair could not be mistaken. What on *earth*? Why, that wasn't *him*! People had often confused Chachi and his father in pictures, but *he* never had. But what were *they* doing together? Could this just be clever work of the camera?

Heart racing, he raised the paper so close to his face, his nose was touching it. The date said the picture was taken last Wednesday. *Wednesday*? His brain sorted through its storage. He was with Michael Wednesday. There was no mention of… He looked at the photo again. Michael was leaning forward, a forkful of something half raised to his mouth. His father appeared very interested in whatever Michael was saying. They didn't seem at all uncomfortable with each other. How long had they been at this? He felt hot and cold at once. Whatever was going on was happening right under his nose.

Anger and fear seized him together. He was deliriously anxious to find out what was going on. Shaking, he folded the paper and placed it in his breast pocket. Renee was napping. He left a message with her nurse and grabbed his coat.

He sped toward the hotel. His father's earlier messages had said that he'd be leaving that evening. He wondered why Spencer stayed in town so long, extending his initial visit. Now he knew. Not wanting to stop at the desk and draw a crowd, he tilted his hat over his face and headed straight for the elevators. He knocked on the door and held his breath.

When Spencer swung the door open, his eyes widened to the size of silver dollars. Chachi charged inside and paced back and forth.

"What is it, son?"

Panting, he stopped and produced the newspaper photo, holding it close to his father's face. "What is *this*?"

"Those vipers don't let up do they?" Spencer chuckled.

Chachi glared at him.

"What?" Spencer asked. "Jasper, what is it?"

Chachi had to take two very deep breaths before he could speak again. "What were you doing with him?"

Spencer's brows converged on his forehead. "We had dinner. What do you think we were doing?"

Chachi stood glowering.

"Come on, son, you don't think—"

"You're up to something!"

"Chachi, think about what you're saying!"

"Don't call me that!"

"All right.

"I don't want you anywhere near anyone I love again, you got that?"

"Now wait a minute—"

"Don't touch me!" Chachi jerked away from Spencer's attempt to touch his shoulder. "You just stay away from my friends! I don't want you near them, I don't want you talking to them!"

"Why?"

Chachi blinked. "Because! That's why! Just go away—get out of my life!"

His father's concerned gaze passed over him. Spencer contemplated him with knitted brows. "You really *do* hate me, don't you?"

"Yes, I fuckin' *hate* you! What did you *think*?"

"Why, Chachi? What do you think I've done to you?"

"Whatever…just…" Chachi ripped the photo to shreds and turned to leave.

"Just a minute ago you were demanding answers. Now I ask you a simple question and you clam up. What, are you afraid I'll tell your friends? Everybody knows, Jasper—"

"Knows *what*!" They stood toe to toe.

Spencer sucked in air. "What you've been afraid to know all this time! What I did was wrong. I know that now. I should have stayed and helped your mother deal—"

"I'm leaving." Chachi turned again.

"Instead, my instinct kicked in and I acted without thinking, but I never meant to hurt you. I thought I was protecting you!"

"I'm gone, Dad," Chachi said, reaching the door.

"When I saw him—that filthy carcass with my little boy…"

Chachi froze, his hand on the door knob. "You're a liar," he said without turning around.

"Am I?" Spencer took a few steps toward him. "It was your birthday, remember? You had a big party in the back yard."

Chachi stood still, listening, his back to him.

"It was a beautiful, sunny day. We rented ponies and a carousel. But you felt ill and wanted to go inside, remember?"

"Shut up!" Chachi spun around and charged him. He stopped just inches away.

"You hadn't been feeling well for days. You'd been withdrawn and sad. I thought it had something to do with my showing up unexpectedly. Your mother took you to your room so that you could lie down. That's when I noticed your uncle—"

Chachi clenched his fists. "I'm not playing, man," he warned.

"Neither am I. You remember, don't you?" Spencer said, tears swimming in the rim of his eyes. "Now that I think about it, you were doing fine until he showed up. I noticed the way he watched your mother take you inside. He looked…anxious."

"I said shut up!" Chachi raised his fist.

Spencer blinked, but didn't flinch. "You're gonna hit me? When he announced he would look in on you," Spencer continued, "it felt wrong."

"I can't hear this…" Chachi dropped his fists and closed his eyes.

"I wanted to follow him, but I didn't at first. My position was already precarious at best. But your brother Liam had been trying to tell me something."

Chachi moaned in his chest.

"He was scared, but I sensed something was amiss, so the first chance I got, I slipped away to check on you. I shouldn't have waited. He was raping you when I walked in."

Chachi growled and raised his fist mid-punch. A sob escaped him. He walked over to a nearby chair and sank into it.

"We fought. I tried to kill him. If they hadn't pulled me off him, I would have." Spencer paused and sighed. "Your mother was prostrate. I was so angry with her—I couldn't believe she didn't know. The man was living in her house half the damn time, for God's sake!" He paused again. When he continued, he sounded exhausted. "They took you to a hospital. They said I couldn't come until I had calmed down. But I got up in the middle of the night, I bribed the nurse and she let me see you."

"I can't do this now," Chachi pleaded. "I'm having a baby…I can't do this."

"That's the very reason you *must* do it." Spencer walked over and knelt next to him. "You looked so tiny in that bed. All I could think about was that I had to protect you. If Zeak had gotten past Murani and Papi so many times before, he'd find a way to do it again. I had to get you out of there." Spencer paused again and this time when he spoke, his voice was even softer. "I couldn't believe my luck when the nurse left her station—for what, I don't know. Without a moment's hesitation, I grabbed you and as many blankets as I could and hustled you out. Money goes a long way and before daylight, we were on a plane…"

Chachi shuddered and Spencer pulled his head into his chest. For over thirty years, he had given his demon the face of his father, but deep down, he had known the pieces didn't fit.

"I thought I was rescuing you," Spencer went on, "but what I had done was taken you from your home, your family, and brought you to a strange land with strange people and a father you didn't know. It was the worst possible thing I could have done after what you had gone through. You were so close to her and she loved you so much—still does. By taking the law into my own hands, I robbed you of her affections, robbed her of yours. I am so sorry!"

Chachi's arm curled around Spencer's neck and tightened. They talked that evening. Tempers flared and cooled, emotions flowed, tears fell. But they were talking.

When darkness fell and Spencer had long missed his flight, he reached for Chachi's hand. "We've lost so much," he said, "but it's not too late, is it?"

Chachi drew himself up and wiped his eyes. His father handed him a handkerchief. He sniffed, pulling himself together. "I've got to get back. I've been gone too long."

"Oh yeah, that's right." Spencer smiled. He used a spare hanky to wipe his own face and smoothed his clothes with his hands. "What're you wasting your time with your old man for? You could be a father any minute now!" He laughed shakily.

Chachi forced a smile. It was weird, standing there with his father yet not screaming at him, awkwardly trying to figure out how to have a friendly conversation since they'd never had one before. "I'd better go," Chachi said, not looking at him.

"I understand. Maybe I can call you later?"

"Sure." Chachi nodded at the floor. He moved to the door leaving a trail of silence. "Do you *have* to go back?" he asked.

"No!" Spencer said, clasping his hands.

Chachi smiled and looked into his father's eyes without anger for the first time. "Your grandson should be here any day now, if you wanna hang around for it."

Spencer gripped the back of his chair. "Oh son, I'd love to."

After a late night of adding beats to a few rhymes he had written for Chachi, Michael slept late into the morning. He played basketball with his boys and met up with Illian for a movie. He kept himself busy so that his mind was occupied. He checked messages to see if Chachi had called. He felt a strong presence behind him and spun around.

Chachi stood in the doorway of his bedroom, his head cocked.

"I told you about sneaking up behind me," Michael said playfully, but his smile faded quickly. This was not a social visit.

Chachi spoke with an eerie softness. "Let this be the last time, in your life, that you go behind my back and meddle in my business."

I thought your business was my business, Michael wanted to say.

"Don't let me *ever* have to tell you again."

Michael stood with his head down. He had only tried to help. He hoped to God he hadn't made matters worse. Shoulders sagging, he wanted to apologize, but something told him not to even do that. Simply don't speak. He swallowed hard and looked up to face him. The space was empty. In that uncanny, soundless way that he could, Chachi had gone.

Renee went into labor mid-morning the following week. Michael was already suffering from a migraine and one of his dark moods. Still lying in bed in his pajamas holding two pillows pressed against his face, he winced when his sister burst into his room to make the announcement. He groaned his response. He hadn't actually spoken to Chachi since his little speech in the doorway. He had missed a couple of his calls. The messages left were short and non-committal. "Nothing yet, we're still waiting. Hope you're okay. I'll call you later." Then the dial tone. Michael didn't call back.

The phone began ringing off the hook. Back to back, family and friends called in anticipation of some news about the baby. As godparents, Joe and Lydia became the dispatchers of information. Michael tried to tune them out as they rushed past his bedroom door issuing updates to David and Leah in urgent voices. He was glad when they got dressed and went to the hospital.

They were kind enough to call him first.

"He's here," his father sang softly.

"Really?" Michael felt pain in his stomach. He was going to be sick.

"Big boy too: eight pounds, eight ounces."

"How's Renee?"

"She had a tough time of it. Twenty hours of labor, most of it hard. It all ended in a caesarean."

"How's Chachi?"

"Proud. You should see him."

Michael's lip trembled and he had to clamp down on it.

"How are *you*?" Joe asked.

"Fine," he mumbled.

"No you're not, but that's okay," Joe said quietly. "I wanted you to know first. Go back to sleep now. I'll see you when I get home."

Moments later, he heard the phone ringing in his sister's room and heard her squeal. He clutched his pillow close and sobbed into it.

He woke to the phone ringing again.

"Wake up, sleepy-head," Chachi said.

"Congratulations."

"Thanks." Chachi sounded tired.

"Tell me about him." Michael could hear the baby crying in the background.

"He looks like me."

"You're kidding…"

"No. I see it already."

The baby bawled. Chachi turned and said something unintelligible.

"I see he's got your pipes," Michael said.

Chachi chuckled softly. "He came out screaming. The way Renee's been behaving lately, there's no wonder."

"How's she doing?"

"She's not looking too good, but she'll pull through. She's so full of hell."

"Who's got the baby?"

"My dad."

"He's there?" Michael felt a flicker of promise.

"Yeah…look, about the other day—"

"Forget it."

They fell silent.

"Michael, I appreciate you being there through all this. I want you to know that."

"Where else would I be?" He took deep breaths to control his voice.

"I don't know how I would have gotten through it without you. I just wanna thank you…for everything. I'll make it up."

Michael sniffed.

"I know I put you through a lot. I'm sorry. It should get better from here."

"I'm not going anywhere." Michael hiccupped. "For better or worse."

"I love you, Michael Simpson."

"I love you too, *Daddy*."

Chapter Thirty-Three

He had been able to avoid the little critter. Renee had been adamant about not bringing the baby out of the house until after his six-week appointment with the doctor. During that time, he could pretend there really was no baby at all, that nothing had changed—except Chachi wouldn't stop talking about him.

"He looks just like me," he said for the hundredth time. "You should see how strong he is. I swear he knows who I am…"

Blah, blah, blah. Michael could not believe how jealous he was of a little baby. Everyone had seen the bugger except him.

They had to trek over to Renee's house to see the baby and, of course, he wasn't doing that. His jealousy was further ignited when he saw, from pictures, that the baby really did look like Chachi—a lot! Well, so much for the question of paternity.

The long-awaited six-week check up went fine and now they were bringing the baby over for the regular weekend get-together.

Michael wanted nothing more than to skip out, but Chachi made it clear that he expected him to be there. Even David was home on school break.

He drifted in and out of the festivities just long enough to have been able to say he was there. He tried hard not to look at the baby as he was passed around the room from arm to arm, tried hard not to look at Chachi's proud face, tried hard not to spit in Renee's smug one. He had to escape to the sitting room to get away from them…all that oohing and ahhing… Even when Chachi found him and sat down next to him with the baby on his lap, he wouldn't look at him.

"You wanna hold him?" Chachi asked.

"Um, no thanks. I'm not good with babies." In fact, he couldn't recall holding one baby in his life.

"All you have to do is put one hand under his head and one under his bottom." Chachi demonstrated.

"Chachi…I can't. I'll drop him!"

"You won't drop him. I'm right here."

Chachi gingerly placed Lil' Jasper in Michael's arms. How little and weightless he felt! The baby began to wriggle and Michael panicked, nearly tossing it back to its father.

"Michael!" Chachi laughed.

He tried to relax. Once he was finally able to, the baby settled comfortably in his arms. "He *is* kinda cute." Michael smiled. Lil' Jasper's hands were balled up into tiny fists and pressed against the sides of his face, his ruby red lips pursed into a little bow.

"Now wait right here. I need to get his bottle."

"No! Don't leave!" His panic resurfaced. "I don't know what to do!"

"He's sleeping!" Chachi laughed. "There's nothing to do. I'll only be a moment."

Lil' Jasper's lips began to pulsate as if he were suckling.

Michael laughed. He was *so* cute. "Hurry, Chachi!" He glanced sideways and caught a glimpse of Renee's apricot dress out the corners of his eyes. She stood with her mouth wide. The baby became a heavy stone in his lap.

"How *dare* you!" In a flash, she dashed over and ripped the baby from his arms. "Don't you ever touch my baby!"

"Renee!" Chachi had come in before Michael could respond. "*I* told him to hold the baby. Give him back!"

"I will not let you use my child to play house with your *boy*friend!"

"Play house with my *boy*friend?" Chachi shouted. "Give me my goddamned baby!" He yanked Lil' Jasper from Renee's grip. The baby's arms and legs flew out with surprise. Michael gasped.

"Renee! Chachi!" Lydia charged toward them, her arms outstretched. "This is not a doll! This is a baby! You're acting like children!"

They all began talking together. Others came to see what the commotion was about and help sort it out. Michael lifted a glass of champagne from an abandoned tray and slipped into the kitchen.

This could not work. He leaned against the counter and pressed the cool glass against his face. He couldn't stand one more encounter with Renee, she was going to make him—"

"I'm not playing games with you anymore, little *boy*!" She had come in behind him.

"Your little *boy* is in the other room, you fuckin' bitch!" he shot back.

Renee's mouth gaped open. "How dare you, you brat! You fairy! You homo!"

"I know somebody that likes it." He tried to sound clever but he was trembling under her insults.

"Don't fool yourself, kid. You're a snack for him, a novelty, that's all. He's tiring of you already."

"Yeah, you wish..."

"Oh, please honey, don't get full of yourself. You're just one of many. Soon you'll be gone too."

Michael forced a laugh.

"Go ahead, laugh. But every time you fuck him, you're fucking *my* man!" she snarled.

"Yeah?" He fired back. "And every time you *kiss* him, you're sucking *my* dick!"

Renee gasped. "You don't want to keep fucking with me, because you *will* lose!" She poked his nose with her finger and without thinking about it, he emptied his glass in her face.

"You freak!" she shrieked and slapped him hard with her open hand.

Michael drew back his arm.

His father grabbed his wrist. "Don't you dare!" Joe's face was close to Michael's, his eyes threatening. "To your room!"

Michael glared at him before pushing through the little crowd. He charged up the stairs. He couldn't believe he was being sent to his room. Behind him, he could hear them shouting.

"Renee, you need to leave!" his father yelled.

"What! You're throwing me out?"

"This is *Michael's* home. If you can't find a way to get along with him, you're not welcome here."

Michael shut the door behind him, hoping to shut out the voices. He could still hear them, but could no longer make out what they were saying.

Until he heard Chachi shout above the rest of them: “This is my fuckin’ baby too, and I’ll do as I fuckin’ well please!”

Michael grabbed a pillow and flopped onto the bed. Now he was causing a rift in his parents’ friendship with Renee, a friendship that spanned twenty years. He sighed heavily. He just didn’t know what to do. The bitch just wouldn’t leave him alone. It felt good to throw that drink in her face. He smiled. It felt almost as good as when he threw up all over her.

A knock on his door shattered his thoughts and he sat up.

His father charged inside. “You were going to hit her!”

Michael only looked at him. He couldn’t deny it. The only thing that would have been better than throwing that drink in her face would have been to pop her a good one.

“You have steel in your fists,” Joe said. “Physically, she is no match for you; mentally, you are no match for her. That’s why I told you to let me handle her!”

“Yeah, you guys have done a bang-up job handling her,” he muttered.

“*What* did you say?”

Michael dropped his head.

“Until Renee can apologize and behave appropriately, she is not welcome in this house.”

Michael looked away.

“I just want you to know, that if you hit her,” Joe said, “if you ever raise your hand to hit any woman, I will beat your ass senseless.”

His father was right. He could have really hurt her. He nodded.

Joe nodded in return and went away.

He heard the baby cry and Chachi appeared in his doorway. He walked over to Michael and sat on the bed, his face flushed, his eyes glittering golden-brown. “Here, take him.”

“Chachi, I don’t want to.”

“He’s my baby, Michael. I want you to hold him.”

“He’s not *my* baby!” Michael shouted.

“But he’s *mine*!” Chachi shouted back.

“She don’t want me to touch him!”

"I don't give a flying fuck what she wants! Here, hold him!"

Lil' Jasper cried, his arms and legs flailing. The poor little thing.

"He's crying," Michael protested.

"*Michael*," Chachi said with forced patience. "This is my son. I don't care if you hate Renee to her dying day, but I need you to accept this child. 'Course that will never happen if you can't even look at him."

Michael lowered his gaze. "Can't we do this a little at a time? Do you have to lay this on me all at once?"

"All at once? You've had months to prepare for this." Chachi's voice softened. "All I'm asking you to do is to acknowledge him."

Michael looked past the fleshy baby in Chachi's arms. Lil' Jasper's thick legs kicked out as he cooed. One of his booties had come off his foot. Michael sighed and held his arms out for a second time.

Chachi wrapped his arms around both of them. Lil' Jasper stuck his fist in his mouth.

Michael leaned into Chachi while he stroked the baby's hair with his thumb. He *was* just a baby. "I'm sorry I let her get to me," he said.

"She won't find it easy to get to you again. Other than the baby, I have nothing to do with Renee. Her doctor says they're fine, so I'm moving back home, and Joe says she's not welcome here anymore."

"Where is she now?"

"She was asked to leave. She didn't want to leave without the baby, but she knows how to pick her battles."

"What about the baby?"

"I'll miss seeing him every day, but we'll have to work something out, even if we have to do it in court."

Michael gazed down at the baby and smiled. Jasper had totally relaxed into sleep, his face peaceful. His tiny chest rose and fell in rapid, jerky movements. Michael thrust a finger between one of the baby's clenched fists.

Chachi tightened his embrace.

With the last few anxious moments behind him, Lil' Jasper slept, oblivious of the storm brewing around him.

Renee met him at the front door. He put the baby in her arms and headed for the guest room.

"It's late, Chachi, I was worried sick!" she cried.

He didn't answer. Chachi hurled objects into his suitcase. He was nearly done when she walked in.

"I'm so sorry," she breathed, "don't leave me, baby."

Chachi turned to glare at her.

"I-I don't know what it is about him that makes me crazy," Renee stammered.

"Get over it," Chachi said and resumed packing.

"I've tried, Chachi! I've tried, but I just can't! I love you so much. I do!

Chachi sucked in his breath and closed his bag.

"I'll apologize to him if that's what you want!" she said.

"What *I* want? What about what's right?"

Renee inhaled through her nose and wiped tears away. "Okay. I'll apologize."

His anger fizzled. "Just leave him alone, Renee."

"Consider it done," she said with a sweet smile.

He watched, skeptical. Her tears seemed real. Perhaps she was sincere this time.

"It's late." She touched her hand to his shoulder. "Stay this last night. Don't leave."

He glanced toward the bed. He would love to wake up one more morning to his son's smiling face. "All right."

"Can I get you something to drink?"

"No. Thanks." He moved the luggage to the floor and lay across the bed, not bothering to take off his clothes. He was bone tired. He and the baby had stayed with Michael and talked well into the night. Before long, he drifted off to sleep.

He tossed and turned, uncomfortable in his clothes. He awakened to Renee, wearing little more than her favorite perfume, tugging at his pants.

"What are you doing?"

"You fell asleep in your clothes. I was trying to help."

He sat up and ran his hand over his head. He felt like he had slept in reverse. He was more tired than when he first lay down. "Renee, cut it."

"My doctor says I'm good to go." She sank her knee into the bed to climb over him and began massaging his neck, moving lower. "We have about one hour before Jasper wakes up for his feeding."

He shrank from her kiss. "You really are crazy, aren't you?"

"What?" She pouted. "I said I was sorry."

He removed her hand from his crotch and leapt from the bed. "I'd better go."

"What did I do now?"

He stared at her, trying to determine whether she was up to her old tricks or whether she had really snapped this time. It didn't matter.

"I said I would apologize and I said I would try to get along with him!" She hugged him, pressing her near-naked body against him. He may not have been in love with her, but she had always been able to turn him on. Now he felt bitterness close to disgust when she touched him and he nearly pushed her away. He shrugged out of her arms.

"What? You don't want this anymore?" she asked, hands on her hips.

He actually laughed. She wrapped her arms around herself.

"I don't believe you just asked me that," he said. "You have completely lost your mind." He pulled on his coat and reached for his bag. "I'm gonna say goodbye to Jasper." He hoisted his bag onto his shoulder and hurried to the nursery taking long strides.

Renee trotted after him. "You're going to leave him? You're going to leave Jasper?"

"I'm not leaving Jasper, I'm leaving *you*! I want to see *him* as much as possible. We'll either work something out, or my lawyer will be in touch."

"Well, I'll go away, Chachi. There's no reason for me to stay. I'll take Jasper and—"

"I'll find you!" He rounded on her, eyes blazing with an animalistic fury. She took a step backward. He turned and continued on to the nursery. He leaned over the crib and caressed the sleeping baby. "See ya, sport." He kissed the baby's face and watched him stir. "I love you." He hurried down the stairs, headed for the door.

She half ran, half slid down the stairs after him. “This is it, Chachi! This is the last straw!” she screeched. You walk out on me again, we’re enemies! I swear!”

He refused to stop or even turn around.

Renee grabbed a lamp from a nearby table at the foot of the staircase and hurled it after him. No sooner had the lamp crashed against a wall did she find herself having to duck to avoid a crystal vase that shattered right over her head. “I hate you!” she screamed. “I’ll get you, you’ll see! I’ll get you and that little—”

He slammed the door on her last words, shutting out that awful voice. He paused outside, allowing a flood of unexpected relief to wash over him, and knew in that moment that she was truly gone from his life.

Chapter Thirty-Four

By the time he was six months old, Lil’ Jasper was trying to crawl. He would balance himself on his hands and knees and rock backward and forward, babbling loudly. Chachi had both his ‘babies’ for an overnight stay. Joe had relaxed his rules a lot lately, allowing Michael to pull all-nighters with him from time to time, and Renee had begun to leave Jasper with him quite a bit as she ran ‘errands’. He was probably babysitting while she planned her next attack, but he didn’t care. He was just glad to spend time with his son.

“All right, Dude, you have to raise your hand and foot one at a time and move forward,” Chachi instructed. “You’ve been doing this rocking thing long enough.”

Jasper responded with a big, gummy smile.

“You see that smile!” Michael exclaimed. The baby’s smile had just about the same effect on him as the father's did.

"Yeah." Chachi grinned. "It'll look a lot better with some teeth in it."

Michael laughed.

Chachi positioned the baby on the floor next to the bed. "Come on, boy!" He clapped his hands. "Come to Daddy!"

Jasper rocked faster, drool slowly streaming from his lips to his father's imported rug.

"You're not moving, Dude!"

Jasper responded with a spit bubble that went sliding down his chin.

"Ugh!" they said simultaneously.

"Cool then. You stay there and do the rock." Chachi turned and slid up against Michael. "I'm gonna play with your friend here."

"No!" Michael elbowed him roughly and scooted away. "Not in front of the baby, take him back to his room!"

"Okay. Let's just put him in there." Chachi motioned with his head at the crib across from his bed.

"No!"

"Why?"

"I just don't feel comfortable."

"He can't see anything. Beside, babies don't understand what they see. They only understand what they feel and all he's gonna feel is a lot of love in this room." With a swift move, Chachi had Michael pinned, kissing his neck. Jasper stopped rocking to watch.

"See! See! He's looking at us!" Michael pointed at the baby whose bright eyes had widened in anticipation of a new game. He gave them another winning smile.

Chachi laughed out loud.

"What's that?" Michael jumped.

"What? Why are you so paranoid?"

"I heard something. I think someone's at the door."

They paused to listen. The knocking persisted. Chachi picked up his phone and listened intently. "The phone's working," he said, returning it to its cradle. Who is it?" he called.

They could hear a response but couldn't make out the words.

“Hold on. I’ll be right back.” Chachi pulled on his robe and stepped over the baby on his way to the door. Muffled voices exchanged dialog. Michael could hear some of what was said.

“Hey, what’s wrong?” he heard Chachi say.

“You’ve got a letter.,” Papi replied.

“Okay. You couldn’t call me?”

“This one is important. You should read it now.”

“I’ll read it later.”

Chachi’s voice drew nearer as he walked away from Papi. Michael grabbed his pajama bottoms and slid them on. He sat on the side of the bed and put the baby on his lap.

Chachi reappeared with a little less wind in his sail. Papi was close behind.

“What are you going to do with it?” Papi asked. His face was deeply lined, more than Michael remembered.

“I said I’ll read it later.”

“But you won’t.” Papi sounded distressed.

Chachi swung around. “Did something happen?”

“My brother, your uncle,” Papi began, “Zeak. He’s dying. He’s got the cancer. They gave him months to live and that was weeks ago.”

Chachi was quiet for a time. Michael had yet to take a breath. “So, what do you want *me* to do?” Chachi asked with an edge of impatience.

“I need to go back. So do you.”

“You don’t need me to go back. You can go by yourself. I’ve always told you that.”

“You know I promised!” Papi shouted. Michael had never heard him shout at Chachi or anyone before.

“Well, *I* didn’t!” Chachi walked over to Michael and took the baby from him, squeezing Jasper to his chest.

Papi shuffled up after him. “He did a bad thing, but he’s not a bad person. Just—a sick person! He’s still my brother and I need to say goodbye, if only that!”

“Then say goodbye! But I don’t want to talk about this in front of Michael!”

"You gotta make him accountable!" Papi's whole body shook. "And then you gotta forgive him or you will never be rid of him!"

Bathed in a strained silence, the room amplified Jasper's babble.

Papi spoke softly, "Please?"

"I'll think about it," Chachi said. "Just...leave me alone for now."

Papi left without even saying good morning to Michael and closed the door behind him. Chachi stood rooted with the letter in his hand, turning it over and over.

"Are you gonna read it?" Michael asked.

"No."

"Have you ever read any of them?"

"No," he whispered.

"Your uncle...Zeak, is he the *one*?"

Chachi nodded and pressed his face into Jasper's neck.

Michael went to him, removing the baby from his arms.

Jasper grabbed a fistful of his father's robe and tugged.

"You have to go, you know." Michael rested his chin on Chachi's shoulder, making it easier for Jasper to use the other hand to claim a fistful of his hair.

Chachi mouthed, "I can't."

"You're ready." Michael balanced the baby in one arm and used the other to slip around Chachi's waist. "Look at how you handled your father."

"It's not just *him*, it's *her*. It's too much at one time!"

"You kill two birds with one stone, that's all," Michael said. "You can handle it." Chachi closed his eyes and Michael moved to look up into his face. "I'll go with you if you want."

Chachi's eyes popped open, but dimmed quickly. "No. I wouldn't want you there—to see me like that. I don't know how I'll react. I might kill somebody."

"You won't. You'll be there for closure and you're gonna go there with that mindset, right?"

Chachi's pupils seemed to recede. He shook his head. "No. I'm not going. Let him die. He deserves to die. If Papi wants to go, he can go without me."

"You *have* to go, Chachi! You can't just not deal with this! You can't let him die with the power he has over you. You have to take that power back!"

"Boy, have you been *shrinked.*"

"Well, maybe you need to be 'shrinked' a little. Look at my relationship now with my father. I mean, nothing turns back the clock. Things can't be undone, but at least you can move forward."

Chachi exhaled sharply.

Michael pressed on. "You have to see him, confront him and all those bad memories, and eventually, like Papi says, you have to forgive him, for your own sake."

Chachi nodded, his brow creased with focus.

"He might not apologize," Michael continued softly. "It would be great if he did, but at least you can put it to bed." Michael waited. The letter in Chachi's hands was sweaty and crumpled.

Chachi's voice was barely audible. "Maybe Joe will go with me."

"Not him."

Chachi met Michael's gaze."

"You know who has to go," Michael prompted.

"My dad," Chachi whispered.

Michael nodded. "He's the final piece. Get all the pieces together and solve your puzzle."

Chapter Thirty-Five

Michael was having trouble sleeping. Chachi was supposed to be gone home only a week, but after three weeks, things were obviously working out better than expected. His calls were always short since he was either going somewhere or he was dead tired from the day's adventures. What if he decided not to come back at all?

Down the hall, Lil' Jasper began to cry again. With Chachi gone so long, Renee let Joe and Lydia keep him for the weekend. Life had become a living hell. Jasper must have cried nearly every moment that he wasn't sleeping. He clung to Michael.

Michael tried to take the baby off Lydia's hands as much as he could, but crying babies were not his cup of tea. He finally had to leave her to it.

Lydia's footsteps passed his door and descended the stairs. He listened intently. Maybe she had found a way to calm him. Michael turned over on his side. Just as he reached slumber's threshold, he was yanked away and came hurtling back to Jasper's exasperated shrieks.

Michael swore and threw the covers aside. He dragged himself downstairs in his bare feet. They were in the kitchen. Raspberry-faced and squirming, Jasper wailed until he was breathless. Lydia jostled him in one arm, eyes wide, hair disheveled. "I've raised two babies," she said to Michael, "I don't understand!"

"I'll take him." He held out his arms. Jasper flung himself at him.

"No, no. You've done enough already. Don't you have to get up in the morning?"

Michael shook his head. "No," he lied.

"Well…" She let him take Jasper from her arms. "I thought maybe he was hungry again; he took some of the bottle, but then he started to cry again."

"You've been feeding him all day. You can't stick a bottle in his mouth every time he cries."

"I know. I had two kids, remember?" she said with slits for eyes.

"And two nannies," he reminded her. He didn't want to be mean, but it *was* her and his father's brilliant idea. He hoisted Jasper on his shoulder and began to massage his back. "Hey, hey, hey," he said softly into the baby's ear. "Come on now, little man. Let's go for a walk."

Jasper began to calm immediately with the sound of Michael's voice. "You get some sleep," he called over his shoulder to Lydia when he discovered she had been following them.

"I don't feel right. He's my problem. I should walk with him."

"Go. I've got him."

"You sure?"

Michael glared at her.

"You think you're gonna need this?" She held out the baby's bottle.

Michael shook his head. He used his chin to knead softly into the baby's neck. Completely quiet now, Jasper's head lolled to one side.

"All right then," Lydia said. "Call me if he starts up again!"

Michael nearly laughed. He walked from room to room, softly introducing each room and describing its décor to Jasper who had no idea what was being said, but relaxed to the sound of the voice. "This is the drawing room…"

They made it back to the kitchen and entered the breakfast room. Michael drew the curtains so that Jasper could see the stars...what was that light? He peered through the glass at what must have been a flashlight beam from one of the guards. He shrugged it off.

After a while, Jasper belched.

"So that was the problem, huh?" Michael patted his back. "Let's see if we can do that again."

The baby belched again.

"Oh, good baby!"

Jasper sighed, whisper soft with a hint of sadness.

"Me too," Michael whispered, staring out into the darkness. "I miss Daddy too. What're we gonna do, Jazz?" He stroked the baby's hair and kissed his head. "He'd better come back soon. I'm about three days from being totally mad at him—"

Michael stopped. He heard, or rather felt something. He resumed stroking the baby's head. "The hard part will be getting you to lie down."

"That's the easy part." Chachi's arms came coiling around him and the baby.

"Oh, god…"

Chachi laughed into his neck and kissed him, then the baby, over and over again.

"How did you get in here!"

Chachi kissed Michael's neck again. "Lydia opened the door for me."

"But I didn't hear nothing! When did you knock?"

"I called Joe's cell phone."

"You—"

Chachi's mouth was over his. If Lil' Jasper hadn't been pressed securely between them, he wouldn't have been able to hold him.

"Come here, you…" Chachi took Jasper from Michael as they kissed.

Then Michael watched him hug and kiss the baby. It paralyzed him to watch that beautiful man with his baby. He looked happier, if that were possible. Chachi looked at Michael and broke the darkness with his brilliant smile.

"Chachi, you're beautiful."

Chachi laughed.

Michael shook his head admirably. "And you're so tanned."

"You really missed me, huh?"

Michael responded by laying his hands on the sides of that beautiful face. "You look radiant. You look delicious."

Then Chachi was kissing him again. "I missed you too," he said in between.

"How was it? Tell me everything!"

"Later. I came here straight from the airport to see you. I couldn't wait."

Michael reached up and took his face in his hands again, moving Chachi's lips from the baby's to his own. "I missed you…I love you." He moaned, his breath coming fast.

"Throw something in a bag," Chachi said. "I'm taking you with me."

Michael glanced warily up the staircase.

"I'll handle him. You go pack."

While Michael threw his things in a bag, he could hear his father greet Chachi. When their voices fell to a soft murmur, Michael knew they were discussing him. He also knew that if his father said no, he would climb out a window. By the time Michael finished, Chachi had Lil' Jasper in his outerwear with a designer diaper bag thrown over his shoulder and Lydia and Joe were walking him to the door.

Michael paused at the top of the staircase, not wanting to be presumptuous.

"This weekend…" Joe was saying, "I'll call the fellas…"

"I'm there." Chachi touched fists with Joe, then hugged Lydia. "You coming?" He smiled at Michael from below.

If someone had asked him how he got down those stairs so fast that night, he couldn't say.

* * * *

"So," Michael turned onto his side and leaned on an arm. "How was it? How'd you do?"

Chachi sighed. "I did pretty well with my mother, I guess, though I became a blubbering idiot."

"Aw." Michael stroked his arm.

"My uncle. It was awful at first," Chachi said, his thoughts hurtling back to his confrontation at the hospital...

He was lying in bed with his eyes closed, an old wasp of a man, gray haired and small in such a big bed. Chachi turned away from the sight. The Uncle Zeak he remembered was a robust mountain of a man, or so he seemed. Chachi felt like a bully that had come to beat up on a senior citizen. Papi walked right up to the bed.

Zeak opened his rheumy eyes and studied him. "Well, well," Zeak said after a while. A sly smile tweaked one side of his wrinkled face. "Look what the cat dragged in."

"If we're talking about cats dragging things, I wouldn't say too much if I were you," Papi said.

Zeak began to laugh, a slow creaky growl in his throat that grew into vigorous laughter.

"Papi!" Zeak grinned. His eyes, like Papi's, twinkled with mirth. "So this is what money does for you, huh?" His cataract eyes scanned Papi from head to foot. He took in the manicured nails, and clear skin. "So you come all this way to see what I look like dead?"

"Unfortunately, and I know it's hard to tell, but you're not dead yet, Zeak."

Zeak laughed again, loud and boisterous. He sat up and squinted at the rest of them hanging around the door. "Who's that?" he grunted.

Chachi's mother, Murani moved slowly toward him. His smile evaporated.

"Murani," he said quietly. Tears welled up in his eyes and he trembled as he struggled to sit up. "Baby sister..."

"I'm not here for you," she said in a proud, clear voice. "I'm here for my son."

"Your...son?" Zeak glanced around, confused.

"Chachi. Jasper. You remember him, don't you?" New anger flashed across her face and her fists clenched.

Zeak's old face twisted and he went into a dissertation that he must have repeated over and over through the years. "I told you woman I never touched that boy! You're gonna believe some dead-beat foreigner who left you with the boy to raise by yourself in the first place! I raised that boy! Papi and me! But you let him come here and feed you them lies...and then what? He took the boy from you anyway! Just like that!" He made a failed attempt to snap his arthritic fingers.

"Don't you lie, Zeak, not now!" Murani shouted and advanced on him with targeted fury. Papi had to hold her back. "Don't you lie!"

"Me? Lie? I'm not the liar! He's the liar!"

"Who, me?" Spencer stepped out of the shadows.

Zeak's face went ashen. "W-what is this, some kind of plot? Some kind of plan…w-what are you doing here?" Zeak looked frantically from Murani to Papi. "What? You come to finish me off?"

"No one came to finish you off, Zeak." Papi sighed. "We came to reconcile this thing, put it behind us. You have the chance to go with a clear conscience, but you can't do that if you can't tell the truth!"

"The truth! What do you know about the truth! You weren't there!" Zeak shouted.

"I was," Spencer said, examining his nails coolly before raising his scorching gaze to meet Zeak's frightened one. "And you're a rapist."

There was no sound in the room save the buzzing of machines.

"You're a liar!" Zeak bellowed. "Did you hear him? This…American piece of shit called me a rapist! You're gonna take his word over mine?"

"No, of course not," Papi said.

The lines in Zeak's face relaxed but his gaze continued to dart from face to face. "Okay…so, what's he doing here?"

"I brought him," Spencer looked in Chachi's direction.

It was his cue to step forward, but Chachi was having that lead-in-the-leg problem. He couldn't remember being afraid of anything in his life.

Zeak stiffened and gripped the bed railing. His mouth sagged, then his eyes widened with fear before squinting with pain as he strained to see the shadow standing close to the door.

Murani held out her hand. The moment Chachi took it, his legs were propelled into motion as if a switch had been turned on. He stood over the old man, just looking. The room was dead silent except for the apparatus keeping his uncle alive. It was hard to believe that the dried-up old man in the bed was the muscular, loud-mouthed uncle of his nightmares.

"But…that was a hundred years ago!" the old man whined. "I only tried to help you…Chachi? Is that you?"

Chachi didn't answer. He couldn't answer. He just looked at the man that had been so enormous and overpowering in his head, lying in that bed, connected to tubes and concoctions, looking so…pitiful. All he could think of was that he'd wasted so much energy being afraid to face…this.

Zeak's countenance fell. "I-I-I wouldn't hurt you… You were my favorite. I loved you…all I did was love you…"

"That's what you called it?" Chachi was surprised to hear his own voice. "That's not what it felt like."

Zeak looked down at his hands; Gnarled, old, and leathery, they looked like swollen lobster tails. The arthritis had them curled toward each other.

"Don't worry about it anymore," Chachi heard himself say. Papi, Spencer, and his mother looked at him, surprised. "Go in peace, old man." Chachi smiled and left them in the room.

"But you're better now."

"Yes. Much. Papi and my Dad helped a lot."

"You must've had a great time."

"Fantastic."

"I was beginning to think you weren't coming back."

"Don't be ridiculous." Chachi moaned and stuck his tongue in Michael's ear.

Michael chuckled and shrank from him. "Tell me about your mom, Murani," he said, reaching past Chachi for the pack of cigarettes on the nightstand.

"Wonderful!"

"Really?" Michael grinned and dug in the drawer for a lighter.

"Kind, smart, and very, very beautiful. Here, let me show you." He leaned across Michael and pulled a package from his bag. Michael couldn't resist smacking his naked bottom as he leaned over him. "Hey!" Chachi protested, handing Michael the package and taking the lighted cigarette from him, extinguishing it.

"Photos!" Michael exclaimed. "Oh, look, the flowers are spectacular!"

"You would love it there."

"What are these?" Michael squinted at the rare bloom.

"I have no idea."

"This isn't your mother, is it?"

"That's my sister, Deja, and her kids," Chachi explained. "She named that one for me," he said, pointing to the seventeen-year-old Jasper still holding onto his basketball.

Michael gasped when he came to the photo of Murani. "This has to be her."

"Yeah." Chachi grinned.

"You're right. She's stunning."

"That's what she said about you."

"Me?"

"Yeah. She can't wait to meet you."

Michael examined the photograph. "You've got her smile."

"These are my brothers…Liam and Troi."

"Liam and Troi…" Michael repeated. "You don't look like any of them, except you all have your mother's smile."

"We talked a lot about you, my mother and I," Chachi said, snuggling up to him.

"What did you say?"

"I told her how much I love you."

Michael blushed.

"She understands me, Michael. She's been the only person I've been able to speak frankly with about us. She totally gets it."

"I can't wait to meet her," Michael said, shuffling the photos.

"So, tell me what you've been doing while I've been gone."

"Okay, you ready?"

Chachi lifted a brow.

"We've been working on the plans for the new haven for the homeless!"

"We who?"

"Dad and I!"

"Haven for the homeless…"

"Like a homeless shelter slash half-way house, but I don't want to call it that. It's gonna be more than just a shelter. It's gonna be a place where the homeless can go and learn life skills to get back on their feet or get medical attention—whatever!"

"You serious?" Chachi asked, his brow creased.

"I've dreamed of doing this. I wish there was something like that when I was out there. The nearest shelter was so far that my friends and I just slept wherever we could. We're building it right at the bridge, where I used to stay most of the time. I'm calling it Longbottom Haven for the Homeless."

"After your friends."

"Yeah."

"That's good stuff, Michael. It sounds huge."

"Dad's helping me with it. It's really needed, Chachi."

"That's why I love you," Chachi hugged him, "you're so not selfish."

"The groundbreaking is next month."

"Already?"

"It's just the groundbreaking. The builders anticipate the project completion in about eighteen to twenty-four months."

"I'll be on tour."

"I know." Michael grimaced. "I was hoping you could make a stop—just for a quick ceremony."

"I don't know, Mike. The schedule's pretty tight."

"Please?" Michael pouted. "Nobody could bring awareness to this thing like you could."

"Oh, come on. You've been all over the papers as the boy-wonder who turbo-charged Duke's career. You carry enough weight to bring awareness to your own project."

"It's not just that." Michael moved in closer and lay on Chachi's chest. "I need you. You and Dad. I just gotta have you there."

Chachi screwed up his face. "I'll figure it out."

Michael raised up on his elbow and kissed him tenderly. The kiss went on longer than intended, and soon, everything, photos and homeless haven, were forgotten.

"Hey." Chachi drew Michael close 'til their hips fitted tightly together, his eyes now amber and glistening. "Wanna have breakfast with me?"

"Breakfast..."

Chachi yanked the covers over their heads.

"Hey, Chachi! What are you doing—Ah!" Michael wiggled and laughed underneath the blankets. A piercing cry came from Jasper's room.

"His turn." Michael sighed.

"Yeah, I don't think I can avoid him forever." Chachi climbed out of bed and donned his robe. "I'm not through with you. I'll be back soon."

"Good," Michael called after him. "And when you come back, bring some *real* food!"

Chapter Thirty-Six

They had lamb that evening. Lamb encrusted with some kind of apple-walnut substance and potatoes with an herb-butter sauce with steamed asparagus. As Maxi and her assistants were clearing the table, Joe's cell phone rang.

"You promised to stop answering the phone during dinner," Lydia chided.

"Dinner's over," Joe responded and answered the call. "*What*!" Joe shouted at the caller. Then he turned to his wife, his eyes bulging, and said, "Go turn on the television. Channel two."

Everyone began scrambling from the table. They all followed Lydia to the T.V. room where she found the remote and activated the wall-sized screen. Joe was already making another call. *Claudia*, a popular talk show named for its high-profile host, was in progress.

"Renee!" Lydia gasped.

"Tape it!" Joe barked.

Renee looked striking in a red Chanel suit. She dabbed at her eyes with a tissue. Michael's stomach churned. The camera wide-angled to include Claudia and her ravishing second guest. Michael staggered and fell backward against the wall.

Speechless, his gaze found his father's, but he too had been disabled by the shock of it. Joe's pupils dilated and his mouth gaped.

Sarah sat, resplendent in lavender, next to Renee. Her hands were folded in her lap, her eyes downcast, as she listened quietly. Two years he hadn't seen his mother, but there she sat on national television. Michael stared at her, his brain in chaos. She had lost weight, but she was still captivating.

Michael was ripped with emotion. Anger and relief fought it out as tears burned the back of his eyes. His stomach bottomed out with fear, his fingers tingled with shock.

"Oh, Michael..." Leah murmured.

Joe labored to breathe. David and Eric exchanged wide-eyed stares.

"If you are just joining us," Claudia said as if especially for them, "we are talking live to Renee Lancaster, longtime girlfriend and recent fiancé of superstar Duke Spencer, and Sarah Bagley, mother of boy-wonder and songwriting extraordinaire, Michael Simpson. Renee just dropped a bombshell, alleging that the superstar and his muse have been engaged in a *sexual* relationship that began as early as when Michael was seventeen years old!"

"Bitch…" Michael muttered.

"Renee also admits," Claudia continued, "that the relationship had been concealed by many of the adults in Michael's life, including Michael's billionaire father Joe Simpson, who she describes as one who would 'do anything for Duke Spencer,' even if it meant handing over his innocent son. Also involved in the conspiracy was Joe Simpson's wife, Lydia, and many of their friends."

"What!" Joe exclaimed.

"So, Renee," Claudia went on, "you've been Duke Spencer's girlfriend since high school?"

"College."

"College," Claudia confirmed. "And he's never exhibited an interest in young men before?"

"Well, he liked variety, to put it mildly, but never so young."

"You just recently gave birth to his son."

"Yes."

"He did this while you were carrying his baby?"

"Yes."

"How did that make you feel?"

"Terrible. Cheap." Renee sniffed. "I was stupid enough to believe a baby would change him. I thought we could be a family."

"Sarah," Claudia tried to look sympathetic, but her grey eyes were dancing with the anticipation of a ratings bonanza. "You lost custody of your son nearly four years ago. Why?"

Sarah cleared her throat and blinked nervously. "He had gotten into some trouble. I didn't have any money to help him. He needed a lawyer."

"He was charged with shooting his stepfather, was he not?"

Sarah's head jerked in surprise. She glanced suspiciously at Renee. She shook her head wearily and dropped her gaze before lifting it to fix Claudia with a fierce glare. "It was an *accident,*" Sarah stressed. Her eyes sparked with resentment. "Look, I love my son very much. I swallowed pride and fear to find his father. I was prepared to *beg* for his help."

"His father has billions, yet you struggled to survive. You thought you might have to beg him to help his own son?"

Sarah's eyes blazed at Claudia, who quickly changed her line of questioning. "The judge awarded him custody. Were you surprised?"

"I-I was stunned," Sarah said. "But what could I do? I was devastated."

"When was the last time you saw Michael?"

Sarah took a deep, steadying breath. "Right before I was admitted into the hospital."

"Over a year ago?"

"Nearly two."

"He put you there, the child's father?"

Sarah's brows creased. She sat up, indignant. "Yes, but I needed help! He was trying to help me!"

"Were you in a mental institution?"

"I—No!"

"Reports were that you were in a mental institution, you were not?"

"No. Well, yes…but I'm not mentally ill. My diagnosis was physical—"

"How often did you see Michael when you were in the hospital?"

"Only once, I wouldn't let him visit any more after that. He was denied access. Everyone was."

"Why?"

"I didn't want anyone, especially my son, to see me like that. Michael had been," she sighed, "having a difficult time bonding with his new family. I was sick. I didn't know what would happen. I didn't want him to see me go through the treatment. I knew he would need Joe, so, it was my way of backing off and letting him get to know his father better. I thought I could trust Joe. I had no idea…he would allow this…"

"How did you find out about the relationship?"

Sarah cut her eyes at Renee. "Renee told me."

"Do you blame Joe Simpson?"

"Wha—I, I absolutely blame Joe Simpson! And Lydia and Steven and that…that…child molester!"

"Would you describe Joe Simpson as a good father?"

"I…thought so…"

"Do you believe Joe Simpson turned his head while his best friend had inappropriate sexual relations with his minor son?"

"I…I don't know. I don't understand it!" Sarah cried.

"Why this show? Why do this on national television?"

Sarah sighed. "Renee convinced me," she glanced at Renee, "and I agreed that these men and their friends are so powerful—we would need the reach of television. We have to expose them before they could clean this up…while they aren't expecting it. Michael is just a child. He's impressionable. He's idolized Duke Spencer all his life. It's only natural he would succumb to his influence."

"What should happen to Duke Spencer?"

Sarah growled with venom. "Duke Spencer will go to jail!"

Even Claudia flinched. "Renee, he is the father of your son. How would you feel if he went to jail for this?"

Renee shook her head and closed her eyes, as if her next words were the most difficult she'd ever have to say. "No one is above the law," she said softly.

Claudia turned to face the camera. "More after the break."

"Turn it off," Joe said.

Joe turned to Michael, one brow lifted.

Still in shock, Michael hadn't found his tongue, but he looked back at his father and nodded, almost imperceptibly. There was an eerie stillness. Then every phone in the house began to ring.

"Get Chachi on the phone," Joe said to Lydia, though he was still looking at Michael. "Leah, call Steven and tell him what's happening."

"How'd they get our lines?" David asked, breaking Joe's reverie.

"Who knows," Lydia said, taking the cell phone still clutched in her husband's hand. "Probably Renee."

"Dad, Steve is on his way," Leah shouted from a corner in the room.

"Chachi?" Lydia shifted the phone. "I'm sorry to bother you…no, no…everyone's fine. You haven't heard?" She listened intently. "It's all over the news!"

Joe snatched the phone from her. "Renee is on national television airing your shit out, *everything!* In about five minutes, you will be hemmed in by reporters. You need to excuse yourself and get your ass here directly. Steven is on his way." Joe terminated the call and placed his hands over his face.

Steven arrived with a team of his legal beagles. Joe had his personal assistant call the rest of their staff—publicists, image consultants, managers... The servants were dismissed for the day. They straggled out slowly, trying not to look jubilant.

Chachi arrived shortly afterwards. Michael moved toward him. Distractedly, he gave Michael a hug and a squeeze, briefly brushing his lips against his forehead. "You okay?" he asked, though he looked shaken.

"I'm okay," Michael lied and took a seat.

Steven started in right away. "We knew this could happen, eventually, right?" He looked around the room at the various faces, their eyes downcast, jaws set.

Lydia spoke up. "There's no way to really prepare for something like this. I mean, I had no idea that Joe and I would be attacked the way we have. Have you seen the news?"

Chachi lifted a shoulder.

Michael gripped his hand for support.

"I think we have to issue a statement before opinions are firmly entrenched," Steven said. Beads of sweat glistened on his upper lip.

"A press conference?" Chachi asked.

"Yes, but not you. It'll have to be Joe. We can't put you out there until we know the temperature."

Lydia asked weakly, "But…why Joe?"

Steven's eyes softened. "Joe is Michael's father and Chachi's business manager. His character is being attacked. He has every right to respond. He *has* to respond. We'll put Chachi out there as soon as emotions ebb." Steven turned to Chachi. "Okay, here it is. We can either deny everything or we can tell some version of the truth."

"What version?" Chachi asked in a flat voice.

Joe glared at Chachi scathingly.

"I don't think it would be a good idea to admit you were sleeping together when he was seventeen."

"We'll deny everything!" Michael tugged at Chachi's hand. "I thought that's what we discussed!"

"Witnesses will say otherwise," Steven said. "Renee claims to have confiscated evidence—"

"Kids, go upstairs." Joe shooed them away. Eric, David, and Leah took to the stairs. "You too, Michael."

"Dad, I'm talking to Steven!"

"Joe, I think Michael should stay," Steven agreed.

"No. I don't want him to have to do this."

"He's *part* of this. This is his life, his career. He's old enough now."

"No. Michael, go to your room."

Michael rose slowly, glancing at Steven.

They all huddled in Michael's room like refugee children. Eric and David looked tentatively at one another.

All Michael could think of was his mother. Why was she doing this to him? How could she work with Renee? Where had she really been all of this time? She looked fine to him, why wasn't he able to see her before?

Michael tapped his foot against the floor with increasing speed. His mother purposefully sat next to Renee, his enemy, and set out to destroy him—her own son! He couldn't believe it! "That was my mother, wasn't it?" he kept asking the others.

A commotion downstairs brought Michael to his feet.

"Dad said to stay here!" David called after him.

When Michael reached the entryway, he gaped at the number of people clamoring about, all talking at once. "What is it?"

Joe turned around, exhaling with annoyance. "It's your mother." He had aged fifteen years in the fifteen minutes since Michael saw him last. "She's at security clearance. She wants to talk. She's coming to the house."

"Good." Michael snarled. "Let her come."

Chachi touched his shoulder. "Let us handle this, Michael."

"No!" he spat. "I wanna talk to her!"

"Come here." Chachi tried to embrace him.

Michael pushed him away, fuming. "I want to see her!"

"She has her attorneys with her," Steven announced as he peered through the curtains. "Chachi, don't say *anything* to her—nothing! Do you hear me?" Steven opened the door and Sarah stepped inside. All speaking desisted. Her beauty had that initial arresting affect on people.

She lit into Joe like a firecracker. "How could you!" she yelled. "You were supposed to look out for him!"

"How *dare* you accuse me, where the hell were you!" Joe roared.

"You know damned well—"

"I know nothing!" he shouted, veins protruding from his neck. "And you know nothing about your son or his life or what is really going on, yet you had the audacity to sit your hot ass on national television and *rip his fuckin' heart out*!"

"Joe…" Lydia murmured. He was going to break a blood vessel.

"I'd like to rip *your* fuckin' heart out!" Sarah screamed. "That woman showed me pictures! Pictures, Joe! Of my baby with that…that…" She swung around toward Chachi.

Michael gripped the arm Chachi held firmly across his chest.

Sarah's eyes lit up and softened at the sight of him.

"Michael…" she breathed.

"Don't come near me," he whispered, only because he couldn't speak louder yet. He was too angry.

"Look at you!" She stepped closer. "You've grown so much!"

"Don't touch me," he warned her outstretched hand.

"Mike, I want to explain—"

"Get out. I don't ever want to see you again!"

"W-what? I am your mother!" She stamped her foot. "They were able to get me to run once, but not again. I won't go away this time!" She glared menacingly at Chachi who only blinked with boredom. "Do you know who this is?" She pointed accusingly at Chachi. "Do you know who this man is?"

"Yes, I know!" Michael shouted. "Do you know who *this* man is?" Michael countered, slapping his own chest open-handed for emphasis. "I am not your little boy anymore! Had you been around, you'd have noticed!"

"I was *sick,* Michael!"

"Yeah, yeah, sick." Michael waved his hand, unsympathetic. "So you shut me out, right?"

"I had to! Is that why you turned to him? I expected you'd turn to your father, not this…pedophile!"

"Don't you call him that!" Michael moved toward her but Chachi held him back. "I love him and don't you ever call him that!"

"You *love* him?" Sarah stumbled backward. "Michael! This man is the cause of all our problems." She scowled at Chachi. "You didn't tell him *that*, did you Casanova!"

Following Steven's advice for once, Chachi calmly gazed at her. She could have been reciting poetry.

"He threatened my life, Michael, when I was pregnant with you! He lied to me and to Joe and sent me away! I had you all by myself and had to raise you on the street while they lived like…like…kings!"

Michael glared over his shoulder at Chachi. His mother wouldn't lie about that, still, he didn't care. Chachi was a different man now.

"Here, honey." She stuffed a slip of paper she'd scribbled on into his hand. "Call me. We can talk about it, just us. I want you to understand—"

Chachi began, "Sarah—"

"Don't talk to me!" she shrieked. Steven's raised brow echoed her sentiment. "I will see you behind bars you…rapist!"

Joe said evenly, "I think its time for you to leave."

"And you!" She turned to him. "You are no father! You ought to be ashamed of yourself! You couldn't stand up to him for me and you can't stand up to him for your son either!"

"How dare you!" Lydia snapped. "You forget the small part in the story about his being a married man when you threw yourself on him like a trashy whore! And don't forget Steven, right?" Steven shriveled in his little space by the door. "Weren't you fucking *him* 'til you set your sights on bigger fish to fuck?"

Whoa. Michael thought he had detected a connection between his mother and Steven.

Sarah turned crimson. "You little waif, your husband loved me then and he loves me now! You're just too pitiful to see it!"

"You wish!" Joe sneered. "Now you heard my son. You said what you came to say, now get out."

"No!" Sarah spun around to Michael, her eyes wide with desperation. "I haven't said what I came to say! Michael, I need to talk to you. It's important. Alone—"

"Goodbye, Mom. There's nothing else to say." Michael turned dramatically and walked back up the stairs.

He stood listening at the top of the stairs with Eric and the others.

"Joe, this is important," Sarah pleaded. "There's something I didn't tell you…or Michael—"

"Have a nice life, Sarah. See her out, please," Joe said to no one in particular. Then he too mounted the stairs.

The day dragged on like a long, slow death. The security staff worked overtime to keep reporters and photographers at bay. The public-relations team took up residence at the Simpson mansion to answer calls and issue generic statements. One good thing came out of all the mess. Chachi had to stay overnight. It was impossible to get past the throng camped outside his home.

Papi was practically accosted just trying to get in. He brought fresh clothes and Chachi's bag of toiletries. The phones rang constantly throughout the night. Joe unplugged them at some point. Joe banned the kids from both television and radio. Only Steven and his team kept an ear bent to them while they worked.

Michael made it through the entire day without shedding one tear, which said a lot. He was trying hard to behave as much like a grown up as possible. They lay on the bed, in darkness, on top of the covers, their bodies curving into one another like spoons. It was the first time Chachi was allowed to stay in Michael's room, let alone lie on his bed so late at night.

"You scared?" Michael asked quietly.

Chachi hesitated. "A little," he said.

Michael rolled over so that they were face to face. "Not for myself really," Chachi added, "for you. I hate having brought this on you. I mean, I knew it was coming someday, but now, I just wish I hadn't—"

"I don't regret anything!"

"Be honest, remember?"

"Okay." Michael exhaled loudly. "Well, I'm a little worried about you…and Dad. I'm really sorry Dad got caught up in this."

"He doesn't deserve it."

"No. He doesn't." Michael sighed and lay his head on Chachi's chest. Outside they could hear faint sounds of life, in spite of the late hour.

"What about Jasper? What's gonna happen with him?" Michael asked.

"Jasper will be fine, even if I'm not. Fortunately, he's too young to understand."

Michael could hear Chachi's heart beat through his chest.

"Mike."

"Hmmm?"

"About today…what your mother said—"

"I don't care."

"Sure you do."

"I don't." Michael looked into eyes that had become liquid gold. "I don't care about what happened years ago, before I was even born."

"Still, you should know the truth."

Michael played with a loose string on his comforter.

"She's right, Mike. She told the truth. I told Joe I would offer her the money just to see if she was on the take."

"She took the money," Michael guessed. He had heard stories of his mom surfacing out of nowhere, very pregnant with him and carrying lots of money. No one knew where the money had come from. Now he did.

"She didn't want to take it. I didn't give her the choice Joe thought I had. I told her…that if she didn't leave town…and if she ever showed her face again…"

Michael's gaze bored into Chachi. Even after all that happened, his instinct was to protect her.

"I told her we'd kill her."

Michael sat up and turned away from him. He didn't want Chachi to see how badly he wanted to hit him. "Did you mean it?"

He felt Chachi shrug behind him.

"Well." Michael turned slowly back to him. "She was out to break up a family, steal another woman's husband. Maybe she deserved it."

"But did you? What would have happened had I not interfered? That wasn't my decision to make for him." He paused and sighed. "He would have taken care of you, Michael. Your life would have been different."

A stiff silence ensued. Michael realized he was holding his breath and let it go slowly.

Chachi pressed his forehead against the base of Michael's spine. "I didn't believe her when she said she was pregnant. When she took the money, Joe no longer believed her either." Chachi paused again and rolled onto his back. "I never saw him in so much pain."

Michael sat on the side of the bed. Had Chachi not interfered, he may never have had to sleep in the cold, be sick in the cold, eat out of garbage cans…

"Will you accept my sincerest apology?" Chachi asked quietly, "for you and your mother?"

Michael turned to look at him. He lay back close to him. "Yes. I do," he said and kissed him gently.

Chachi shifted and re-settled his body, holding him close.

Tomorrow loomed ahead of them, threatening and ominous, but that night they lay in a cocoon of safety with family and friends surrounding them, tackling accusations, erecting a fortress of protection around them, preparing a plan of defense on their behalf. It might be the last night of peace for them in a long time. "Chachi?"

"Hmmm?"

"What's gonna happen to us?"

"We'll survive," he said sleepily. "I promise."

"Think you'll perform again?" Michael felt the air being sucked away from his neck.

"No. I'm finished. I'm retiring."

"You don't deserve to go out like this."

Chachi chuckled softly. "What other way is there for Duke Spencer to go out but in a blaze of controversy?"

Michael laughed. He lay still in the darkness. The house had finally come to rest and the sounds outside the door settled into nothingness. All he could hear now was the faint sound of Chachi's breathing. "Things happen for reasons," Michael said softly, "and I'm glad you did what you did to my mother."

"Don't be silly," Chachi mumbled.

"Look at it this way," Michael said. "I could have been David."

Chachi laughed.

"And…you would be my Uncle Chachi, not the love of my life."

"Ummm hmmm," Chachi moaned and held him tighter still.

Chapter Thirty-Seven

They woke to a plethora of news stories involving them. When they came down to breakfast, the table was littered with newspapers and magazines, many of them with their faces on the cover. Joe sat pouring over the periodicals with a cup of coffee. Eric sat next to him, his face buried in a newspaper with the bold heading that read: 'SUPERSTAR SEX SCANDAL' on the front page.

"How much damage?" Chachi asked as he sat down to a cup of Maxi's fresh brew. He nodded his acceptance of a plate of toast but raised his hand to refuse eggs and bacon.

"Lots," Joe said without looking up. "Look at this." He took a sip of his coffee and set down the cup just as Maxi moved to re-fill it. He read: "CELEBRITY HUNKS FIND LOVE—WITH EACH OTHER."

To everyone's surprise, Chachi began to laugh.

Michael, seated next to him with a plate of pancakes, began to laugh too. "Oh, I'm a celebrity now, huh?" he said.

"What about this one." Eric held up a popular magazine: "STARS MAKING MUSIC TOGETHER HIT A SOUR NOTE WITH POLICE."

"Here's one." Joe picked up another publication and read: AMERICA'S HOTTEST BACHELORS HOMOSEXUAL: IS THERE HOPE FOR WOMEN?"

"Glad you're in a good mood this morning," Steven said as he trot in, wearing drawstring jogging pants and a matching sweatshirt. "You're gonna need it." He sighed accepting a cup of coffee from Maxi.

"What happened?" Joe asked, letting the periodical fall to the table.

"Sarah filed criminal charges. They'll have a warrant for Chachi's arrest by end of day."

Michael lost his appetite. Joe put his hands over his mouth.

"What!" Eric exclaimed.

Chachi quietly went on eating his toast.

"It gets worse," Steven said.

Chachi paused, but did not look up. Michael hated the idea that he might be scared or ashamed, or both. He hated the world for making him feel that way.

Steven blew air out of his cheeks. "I think we should turn ourselves in."

"No!" Michael shouted vehemently.

"Michael," Chachi began.

"No!" Michael persisted. "We're not doing that!"

"I'll have him out in forty-eight hours." Steven sighed. The shadows underneath his eyes said he didn't sleep much last night.

Michael turned to Chachi. "I thought we said we weren't doing this. You're not going out like that, are you Chachi?"

"Mike—" Chachi pinched the bridge of his nose. "That was before we could even imagine this shit truly going down. I don't think I have a choice. I trust Steven's judgment, don't you?"

Michael tossed his napkin into his plate, pushed away from the table and stood up. "You haven't done anything wrong! What we do is our business!"

"Not according to the law, Michael, not when you're a minor," Steven said.

"I'm not a minor! I'm a grown, fuckin' man!"

Joe snapped, "You weren't a grown, fuckin' man in those pornographic photos Renee claims she has, so sit down and watch your mouth!"

Michael sat down, trembling, his chest heaving, his teeth clamped down into his bottom lip. "This is ridiculous!" He felt the reassuring touch of Chachi's hand on his knee.

Dominic came storming in, his grey eyes wide. "Problem," he announced between gasps of air. "They're coming to arrest you," he said to Chachi.

"We know," Steven droned, "we're going to turn ourselves in this afternoon—"

"Not this afternoon." Dominic panted. "Now. They're coming now."

"What!" Joe and Steven barked simultaneously.

"I got a tip a while ago from a friend on the inside." Dominic looked at Chachi with apologetic eyes. "I got here as fast as I could."

"I'll get dressed." Chachi stood.

"Sir..." Pratt appeared at the threshold twisting a handkerchief in his hand.

Joe's cell phone rang. "Hold on." Joe put the phone to his ear and listened. "They're at the gate!" he said in disbelief.

"No!" Michael groaned.

"That's what I came to tell you, sir."

Joe turned unfocused eyes on Pratt. "Thank you, Pratt." He turned to Steven. "What's going on? How can they get a warrant that quickly?"

"Can you say 'Witch Hunt'?" Steven answered wearily. "They want him now. They're determined to get him to satisfy the public appetite." He turned to Chachi. "Get dressed as quickly as you can, Chachi. Joe…"

"Yeah."

"Be ready for that press conference at 4."

"Sir..." Pratt had returned.

Joe spun around, enraged.

"They're at the door..."

They all froze. Then Chachi kissed Michael and nudged him toward his father. "Joe, take Michael upstairs."

"No! No, Chachi! We can go away! Don't just walk into this trap, this is bullshit!" Michael gripped Chachi's sleeves like a tourniquet.

"Please take him, Joe." Chachi wouldn't look at Michael.

"Michael…" Joe went to him.

"No!"

"Michael…"

"This is bullshit!"

"*Michael*!" Joe pressed his mouth to Michael's ear. "He doesn't want you to see him get arrested. You wanna see that? Huh? You wanna see them place the cuffs on him and drag him out?"

He didn't want to see it and he didn't appreciate the picture his father painted. "This is crazy," he whispered and let his father escort him and Eric upstairs.

* * * *

They sat on his bed; Joe's arm draped across Michael's shoulder, Eric on the other side of him, solemn.

"How can people dictate who you can be with?" They couldn't hear what was happening downstairs, but he couldn't shake the image of Chachi in handcuffs.

"You had to know that this could happen, Michael." Joe squeezed his shoulder affectionately. "We talked about it."

"I know we talked about it, but Chachi's arrest was not part of the equation. Renee has no proof. There are no *pictures*! If she had pictures, why didn't she give them to the show? And even if she had pictures, who's to say I was a minor when they were taken?"

Eric scowled. "They probably have dates printed on them—*if* they exists."

Joe lifted his hand in an abrupt gesture. "There are ways, but...let's not discuss that right now. We'll just follow the plan."

"What plan? I'm obviously not included in the *plan!*"

Joe rubbed a comforting hand up and down Michael's back. "Lydia's working on Renee. Steven will work on Sarah—"

"I'll *work* on Sarah..." Michael snarled.

"You'll do no such thing. Just the sight of you sets her off. Now we've *got* this. I hate it, but I'll do what I have to for your protection. Public relations are contacting key members of the press to start the damage control and Steven and I will be addressing the public shortly. You just sit tight and keep your mouth shut. Chachi expected this. It's just..." Joe sighed and looked away, mumbling to himself. "As Lydia said, we couldn't have prepared for the way it feels."

"Yeah, but Chachi's still in jail!" Michael shook his head. "I just don't understand it."

"Chachi'll be okay," Joe said, "he made this bed."

Dominic appeared in the doorway. "They're gone."

Joe patted Michael on the back and stood up. "Steven said he'll have him out in forty-eight hours, so don't think on it too much. I've got to prepare for this press conference. You gonna be okay?"

Michael nodded and watched his father join Dominic at the door. "Dad."

"Yeah?" Joe looked back at him.

"I'm sorry about all this."

"Don't *you* be sorry about anything." Joe's face was set in stern lines, but his eyes were soft.

Michael tried to smile, but it came out as sort of a twitch.

"Eric, stay with him, please."

"No, Dad, I'm fine. I wish everybody would stop babying me. Eric, you go. I have something important I need to do."

Michael waited until they were gone. He gazed at the telephone. He hated to do it, but what choice did he have? Steven was right when he said that this was a witch hunt. Chachi's offense was no small one; he might not get out of this one unscathed. He picked up the phone, and dialed.

* * * *

Joe's mouth sagged, surprised to see Sarah back at his door. She was a lot worse for the wear with her tear-stained, swollen face.

Michael called to him from the top of the staircase. "It's okay, Dad."

Michael led her up the staircase to his room, closing the door behind them.

"This is nice, Mikey." She hadn't called him that since he was five. She scanned the opulence as she tried to suppress her envy. "You still have this old thing?" She eyed a portrait of herself on the wall. A life-sized image of Duke Spencer hung next to it.

"Mom, I need you."

She turned to him, her eyes brimming with fresh tears.

"Help me, please?"

"Oh, honey, yes! *Anything*!" In a few long strides she was holding him again.

"I need you to take it back," he whispered.

Sarah stepped back and looked into his face. "What?"

"I love him, Mom. I *love* him. Don't do this to him. For me, please?"

"Michael!"

"This'll kill him. I know, 'cause it's killing me! Renee put you up to it. You can say…that…she made it all up or something…"

"I don't believe what I'm hearing!"

"I swear, Mom, I'll die without him. You have to help me get him out of there."

Sarah stood ramrod still. "How did this happen?" she asked, tears spilling from her eyes. "Did you hear *anything* I said to you earlier?"

"I heard you," he said softly, without taking his gaze off her. "If you want to do something for me, if you want to make it up to me, go to the press. Tell them how Renee tricked you, how she lied."

"But…she didn't lie, did she?"

"'Course she lied!" His eyes went from a liquid calm to smoldering coals. "It isn't like you think!" The fire burned out of his eyes as quickly as it had ignited. "You love Dad, don't you, Mom? People say you're wrong, but you love him still, don't you?"

She stared past him.

"And I was wrong to interfere with that." He took her hands in his. "I'm sorry. But you understand, to love someone you're not supposed to. I know you do. You love him anyway. You have no choice. Will you help me, Mom?"

"Michael, I couldn't take it back if I wanted to. It would be the equivalent of filing false charges."

"You made a mistake!"

"Prosecutors have it now. It's out of my hands."

He turned his back to her.

"I'm sorry, honey."

He shook her hands from his shoulder.

"Michael…"

"You won't keep us apart," he said quietly. "Dad couldn't and neither will you."

For a while, neither of them spoke.

"Michael, there's something I've been trying to talk to you about." She waited for a response. "I told you honey, I've been sick…"

"Mom, I don't want to talk about *you*! Everything doesn't revolve around *you*! If you won't help me, you'll have to excuse me. I have stuff to do."

"Eric and David are here. Leah is in her room. Your mom is going with me." Joe stood at the door of Michael's room with Steven at his side.

Michael could hear the nervous ripple in his father's voice. It also hadn't escaped him that Joe had already begun referring to Lydia as Michael's 'mom,' as if he could erase Sarah.

"You hear me, Michael?"

Michael lay on the chaise in his room, his face buried under his arm. Chachi was in that terrible place for loving him. The helplessness he felt was paralyzing.

"You go. I'll meet you downstairs in a minute," Steven said to Joe. "I wanna talk to Michael."

Steven knelt beside Michael. "Pooch called again. At some point, you should call him back. Joe had to talk him out of leaving school to come see about you."

"I'll call him," Michael said dryly, not bothering to look at him.

Steven sighed wearily. He lifted Michael's arm away from his face. "Your father's getting ready to go out there and stand bare-chested between you and the world.

Michael sat up. "I know. I feel awful."

"Chachi knew what he was getting into. We warned him repeatedly."

Michael's gaze probed Steven's face. "How was he doing when you left him?"

Steven shrugged. "He won't let them see him crack, but you know what it's like."

Michael nodded in painful remembrance.

"It could be worse when you're a star," Steven added. "Who can resist watching a falling star?"

Michael closed his eyes.

"You were too young for a relationship like that. Chachi was wrong to touch you, but you went after him, didn't you?"

Michael blushed, but nearly smiled.

"Your father did everything he could to stop it, but he couldn't stop it, could he?"

"No," Michael said breathlessly. Where was Steven going with this?

"The travesty in all this is that Joe is going to take a major blow to his reputation. He's got issues of his own, but he's a good man. He's always tried to protect you and he loves you immensely. He might have to leave the center."

Michael raised his gaze to meet Steven's. What was he trying to say? "What should I do?" he asked.

"I can't tell you what to do," Steven said calmly, but he gripped Michael's wrist, staring into his eyes. Then he stood and smoothed the wrinkles from his pants. "I have to go. We have a press conference at 4 in meeting room 'A' at the center," he said, as if Michael didn't already know that.

"Tell me what to do!" Michael reached out to detain him.

Steven only took his hand, squeezed it and let it fall. "Grow up," he said and walked out the door.

The room was filled to capacity and buzzing with reporters, camera men, and photographers. The excitement hung on the air, producing a sound similar to the hum of bees. Joe wiped his hands on a towel for the hundredth time while Steve prepped him—again.

Michael peered from behind a curtain, gauging whether it was safe for him to emerge. His father's goal was to gain some measure of public sympathy, stave off the gossip hemorrhage, and maybe even save a career or two. His own was a bit different.

"Don't look so severe! Take a breath!" Steven was straightening Joe's tie.

"I'm trying, I'm trying…"

"Okay," Steven grabbed Joe's shoulders and looked into his eyes. "Be confident. Think before you speak; I don't want you to stumble or stutter, it sends the wrong message. I would do this for you, but in cases like this one, it looks pompous."

Joe nodded and inhaled a ragged breath.

"And remember, I'll be right beside you to jump in if you need me to. Now let's go."

The gay buzz rose exponentially as Joe took his place at the podium. Members of the Spencer-Simpson management team along with his wife and friends stood behind him. He cleared his throat. The buzz fell to a soft hum, then dissipated. Steven began by explaining their purpose. He relayed the rules regarding questions and comments. Then he turned the floor over to Joe.

"Thank you for taking the time to come out and meet with us," Joe began. *"On behalf of my son, Michael, my family and my friend and partner, who you know as Duke Spencer, I would like to—"*

A growing whir of voices rose into a chorus. People pointed and scribbled on pads, cameras clicked and flashed.

Joe looked questioningly at Steven. "What is it?" he asked.

Michael stepped up to the podium next to him.

"No!" Joe said firmly under his breath.

"I'm doing this, Dad," Michael said using the same tone.

"No."

"This is my fight! Not yours!"

Joe sucked in his breath.

Steven stepped between them, his back to Joe. He smiled at Michael. "You sure you wanna do this?"

"I'm ready." Michael rolled his shoulders, exhaled a deep breath and gripped the podium.

"All right then. You know what you're gonna say?"

"Wait a minute!" Joe grabbed Steven by the shoulder. "You haven't even prepped him! You can't let him speak to the press!"

"He's the person most equipped to do it." Steven winked when he turned back to Michael.

The room was nearly in an uproar. People were calling out Michael's name, begging for his attention or just a good shot.

Steven said, "All right, you don't admit to *any* sex, you got that?"

Michael rolled his eyes. "All right."

"Take control from the beginning without anger. You want to show you're mature, not rebellious."

Michael nodded.

"Okay, let's go!" Steven moved to give Michael room at the podium, edging Joe aside.

"Ladies and gentlemen." Steven's voice hushed the crowd. *"Michael Simpson appreciates his father's support,"* Steven glanced at Joe's mortified face, *"but he would like to respond to these allegations himself."*

"Thank you, Steven," Michael's velvety voice coated the room like a tranquilizer. *"As my father said, we thank you for coming."* His words hit silence. *"You represent selected members of the press who have, in the past, demonstrated fairness and compassion in your reporting, and besides a few bad photos here and there—"* the room broke into laughter. *What I'm trying to say is that you've been fair to me. So you've been invited here in hopes that, in this time of crisis, you'll be fair to me now."*

A new hush settled over them.

"I met my father late in life as meeting fathers go. I was fourteen, almost a man. Ideas were already formed, habits made, ways set. I presented more than a problem for this man and his family. Until then, I raised myself. No one told me when to eat, when to sleep, when to leave the club... I had no place to go. I slept here, I ate there, I sold my body for showers, for food, for money. I ate out of trash receptacles. By the time I got to him, I was formed. A soft and vulnerable center with a hard scab. He did what he could and a damned good job of it. He saved my life. And though he could fix some things, he couldn't change who I was no more than you could." Michael swallowed before continuing, *"I hadn't seen healthy relationships. My aunt had six children, yet I never saw her with a man. I saw my mother with too many, and when they weren't beating the shit out of her, they were using her in one way or another.*

"The most love I ever saw between two people before I met my father was the love between a homeless old lady and a homeless old man who slept under a bridge with me wedged between them at night to keep me

warm."

Tears were now in many eyes including those on the set with him. Lydia sniffed.

"I didn't think I would ever know what true love was like. I didn't think I cared. Then one day I did. I don't need to go into details," Michael said, *"it's none of your business."* He paused and glanced at his father. Joe's face was taut and drained of blood as he clutched Steven's arm. *"Please understand my position. I put out the best music I can for Duke and his fans and if they didn't like it, I'd be right back in that studio trying to do better. That's my job. But when it comes to my sex life, my love life, who I fuck or what I fuck is nobody's business but mine and it's my choice...not my mother's or my father's, mine!"* The crowd was so attentive, they nearly stood on their toes. Every gaze was riveted on Michael.

"I know my mother loves me, but she's been misguided. She spent the last two years in a hospital, cut off from me. She has no idea what my father has done, and to say he would allow a friend or anyone to harm me is preposterous! He gave me what she could not and I'm not talking about things money buys. I'm talking about stuff she could have given me, that didn't cost her anything, but she didn't have them to give. I don't blame her. I love her. I'll die for her if I had to. But I'll be damned if I let her or anyone else slander this man." Michael turned to look at his father. *"I don't care who you are."*

Tears glazed Joe's eyes.

"Now, I understand the law and I know right from wrong. But sometimes, everything really isn't as it seems." He leaned over the podium. *"That-man-does-not-belong-in jail. Let him go!"*

If the room could get anymore quiet, it did.

"I also understand and appreciate your concern. There are a lot of abused kids in the world, I know. Don't focus on me because of who I am. Shine your spotlight in those dark places in the world where kids need you. People are outraged, they want to help me, they want to protect me. The world demands a response; so, friends, I ask that you relay this message to those that are so concerned about me. You tell them that when I was hungry, they did not feed me. When I was cold, they did not provide me

shelter. When the federal government cut me out of its budget, they did not fight for me then, don't fight for me now. I have learned to fight for myself."

Michael was breathing hard now. *"You are either for me or against me. If you are for me, trust that I am mature enough to know what I am doing. If you are against me,"* Michael paused a long time, scanning the crowd, *"then kiss my ass."*

The room burst into sound and Michael let security lead him into the next room while Joe and Steven took questions. Once inside, he let himself fall into a chair, deflated. He stood up again when his family came in to join him.

"Holy Christ!" Joe looked like he would fall any minute, but he hugged Michael long and hard. "I didn't think I'd make it through that." Then he slapped Michael promptly upside the head.

"What's that for!"

"Your foul mouth!"

Michael laughed.

Steven looked as though he could have danced a jig. "We'll know soon if it worked." He grinned.

"How do you think I did?" Michael asked.

"Not quite the ending I expected, but, couldn't have been done better."

Chapter Thirty-Eight

Steven was good for his word. Chachi was out within forty-eight hours. Spencer Sr. made it into town by then and went with Joe and Steven to collect him. Michael waited impatiently in the family room with the rest of his family.

"This article says that you said 5 cuss words, mind you, all in the span of a three minute speech." Eric was reading the newspaper. The day's headline, 'LET HIM GO' was in bold face across the front page.

"Whatever." Michael sighed and wiggled his leg anxiously. He was disappointed to see h is father come in alone. "Where is everybody?"

"Steven went home to get some much deserved sleep."

"Where is Chachi?"

Joe peeled off his jacket and sat down. He shut his eyes and massaged his temples. "He wanted to go home, Michael." When he opened his eyes, Michael noticed the dark shadows underneath. "This has been an ordeal for him. He didn't want to see anyone."

"Anyone? He'll want to see me."

Joe leaned back in his chair, exhausted. "I'm sure he'll call when—"

"No. I'm going." Michael turned to leave.

"Michael, give him time…"

"Time for what? He needs me." He was already down the hall.

"There are reporters everywhere still!" Joe called wearily after him. "You'll never get through!"

"I'll get through!"

He was so glad to see Spencer he jumped on him and hugged him tight around the neck.

"Hey, you! It's good to see you!" Spencer smiled, *really* smiled.

"How is he?"

Spencer shrugged. "Who knows? He won't tell me."

"Well, he'll tell me." Michael started up the double staircase.

"His door is locked. He may be sleeping."

When he reached Chachi's door, he found that it was indeed locked. "Hey Chachi, it's me. Open up," he called.

Nothing.

"Chachi?"

Still nothing.

"You know I'm not going…"

The door swung open. Chachi leaned against it fresh from the shower in sweats and a t-shirt. His face was as blank as a wall, but Michael could see sadness in the faded depths of his eyes.

"How you doin'?" Michael asked.

Chachi shrugged in the same manner that Spencer had just done moments ago.

"You *look* okay."

Chachi looked down at Michael's feet.

Michael suppressed an involuntary shiver. "Can I come in?"

Chachi opened the door wider to admit him.

Michael walked slowly around him in mock inspection. "Everything in tact?"

"Please..." Chachi rolled his eyes and walked into the bedroom area.

"I'm just asking," Michael said, following close on his heels. "You know what can happen to a pretty boy like you in lock up."

Chachi frowned playfully. "Well, you should know."

Michael laughed and placed a hand on each side of Chachi's face, making him look at him. "You okay?"

"Yeah."

"You sure?"

"Sure."

"You promise?"

"No."

Michael hugged him hard.

For a few seconds, Chachi didn't move to respond, then he wrapped his arms around him so tight, Michael gasped.

"Were you gonna call me?" Michael whispered in his ear, arms still tight about his neck.

"Of course."

"When?"

"Later."

"That would have been too late."

"I know. I'm sorry." Chachi pressed his face into Michael's warmth.

Michael kissed him, slowly at first, then with everything he had. "No one hurt you, did they?" he asked, breathless.

"No." Chachi assured him. "It's just that—"

"What?"

"That…" Chachi exhaled through his nose and released his grip. "Joe and I spent so much time discussing how to protect *you* when the shit hit the fan, that when it actually hit, *I* was so caught off guard."

Michael laughed and pat him on the back.

"You held me down on this one," Chachi admitted. "You were great at that press conference. I don't deserve it."

"You deserve…" Michael kissed him again, "whatever I choose to give you," another kiss, "Okay?"

"I'm better now," Chachi looked into his eyes and stroked his hair. "You?"

"I feel great, now." Michael grinned, pulling off his shirt. "So come over here and molest me." He loosed Chachi's sweats and let them fall to the floor. Kneeling, he slid his tongue from the navel down, then stood up abruptly.

The look on Chachi's face, eyes wide, skin an explosion of crimson, made Michael freeze, mouth open, horrified at his own insensitivity.

"Oh, Chachi…I was just joking…I just…"

Chachi's face collapsed.

"That wasn't funny, was it?" Michael asked. "Chachi, I'm so sorry! I would never…"

Chachi lifted his pants, went over to the bed and climbed in.

Michael followed and climbed in beside him. "It was a joke. You know that!"

Chachi lowered his head onto Michael's chest and cried.

Michael was so surprised that he began to cry too.

"I'm sorry! I didn't mean to hurt you!" He sobbed. "You know I didn't. I was only kidding...I'm sorry…" His apologies seemed to have no effect so he just shut up. After a long time, they just lay in each other's arms.

"Guess I should get used to it, huh?" Chachi said quietly.

"I'm sorry," Michael said again.

"I thought I was ready for it. I could never have imagined being handcuffed, arrested, charged, *taunted*...watching my career go down the tubes after all I worked to achieve...having to be finger-printed and mug-shot...registered a pedophile..."

"It's all bullshit," Michael sniffed. "I'm sorry..."

"And then—"

"What?"

"She says..." Chachi shook his head.

"Who? Renee? What did she say?"

"Her lawyer called Steven. She's tryin' to take my baby from me." Chachi pressed his face into the bend of Michael's arm, his shoulders shaking.

"Let her try. You're a wonderful father and Steven is the best. This shit has nothing to do with your ability to raise your son." Michael heaved a sigh and held Chachi tighter.

"I'm so sorry, Chachi."

Chachi wiped his face. "Hey," he said, "for you, I'd go through it all over again and again."

Michael slipped his arms around him. "Promise me you'll never leave me," he whispered into Chachi's neck.

The phone rang, startling them both.

"It's your red-line," Michael said.

"God, I hope it's not more bad news." Chachi picked up the phone. "Yeah?" He shut his eyes tight. "He's here. We're on our way."

"What now?"

"It's your mother," Chachi explained, still drying his face on his arm. "She's in a coma."

They drove at break-neck speed, nearly toppling a couple of photographers to get out of the gates.

"Michael, please calm down!"

"It's my fault!"

"Now how do you figure that?"

"She tried to tell me!" Michael groaned. "I wouldn't listen. I upset her!"

"So she tried to tell you something and you wouldn't listen. How does that make it your fault she's in a coma?"

"The stress…the shock…I don't know!"

"Okay. I can see *that*," Chachi said.

Michael groaned. He leaned his head against the tinted glass of Chachi's Mercedes and gazed, unseeing, at the images speeding by.

"Look." Chachi placed a hand on Michael's thigh and squeezed. "Parents expect their kids to get angry and stop speaking to them—even say nasty, mean things once in a while. She knows you don't really mean it, even when *you* think you do. Ask my father. He's an expert."

Michael cut his eyes at Chachi.

"Okay. So I was a special case." Chachi lit a cigarette and took a long pull from it. "She could have just over-taxed herself and had a small brain attack. Your mom is gonna be okay!"

They pulled into the hospital parking lot and jogged to the entrance.

The receptionist's face brightened and all the nurses behind the counter huddled around her when they saw them. The receptionist, a twenty-something gum chewer wearing too much lipstick, typed Sarah's name into a computer and handed Chachi a slip of paper.

They hurried down a long corridor where they found Joe, alone, standing at the end, pacing before a set of cushioned settees. Michael broke into a sprint.

"Hey!" Joe hugged him to his chest. "You made it."

Michael groaned. "I can't believe…we were just *screaming* at her! I said awful things and she could have died…"

"Don't torture yourself," Joe said. "We were angry, all of us. I still am. She's going to be fine, though."

"What did Lydia say about you coming out here?"

"What could she say? Someone had to come until you could get here. They called me and I didn't even think about it."

"Thanks," Michael muttered.

"The doctor is in there now. She'll be coming out to speak with us shortly—hey, Chachi." Joe and Chachi embraced and Michael noticed how his father leaned into Chachi for support.

They waited, mostly in silence, another ten or fifteen minutes before the doctor came out. She was smiling, a good sign, and had bouncy brown hair. She smiled at Michael with her kind face and he was grateful that she wasn't one of those stoic, doomsayer types.

"You must be that golden child she never stops talking about. I'm Doctor Reynolds."

Michael took her hand and held it, more out of desperation than anything.

She placed her hand on top of his. "She's resting," Dr. Reynolds said. "It was a stroke, a small one. We expected this might happen, especially after she signed herself out of the hospital."

"A stroke! What's wrong with her?" Michael asked.

Dr. Reynolds's eyes widened, then softened. "That's right. I forgot. You didn't know."

"We admitted her for drug rehabilitation," Joe offered.

"Yes, I remember." Dr. Reynolds' gaze drifted to the medical chart in her arm. "She didn't want her family to know. She wanted to protect you," she said to Michael.

"Well, it didn't work," Michael said.

"It never does." The doctor smiled. "Would you like to chat in my office?"

"Can't we chat right here?" Michael asked, shifting impatiently.

"Michael," Joe chided.

"No, it's okay." Dr. Reynolds patted Michael on the shoulder. "I understand. You've waited long enough, right?"

When Michael didn't answer, she continued. "It was a brain tumor."

Michael gasped. Joe staggered a bit.

Dr. Reynolds continued, "You're correct. She was initially admitted for drug rehabilitation and that's what they focused on. But when the treatment failed to produce the expected results, they began to suspect other culprits."

"She's always complained of headaches," Michael recalled.

The doctor nodded. "She admitted she got into trouble with the drugs when she began using them to ease the pain after her headaches became worse. They called me in after a team of doctors found the tumor. We removed it."

"Brain surgery?" Joe asked, amazed.

"Yes. The tumor grew rapidly, pressing on the brain. She began hallucinating and losing consciousness. We removed as much of it and the surrounding tissue as we could manage, and promptly began radiation therapy."

"You cut out her brain!" Michael shouted. "You cut out her brain and I didn't know?"

"It was her choice that you not be told," Dr. Reynolds reminded him. "She worked hard to spare you a lot of pain."

Michael was glad to feel his father's hand slip inside his own and Chachi's comforting arm on his shoulder. "How is she now?" he asked.

Doctor Reynolds shook her head. "She was doing fantastic. Then suddenly, she stopped the therapy."

"Why?"

The doctor shrugged. "I tried to talk her out of it. She felt she was well enough. She said there was something she had to do."

"Renee," Michael spat bitterly.

"We think it had already begun to metastasize. The cancer returned."

"No." Michael struggled to breath. "No."

Joe clutched his hand tighter.

"Can we see her?"

Dr. Reynolds shook her head sadly. "Tomorrow." She looked at Michael with the concern of a mother. "We won't know until we run some test but, be prepared for anything."

* * * *

"Can I get you something else before I go?" Joe knelt in front of Michael with a cup of cocoa.

"Can you bring me some clothes?"

Joe came to the hospital every day. Michael never left. He slept in the room with his mother, on a couch near her bed. For three days he had done that. Chachi slept outside the room, pulling the two cushiony settees together as a makeshift bed.

Michael lay with the hospital blanket thrown over him and watched his mother's still form. Doctor Reynolds said the prognosis would darken with each day she failed to regain consciousness.

Before long, the hospital sounds quieted and the lights in the hall dimmed. He could hear the faint rhythmic sound of Chachi breathing. Instead of counting sheep, he studied the contours of his mother' delicate face until he fell asleep.

"Michael," Sarah called softly. "Michael…"

"Mom?"

Michael threw the covers aside and was at her bedside in a flash. "Mom…you okay? Should I get someone?"

"No. I'm fine. I'm glad you came, sweetheart!"

He kissed her. "You scared me, lady."

"I know. I'm sorry," Sarah whispered.

"Dad's been here. Everyday."

She smiled. "That's nice."

Michael smoothed her hair. "Mom, I'm so sorry. I'm such a brat."

"Shhh. You're here now."

"I should get the nurse."

"No, no. I just want to spend this time with you. Come over here, closer." She moved to make room for him. He climbed in beside her and laid his head against hers.

"Michael…"

"Hmmm?"

Sarah cleared her throat and blinked. "Do you see that man there?"

"That's Chachi, Mom!" Michael laughed. "You don't mind, do you? He hasn't once come into the room."

"I don't mind. I've had time to think about this mess. I'm glad he's here to support you."

"He's been here the whole time."

Sarah smiled and ruffled his hair. "He really loves you, huh?"

"I suppose so." Michael blushed.

Sarah chuckled softly. "It's hard not to, you know."

"I know," he said and they both laughed. "I love him too, Mom. I used to wish I didn't, but I do."

"I know, baby." She hugged him gently. "I know exactly what that's like."

Chapter Thirty-Nine

"What's wrong?" Sarah sat up and frowned upon seeing Joe enter her hospital room.

"Nothing," he said. "You look beautiful."

"What, this thing?" She pinched the neckline of her imported lace nightgown nonchalantly. "I just threw this on. I didn't really expect you to make it."

Joe laughed. "You don't look like you wasn't expecting me to make it."

Sarah laughed too. After all, having her hair pinned up and curled, her nails done, wearing full makeup, and sporting an $800 nightgown was sort of a dead giveaway. She let Joe kiss her, just a soft peck, on the lips. She scooted aside to make room for him to sit on the side of her bed. "You okay?" she asked when he was settled.

"I just had a little trouble getting here."

"Lydia?"

Joe nodded.

"Maybe you shouldn't come everday. Maybe—every other day."

"You think it would matter?"

"She hates me, doesn't she?" Sarah pouted.

"Well…yes." Joe chuckled.

Sarah's pout dissolved. Her eyes narrowed seductively. "I'm sorry," she said.

"No, you're not."

Dropping all pretense, she wrapped her arms blissfully around his waist. "You're right. I'm not." She sulked playfully. "Am I terrible?"

"You are," Joe said, smiling, "but I brought you something anyway," he reached inside his bag and fumbled around.

"Wine!" she squealed as he pulled the vintage bottle from the bag. He also unveiled grapes and a wheel of cheese. "You were always so romantic."

Joe went to the wall and flipped the light switch, turning off the harsh halogens. He produced candles from the bag and lit them, arranging them on her bedside table. After he finished, they sat smiling at each other like teenagers.

"How's your pain?" he asked.

"What pain?" They both laughed.

Joe poured the wine into crystal goblets he brought with him and they talked and laughed about everything from the time they were dating to their breakup—subjects that were once too painful to even discuss. Sarah talked a lot about Michael's baby years too, a subject Joe never got enough of. After several hours of this, Joe noticed something abnormal. "Where's the staff?"

"Oh. I gave them the night off." When he lifted a puzzled brow, she explained. "I asked them not to bother us until visiting hours are over."

"What about your meds?"

"I took them before you got here. I can be a little late with the next dose."

"What about—"

"They can be quite discreet. They kept the cancer a secret, didn't they?"

There was an awkward silence after that.

"Joe," Sarah said softly, "let me tell you how sorry..."

"I would have reacted the same way in your position, Sarah."

She nodded sheepishly and toyed with the lace on her gown.

"But you can see now," Joe continued, "what I was up against. I did my best to stop it. I tried to *kill* Chachi, but you know Michael when he wants something. He is *so* enamored with Chachi."

Sarah snorted. "Chachi," she spat, "of all the people in the world, it had to be *him*."

"He's been here, you know," Joe pointed out, "every night."

"Not for me, you can bet on that!" Sarah scoffed.

"Still, it shows how much he's changed."

She put a grape in her mouth and chewed it. "He does seem very different."

"Michael's caused a great change in him."

Sarah gazed at the ceiling. "Do you think they'll last?"

Joe sipped his wine and shrugged. "I love them both and I want them to be happy, just not with each other. I was hoping one of them would have tired of the other by now."

"I saw them together."

"Where?"

"Right over there," she gestured toward the door, "on those settees. Kissing. Michael was all over him. I was shocked."

Joe had grown past the point of being shocked anymore.

Sarah gazed past him as if she were visualizing the scene anew. "Boy," she exhaled dreamily, "to be kissed like that again…"

She locked eyes with Joe, their gazes joined for a long time, contemplating.

Joe rose slowly and locked the door, glancing at the wall clock. He sat next to her and placed his hand on the side of her face, just resting it there. He bent to kiss her and she parted her lips. Then he was on top of her.

She wrapped her legs around him, clutching at the buttons of his shirt.

He froze, panting.

"Why'd you stop?" The desperation in her voice wasn't concealed..

Joe lay still, his faced pressed into her hair, his eyes closed.

"Joe?"

"Sarah...I want to, but..."

She sighed and released her grip. "Don't say another word."

* * * *

"You're refusing the chemo!" Michael chided Sarah as he scooped spoonfuls of her Jell-O into his mouth.

"I *was.*" She glanced quickly at Joe. Michael caught it and felt a pang of jealously. "But I changed my mind. We don't give up, right?" She was talking to him, but there was someone else in her eyes.

"Yeah, right." He tossed the empty Jell-O container onto the tray and started on her applesauce.

"Poochie!" Sara squealed.

"Hey!" Michael abandoned the applesauce to hug his cousin. "Look at this!" He fingered Pooch's newly sprouted beard. "A beard, Pooch?" Michael said, half admirably, half envious.

"How ya doin'?" Pooch gripped Michael's chin with one hand. "I was worried about you with all the shit going on."

"I'm cool," Michael said, returning to the applesauce.

"Hey Auntie, how ya doin'?" Pooch knelt to kiss Sarah. "I got here as soon as I could."

"Pooch, look at you!" Sarah sniffed. "I'm gonna cry!"

"Don't do that!" Pooch laughed. "Hi, Joe."

"Hey, partner. How's school? You done yet?"

"Just about." Pooch smiled at his benefactor and put an arm around Michael's neck.

"Is my sister coming?" Sarah asked, sitting up.

Pooch shrugged. "You know Mom." He chuckled, uncomfortably.

Sarah fell back onto her pillow.

"Steven!" Michael shouted.

Steven entered the room with Chachi close behind him.

Chachi and Sarah exchanged awkward glances.

Steven bent clumsily to deliver a wisp of a kiss. "How are you?" he asked Sarah. Without waiting for an answer, he turned to Joe. "I was just telling Chachi that a contact of mine called with some strange news."

"What?" Joe rose.

"The evidence, the photos or whatever Renee allegedly submitted to the police…"

"Yes?" Joe pressed.

"They're suddenly missing."

Joe glanced at Chachi before turning his gaze on Sarah.

Sarah shrugged.

"What do you mean, missing?" Joe glanced again at Chachi, who shook his head.

"What do you think could have happened?" Michael asked.

"Someone obviously took them, but who?" Joe said absently.

"Renee?" Michael frowned.

Steven said, "Whoever it was knew someone on the inside."

Chachi asked, "So, what does this mean?"

"Can only be good news for you. Perhaps this whole thing will be dismissed—that is, unless enough witnesses to the photos come forth." Steven stole a glance at Sarah who gave him a subtle shake of her head before looking away.

"Anyway—"

"You okay?" Joe placed a hand on Sarah's shoulder. Michael frowned at the look of concern on his father's face.

"I'm fine." She smiled shakily. Her breathing had become shallow.

"Here, let me help you…" Joe began fluffing her pillows.

"Dad…"

A flush of discomfiture crossed Joe's face.

"Can we take a walk?" Michael asked.

Joe straightened up and smoothed his clothes. "Sure."

"Uh…I should go too." Steven smiled. "Get well, Sarah." He gave her another peck on the cheek. "Pooch." Steven nodded in Pooch's direction before slipping out of the room.

"I'll walk Steven out," Chachi mumbled and hurried after him.

Out in the hall, they waited until Chachi and Steven had gone.

"What were you doing in there?" Michael asked.

"Nothing!" Joe put on his best display of wide-eyed innocence. "I'm just trying to make her comfortable."

"Dad."

"What!"

Michael stared at Joe accusingly.

"Michael, really, I'm only trying to help!"

"Dad."

Joe sighed. "All right," he confessed, "I thought you'd be happy to see we'd gotten closer."

"Not *that* close!"

"Well, I know how much you love your mother."

"I love Lydia too!"

"I know…I know, so do I!" Joe walked away, war-weary.

Michael followed.

"I don't know, Michael. I'm having all these feelings…"

"Dad! This is Mom, remember? Nothing's changed. She's sick, and I know that evokes all kinds of emotions but…don't get it confused…"

Joe spun around to face him. "What if I'm not confused, Michael?"

Michael stared at him. "Lydia would be crushed."

"Auntie Sarah!"

Pooch's shrieks shattered the tension between them and they went flying down the hall. When they reached Sarah's room, she was convulsing.

"I don't know what happened," Pooch gasped, "I was talking to her, when all of a sudden, her eyes rolled back into her head—"

"Did you ring for help!" Joe was going for the emergency button, but the room was instantly flooded with white coats jostling them outside.

"My God! She was fine when we left her! Pooch, what happened?" Michael howled.

"I don't know! We were just talking!"

"About what! What did you say?"

"Hey, hey, come on, calm down." Joe put an arm around each of them. "It couldn't have been anything Pooch said. She was looking a little off. I thought something might be going on."

"Jesus, Pooch. I'm sorry." Michael whimpered. "I'm sorry…"

"It's okay. Hey…" Pooch wrapped his arms around Michael.

"What happened?" Chachi returned to find them huddled in the hall.

"We don't know." Joe swallowed. "Looks like she went into convulsions."

Michael left Pooch's arms for Chachi's.

"It's gonna be okay," Chachi whispered. They waited on the settees.

When the doctor finally emerged, they all stood at attention.

"A seizure." Dr. Reynolds sighed as her staff spilled out of the room behind her.

"Is she awake?" Pooch asked.

"Yes, but she's resting."

"What does this mean?" Joe asked.

"It means we start the treatments tomorrow, first thing." The doctor scratched her head tiredly.

"Can we see her?"

Dr. Reynolds nodded. "Only for a short while, though. Fifteen minutes, and I'll have to boot you out. We gave her a pain killer that should put her out in about that time."

They thanked her and slowly filed into Sarah's room. The lights had been dimmed to protect her eyes. Joe and Michael sat on each side of her. Pooch stood next to Michael. Chachi stayed by the door.

Sarah was crying softly and writhing in pain.

Michael began to sob.

Joe placed a comforting hand on her forehead. "Hey, is it too bad?" he whispered. "If it's too bad, we'll ask for more medicine…"

"No," she moaned, "Joe…"

"I'm here, sweetheart. We all are. Just try to rest."

"Joe…Joe. I need to tell you…Michael…the medical records..."

"Mom." Michael sobbed. "What is it?"

"Oh, God…" Sarah gasped, sucking in lungfuls of air, her eyes intermittedly bulging and closing. "Oh God…"

"Mom…" Michael held her hand. Pooch held on to Michael and cried silently. Unable to watch, Chachi turned away.

"Mom, don't you leave me…"

Sarah's hand flew to her head. Her body tightened and she let out a shrill cry.

Michael screamed and held his mother but her cries did not stop. She screamed and screamed. In moments, they were again rushed out of the room.

Joe fell back against the wall and covered his face. Pooch slid to the floor and cried.

Chachi had to throw both arms around Michael. He helped Michael sit.

Michael hugged himself and rocked. His lips trembled as he began to mumble. "He maketh me to lie down in green pastures, he leadeth me beside the still waters, he restoreth my soul, he leadeth me in the path of righteousness for his namesake…" Michael paused.

"Mike," Chachi pulled him close.

Frustrated, Michael pushed him away. "Yea…though I walk through the valley in the shadow of death, I will fear no evil, for thou art with me, thy rod and thy staff, they comfort me, thou preparest a table before me in the presence of mine enemies, thou anointeth my head with oil, my cup runneth over…."

Dr. Reynolds came out. Her face was drawn. She looked at Michael and smiled, but it was laced with sadness. "She's sleeping now," she said quietly. "I don't think it would be a good idea for you to see her again tonight. Go home and try to rest. She's going to need you tomorrow."

"You'll start the treatments in the morning?" Joe asked.

"Yes, if she's up to it." The doctor sighed. "But, I can't promise anything at this point. Good night." She turned and her heels clickety-clacked down the quiet halls.

Michael inhaled through his nose. "…surely goodness and mercy shall follow me all the days of my life, and I will dwell in the house of the Lord forever..."

* * * *

Between the chemotherapy and radiation treatments, Sarah looked old and wasted, but Dr. Reynolds said that the tumors appeared to be shrinking.

Michael sighed and lowered the book he was trying to read. Chachi was planning to go away on business. He had to meet with certain sponsors who wanted to cancel his endorsement contracts due to the recent scandals.

"Psst," Chachi hissed from the doorway.

Smiling, Michael dropped the book and met him at the door with a warm hug.

"How is she?"

"Fine. She's in and out."

"Where's Joe?"

"Gone home to shower and for dinner with Lydia,"

"Good."

Chachi cupped Michael's face and tilted his head back for a long, sensuous kiss.

"What time is your flight?" Michael asked after Chachi let him up for air.

"In the morning."

"Commercial?"

"Yeah, red eye."

"When are you gonna buy that plane?"

"It's just so much money, and since I don't travel nearly as much as I used to…I don't know if it'll be worth it."

Michael grinned. When they met, it was nothing for Chachi to think about dropping thirty to forty million dollars on a plane.

Michael sensed movement in Sarah and turned to look at her. She appeared to be sleeping soundly.

"I told you your mother was a warrior," Chachi said with a wry smile. "It's gonna take more than cancer."

Michael laughed and flat handed Chachi in the chest, ending up with a fistful of his shirt, which he used to pull him closer. "How long will you be gone?" he whispered, his forehead pressed against Chachi's chin.

"Three days..." Chachi whispered back, his eyes closed. He had his hand inside Michael's jogging pants squeezing his left buttock.

"Mmmm…" Michael moaned.

"Come on." Chachi smacked his butt and pulled away. "I just came by to see how things were. I don't wanna leave you if—"

"Everything's fine. Go." Michael stood on his toes to kiss him again. "Go so that you can hurry back."

Chachi would remember everything about that night from the sickle-shaped moon that stared down at him through his skylight, to the way he seemed to awaken just in time for her phone call to shatter his dreams. Icy fingers crept across his skin and he let the phone ring a few extra times before answering.

"Sarah who?" She was the last person in the world he expected would call.

"I need to see you," she said in a breathy voice that reminded him of Michael so much, that his feet and palms went moist. Having never spoken to Sarah on the phone before, he hadn't realized Michael had gotten that sexy voice from her too. Seems when he'd exchanged words with her in the past, she was usually squawking. Now, sedate and serious, her voice traveled through the phone lines as smooth as a wave of silk. "I know I have no right to ask…"

Nestled in the rear seat of the limo with a mimosa in his hand, he watched the landscape float by and pondered the possible purpose of this visit. Finally, just her and him…

He pulled into the service area as she instructed and was met by an orderly who let him inside, locking the door behind them. Save for the security guard at the desk and a lone nurse pushing a rolling cart, all was still and quiet. They stepped onto the elevator and rode up to Sarah's floor.

Passing the door behind which he knew Michael slept, he fought the impulse to stop and look in. He continued past until he came to her room, where she waited.

She appeared too small and the room, usually alive with people and sounds during the day, seemed artificial and cold during the night. Sarah lay with her hair spread out, like wings, across the king-sized pillow. Her eyes were shadowed with dark circles underneath. With some effort, it seemed, she tilted her head to acknowledge him. She was still beautiful.

Out of habit, he stopped at the door.

"At the risk of sounding cliché," she began, "come in…I don't bite."

"Maybe you don't, but I do," he said as he approached the bed and sat down.

She laughed, a light tinkle that stabbed the air and faded. He looked down at her hands. She was small-boned, her hands so tiny, they could have been a child's. Her body, covered by a sheet, seemed to be disappearing. Finally, his gaze met hers. He understood.

"So you were right." She smirked. The voice coming from her frail body was oddly strong and sexy. Chachi's brow crinkled. "You said you'd see me dead before you'd let me have Joe. I guess you meant it."

His eyes widened with horror.

She lay a hand on his arm. "I was only kidding," she whispered.

He trembled and a glimmer of a tear wavered precariously on his lash.

"My, my," she teased, "is the great Duke Spencer crying?"

He clutched her tiny hand and the tear fell, making a path down the side of his nose before falling softly onto their hands.

"It's okay," she said quietly, but her own tears were streaming down her face.

He loosened his grip and she slid her hand from underneath his. He cleared his throat and dried his tears. She pulled the sheet further up her neck as if to hide herself.

They sat, listening to the sounds of night for a long time before she spoke again. "I forgive you."

"What?" He leaned toward her.

"I forgive you. That's why I called you here. To say that."

"Thank you," he mumbled without looking at her.

"And…I'm sorry," she added.

He looked toward the ceiling and then down again. He breathed deeply.

"I called you here to say that too, and to ask you a favor." She took a breath so deep, her fragile body shuddered as she let it out. "I know you hate me…"

"No, I don't."

"I helped ruin your career; a lucrative, longtime, successful career."

Chachi exhaled hard and closed his eyes.

"You were…great," she continued, "the best in the business. You know that, don't you?"

He opened his eyes, but he couldn't look at her.

"I'm really, really sorry. You *should* hate me…but you love him, don't you?"

His jaw tensed.

"Our only crime against each other, Chachi, is that we love the same people. And when we love, there is no room for anyone else. Chachi?"

He inhaled long and slow. Sarah seemed to sink into the pillow, exhausted already. "Have you told him?" he asked.

"No." She fingered her hair nervously. Long strands of it came out in her hand. She looked at them strangely. "No."

"He has a right—"

"I want these last days for him to be…hopeful ones…happy ones."

"And Joe?"

Sarah sighed and gazed wistfully past Chachi.

"Joe was a beautiful dream."

"What do you want me to do?"

"I want you to look after Michael." Her eyes were too large in a face that had become thin and drawn. "Always," she said, "no matter where you are in the world, who you're with or why. Promise me you'll always look after him."

"Until my heart stops," he said as fresh tears sprang to his eyes.

"Thank you. Joe has his wife and other children, and though I know how much he loves Michael, no one loves him like I do, except you." She smiled, a genuine gesture of friendship.

"When?" Chachi asked.

Sarah looked down at her hands. "Oh, I don't know."

"Should I stay?"

"No, no. Take your trip. I have things I need to take care of too."

Chachi covered her hand with his own. Her fine bones seemed to give-way in his grasp. "You're no quitter."

"Oh, but I am, Chachi. I am." She turned onto her side and grasped the pillow tightly. "I just can't do it anymore. I don't want to waste away. I don't want Michael to see me waste away." He held a hand out to her and she took it, allowing him to lift her up for a hug. She cried into his chest. "Well," she sniffed when she was done, "that was a historical moment."

They laughed softly before he lowered her gently onto her pillow.

"You shouldn't miss your flight."

"Oh, yeah." Chachi stood. "I should be going."

They held each other's gaze a while longer.

"Thank you for coming, Jasper Dukakis Spencer." She gave him a look reminiscent of the old, feisty Sarah. "I'm glad we had this chat. Wish I could have known you better."

He nodded and walked to the door. When he opened it, he saw that his guide, the orderly who escorted him before, was dozing on the settee. "Oh, and Sarah..." He turned to address her one last time. "I forgive you too."

He walked away, leaving the tinkle of her laughter behind him.

Chapter Forty

"Look, Mom, it's a Viggo Vantelle original." Michael held up the designer hat Eric picked up for him and brought to the hospital. It was not what he had in mind, but then, that's what he got for assuming everyone had his good taste.

"I am not wearing a hat in a hospital bed, Michael," Sarah grimaced, "though it was sweet of Eric," she added to the embarrassment on Eric's face.

"Your hair is falling out." Michael abandoned the hat and reached for the lip balm, slathering some on her lips.

"I say cut it all off," Joe said.

"My hair?" Sarah and Michael gave him identical frowns.

"It'll grow back..."

Michael finished her lips and began to gently gather her hair into his hands. "Here," he said, thinking out loud, "we can pull it into a soft bun, so that there's not much tension on it."

"No, no, no, Michael!" Sarah swatted his hands away. She slumped into her pillow. "Joe, get him..." She lay gasping. "I'm sorry, honey," she tried to reach out for Michael, but her hand fell weakly at her side. "I know you're just trying to help."

"One more treatment, Mom, one more. Dr. Reynolds said one more should do it."

"Yeah, one more should do me in." Sarah rolled her eyes. She reached up, this time successful in touching his face. "Does it really matter, sweetheart?"

Michael frowned, puzzled

"You know I'll never really leave you, don't you? You know that."

"Don't talk like that!"

"Michael, we have to face the possibility—"

"I said don't talk like that!" Michael shouted and stepped back.

"All right," Joe said softly, his voice strained. "Eric, won't you take Michael to lunch—"

"I'm not leaving her!"

Eric began, "Actually, dude—"

"I'm not going!" His breathing was coming faster.

"Come here, baby," Sarah said.

He lay his head on her fragile chest and closed his eyes.

"You can never lose me," she whispered. "Never. No matter what happens, you are gonna be okay." She made a weak attempt at stroking his hair. "Now go. Go with Eric and have a nice lunch. I need some time with your dad."

"It can work if you fight, Ma."

"I know. Okay." She nudged him so that he sat up. "Go get some fresh air. Eat a big, greasy steak for me. Don't worry about me; your mama is just fine." She smiled.

"Okay." He stood and Eric took his arm before he could change his mind.

Her pain was great, making her agitated. Joe held her hand.

"Joe…" she rasped. "Joe…"

He looked at her, but only briefly. He couldn't stand it and returned his gaze to his feet.

A nurse interrupted their silent battle bringing Sarah's pain medication. The nurse bid them good evening and left the room.

Sarah lifted her frail arm with great effort and removed the pill from underneath her tongue. She opened the side table drawer and added the little miracle worker to the rest of her collection. She should have enough now. She fell back, exhausted.

"No," he whispered.

"Baby, we talked about it."

"No, we didn't!"

Sarah lay quiet, her chest working furiously to accommodate the beating of her heart. "It hurts so bad, Joe."

"Sarah, no! It'll get better once the treatments—"

"Joe, look at me!"

He *had* looked at her. He saw the shedding hair, the charred, dry skin, the skeletal body. But he loved her.

Her dark eyes blazed at him from their sockets. "You and I both know the truth."

He looked away. He just couldn't let her do it. He could live without her, knowing that she was somewhere in the world, but what would life be like without even the possibility of her in it? "Let's just see, honey," he said. "Let's just see what the tests say."

"I'll never get another chance. Not with Michael around, not once the doctor returns. I may not be strong enough next time and I cannot do this anymore!"

"Sarah..."

"Joe, please! I—" Her head jerked back.

"*Sarah*!"

"What time is it?" Michael asked, looking at his watch.

"Ten minutes to 8," Eric confirmed.

"We'd better get back. We won't be able to get back in after visiting hours."

"Come on." Eric took Michael's arm and led him through a sea of gazes to the door. A small group of people at the entrance clamored to get in. The Maitre-d had his arms spread wide to hold them back. "Photographers!"

"There he is!" A woman pointed at them. The group rushed them. The restaurant manager joined the Maitre-d in trying to keep them at bay.

"Michael, did you hear the news about your mother?" the woman asked, holding a microphone in his direction. Her eyes danced with ambition.

"My mother?"

"Come on!" Eric grabbed him and pulled him in the opposite direction.

"Did they say my *mother*?" Confused, Michael let himself be led, nearly dragged by his cousin, but he couldn't stop watching the cluster of reporters calling his name.

"Michael, are you devastated?"

"Is there another exit?" Eric yelled. Guests were standing and craning their necks, trying to see the cause of so much activity.

The restaurant manager caught up with them. "Your car is surrounded, but I'll have someone drive you. This way, please." He led them through the kitchen and onto a service elevator.

They rode down to the basement level, cut through a parking garage, and came out at the back of the restaurant. A delivery car was waiting.

"No one will suspect you'd be in this vehicle. I'll make sure your car is delivered to you safely," the manager promised.

Eric's cell phone rang. He stopped in his tracks, listening intently.

"Who is it?" Michael asked.

"Get in the car. I'm coming." He pushed Michael toward the vehicle, climbing in after him.

"What?" Michael asked anxiously.

Eric disconnected the call and pulled a business card from his wallet. He scribbled something on the back.

"It's my mom, isn't it?"

Eric nodded, but he kept to his task.

"What happened?" Michael's voice cracked, on the verge of tears.

"She had another seizure," Eric said evenly.

Michael's breath caught. He gripped the leather seat beneath him. "Is she conscious?"

"No," he said softly. He squeezed Michael's knee with one hand and handed the card to the driver with the other. "As quickly as you can, please."

The press had the gates surrounded so that security was unable to admit the car without risking admitting half the press too. Security had to abandon the tower and physically restrain the crowd while the car rolled slowly inside.

People hung onto their car, faces pressed against the window, mouths moving wordlessly. Several tried to climb the twenty foot wrought-iron fence. Eric offered a hand to Michael for comfort, but Michael sat rigid, stoic, watching.

As they exited the car, Lydia, David, Steven, Dominic, and Leah stood at the door. When Michael stumbled, Steven moved to assist him.

Lydia touched his face and Dominic put an arm around him.

He shook them off. "Dad…" he pushed past them.

The house was dark with the stillness of gloom and the entryway seemed to grow with every step.

"Joe, Michael's here," Steven said.

When Joe appeared puffy faced, red eyed, and shaking, Michael's world twisted. He cried out and gripped his belly with both arms.

"I'm…sorry, baby…" Joe stammered.

Michael hit the marble floor like a sack of bricks.

* * * *

"I'm here," Chachi whispered softly.

Without opening his eyes, Michael rose and threw his arms around Chachi. "You came."

"You knew I would."

"They're saying she's dead."

"I know. I'm sorry."

"But I don't feel it."

"It's such a shock."

"No, I would feel it if she were dead. Wouldn't you feel it in your heart if I was dead?"

"Yes. I think so."

"I don't feel it in my heart."

Chachi eased Michael down onto the bed.

"I need to see her." Michael sucked in a ragged breath. "I wanna see for myself."

Chachi nodded and thumbed fresh tears away from Michael's eyes. "Tomorrow," he promised. "If you're up to it tomorrow, we'll go together, but right now, you should sleep. What happened to your face?" Chachi traced a bruise down the length of Michael's cheek.

"I fell..."

"Ah. Poor baby."

"Are you leaving?"

"Not until you say I can go. I'll be right next door."

Within minutes, Michael was asleep again.

On another day, they could have all passed for a wedding party. His father looked handsome enough in his black suit to be the groom on top of a wedding cake. Lydia was pretty in a cream chemise with black piping and a wide-brimmed black silk hat with little cream roses. Michael wore navy, an outfit Chachi in his infinite good taste chose for him. It had a straight-collared, three-quarter length jacket with matching pants. With it, he wore a high-buttoned shirt in the palest pink, no tie. Chachi, as usual, looked like a god in grey. Pooch wore black with brass buttons, David and Eric also wore black and his sister wore a 50's style white dress revealing pretty legs and a tightly cinched waistline. They could have been a handsome group on their way to celebration, had it not been for their swollen, red eyes and the hearse parked out front.

Rain fell all morning and the night before, but the skies were clear now that the weather decided to be friendly. As Michael stepped out into it, he was assaulted with many emotions: appreciation for the beauty of the day, love for his family milling about him, and bone-crushing sadness. He climbed into the hearse with his father, Lydia, his brother and sister, his auntie Melanie and Pooch.

Chachi smiled sadly down at Michael. "I'll meet you there. I'm driving my own car." He blew Michael a kiss and closed the door before he could protest.

Joe began to cry again. Michael put both arms around his waist and lay his head on his shoulder. He had been doing that a lot lately, comforting his father. It kept his mind from giving his heart up to his own grief. Lydia reached over and held Joe's hand, but she sighed as she did each time he broke down in her presence.

The car stopped and they waited, glancing nervously at one another. Just as he began to wonder at the delay, he could hear them removing his mother's casket from the rear of the vehicle. Outside, Chachi, Jake, Dominic, Spencer, and Uncle John all gathered round for pallbearer duty.

Michael turned to avoid glimpsing the casket draped with tufts of tulle and pink tulips. After a while, the doors opened and they all stumbled out.

How full the church was. Nearly everyone from the center was there. He waved at Illian, who was holding a tissue to her tear-stained face.

He averted his gaze when they reached the front and an attendant motioned for him to take the front pew. Pooch and Eric each sat on a side of him. Aunt Melanie and her children completed the row, while his father and Lydia slid into the row behind him.

The coffin remained covered as the services began. After the choir, friends close to them spoke. Michael choked on tears and had to steel himself when his old minister stood up to deliver the eulogy.

The mood shifted and the attendants surrounded the coffin. Pooch began to wail. Michael gripped the edge of his seat and watched out of the corners of his eyes as they stood, one at each corner, and to his horror began to lift the tulle and tulips covering Sarah's casket. A soft, pink light glowed inside and his mother lay bathed in it, in her glass bed on white satin cushions trimmed in fur. She was wearing a white mink; one bare leg strategically on display, illuminated for all to see. Her hair was spread about her shoulders in soft highlighted ringlets, a very good hairdresser's magic. People lined up for viewing. One by one, they stood at her coffin and looked in, more awe on their faces than sadness. They filed past Michael and his family. Most stopped to offer kind words. Others touched his hand, hugged, or even kissed him. He wished they would leave him alone.

Once all the guests had viewed the body, the family was led to the coffin. Pooch linked arms with Michael, but he pulled away. He had wanted to see her. He wanted proof that his mother, who he thought would live forever, was dead. But now, he couldn't bring himself to it. Besides that, he couldn't have stood on his legs if he wanted to. Joe tried but Michael held firm, staring straight ahead, vigorously shaking his head against the words his father was speaking quietly into his ear. He thought of making a run for it. Where was Chachi?

Chachi appeared and nodded at Joe, sinking down beside Michael and wrapping his arms around him.

Michael ignored the gazes on them and melted into Chachi's chest, weeping as the others went without him to view his mother's body. He could hear Pooch's loud cries peppered with the sniffles of others. He held onto Chachi tighter.

Michael breathed a sigh of relief when they returned to their seats, grateful he wasn't going to be made to go see her. He may have had to make a fool of himself if that happened.

To his dismay, he saw Chachi nod to the attendants. They began to roll the coffin toward him.

"No..." he mumbled and shook his head, but his gaze locked on the tiny form in the casket, resplendent in white fur and silk, nearly as beautiful in death as she was in life.

“No…” he said again, but he sat up and looked at her, his mother, lying peacefully in her coffin, her hair splayed about her shoulders, her lips frosted a petal pink.

He identified every familiar inch of her. It was all there: the beauty mark barely visible on the right side of her nose, the faded scar near her left ear where she had once been slapped so hard by Jaye the skin had broken, the faintest hint of an almost crooked smile…

“*Mom*!” He arched his back so far over his pew in spite of Chachi’s restraining arms that Joe, sitting behind him, had to grip the back of his neck to keep him from toppling completely over. His pain shot out in all directions. The soft rise and fall of weeping permeated the room full of people, most of whom did not even know his mother. His heart writhed and twisted inside of him. He didn’t feel the strength of Chachi’s arms holding him nor Pooch’s hands on his face. He didn’t hear his father’s comforting words in his ear. All he could hear was his own cries in his ears, desperate and gut wrenching, and knew his heart had permanently broken.

* * * *

Morning was brutal. Michael woke to rays of sunlight on his face, a beautiful clear day, and emotional paralysis.

Joe let him sleep, if you could call it that. For nearly a week, he lay between sleep and wakefulness in so much anguish he could no longer cry. He took spoonfuls of Maxi’s soups and sips of water just so they’d leave him alone. He slept but he didn’t rest. He didn’t bathe, he didn’t even have the energy to speak.

His family hovered over his bed.

“Michael,” Chachi said. “Joe, when was the last dose of medication?”

“I stopped giving it to him. I don’t like him sedated all the time. Dr. Murphy’s bringing another antidepressant.”

Michael gazed sightless and unblinking past them.

“Hey.” Chachi leaned close. He drew his head back in surprise. “Okay, this has gone too far." He began yanking Michael's bedding away from him.

"What?" Joe asked.

"In all my years with Michael, I've never known him to stink." Chachi tossed pillows to the floor. "Have somebody clean this bedding!" He disappeared into Michael's bath. When he returned, he lifted Michael from the bed. Michael began to struggle. "Good. Still got some fight in you, huh? Come on, Mike! Let's fight!"

Michael grit his teeth and growled. Chachi hesitated, brow raised. He hoisted Michael, kicking and flailing over his shoulder.

"Good," Chachi shouted, "let's get that blood flowing…phew!"

Chachi dumped him into the tub, splashing water all over. He gripped Michael's struggling arms and held them behind him. It wasn't a small task, Michael had inherited his father's unnatural strength.

With one hand, he finally had Michael pinned and gasping. He used the other to reach around him for a bottle of bubble bath.

"Here, smell this." He grabbed a sponge and poured a generous amount of the purple goo onto it. Michael turned his head away.

"Chachi…" Joe was in the doorway, blocking the view of this scene from the kids in the room behind him.

"Smell it!" Chachi demanded and thrust the sponge under Michael's nose. "Remember that? You love this stuff…" He began to rub the sponge around Michael's neck. Michael released the grip on his arm.

"Chachi," Joe said.

Chachi began to peel off Michael's clothes.

"Chachi!"

"What!"

"You're not going to give Michael a bath!"

"Yes, I am!"

Joe lowered his voice. "I don't think Eric and the kids need to see you do this!"

"Then get them out of here!"

"I don't believe you!" Joe said.

Chachi went back to his task. Michael tried to fold himself, but Chachi forcibly made him straighten up.

"Here, I'll do it!" Joe moved to take over.

Chachi stood up in challenge, his legs spread apart.

"Have you lost your mind too?" Joe asked.

Chachi only blinked. Maybe he had.

"We all know you and Michael have a *relationship* but if you think you're gonna rip his clothes off and bathe him—"

"Get over it already, Joe!"

Joe sighed. "Can we talk calmly about this? I don't wanna fight with you in front of Michael on top of everything else."

"Cool." Chachi said calmly. "Step outside."

Joe glanced at Michael who had curled himself up, his knees drawn to his chest, his head resting on the ledge of the tub.

"He'll be okay." Chachi nudged Joe toward the door.

When he had him across the threshold, he closed the door, locking it.

Minutes later, Chachi opened the door. Joe was still standing there, his mouth a grim line.

"Get me a robe, please," Chachi said tiredly.

They lifted him out of the water. Chachi threw Joe a towel and went about the business of drying Michael's flawless skin.

Michael lay against Chachi as he moved the towel smoothly across his body.

As he neared the boy's genitals, Joe objected.

"That's enough," he said, wrapping Michael's robe about his shoulders. He held Chachi's light brown eyes with his own midnight black ones. "Those can air-dry."

They propped him in a chair so that Chachi could brush and floss his teeth and scrape his tongue. Then Chachi carried him gently into the bedroom and lowered him onto the freshly made bed.

Joe knelt so that he was looking into his son's face. "Better?" he smiled. "You look better."

Michael blinked and turned his head away.

"If you don't get out of this bed soon, Michael, I might have to put you in a hospital. I don't want to put you in a hospital."

"He's not going to any hospital," Chachi snapped, rubbing oils into Michael's feet. "I'm gonna stay with him 'til he snaps out of this."

Joe's eyes narrowed. "I know what you think you're doing, but you're not doing it here!

"What?"

"You know my rules. You know what I mean!"

"Look, Joe, you know Michael when he shuts down. He can practically will himself into a coma. You can't just let him lie there day after day and hope he pulls it together, not after he's been down a week!"

"You stay in the guestroom, Chachi. That's the rule."

Chachi finished with Michael and sat down on the side of the bed. He began removing his socks and shoes.

"I mean it, Chachi."

"I'm sure you do, Joe."

"I'm serious. I know you. Don't you see? He's sick! I don't want you touching him!"

"Okay." Chachi stood. "I'm tired. I'm just gonna lie here and keep an eye on him. Tell Maxi I won't be down for dinner."

Joe screwed up his face and raised an accusatory finger.

"All right, all right, I heard you!" Chachi nearly pushed him to the door.

Joe stole a glance at Michael. He had buried his face in his pillow. "All right then," Joe said. "You call me at the slightest change."

"Okay."

"I mean it!"

"I know. Bye."

For the second time, Joe had his own door closed in his face.

No sooner had Joe's footsteps faded than Chachi shed his clothes and climbed into bed with Michael, taking the oil with him.

"Let's see if we can't get a rise out of you," he whispered. He began at his neck, massaging the oils gently into the skin, and moved up to the face and head, applying pressure at the temples. "Come on, give it up..."

He moved downward, using his thumbs to press into the grooves of the shoulder blades and down both sides of the spine. He felt the tension release—a little. "There you go…"

He used the balls of his fists to apply pressure at the base of the buttocks. Michael groaned. He moved down to work on the feet and slid both hands up the body, up the neck for another scalp massage. "You told me you would never let me go," he whispered, "remember that?"

Michael didn't respond, but Chachi could tell that his breathing had picked up.

"You're alive, Michael. You're not dead. Feel something!"

Chachi gently pulled his head back and kissed his lips. "You feel that?" he breathed before kissing him again. He turned the limp form toward him and ran his tongue down the length of his body, lingering in selected places. He got traces of the response he was looking for. "You feel that, don't you?"

He retraced his path back to the mouth and, this time, his kiss was answered, slowly at first, then hungrily. He gripped Michael's buttocks and used them to press his body close. "You feel that?" he muttered into Michael's mouth against the first real sounds of awareness he had uttered in a week. "That's me, baby. I'm here. I'm here with you. I love you, Michael."

He moved hard against him, losing himself in his task. Michael wrapped his legs around him. With every stroke, Chachi felt him give him a little more. "That's right, give it to me. Give it to Daddy…"

He had to press hard against Michael's mouth so that they would not be heard. By the time it was over Michael was sobbing. "That's okay. That's good." Chachi pressed Michael's face into his chest. "I'm here."

It seemed a long time before he slowed to a sporadic sniffle. The room darkened as daylight failed. They could no longer see each other's faces.

Chachi began to hum to him, then to sing. He sang in soft, low tones. Michael became very still. When he finished, they lay in each other's arms in the moonlight, their breathing synchronized.

Chachi's voice rose above them in the darkness. "Talk to me, Michael."

Michael removed his arms from around Chachi's waist and placed them around his neck.

"Tell me something, anything, just say something."

Michael pressed his mouth against Chachi's ear. Nothing came for a while, though Chachi could tell he was trying to get something out. Hopeful, he inclined his ear for better listening.

Michael's voice, when it came, was raspy, but clear: "My dad is gonna kill you."

Chapter Forty-One

Michael awakened in the middle of the night with the sensation that he was being watched. The moon was a smile in the sky, glowing through his glass balcony doors.

"Chachi..."

Michael sat up when Chachi didn't answer. Usually, he could barely shift positions without waking him. He nudged Chachi. Still no response. Something wasn't right. His skin felt sensitive, exposed. "Chachi!" he called a bit louder. His voice was so shot, calling was useless. He was about to give him a good shaking when his eyes landed on an apparition so clear and real, he nearly released the fullness of his bladder.

His scream faded into nothing before it left his mouth, absorbed like a mist into the night.

She was sitting on his chaise, her knees drawn up to her chest, her hand twisting a few strands of her hair, the ends of which were in her mouth. When Michael was really small, he could remember her doing that. His mouth opened and closed soundlessly. Her young, beautiful face watched him, wide-eyed and apprehensive.

"Mom," he only mouthed it, or maybe he said it, but his language had no voice or his voice had no sound…or something or other.

She smiled, a slow spreading show of light. She stood and moved to the foot of his bed, playfully kicking out her bare feet. She reached for his bedpost and leaned against it, her head tilted playfully to one side, her face happy.

Was she a ghost? She didn't look like a ghost. She had regained lost youth and must have been in her prime. Her hair was full and tousled with waves and loose curls hanging down the length of her slender back, separating into lady fingers at the base of her spine.

Michael looked over at Chachi and knew that Chachi was not asleep. Somehow, Chachi had just…stopped. Everything had, except Michael and his mother. He dug his nails into Chachi's forearm and watched his skin bruise. Nothing.

His fear was replaced with fireworks of joy that lit him from the inside and expanded to the tips of every extremity until his smile mirrored hers. "Mom!" he grinned and she laughed, but only inside his head.

What do you say to your mother's ghost? He needed to see her like that, healthy and happy, as far from dead or sick or sad as he had ever seen her. Using his post, she swung herself around and examined him.

With one final smile, she took a step away but then stopped to look at Chachi as though she hadn't noticed him before. She frowned thoughtfully, her eyes narrowed and the familiar half-smile tugged at her lips. In an instant, the covers flew off Chachi, baring his nakedness. She covered her mouth to stifle a laugh and was gone.

Trembling, he turned to Chachi, whose eyes were already opened, dull with annoyance. "Why'd you do that?" he asked tonelessly.

"I didn't. Chachi, you wouldn't believe what just happened!"

Chachi sighed and pulled the covers over himself. He was already a light sleeper, a good night's sleep didn't come easily. "Well, you've made a miraculous recovery," he said.

"Chachi, it was her! She was here!"

Chachi slowly sat up, his mouth hung open for a spine-chilling moment.

"My mother…she was here! It wasn't me that yanked the covers off you, it was her!" Michael laughed. He drew in a deep breath. "God knew I needed to see her. He *knew* it!" He noticed Chachi's doubtful expression. "You don't believe me, do you?"

"Of course..."

Michael laughed. "You don't believe me! I understand you not believing me, but oh, shit, Chachi! It was her! She didn't touch me, but I could *feel* her!" He looked at Chachi's face, framed by the moonlight, and placed a hand on his cheek. "I'm not crazy, baby."

"I know. Come here." Chachi pulled him down with him. "Lay down. Rest your voice. We'll talk more about it in the morning."

"I'm just so excited!" Michael breathed, but he let Chachi pull him into his arms.

"Ow!" Chachi exclaimed, rubbing his forearm where five red bruises marked his skin. "What happened to my arm?"

* * * *

Chachi's space was already empty when Michael woke up. He sat up, feeling weirdly buoyed and a bit frightened, thinking about the bizarre events of the night before. Maxi's standard breakfast tray, covered with its silver dome, lay on his bedside table. Without touching it, he got up and showered. He felt like having a bit of company for breakfast.

He was dressed and about ready to go downstairs when Chachi stopped in to check on him.

"Don't tell me I ain't a healer," Chachi boasted and opened his arms for Michael to fill them.

Michael hugged him. He was deliriously happy. "Not to take anything away from your skills or sound ungrateful," Michael rasped in his grief-torn voice, "but seeing my mother…

Chachi's face drained of color.

"What?"

"I just thought you might have realized that you dreamed that."

"But I didn't!"

"Okay..."

"I didn't!"

"All right." Chachi cupped Michael's face. "You're doing great, let's not ruin it. I'm not trying to upset you."

"I wish you could have seen her too." Michael smiled wistfully. "She wouldn't let me wake you—" He inhaled sharply. "I've gotta tell Dad! I've gotta tell him she's okay!"

"Um, Mike." Chachi took both Michael's hands in his. "I don't think it's a good idea to tell your dad any of this."

"You're right," Michael agreed, sighing. "What am I thinking? It might upset him."

"He's just not having a good day today."

"Why, what's happening?"

"He asked Lydia for a divorce."

Michael ran quickly down the staircase, stopping a couple of times to get his bearings. He headed for the study where his father was said to have taken up residence. He found Joe sitting in his big armchair, a tray of cold breakfast at his side. His eyes had a distant look to them as he sat fingering a half-eaten slice of bacon.

"Dad?"

Joe's face came alive when he saw Michael. He held his arms out to him. "Michael, your voice is gone! And look at your poor face!"

Michael had seen the distorted puffiness of his face, but he didn't care about that now. He wished he could tell Joe about his mother. He looked so sad and thin. "What are you doing in here?" Michael asked.

"Just having a little breakfast." Joe picked up his cold coffee.

"Why aren't you in the breakfast room with the rest of the family?"

Joe shifted and cleared his throat. "I'm giving Lydia her space. I don't want to cause her anymore discomfort. I guess I should tell you—"

"I heard. I think it's ridiculous!"

Joe shrugged and looked at his hands.

"She loves you, Dad. You think she'd have endured all your bullshit if she didn't? And still you ask her for a divorce?"

Joe said softly, "It's none of your business."

Michael picked up Joe's plate and cup of coffee.

"What are you doing?"

"You belong in there with your family. You always have breakfast with your family!"

"Michael, things have changed!"

"Dad, you can't do this to her, or Leah, or David, just because you feel the need to punish yourself!"

"Look, I know—"

"You can't do this to yourself, or me!"

"Michael, stop!"

"No, *you* stop!" Michael took in a sharp breath and let it out. "Mom is…gone."

Joe's eyes filled with new tears. "She shouldn't have to watch her husband grieve for another woman. I just…I don't deserve her."

"Yes, you do," Michael said gently. "If she's willing to fix this, to see you through it, why won't you help her? Please, Dad. I can't take another tragedy that shouldn't have happened."

Joe wiped away the tear that streamed down his cheek.

"If I can get up…" Michael shuddered. "You can too. Come on!"

Joe nodded and stood up.

As they entered the breakfast room, the chatter stopped.

Lydia stared nervously onto her plate.

"Talk about a speedy recovery!" Leah hugged Michael.

"Well, the dead rises!" Maxi exclaimed. "Welcome back!" She gestured for her two assistants to bring more food.

Joe quietly took his seat at the head of the table next to his wife.

"Hi, Daddy," Leah chimed, her pretty face beaming.

"Hi, sweetheart."

Even David had tears glazing his eyes. "How do you feel?" he asked Michael.

"Great."

"You look awful. You sound awful too," Eric muttered through a mouthful of eggs.

"Your coffee's cold." Lydia turned to address Maxi, but she was already pouring Joe a fresh cup before bustling away. Both Lydia and Joe reached for the creamer and their hands touched. They froze.

"I'm sorry…" Joe mumbled.

"No, no…it's nothing." Lydia smiled, blushing.

Michael knew Chachi had something up his sleeve by the way he sauntered into the room.

"Oh, go ahead! Kiss and make up already!" Chachi cupped Joe's and Lydia's heads and roughly banged them together.

"Ow, Chachi!" Lydia complained, but she was laughing, and to everyone's surprise, so was Joe.

He held out his palm, and she placed her hand inside.

Chapter Forty-Two

They were on their way to break ground on Longbottom Center. Michael felt a little guilty that his father had done all the work, supervising the design and managing the details of construction; still, he was excited to be going home. How much had Detroit changed?

Joe and Chachi were to accompany him on this project. Michael was delighted. He had missed Chachi's twenty-four hour availability since Joe made him go home.

The ride from the airport to his old neighborhood was quite different from what he remembered when he rode with Steven in the opposite direction all those years before. He had cried the entire time then. This time, he rode with the thrill of anticipation and sat between the two men he loved most in the world.

The landscape quickly changed from the tall, concrete-and-steel high rises of downtown Detroit's commercial district to rows and rows of neat, brick houses with identical manicured lawns. Michael watched with fascination as areas he had never even seen of the city he lived in all his life whizzed by. Soon enough, the uniformly neat brick houses and lush greenery gave way to neglected frame houses and run-down, graffiti-laden apartment buildings. He wasn't far from home. The town's residents moved hopelessly along as if nothing they were heading for mattered enough to hurry. Surveying the landscape, Michael sat bolt upright when he spotted Ben the Bottle Man.

"Ben! Bottle Ben!" Michael shouted. "That's my friend! Stop the car!"

The driver slowed and waited for Ben, dusty from head to toe in about six layers of clothing including three hats, one of which had ears that flapped about his head as he walked. He pushed a rickety grocery cart filled with stacks upon stacks of bottles and crushed cans.

Michael gripped Chachi's wrist to quell his rising emotion. "Ben!"

Ben slowed and peered cautiously at the shiny limo.

Michael rolled his window down further. "Ben, it's me! Michael!"

Ben blinked and shielded his eyes. Michael grinned at the old man who seemed to have aged another twenty years since he'd left.

"I know that smile…" Ben said with a tarnished brown smile of his own. His whiskers had grown. Ben kept the gray mass braided in a jumbled mess that hung down his chest. "Hey, Pretty Boy!"

"Hey, Bennie! How've you been?"

"Oh, hangin' on…"

"Ben, this is my father," Michael said with pride. Joe waived. "And my friend." Chachi nodded at Ben.

"That's nice." Ben smiled absently. His gaze bounced uncertainly between the five men in the car. Then he turned to his grocery cart and weighed its contents importantly. "You want these, Pretty Boy?" He held up two bottles. "They'll fetch you a dollar for a hotdog at Weitzers."

Michael had to blink back tears. "No, Ben. You use them," he said softly.

Ben shrugged and replaced the bottles, shuffling his feet nervously. "They're about to build that new center down there." He pointed in the direction of Michael's new shelter. "There's gonna be free food today, they say."

"Yeah." Michael nodded. "You going, Ben?"

"Yeah, sure. Headed right there now."

Michael's next words would have been to offer him a ride, but the simultaneous side glances of both his father and Chachi made him hesitate. Besides, they couldn't have accommodated Ben's cart containing his worldly treasure of empty bottles and cans.

Michael felt inside his pocket for money. He never had money since his father bestowed him with the limitless credit card. Taking Michael's cue, Joe felt around in his pockets too for whatever change he could muster, producing fifty dollars. Chachi didn't budge.

"Give me money, Chachi," Michael demanded.

Ben looked anxiously on. Fifty dollars was a small fortune for him, but Chachi was seldom without a bank roll of thousands.

Chachi reached into his pocket, pulled out a bundle, and peeled off two crisp one hundred dollar bills. Michael picked them out of his hand and handed them to Ben with the fifty.

Chachi sneered, "Won't you give him the whole lot?"

"They'll kill him for that much money."

Ben's rotted grin was all the thanks Michael needed. They proceeded toward the new center with Michael's promise not to stop the car again.

The crowd spilled across the landscape like brightly colored ants. Every square inch of concrete within miles was covered with people. Police in full riot-gear lined the sidewalks and directed traffic. Michael's car was led behind the makeshift stage where they were greeted by staff from the mayor's office and the mayor himself, who would present Michael with a key to the city.

Michael had initially declined this gesture. His mayor could have done more for his homeless citizens by providing a key to a kitchen and a hot meal, not to mention a dry bed once in a while, when he and many thousands more lay exposed on the streets. He didn't want his fuckin' key to the city; but Joe had insisted for the sake of 'appearances.' After all, projects of this magnitude didn't happen without favors.

They wasted no time in briefing him and hustling him onto the stage where he was introduced with much fanfare by the mayor and then presented with the key. Camera bulbs flashed and reporters jockeyed for position.

Michael thanked the mayor and took the microphone, but when he looked out at that crowd, he lost his voice.

One thing he had insisted upon for the ceremony was that, besides accommodations for special guests that would include politicians and the press, all other VIP seating be reserved for the homeless. When he looked out at the hoards of these displaced citizens grinning and waving proudly at him from their unlikely places of high position, he let the tears fall. The crowd was alive, a motley of the young and old, big and small, haves and have-nots. They screamed and yelled and called out his name. "We love you, Michael!"

They held up signs that read 'Neighborhood Son, Welcome Home.' At first, he was both touched and angered seeing those he struggled with alongside those he struggled against, those he tried to help alongside those who, for many years of his young life, he begged to help him. Each time that he thought he had conquered those demons, they rose again from another place he'd missed.

"I remember those smiles…" he began, taking a line from Bottle Ben. The crowd erupted. "Even though there was nothing much to smile about for me then. I was one of you." He scanned the destitute faces. "I *am* one of you. I remember what it was like to be so hungry I'd double over in pain. I remember the thrill of finding the half-eaten sandwich of a stranger, sometimes rotted and mixed with trash, and feeling grateful. I know what it is to sleep on damp concrete with only the shelter of cardboards and the meager body heat of friends, like you. The threat of rain or a drop in temperature was not the stuff of small talk for us; it was the stuff of nightmares that threatened our lives. I think I know what you need."

Was that his mother in the crowd? He blinked twice. She was gone, leaving him breathless. The crowd filled his silence with their applause and Joe stepped protectively beside him.

Michael smiled at him and continued. "God, in his infinite mercy and wisdom, has given me the opportunity I dreamed about. He has blessed me to do something worthwhile. He has allowed me the pleasure of saying to you with surety that help is on the way." Michael held out his arm as a drop cloth was lifted to reveal a billboard-sized poster of the shiny new facility, towering over them. The crowd lit up with their approval. Michael smiled through hand-clapping and shouting.

"The Longbottom Center will provide healthcare, job placement, training, reduced-price shopping, entertainment, and education as well as hot meals, showers, and a warm, clean place to stay for those in need. Many nights I lay under that bridge that runs across the center." Michael pointed at the re-habilitated image in the poster of the decaying bridge that snaked behind the makeshift stage. "The Pass. There I slept alongside many of you and your children, your friends and your family in the arms of two of my dearest friends…Sam and Myrna Longbottom." He waits until the applause subsides. "And so this center is thus named."

He cleared the tears from his throat for the next part. "Its crown jewel will be a haven for women. A place where the special needs of women will be met. I'd like to call it Sarah's House."

His voice broke and Joe placed a steady arm about him.

"To help me in this ceremonial groundbreaking is my father, Joseph Simpson." The crowd cheered, Joe nodded. "And my friend and idol, the great Duke Spencer!"

The crowd exploded. Chachi stepped from behind a partition and stood on the other side of Michael. He bowed gracefully and blew kisses to his fans. He seemed surprised at their spirited reaction.

"Let's rock and roll!" Michael grinned and pumped his fist.

He was handed a shovel and led down to the construction area below, followed by his father, Chachi, and the mayor. The hush of the crowd felt like thousands of people holding their breaths. Joe and Chachi each placed a hand over Michael's as he turned over the first patch of dirt to cheers.

"Enjoy and thank you for coming!" he yelled as he was escorted away for press photos.

Most of the crowd spread out amongst the many vendors set up to dole out free food and entertainment. After press, Michael returned to the stage with Chachi to sign autographs. He was tickled to find that his autograph was in demand too.

Michael was signing and chatting with an over-zealous fan and her mother when he heard the repetitive call of a name from the crowd.

"Porter! Porter! Porter!"

"Porter…" Michael turned the name over in his mind. "Porter… *Porter*!" He grinned, handed off the autograph he had been signing, and combed the crowd. "Porter!" he called out.

"Hey, baby!"

Michael spotted Porter waving a dirty red cloth and jumping up and down to compensate for his lack of height. He laughed and reached for one of the guards on the stage. "Go get that young man for me. He's a friend."

"Whatz-up, Bagley!" Porter climbed the stage with exuberance after being thoroughly searched by security.

Michael held out his arms and gave Porter a long, welcoming hug. "How are you, man?" he whispered and held on tight, in spite of Porter's smell of dust and old onions.

"I *knew* it, man! I *knew* you were something special!" Porter grinned, displaying yellowed teeth.

"You okay?" Michael asked.

"I'm good, man. You doin' things *big*, partner!"

"What did I miss?"

"Not shit. Death and starvation, that's what you missed!" Still, Porter grinned.

Michael cupped his face with both hands. "It's good to see you, dude."

"I'm makin' it."

Michael dropped his hands. "You heard from Chauncey?"

"He's still in the joint."

Michael sighed. "I want you to meet a friend."

Chachi had just thrown his hands up, signaling the conclusion of his autograph signing, when Michael led a wide-eyed Porter over to him. "Chachi, this is my friend, Porter."

Chachi forced a smile.

"Well, blow my balls! I'm shaking Duke Spencer's hand!" Porter grinned and bobbed in his usual hyperactive way. "I love you man! You're like a god, man!" Porter beamed.

"Thank you." Chachi gave a nod and took his hand back.

"You *bad*, baby!" Porter slapped Michael on the shoulder. "Writin' songs and shit, givin' the press hell! I'm like, that's my *boy*!" He turned to Chachi. "I got all your shit, man."

"*All* his shit?" Michael teased. "How'd you get all his shit? You been stealing?"

"Me? Stealing? Naw, well, I wouldn't call it stealing…but I got my ways." Porter winked.

Michael smiled at this young man, not more than two years older than himself, who looked as though he'd lived three lifetimes.

"Hey." Porter moved in close and jerked his head toward the dwindling crowd around the stage. "Somebody's here to see you."

Michael looked around Porter and saw her right away. She was standing alone holding a bright yellow sweater tightly about herself. "Blaine…"

Michael's senses were flooded with memories upon seeing her. He drew a sharp breath and held it. As she climbed the stage, his face grew hot and he closed his eyes. When he opened them, he was smiling. After all, she did take care of him. He was standing on that stage because of her. She had saved him once.

She watched him from underneath her lashes, her head bowed, her face a crimson oval. She had to have been close to fifty by now.

"Hey you." He smiled and her eyes filled with tears. "Don't cry—" But she had already begun. Her shoulders shook and she used the hem of her sweater to dab at her eyes and nose.

"Blaine, don't cry." Michael put his arms around her. "It's okay," he said.

"I'm so proud of you." She sniffed through her tears. She looked up at him, now several inches taller. "You look wonderful." She smiled. "You were always so beautiful—" Her hands flew to her mouth. "Your mother!" she gasped. "It nearly killed me to hear about your mother."

"Yes. I know." Michael said, but he had to look away. At the edge of the stage, Porter gesticulated, making teasing remarks to his friends in the crowd.

Michael followed her gaze to where Chachi stood. "Come on. I want you to meet him."

Chachi's eyes rolled as Michael shepherded another one of his 'friends' in his direction.

"Chachi, this is Blaine."

She offered her hand and he raised one neat brow in interest as he took it. Blaine. They exchanged knowing looks that made Chachi shift his weight and Blaine's cheeks blush. They let their hands fall away. Chachi nodded and turned abruptly.

"He's gorgeous." She blushed again and looked down at her feet. "But then, look at you."

"How've you been, Blaine?"

"Good."

"The store?"

"Had to close it." She bent her head toward the billboard-sized poster of Longbottom Center.

"No!" Michael gasped. He hadn't thought of the surrounding businesses that might have been sacrificed for this project. How about that for irony?

"It's okay." Blaine smiled. "I'm doing okay. I got a good price."

"Are you sure? You can tell me. I'll make it right."

"I'm fine," she said softly. She began to cry again. "I didn't deserve you," she whispered.

Michael thumbed away her tears.

She turned and started for the stair leading off the stage before turning around again. "I'm so sorry, Michael."

"Blaine…don't—"

"I just…" She swallowed. "I just want you to know that I know I was wrong. I've been blaming myself for years."

"It's all right."

"I loved you. I need you to know that."

He smiled and leaned forward to kiss her on the cheek.

"Michael." Chachi's call from the other side of the stage saved him.

"Good seeing you," he said, touching her face.

"Take care of yourself." Blaine looked over at Porter, who had the crowd laughing at his antics. "Porter, let's go."

Michael watched them descend the stairs from the stage. A piece of his heart wanted to follow.

Chapter Forty-Three

They were heading toward Aunt Melanie's where Pooch and the rest of his family were working on an early dinner in his honor.

"Turn around and go down that ramp behind us," Michael instructed the driver. "It'll just take a moment," he promised Joe's and Chachi's protesting faces. The driver complied and soon he found himself transported in time, under the pass.

He stepped out of the car and looked around. The area had been cleaned, scoured even, and cleared of all its old residents in preparation for the new center. Had it not been for the chip in the wall where the concrete was missing a piece, he would not have been sure of the exact spot, but he found it. How many times had he stared at that chipped space in the wall, trying to fall asleep?

"This is it," he said to his father who had climbed out of the car to follow him. "This is where I slept most nights—" He stood shaking until Joe wrapped his arms around him. He cried for Sam and Mrs. Longbottom and Bottle Ben and Porter and everyone that was a part of the fabric of his difficult past. He gazed one last time at that place he once called home and took his father's hand, leaving it forever.

At his aunt's apartment, Chachi groaned loudly at the throngs of people moving up and down the dank, narrow staircase leading inside. In spite of Michael's and Joe's repeated offers, Melanie had proudly refused a new home. Pooch left her, accepting Joe's gift of a full scholarship to film school and a paid-for condominium apartment near campus.

They were back to shaking hands and smiling 'til their faces hurt. Members of her church helped Melanie prepare a bountiful meal for their guests and, in return (in addition to a fat donation from Joe), they were allowed to wait around and greet Michael and the famous Duke Spencer up close and personally.

"Come in, come in," Melanie summoned them. They inched into the living room that did double duty as a dining room. On one side was a large dining table and on the other side a sofa, television, and cocktail table with barely room to walk in between.

"Sit down; you're late," Melanie said. "Dinner is served."

"Where's Pooch?" Michael took his seat between Chachi and his father.

"Hey kids!" Pooch materialized from the kitchen area as if on cue, pulling Gherri by the hand behind him.

"Gherri!" Michael stood to embrace them.

"Grace, we have to say grace!" Melanie reminded them. She closed her eyes and everyone followed suit, clasping hands as she belted out a heartfelt prayer. "Dig in," she said finally.

Chachi frowned at the array of foods, most unrecognizably soaked in gravies, broths, and sauces. As steaming platters and bowls were passed around, he said to Michael, "I can't eat this stuff."

"Chachi, don't embarrass me!" Michael admonished in a whisper while smiling at his blushing young cousin Dania, who had become a young woman in his absence.

"Try my homemade biscuits," Melanie said, rising.

Michael had never seen her so pleased with herself. She reached for the biscuit platter and placed a mound of the bread on each of their plates; then she used a spatula to spread her home-concocted honey butter across the tops.

Chachi nudged Michael. "Did she just spread fat on my food?"

"It's called butter, Chachi!"

Melanie poured a stream of her red-eye gravy across Chachi's biscuits before moving on to Michael, then Joe. Chachi looked stricken.

"It's only this once," Michael pleaded.

"I'm sick already!"

They made it through dinner, though in Chachi's case, it was under Melanie's accusing gaze as she glared at him pushing food around on his plate.

"Hey," Pooch said to Michael, "let's hit the block like we used to, see who we can find!"

"Yeah!" Michael agreed.

"No!" Chachi yelled, then lowered his voice. "Um, you can't just go traipsing down the street, Michael; things have changed."

"Like what? I'm the same person, this is my turf. This is where I grew up."

"Chachi's right," Joe added. "You have too much celebrity now. It's too dangerous."

"We can take the guard and driver," Pooch said.

"Okay," Joe agreed. "But you got one hour. If you're not back in one hour, I'm sending someone to look for you and we're hopping a plane straight home."

"One hour," Michael confirmed, pushing Pooch toward the door lest his father changed his mind.

Things stayed the same in the hood. They stopped at the cleaners, the candy store, and the motel. Each establishment they left produced a trail of people eagerly following their slow-moving limousine.

They passed the Tire Shoppe and the Dollar Bonanza. They passed the Laundro-Mat and Mrs. Benneton's porch. Before long, they spotted Fleet and Booker leaning on the hood of an old, rusted car, getting wasted.

"Stop here," Michael said.

The two guys eyed them suspiciously.

"Hey, Booker," Michael called.

Booker peered at Michael's approaching form, then flashed a charming grin. "Hey, Pretty Boy!" He held out a brotherly hand. "I heard you were in town! I was on a run. I missed that shit down the road."

"What's goin' on?" Michael grinned.

"Ain't shit poppin', dude. 'cept you! You all from rags to riches and shit, all over the newspapers gettin' scandalous! You tell *me* what's goin' on!"

"Nothin's changed." But Michael felt his face flush. "Just stopped by to check you guys out, that's all."

"Who the fuck is all these people?" Booker spun around, gaping at the growing crowd.

"You heard from Chauncey?" Michael asked.

"Naw. I get up there when I can." Booker spat on the ground, still eyeing the crowd.

"Time to go." The bodyguard moved in close to Michael and Pooch, nudging them away from the volatile crowd.

"Brought your heat with you, huh," Fleet leered.

"I don't need heat, do I, Fleet? I'm among friends—"

"Hey," Booker said. "You should try to get up there to see Chauncey. He'll get a kick out of it."

They had fifteen minutes left and Michael wanted to see the strip.

"Five minutes," Pooch warned.

Michael didn't recognize any of the girls who pranced about in scraps of clothing. So many new faces, he thought sadly. A pretty young girl wearing too much makeup and too few clothes spotted them and tipped over in her too-tall heels.

"Looking for a party?" She smiled. She couldn't have been more than seventeen. "I know you!" her eyes widened.

"Back to the car," Pooch ordered.

They drove to the spot where Lazy Jaye sat parked the day of the shooting. A green Chevy sat in its place. Michael got out and stood, staring at it.

Pooch got out too and stood beside him. "Seems like a long time ago, doesn't it?" he said.

Michael said nothing.

"Hey! What'cha doing to my car!" A man, still zipping his pants, came running from an alleyway. The young girl who had been servicing him teetered behind.

"Let's go, Mike. There's nothing for you here anymore." Pooch placed a massaging hand on his cousin's neck and pulled him along.

They made it back to the apartment with less than a minute to spare.

"Good," Chachi said meeting them at the door red and damp in the face.

"What's wrong with you?" Michael looked him up and down.

"This room is stifling," he whispered. "I've gotta get out of here!"

Michael glanced away sheepishly. "Um, my aunt is expecting us to spend the night."

"What?" Chachi lost all semblance of discretion. "There's no room!

"Nonsense," Melanie barked from the sofa where she was seated in conversation with Joe. "Joe, you can take the girls' room. The girls can sleep on the couch."

"I wouldn't dare take a room from the girls, *I'll* take the couch," Joe offered.

"You take my room, Chachi," Pooch volunteered. "I'm gonna crash at Gherri's." Gherri hid her face in his shoulder.

"You're not married yet!" Melanie spat.

"I know, Mom…" Pooch took Gherri by the hand and bid them goodnight.

Chachi gasped, mortified.

"Michael, I'll make you a pallet on the floor with the boys," Melanie said.

"What about our clothes…at the hotel?" Chachi sputtered.

"I just sent for them," Joe said evenly, his eyes narrowed at Chachi.

"Come on, I'll show you to the room." Michael took Chachi's arm and led him up the short, narrow staircase.

Melanie called after them. "I'm making you a pallet on the *floor*, Michael!"

"I *know*, Auntie Mel..."

He had to step over his cousin Thomas, already asleep, to get to his pallet on the floor beside the sofa where his father lay sprawled like a giant on a trundle bed. Icy teeth gripped his gut like a vice. She was back. Sitting on the arm of the sofa where Joe lay, she studied his father's toes with childlike curiosity. Her face, framed by her soft mass of wavy hair, seemed ready to burst into laughter.

For a second, Michael thought his father saw her too, the way he wriggled his toes this way and that. But when Joe turned upon hearing Michael gasp and stumble, his face displayed a commonness that would not have been possible had he seen her. "Careful, Puppy. You okay?"

Michael stood stock still. She smiled at him, more radiant than when he'd last seen her in his bedroom.

"Michael?" Joe let his gaze follow Michael's to the empty space at the foot of the sofa. "What is it?"

'Don't say anything to your father. He's not ready...' Michael recalled Chachi's words. Joe wouldn't understand, neither had Chachi for that matter.

"Nothing. I thought I saw something." He lay down on the pallet, his heart hammering in his chest, and pulled the thin blanket over him. He could feel the floorboards through the layers of towels Melanie had laid out for his bed.

"Let's switch." Joe was leaning over the side of the sofa, gripping the edges to keep himself from falling over. He looked like an oversized boy to Michael at that angle, with his face leaning in so close. "You get up here and let me come down there."

"No, Dad. I'm fine."

"I'm too big for this thing. I won't get an ounce of sleep."

Sarah held on to her knees and hummed to herself. He couldn't hear what she hummed, but somehow, he knew that she did. Her bare feet were only inches from Joe's. What would happen if they touched?

"You did a great job today. I was proud of you," Joe said, turning onto his back and placing his hands behind his head. "You're gonna help a lot of people with that shelter and it's something for you to focus on."

Michael nodded in the darkness and watched as his mother crawled over the sofa's headrest and lay down.

"Well," Joe yawned and shifted so that he was facing her, his back to Michael. "I doubt if any of us will get much sleep, but let's try."

Michael fell asleep to the sounds of soft snoring and the image of his mother staring down into his father's face.

He awakened with a start, angry with himself for having fallen asleep. He meant to watch her longer, memorize her. Who knew when he'd see her again? Joe was alone on the sofa, snoring softly like heavy sighs.

Michael lay in the semi-darkness and watched the sickle moon through his aunt's lace curtained windows. Those curtains had to be older than he was, maybe even Pooch. He tried to make out the sparse furnishings, the water stains on the walls, the eclectic collection of photos of Christ with different shades of skin color, hair color, and even hair length scattered along the walls, the things he had grown most familiar with and somehow had forgotten. He used to find that his aunt's house was cozy and inviting with its changing smells and too many children. Now he found it cramped, as Chachi voiced so eloquently, stifling, and smothering. He rose quietly from his pallet, stepping over bodies, and was at Pooch's bedroom door before he realized it.

Chachi's eyes opened in that uncanny way he had as if he'd been awake all along. " 'Bout time." He groaned and made room for Michael.

Michael pressed his body close and felt Chachi respond. "Sorry to wake you."

"Who could sleep on this slab of concrete?" Chachi grunted and shifted so that Michael could lay in the bend of his arm. "It's kind of hard trying to sleep with your own face staring down at you from all sides, too."

Michael laughed. He knew by memory every Duke Spencer poster he and Pooch had pasted to the walls despite Melanie's protests.

Chachi nuzzled closer.

Michael tightened his embrace. Chachi responded by finding his lips. The passion between them created a layer of heat, like fever. "Not here," Michael reminded him.

"I wouldn't."

Michael kissed his chest, savoring him. Years now and his love for this man only continued to grow. He wanted to tell him that he saw his mother again…

"What?" Chachi asked quietly as if reading his mind.

Tread carefully. He hadn't forgotten the look on Chachi's face when he confided in him that he saw his mother's ghost. "I just love you, that's all."

"You nervous about tomorrow? Chachi asked.

"Yeah. I don't know why. It's just an empty house."

"I'm sorry I've been such a shit-head. I really am trying."

"You like being a shit-head and you're not trying," Michael said. He could feel Chachi's brow lifted in surprise in the darkness.

Chachi laughed. It began as a chuckle and grew until, soon, Michael was laughing along with him. Then Chachi said, "I want you with me always. You know that?"

Michael rested his face against Chachi's.

"What do you think about that?" Chachi insisted.

"What?"

"What I said. Could you spend the rest of your life with me?"

"Are you kidding? Where else would I spend it?"

"I'm serious." Chachi clutched him around the waist. "I tried to talk to you about this before," he said, moving Michael's hair around with his fingers. "You're still so young, and you've got so many choices ahead of you, I hate to push but sometimes…I can't seem to help it."

"Tell me what you want me to do."

Chachi paused before answering. "I want to take you home with me."

"Home?"

"Yeah. I've been thinking of home a lot lately."

"To…live?" Michael didn't want Chachi to hear the panic in his voice at the thought of leaving his father, Pooch, his family.

"Just for a little while, just to get away for a while. To shake off this grief and tragedy, to not have people making judgments about me or see my name in the papers everyday."

"Where on earth can you go and not have your name in the papers?"

"It's different there. They're so proud of me, they never have a bad thing to say." Chachi cleared his throat. "I thought, maybe when we returned, you...could move in with me."

Whoa. Michael rolled the idea around in his head. "You think my father would let me move in with you?"

"'Course not. But you're old enough to make these decisions now."

He had nearly forgotten. Michael turned onto his back and smiled. To be with Chachi every day and every night.

"You don't have to answer now. But think about it."

Michael looked up into Chachi's pretty brown eyes. The dawn breaking into the room gave them that kaleidoscopic look they got from time to time. "I don't have to think about it," he said. "I go where you go."

* * * *

Michael expected the house to be alive with his mother's spirit, but it lay still and desolate, an unremarkable shell with doors and broken windows.

The smell of mildew was overpowering, but otherwise, everything was as he remembered it. An old table that used to be in the kitchen sat out in the hall near the stairs. On it sat an astray and an empty bottle of beer, remnants of an old card game.

"Where was Sarah's room?" Joe asked.

Michael pointed to an open door off from the living room. He could see the bed, stripped of its linen.

Joe disappeared inside.

Michael led Chachi up the stairs. "Here's my room." He held his arms out and made a complete turn.

"Um hmm," Chachi said.

Michael walked over to his dresser and sorted through knick knacks. "Look," he said, holding up the ticket to his first Duke Spencer concert. "Look," he said again. This time, he held up a photograph.

Chachi walked over and took it out of his hands. It was a picture of Michael and Sarah, probably taken by Pooch. Sarah was dressed in a tight micro-mini skirt with long dangling earrings and too much makeup. The boy who stood beside her was the poster child of poverty with his too-skinny arms and shoulder blades protruding through a t-shirt that was way too large for him. Chachi tossed the photo onto the dresser. "Let's go find your father."

They found Joe sitting on her bed with his eyes closed.

Michael sat down beside him.

"You okay?" Chachi asked

"Yeah," Joe rasped, then cleared his throat.

"You?" Chachi asked Michael, who nodded. "Come on." Chachi led them to the front door.

Joe looked back one last time before letting Chachi take his arm.

Michael knew his father would go back and change the past if he could. But past was past. And nothing any of them could do would change it.

He stood by himself for one last look. He used to love that house, before, when he was very little and he still felt safe. Maybe he'd fix it up and give it to one of his homeless friends.

He discharged a final sigh and turned the knob, swinging the door wide. "Goodbye house."

They had several hours to spare before heading to the airport. They grabbed sandwiches on the run and pondered what to do next.

"I'd like a shower and a nap," Chachi said with a groan. "That matchbox of a house was so small, you could barely wash your ass properly."

"Don't be a prude," Joe chided.

"I'm not being a prude. You gave her a chance to get a bigger place. She's got to be outta her mind to stay in that trap."

"I know what we can do!" Michael brightened.

Chachi moaned and Joe's shoulders slumped.

"Please?"

Hours later, the coldness of steel made Michael shiver as he was stripped of all things that symbolized his freedom: his wallet, keys, jewelry... He emptied his pockets and stepped aside, as instructed, for the next officer to search him.

"Michael Simpson?" the officer examining his belongings swung around, his mouth slack.

"Yes sir," Michael mumbled.

After being searched, he was led down a long, narrow corridor. They came to a gated door, his escort entered a code, and the door slid aside. Once they were admitted, they had to wait for the doors to close before the next one could be activated and this went on for two more doors. Finally, he was placed in a secure room with only a desk and chair.

Chains clanked in the distance, the sound growing nearer with each of its victim's steps. He took a deep breath just before Chauncey's bearded face appeared, smiling even under his present conditions.

"It's me, Chauncey. Mike!"

They left his feet bound but undid his hands. Chauncey's mouth widened just as he was shoved downward into his chair by two burly guards. "Damn man! You almost made me bite my tongue!" He frowned up at the men before turning to grin at Michael. "Pretty Boy, Mike!"

"You remember." Michael smiled, blushing.

"How can I forget?" Chauncey leaned back in his chair, his knees spread. "Well, don't this fuckin' beat all!" He began to laugh. "Goddamn! I mean that in a good way," he added.

Michael smiled and looked down at his hands.

"Famous and shit..." Chauncey paused to look Michael over. "Lemme have a cigarette."

Michael shrugged that he had none.

"Hey, Duck!" Chauncey looked around the room at one of the guards who seemed perpetually annoyed. To Michael's surprise, the guard dug in his pocket, pulled out a pack of cigarettes, removed one, and handed it to Chauncey.

"I see you're doing okay," Michael said softly.

Chauncey let the guard light his cigarette, took a drag from it and nodded through the smoke. "I see you're doing okay too," he said in a way that made Michael look off to the side. "Still pretty too."

Michael gave him a look that said 'don't even try it.'

"So you flipped on me, huh?" he teased. "You should've told me you slept on that side of the bed. I'd have taken care of you." Chauncey grinned and Michael noticed, oddly, that he had perfect teeth. "I'm just fuckin' with you!" He laughed.

Michael laughed with him. After a while, he sighed. "Look, I had to say thank you."

Chauncey leaned further back in his chair. He squinted through a halo of smoke. "No prob." Chauncey sat watching him. A smile crept at the corners of his generous lips and slowly spread across his bearded face. "Hey, remember how we used to run game on fools, tradin' phoney money and shit?"

"I remember your valet parking service…"

Chauncey nearly fell over backward laughing. "What about Booker, sittin' on his legs all day, collecting money in a tin can?" Chauncey guffawed.

Michael didn't want to tell him that the mere thought of those schemes brought him shame.

"You need anything?" Michael asked.

Chauncey narrowed one eye at Michael before beaming fondly. "I got a son," he said, his chest puffed with pride.

"Yeah?" Michael smiled.

"Yeah. Me with a son." He laughed again, a short burst of sound. "You got kids, Pretty Boy?"

"Naw. No kids."

"No kids, huh?"

"No kids."

Chauncey's smile faded until it became a shadow of itself. "He's with my girl. They're stayin' with my moms. If you could look out—"

"Hey, done." Michael nodded.

"Yeah?"

"Done."

Chauncey's smile made a brief reappearance before fading again. "I heard about your moms."

"Yeah."

"You cool?"

"I'm cool."

"You sure?" Chauncey sat up straight and grasped Michael's wrist with his free hand. He had surprising strength.

"Yeah, I'm sure."

"'Cause you can be straight with me. I understand that shit." He shook ashes from the cigarette onto the floor and extinguished it with his fingers. "People don't know this about me, but I got a soft spot for my moms." He looked directly at Michael and for the first time during their conversation, there was no trace of mirth on his face. "I know how you felt about your moms."

Michael swallowed a lump in his throat. "Thanks," he whispered.

"Her ass was fine too," Chauncey said half to himself. Then he sprang back to the business at hand, his grin returning. "Anyway," he clapped his ankles closer together and saluted, military style. "It was a pleasure being at your service."

They shared another laugh.

"You were a good kid. I couldn't let nothin' happen to you." Chauncey smiled. He inhaled deeply. The crow's feet around his eyes faded as he sobered. "I was never gonna be shit, but you were different." He sighed. "Probably the only good thing I ever done was look out for you."

"Times up!" the guard named 'Duck' barked. Chauncey's grin widened. He held out a hand for Michael to shake.

Michael grasped the hand and pulled him as close as he could across the table. "I'll never forget you," he said as he hugged him.

"Hell naw, I'm unforgettable!" Chauncey stood, beaming, while one of the guards secured his hands behind his back. He shuffled toward the door with both guards flanking him and turned for one last look at Michael after stepping through. "Still pretty…" he said as the heavy door slowly closed in his face.

Chapter Forty-Four

Michael burst through the front door of Spencer Mansion close on Chachi's heels. They scampered up the winding staircase, chuckling all the while at their maneuvers to dump Joe off at home and avoid the press-stragglers still camped outside.

Papi called out something unintelligible from another room.

"Later!" Chachi called back, pushed Michael into the bedroom, and shut the door.

Gripping Chachi's neck, Michael pulled him in for a long kiss. Spending a weekend with Chachi, unable to touch him, tested Michael's limits. Just as the heat rose another notch, Chachi pulled back, his amber eyes soft.

"I was gonna wait..."

"What?" Michael panted, his chest heaving.

Chachi led Michael to his bedside table and removed a box from the top drawer. He opened it to reveal a platinum band embedded with glittering diamonds.

"A ring?" Michael stepped back, confused.

"A token. Nothing more."

"Chachi..."

"I hadn't expected to give you this so soon, and I'm still willing to wait. I just...wanted you to wear this...to remind me.

Slowly, Michael held his hand out. Chachi slid the ring on his ring-finger. "It's...crazy beautiful."

"Like you." Chachi ran his hand through Michael's shock of black hair and pressed his tongue into his mouth, using the other hand to undo his own shirt.

Michael held the kiss while struggling to get out of his shoes.

Chachi forced him backward toward the bed.

While trying to remove a sock, Michael lost his balance and fell against Jasper's crib. The baby's head shot up as he let out a piercing cry.

Michael and Chachi froze. Eyes stretched wide, Michael stared into Chachi's face, now pale and lined with concern.

"What is Jasper doing here?" Chachi whispered.

Michael drew up his shoulders and cut his eyes at the baby who was now up on his knees, sobbing.

"Papi!" Chachi stumbled over Michael's shoe in his rush to the door. "Papi!"

When Chachi pulled the door open, Papi's voice wafted through. "I tried to tell you."

"Tell me what!"

"Renee dropped the baby off."

"Why? Why didn't you call me?"

"I didn't want you running back here. I didn't want to ruin Michael's ribbon-cutting. I figured if she was serious, he'd be here when you got back."

A long silence ensued. Michael held the baby close.

Chachi's voice shook when he asked, "If she was serious about what?"

"She said she couldn't take it anymore. Something about you running all over the country while she babysat—I don't know. Of course, that's not it. She's got baby-sitters at her beck and call. It's you, Chachi. She just wants your attention."

Chachi walked slowly toward Michael and sat on the bed. His gaze focused on a place Michael couldn't see. He pulled out his cell phone and dialed. "Renee, call me!" he said before disconnecting and re-dialing. "Hello, Mrs. Lancaster? This is Jasper. Yes. Um...Renee dropped the baby off with my uncle when visitation wasn't scheduled. Do you know anything about this?"

Chachi stood as he listened. His gaze darted around the room impatiently. "I know...look...that's between Renee and I. But I'm concerned about her now. I just want to know if you know anything or how I can get in touch with her..."

Chachi pressed a hand to the side of his head, as if in pain.

Papi took the baby from Michael and tipped quietly away.

"Mrs. Lancaster—" Chachi sighed. "I know." His voice trembled. "This baby needs his mother—" Brows drawn together, he removed the phone from his ear and looked at it.

"She hung up on you."

Chachi nodded and sat on the bed again.

Michael sat with him and watched him stare at the wall. "She'll come around. She loves that baby."

"She's doing this to hurt me."

"She'll come around." Michael eased an arm around Chachi's waist and continued to gaze silently at the wall until Chachi spoke up again.

"She can't play these games with my baby. I won't let her."

Michael stroked the groove between Chachi's lower back and buttocks.

"But I'm concerned about her," Chachi continued as if in conversation with himself. "I'd never in a million years expected Renee to—"

"Shhhh." Michael lay his head on Chachi's shoulder. "It'll work out."

They sat that way a long time. Then Chachi exhaled sharply. "You're right. I can do this. I'll have to. I'm just worried about Renee."

"If she's as bad off as Papi says, the best thing for Jasper is to be with you now."

Chachi nodded, his fingers tapping lightly against Michael's knee. "You know, I'm gonna need to go home sooner than I thought, Michael. I really need my mother's help."

Michael sat up. "Guess we're talking more than a couple months too, huh?"

Chachi sighed. "Yeah. Too much has happened here. I need a break—to regroup." He pulled Michael closer. "I've gotta get Jasper away from this media circus for a while."

"And," Michael traced Chachi's windpipe, "how long will we be gone?"

A smile curved Chachi's fine cut lips. "It'll kill your father."

"I know. But he'll get over it. David's in school," Michael kissed Chachi's earlobe, "Eric's in school, Leah will be leaving for school soon...where does that leave me? At home with my parents?" The flame of excitement returned to his eyes and he grinned. "No, he'll just have to deal with it."

Chachi traced circles in Michael's hair with his nose. "Are you well enough for this?"

"What do you mean?"

"Your mother..." Chachi said, "I know you're still grieving. You haven't...seen her lately, have you?"

"No. Maybe I imagined her. Maybe not." Michael shrugged. "Maybe I saw her because I needed to...and now she's gone for good."

Chachi placed tiny kisses on Michael's neck. His worry for Renee was replaced with a rising urge to toss Michael onto the bed. Both the simplest and most complex things about the boy aroused him. Instead, he patiently asked his next question, insisting that they have the complete discussion so that the decision to leave and take Michael with him would be an informed and well-thought-out one. "Did you ever mention this to your shrink?"

"She said it was sort of like an imaginary-friend type situation and that it would stop when I felt I could handle...my mother's passing." Michael had wriggled out of his pants and straddled Chachi's lap, well-defined legs protruding from his shirt.

"Joe's worried about you," Chachi murmured, his eyes closed.

"Isn't he always?" Michael alternated between kissing and undoing Chachi's clothes.

"We'll have to convince him that you're well enough to go." One hand was already up Michael's shirt.

"We'll have to do no such thing. I'm a grown man." Michael breathed heavily, working to help Chachi out of his jeans. He smiled at him when he had accomplished his task. "I do whatever the fuck I want."

* * * *

"She hasn't returned any of my calls, not even to ask about Jasper." Chachi sat at the kitchen counter across from Joe eating from a bowl of cherries while Lydia helped Maxi prepare dinner.

Michael stood next to him chopping a carrot for their salad.

Lydia slid a colander of tomatoes and cucumbers in front of Michael and began slicing a zucchini. "She called me, Chachi. She didn't want to see or talk to you. That's why she couldn't wait until you came back." She drew in a deep breath. "Although, I must say she sounded quite off. She wasn't making much sense at all. I tried to get her to bring Jasper to me, but that was out of the question." Lydia gathered the strips of zucchini for chopping. "She'll be fine, just give her a minute."

Chachi huffed. "You think I'm gonna turn my baby over to her because she decides *she's* ready to be a parent? What if it happens again?" Chachi shook his head. "I can't even take Jasper out these days with the press sneaking around, hiding in bushes, trying to get a shot. This'll just add another log to their fire."

Lydia handed the bowl of chopped zucchini to Maxi. "Be patient with her. She'll pull it together...I hope."

Michael reached for a tomato. His ring winked in the sunlight streaming through the palladium windows.

Lydia gasped. "Let me see that ring!" She lifted Michael's hand and bent for a better view. "It's stunning! Must have cost a fortune!"

Her words hung in the air as Joe chewed thoughtfully on a cherry, his gaze on Michael's ring.

"That's a pretty generous gift," he said, turning to Chachi. "What does this mean?"

"It's just a symbol." Chachi shrugged. "For now."

The muscles in Joe's face twitched with the effort to maintain his amiable expression. "A symbol of what?" he asked.

Michael responded. "A symbol of our love," he looked at Chachi, "our commitment."

"It's lovely." Lydia gently nudged Joe and pulled a bowl of radishes toward her.

"Hmph." Joe grunted as he eyed the ring and popped another cherry into his mouth.

After dinner, Joe had to steady his hand from the effects of sweet anticipation as he check-mated Chachi. "Yesssss!" he leapt from his chair, fist pumping the air. "Yesssss!" he repeated.

Chachi smiled and began to return the marble figurines to their starting positions.

"That felt good." Joe blew air out of his cheeks and plopped back down into his chair. "Now, give it up."

"What?" Chachi laughed.

"You let me beat you. That took restraint that only one close to you would understand. What is it you want to tell me?"

Chachi's smile widened. He sat back in his chair and pulled out a cigarette and platinum lighter.

Joe took the opportunity to pour himself a brandy. "So what is it? It must have to do with Michael since you had to have a smoke first," he said, returning to his seat.

Chachi took his time before speaking, not only because he knew leaving again would hurt Joe, but also because saying the words was like making the decision final. In his list of pros and cons about returning home, leaving his best friend was a great big 'con.' "I've decided to go home for a while."

"What's a while?" Joe asked, sipping his brandy.

"Not sure. Could be a stint."

Joe seemed relatively calm. "What about Lil' Jasper? You know Renee will be back for him. She's just going through a tough time."

"Renee and I will have to work that out, but I'm not waiting around with my thumb in my mouth. I'd like my mother to spend some time with Jasper. He'll love it there."

Joe nodded abstractly. "Papi going?"

"Yeah. You know this is what Papi's been waiting for. In fact, he's taking Jasper ahead. I'd be surprised if Papi even came back with me."

Joe nodded again. He chewed his bottom lip, never taking his gaze off the comforting amber liquid swirling in his glass. "What about the house?"

Chachi sighed and shifted. "I'm trying to get my sister to come up and stay in it for a while. She just filed for a divorce and she'll be looking for a place to stay. She can stay there until she's ready to rebuild."

Joe blinked rapidly and exhaled. "What about Michael? You told him?"

"Of course I have," Chachi said. "You think I could think about leaving without Michael?"

Joe shot Chachi a hard look. "This wouldn't have anything to do with that fine-lookin' ring, would it?"

"A little. When we come back...he's gonna move in with me."

"Are you crazy?" Joe asked, his voice eerily soft. Chachi knew it was meant to disconcert him.

"Michael wants to be with me, Joe."

"That's out of the question."

"There's no question, Joe. He wants to do this. He's old enough now to decide and he wants to."

Chachi could feel Joe's retinas penetrating his skin.

"Maybe for a week or two, Chachi, I could bring him down to see you, but to move *in* with you?"

"*Bring* him down? *Bring* him down, Joe? Just when are you going to let him go?"

"When he grows up."

"And when is that in your head?"

"When he starts acting like it!" Joe sprang to his feet. He jammed his hands into his pockets.

Chachi took a pull from his cigarette. "You can't stop him Joe," he said quietly.

"Like hell I can't."

Chachi looked at Joe, surprised. "Why would you want to? Don't you think he deserves this? He's happy."

"Your son is a baby. You know nothing about raising a teenager. You think you turn eighteen and you're a grown up? If you do, you have a lot to learn. That boy's been a loose cannon for more than thirteen of his eighteen years, he's not even close, emotionally, to where the average eighteen-year-old should be."

"Maybe you're right, but it's not like we'll be gone forever, and it's not like he can't come back home if he wants to."

"What am I talking to you about this for anyway?"

"You're right," Chachi said and put his cigarette out in an ashtray on a nearby table. "In the end, it's Michael's decision."

"Hi, Daddy."

"Hi baby." Both Chachi and Joe's voices blended harmoniously. They stared at each other, Joe's face frozen and appalled, Chachi's steeped with amusement.

Michael groaned.

"You're not his goddamned daddy!" Joe barked.

Chachi tried hard not to laugh outright at Joe's anger. He choked back a chuckle. "Yes," he said in a tone reserved for Lil' Jasper, "*you're* his father…*I'm* his daddy…"

"Stop it!" Michael growled at him but Joe had already charged out of the room. "Why'd you do that!" His eyes blazed. "Isn't it hard enough on him?"

"I thought you were talking to me," Chachi said, laughing.

"I've never called you that in my father's presence and you know it!"

Michel turned in pursuit of his father. Chachi followed.

They found Joe in the sitting room. Michael sat next to him, not speaking, watching him struggle with his feelings. "I'm sorry, Dad," Michael whispered.

"I'm used to Chachi, he doesn't really bother me," Joe said slowly, "but you…you should have told me this yourself!"

"I'm sorry. Chachi thought it would be best—"

"Chachi, Chachi, Chachi! Don't you think for yourself anymore? Don't you think you might be investing too much in Chachi?"

"No!"

"*I* am your father! *You* should have told me you were moving out!"

"It wasn't that long ago that we decided—"

"Leave your father and me alone, Michael," Chachi said from the doorway.

Michael hesitated, grounded by the pain in his father's face.

"Go," Chachi urged.

Joe stood and turned his back on Chachi, who walked over and wrapped his arms around him from behind.

"We love you too," Chachi said, rocking Joe gently from side to side. "This'll be good for us, Michael and me, away from all the press and accusations…this place, where both our mother's passed… Can you give us this little break? We'll call every day and come home on holidays. And you'll visit as much as you like. It's not like I'm selling the farm or anything. He's coming back."

"Not to me."

Chachi stopped rocking. He slowly released his embrace. "So we come to it. This is not about Michael, this is about you."

Joe said nothing.

Chachi crossed his arms over his chest. "You don't intend for Michael to *ever* leave, do you? You'll make sure he's classified sick, mentally ill, immature, whatever it takes to hold on to him, am I right?"

"That's preposterous!"

"Joe, you *lost* those years, they're gone! But Michael's here now. He's forgiven all that shit, he's moved on, he adores you; don't fuck that up by smothering him, trying to get back something that you can't get back. You can have something else, though."

Joe turned to face him. "You don't know what you're talking about."

"You do."

Joe snorted and looked away.

"Do you still sit up at night and watch those old videos Pooch sent you?"

Joe's head whipped around. "What is it to you? What are you trying to say? Are you saying something's wrong with that?"

"He's not that baby anymore, Joe. You missed that. That time's gone. Watch them all you want if you want to live in someone else's past, but let him go."

Anger rose like a physical barrier between them.

"Who the *hell* are *you* to tell me that? You have no business and *no say* in what I do with my son!"

Chachi asked gently, "You think your obsession with your son is healthy?"

Joe's eyes ignited. "Do you think *your* obsession with my son is healthy?"

The two men stood, eye to eye, Joe with his angry glare, Chachi with a slight smile playing on his lips.

"Stop. Please, just stop." Michael returned, wedging himself between them. He clasped Joe's arm. "Dad, you've gotta stop. Let me go with Chachi, please?"

Joe turned his smoldering eyes on Michael and clenched his teeth. "You're *here*, in the first place, because a gun you held in your hand nearly blew a man's head off." He said evenly, ignoring Michael's gaping mouth. "Not long ago, you lost your mother. You've been through a lot, Michael. And you haven't been taking the therapy, the medicine, none of it seriously. I'm afraid to think of where your head is." He expelled a lungful of air. "And I think we've been silent about it long enough."

Michael took a step back and caught his breath.

"What are you saying…that I'm crazy?" Michael gasped. "I get angry! I get depressed, but I'm not crazy!"

"I'm not saying that, but what kind of father would I be to let you go gallivanting across the world, settin' up house with a man who hasn't quite grown up himself, knowing you haven't properly dealt with things." He cut his eyes at Chachi. "How responsible is Chachi for even encouraging it?"

"I'm not encouraging it, it's Michael's choice," Chachi said, moving to stand with Michael, "and I happen to think *you're* the very reason he needs to get away!"

"Who cares what *you* think?" Joe spat. "You don't have the patience to stay here and fight for your own son—you'd rather run away with him! What are you gonna do with mine? A teenager! Still grieving! It wasn't long ago that this boy couldn't get out of bed!"

"And who got him out of bed, Joe? If it were left up to you, you'd have doctors boring holes in his frontal lobe to release evil spirits!"

"Just stop!" Michael shouted. He took deep breaths. "I'm not crazy, Dad, and I'm sorry you seem to think so. I know I have some issues…I promise I'll address them. Chachi will help me. But I'm *going!*"

"Talk about the blind leading the blind…" Joe scoffed and closed his eyes. "What would your mother think?"

"My mother is fine—" Michael squared his shoulders defiantly.

Joe stared at him.

"She was…happy when I last saw her." He sighed. "She doesn't come anymore. She doesn't come anymore because I'm fine now."

Chachi squeezed his eyes shut.

Joe inched closer, his furrowed brows lowered to eye level with his son's. "What are you talking about?"

Michael didn't answer.

"What the *hell* are you talking about?" Joe repeated. "You've seen your mother?"

"Sort of…I guess…"

"Your mother is dead!"

"I know!"

Chachi cleared his throat. "Of course he hasn't really seen—"

Joe ignored Chachi and rounded on Michael. "You've seen your mother…*after* she died?" His face was damp and blotchy, his veins pulsing.

"I—yeah…"

"When? When was the last time?"

Michael cast a nervous glance at Chachi.

"Don't look at *him*! *I'm* talking to you!"

Michael's eyes raced in his head. "At the…ground breaking; at Auntie Mel's. She was…watching over you…"

They stood as though ossified.

"You knew about this?" Joe glared at Chachi.

"I didn't know she was watching over you…"

"Can you ever be serious!" Joe bellowed. He turned back to Michael. "Why hadn't you told me this?"

Michael's lips moved to answer. His eyes darted in Chachi's direction with a subtle quickness.

"You see!" Joe shouted at Chachi. "This is why I can't trust you to make the right decisions where Michael is concerned. Why wouldn't you have told me this?"

"Goddammit, Joe, be still! It happens to lots of people in traumatic situations. He talked to his doctor-chick about it! She told him it would stop when he got better and accepted his mother's death, or something or other like that…right, Michael? And it did!"

Michael sort of nodded and looked away from his father's beseeching eyes.

"Hey," Chachi put an arm around Joe's shoulder, "I understand. I hear you, I really do. If he even so much as gets bored, I'll send him back to you. I just think the environment is going to do wonders for him…for both of us…"

The fire in Joe's eyes dulled and fine lines of fatigue crept into his face. "Maybe you could just hold off…let's back up for a while," he sighed. "It'll give us all a chance to think about it some more."

"I've been thinking about it for over a year now, Joe. Michael's it for me. And we need this trip. If one more camera flashes in my face, one more person calls me a pervert, I might kill somebody!"

Joe's gaze wandered sightlessly to an area in the corner of the room. "When…were you planning to leave?"

"Before the month ends."

Michael lowered his head. Joe's footsteps were fading before he could look up again.

Chapter Forty-Five

If he could describe the weight of waking up in a room that had been cleared of his things to a morning heavy with the sadness of separation and the fear of change, he would—but he couldn't. Michael lay for a long time in his bed, clinging to its comfort, shutting out the sounds of the day progressing around him. He got a single phone call from Chachi.

"Get up," was all Chachi said, his voice sounding artificially cheery.

He rose to shower and dress, dragging with the knowledge that his father, a few doors down, had sat up and cried all night. He knew, because he barely slept a wink himself.

Lydia made breakfast as a parting gesture, but he couldn't eat it. He and his brother and sister sat, staring into their toast. Maxi wouldn't even come out of the kitchen. Both Joe's and Eric's chairs sat empty.

He packed the last of his things in a carryon bag and was zipping it just as Chachi's car horn began to blow. "Dad," his voice shook and his heart shrank in his chest. He slung his bag on his shoulder and walked down to his father's bedroom. "Chachi's here," he called through the door. The car horn blew again. He turned, exasperated, and met Lydia, smiling through tears that pooled in her eyes.

"You go down, honey. I'll see to your father."

On the way down, he met Eric coming up. He looked as bad as Michael felt.

"You'll be graduated by the time I get back," was all he could think to say. Eric embraced him. Michael was bedraggled by the time he made it to the foyer and joined his family outside where they were giving Chachi final hugs. He felt the bottom drop out of his stomach. He hugged David. His sister lay in his arms as though sleeping, tears streaming down her face.

"We've gotta go," Chachi said, but his gaze darted to the open door from where Lydia emerged without Joe.

"Where is he?" Michael whispered as he wrapped his arms around her. She shook her head miserably and started to cry too. He thought he would die.

"Come on." Chachi handed Mike's bag to the driver, who had come around to help, then held the door for Michael.

"You first." Michael sniffed, waving him inside. He wanted those last few seconds to see if his father would come. Seconds later, he joined Chachi inside.

The family gathered around. "Bye!"

"Call as soon as you get there!"

Eric pressed his face to the glass, trying to make Michael laugh one last time. As they began to pull off, Eric banged on the door.

"What's he doing?" Chachi frowned.

“Stop!” Michael barked. He jumped out when the car stopped. His father, bleary eyed with mussed up hair, stood in the entryway in his robe and slippers. Michael moved toward him and Joe met him halfway, gathering him into his arms. Michael clutched at his father’s robe.

“You’re going to be late,” Joe croaked, but Michael held on. Joe looked up as Chachi approached, smiling. “Go on,” Joe urged, wriggling out of their grasps and blowing his nose on a tissue. “Go before you miss your flight.”

As the car started to move, Chachi said, “Don’t look back.”

They had dinner in the private dining room of their fancy hotel before turning in for the evening. Michael located his pajamas and stole into the spacious double bath. He watched himself in the mirror as the tub filled with water. He couldn’t believe he had left home. He came out brushing his teeth.

Chachi was on the phone. “Your father,” he whispered with his hand over the receiver. “Everything’s fine. We’re fine,” he said. “Sure…you wanna talk to him now?”

Michael began waving his arms and shaking his head. He’d had enough for one day.

“All right, I’ll have him call you in the morning,” Chachi said. Michael blew out his breath in relief. “Sure thing. Good night.”

He was cozy in bed, watching the moon through picturesque windows when Chachi slipped in beside him. The warmth of the knowledge that it would be this way from now on spread throughout his insides. He smiled and pressed himself into Chachi’s body so that they could lay like spoons. “You think your mom will like me?”

“She already loves you.” Chachi chuckled. “I might be crazy for bringing you along. You know how you have a knack for upstaging me.”

Michael laughed and jabbed him in the belly.

“Ow!”

“I can’t wait to see the flowers, the way you describe them.”

“Yeah…”

"...and feel your sun..."

"Um hmm."

Michael let out a long sigh. "Just think, that's the same moon your mom and my dad sees in different parts of the world."

Chachi, half asleep, did not answer.

"I miss her so much..." Michael breathed, mostly to himself.

Chachi peered around into Michael's face. "You okay?" he asked in the darkness. "What's wrong?"

"Nothing," Michael said before snuggling his back into him and going to sleep.

* * * *

"Everything's fine," Chachi said into the phone as Michael emerged, combing his hair. "I just wanted to keep you abreast of how things were going. Sure. He's right here, you wanna speak to him?" He handed Michael the phone.

"Hi, Dad." He listened. "I slept fine. Are you okay? I miss you already." He paused again to listen, then laughed. "Sure. I will. I'll remember. Okay. I'll call you when we get there. I love you too. Bye."

He handed the phone back to Chachi.

"Okay," Chachi resumed. "We got one more flight after this one and we'll be there. Sure. I will. Talk to you later."

By the time they checked into a hotel for the last leg of the trip, Michael was dead-dog tired. He staggered from the shower. "Is that Dad again?" he mumbled.

Chachi nodded, the phone pressed to his ear. Michael flopped onto the bed. He let Chachi's voice lull him toward sleep as he chatted with Joe. He was at the threshold of slumber when Chachi lowered his voice to a near whisper, a move that pricked Michael's interest.

"I know, I just... I don't wanna make a mistake," Chachi was saying. Michael heard tears in his voice and roused himself. "I know you do, I just... I wish I could be sure." Chachi listened a long time. Joe must have been lecturing. “Yeah,” Chachi said softly. “I will. Bye.”

Michael lay very still listening to Chachi think. After a while, he heard Chachi move into the bathroom and turn the showers on. He must be having second thoughts. Thousands of miles away and Joe was still able to get to him. He couldn’t let that happen. He had to put on a happy face and reinforce that they were doing what was good for *them*, his father be damned. If Joe ruined this for him…he’d never forgive him.

Chachi snuggled up behind him, still wet from the shower and began his habitual stroking of Michael’s downy-soft hair. “You awake?”

“Um hmm.”

“Turn around for a minute. I wanna talk to you.”

Michael shifted so that he was facing Chachi. Moonlight streamed from the parted drapes at the windows, reflecting off his light eyes. Michael’s stomach flipped with the prospect of spending the rest of his life with such beauty.

Chachi didn’t speak right away; he spent a long while just gazing at Michael. “I want you to be absolutely, positively sure you want this,” he said finally. “Please. Be honest with yourself and me.”

“I want this.”

“’Cause, I’m coming back. I said I couldn’t leave you, but I’ll understand if you want to stay with your family and work on some things, take care of your shelter, maybe go on with your career…”

“I asked you not to bring this up again,” Michael said.

“I’ve got to be sure or the guilt will eat away at me.”

“Guilt for what? I don’t understand what the problem is! I thought we agreed that if I didn’t like it, I’d come home!”

“But…you wouldn’t. I know you. You’d stay because I’m there. You think of me before you think of yourself and, though I love you for it, I’m trying to think of you, and I’m trying to get *you* to think of you.”

“I-want-to-be-with-you!” Michael insisted. His face was growing hot with frustration.

“But what’s best for you? I just don’t want you to get across the world and lose yourself to me. It won’t hurt us to be apart a couple of years while we work on ourselves, while you find out who you are…”

"I'm yours. That's all. That's all I want to be. Chachi, I swear, if you try to leave me, I'll follow you. He can't keep me home!"

Chachi considered him a while then smiled. "Okay." He bent to kiss him and Michael wrapped his arms tightly around him. "All right," Chachi whispered. "I'm glad you're here."

Michael slid underneath him for better handling. As tired as he was, there were some things he just couldn't pass up.

Michael awakened in the night with a start. The room was so dark, he thought his eyes were still closed. Someone had drawn the drapes. He wanted to go back to sleep, but every part of him was coursing with energy as though he had never even been asleep. In the morning, they would board their final commercial flight, then take a private jet the rest of the way to a new home, a thought that both excited him and filled him with grief. He closed his eyes and tried to dwell on happier thoughts, but the darkness bled into his spirit. Depression hovered as it usually did at night, and he longed for his mother, his father, his family… He couldn't shake the panicky feeling that this was his last chance…

"Ridiculous," he murmured out loud, but abruptly caught himself. In spite of the little blue pill he saw Chachi taking, he was still a very light sleeper and Michael didn't want to risk waking him. He tried again to still his brain for sleep. He focused in on the quiet and, after a while, welcomed the peace that was the beginnings of sleep. Then something moved out there.

Eyes open again, he trained them on the darkness, squinting hard at something he could feel rather than see. It was moving toward him. He felt the fine hairs tickle his neck as they stood on end. His pulse raced.

Mom, no! his brain pleaded, but his heart won. She was standing before him as though she had materialized from thin air.

Not a foot away, she stared, her arms limp at her sides, her eyes sad.

"What are you doing here?" Michael whispered as softly as he could so as not to awaken Chachi. "I missed you," he couldn't help adding as an afterthought, though his intent was to make her go, not stay. "Mom, they already think I'm crazy! You've got to stop this! You've got to go away. Why can't you rest?"

But Sarah only stood, her head tilted at an angle that made her lovely hair spill over one shoulder, her beautiful face clouded with sadness.

"Mom…what is it?"

Chachi moved behind him and he snapped his mouth shut. He tried communicating with his thoughts, but she just wasn't responding.

He watched her watch him and, after a while, she moved closer. She wanted to say something. Michael's quizzical expression changed to shock when she walked right up to the bed and bent over him. He could feel her breath. It was warm, not cold like a ghost's should be. He could smell the sweetness of her hair. But the voice that came out of her was sad and crackly, as if from lack of use.

"How can I rest!" was all she said. Then she was gone.

It was at least another hour before he was able to stop trembling. Getting out of bed crossed his mind, but he remained—afraid that the movement would wake Chachi before his trembling would. He was surprised his heartbeat alone hadn't accomplished it. He turned gingerly to face Chachi, making sure that he was still sound asleep, thanking the little blue pill the whole time. Maybe he *was* crazy. Maybe his dad was right. He couldn't go on like this. If he *hadn't* gone nuts, he would be well on his way if this continued. But she didn't seem dead. He felt heat from her body. He inhaled her scent. How could she be dead? Yet, he had seen her dead. He buried her…

How many would give their fortune to see a deceased loved one again? How could he send her away—really? Satisfied that Chachi was none the wiser and busy with dreams, he closed his eyes in hopes of catching those last few hours of sleep.

Chachi lay in the dark, unmoving. His spirit was too heavy for movement. His brain too tired. He lay until he could hear the soft, even breathing that said Michael had finally drifted off to sleep, then he rose.

He took his cell phone and went into the bathroom. He always called

Joe when he felt like this. He stood in front of the mirror, gazing at his reflection. After a short while, he dialed the number.

He wasn't surprised that Joe answered on the first ring. Joe hadn't given up his night walking. "Hey, it's me," he said softly. He walked over and stepped into the shower stall. As if someone might see him, he waited until he was inside and had closed the sliding glass doors before he let his tears fall. He backed up against the wall and slid down it to a squatting position. "I need to talk."

Chapter Forty-Six

Michael woke to a set of nerves that rivaled those he felt the first time he stepped foot in New York. Chachi was already up and he was anxious to find out how much, if anything, he heard last night. His belly lurched when Chachi came out of the bathroom suite fully dressed in a starched white shirt and jeans, Michael's favorite ensemble. He looked fresh and handsome. He smiled brightly at Michael, putting his fears to rest.

"Up, up!" He kissed Michael, who sucked in the taste of toothpaste and the smell of cologne. "We don't wanna be late," he murmured, but kept kissing him until Michael felt that warm, tingly feeling in his loins.

Michael gazed deep into his eyes and grinned.

So he hadn't heard a thing last night. Chachi seemed to be in animatedly good spirits as he rushed Michael along. Soon, they had joined their security team in the back seat of the limo.

Excitement danced inside Michael's chest. He slipped an arm under Chachi's and leaned into him, smiling.

"Hungry?" Chachi asked.

"A bit."

"We'll get something at the airport."

Michael nearly dozed again, lying comfortably against Chachi and feeling his strong arm around him. Chachi planted kisses on his head often, but his mother's sad, worried face loomed in his mind and he jerked to wakefulness.

"Okay?" Chachi frowned at him.

"Yeah."

He took to looking out the window at the beautiful landscape racing by instead. Soon they were stopped.

The airport was crowded. Though they wore hats and shades, curious passer-bys stopped and stared after them with puzzled looks. Finally, they slowed and came to a halt.

"Hold these." Chachi handed Michael their plane tickets and his bag. "I'm going to grab something for us to eat."

"Can't you let them do it?' Michael motioned with his head toward one of the burly guys flanking them, looking cold and unapproachable.

"I could, but I don't trust people with my food."

"Can we go together?"

"I want you to get to the gate. We'll attract less attention if we're not together." Chachi dug in his pocket for money. "I'm leaving two guys with you and taking one with me."

"Gate six," Michael said, reading the tickets.

"What do you want, a hot dog or something?"

Michael arched a brow. "You're offering me a hot dog?"

Chachi smiled, but it looked strained. "If you wanna clog your arteries, what can I do?"

"A hot dog sounds good."

"Drink?"

"A soda—anything." Michael shrugged.

"Okay." Chachi turned, but stopped as though he had forgotten something. He turned again, slowly, and gave Michael the softest look. "Come here…"

Standing as much behind one of the guards as they could, he pulled Michael close and kissed him, this time so long and sensuously that Michael stiffened and pulled away, afraid people might notice.

"You're just going to get a hot dog, right?" Michael joked.

Chachi answered with another kiss. "Don't talk to anyone," he warned as he winked and walked away.

Michael watched him until, quite a distance away, he turned and winked again. Something twisted in the pit of his stomach.

"Okay," he said, pulling the tickets out for a glance. "Gate six," he held the tickets up for the guard to see. After nodding, the burly man led the way to the gate.

They arrived without incident. His security guard whispered something to a pretty lady behind the information desk. Her eyes lit up and she smiled, gesturing Michael forward. They would lead him to the VIP room to wait until he could board before the other first-class passengers; he knew the deal now, but refused to budge without Chachi. He wanted to be sure Chachi could see him as soon as he returned. His cell phone rang and he snatched it off his hip.

"Hello?" he said anxiously.

"What do you want on your hot dog?"

Michael laughed as his system was flooded with relief. His stomach unclenched, he stopped perspiring, and that dreadful urge to rush to the bathroom disappeared. "Everything! Anything!" he laughed.

"What's so funny?" Chachi asked quietly.

"I just…I thought—oh, nothing. Just hurry back, will you?"

"I'll hurry back, you just wait," Chachi said and hung up.

Breathing in lungfuls of air now, Michael relaxed. He picked up a teen magazine on the seat next to him. Duke was on the cover as part of a montage of hot music artists. He opened the magazine to see what else was going on in Duke's life that he didn't know about.

The announcement came over the loud speaker that their flight would be boarding in ten minutes. He looked over at the larger security guard. The guard immediately got on his phone. The pretty lady behind the service desk came out to ask him if he was ready to board. He shook his head.

"What did he say?" he asked the guard.

"They'll be here shortly," he said gruffly and picked up a newspaper.

The call to board rang out and Michael, now petrified, leapt to his feet. People lined up at the door. His stomach did acrobatic tricks and his legs struggled to keep him upright. Where was Chachi? They were going to miss their flight. He looked frantically at one guard, then the other. The burly one in charge shrugged helplessly. Michael hurried over to the information desk. "How soon do we take off? My guest is missing."

"About ten minutes." The pretty lady smiled and held her hand out for the tickets. "Are you ready to board?"

"No!" he shouted at her. She blinked and stared at him, her smile fading. "I'm sorry…" he was hyperventilating now, "…I just…we…need to wait…"

"Please calm down," the pretty lady said quietly. "We still have a few minutes. What is your guest's name?"

The security guard in charge cleared his throat. Michael spun around to look at him.

"My instructions are to leave you after boarding," he said. His associate stood and adjusted his pants. They were going to leave him.

"But…I haven't boarded!"

The guard gave him a look that said, 'so board.'

"You're going to just leave me?" he shouted, panicking. "In a crowded airport!" He had never been in an airport alone. The already immense size of the place grew as he seemed to shrink. He looked around wildly, first in one direction, then the other. The pretty lady behind the desk was saying something to him, but he couldn't make out what she was saying.

The final call for boarding came and the doors were closed. Michael thought he would wet his pants. He pulled out his phone and dialed Chachi's number, wondering why he hadn't thought of that sooner. The line was busy. He had expected that. Stupidly, he tried again and again with the same result.

"I'm sorry." The guard nodded slightly in farewell and beckoned for his partner to follow him. A cry of outrage and distress escaped Michael's throat.

"Can I do something for you?" The pretty lady and an acne-scarred, lanky-tall guy were suddenly in front of him. She had a hand on his arm.

"Yes…" he said distractedly. He scanned the corridor where he saw Chachi disappear.

She was speaking again, but he took no notice. A nervous smile broke onto his sweaty face and he was buoyed with exhilaration at seeing the familiar form moving toward him. "Oh God, am I glad to see *you*!" He gushed but then stopped. "W-hat…what are *you* doing here? His gaze darted between his father and the two men with him. They looked ready to grab him at any false move.

"I've been flying a long time to get to you," Joe said calmly.

"We missed the plane," Michael tried to explain, still not grasping the purpose of his father's presence. "Chachi went for food and never returned..."

Joe watched him intently.

Michael stopped, finally getting a clue. He felt as though he had been doused with ice water. "Where is he?" he whispered.

"He took another flight," Joe said quietly.

Michael stared at his father, unbelieving. Joe waited.

"But…how did you get here so quickly?"

"I took a Lear, nonstop. We cut across your path to save time."

"Not again…" Michael mumbled. "Not again, Chachi." He held both hands to his head and spun away from his father. "He can't have left… I have his bag. I have the tickets!"

"Come on, son." Joe held his hand out. "Come on…"

Michael turned to face him. "What have you done?" he croaked, barely able to speak from the jumble of emotions inside of him. "What have you done, Dad?"

"Nothing. I swear. It was his idea." Joe sniffed and swallowed. "But it's best, Puppy," he added quickly. "Take the bags," he ordered the two guards. As they reached for Michael's and Chachi's bags, Michael moved unsteadily in the direction he saw Chachi go, then, in a last-ditch effort, he shot out of there, just barely escaping Joe's clutching fingers, and raced down the corridor. People jumped out of the way, drawing baby carriages close to them as Michael ran, with Joe and the two guards in close pursuit. He passed gates where passengers lined up for boarding and planes taxied.

He ran out of air by the time he reached gate number two and, with his lungs ready to burst, he ran up to the enormous window where a plane was slowly pulling out onto the runway, and heaved against it.

The area was nearly empty. Two attendants were packing up. Michael stood with his hands and face pressed to the glass and watched the winged giant as it came to a halt at the edge of the runway and began, slowly at first, then picking up speed, its graceful journey. Chachi could be on that plane.

He could hear his father somewhere behind him, panting from his run.

The thought of returning home with him made him sick. He flung himself around and met Joe's eyes. He needed to destroy something. He imagined kicking at the chairs, knocking everything he could get his hands on to the floor. He'd let the tantrum consume him, grunting and growling as he wrecked as much havoc as he could until he was left spent and sagging, sucking in ragged breaths. But then what? Chachi would still be gone. After all his promises, he had left him again.

He'll be nineteen years old. Time to grow up.

"Can we go now?"

The flash of a camera bulb pierced the calm. By morning, the world would have his humiliation to feast on. Unaware of how they got there, he found himself in a small, private waiting area, not unlike the ones he and Chachi had sat in before, waiting to board their plane. He let Joe pull him down into a seat next to him. He couldn't go any further. He had said that if Chachi tried to leave him, he would follow him, but knew he would not. He was done. It was finished. He felt his heart glaze over.

When Joe put a hand on his knee and shook it, turning to face him was like shifting a giant lead ball on his neck, but he managed to do it. Joe watched him with a look of mingled concern and kindness and Michael's brain had visions of gouging out his eyes, but his heart was no longer into feeling anything. In a final act of surrender, he lay his head on his father's lap.

* * * *

Chachi hadn't realized he had been semi-holding his breath until the plane was gliding safely through the air. He couldn't believe that, soon, he would be home. He also could not believe that Michael wasn't sitting next to him.

It was the night that did it. He had battled through Joe's constant whittling away at his conscience with his resolve still in tact. But he could not ignore Michael's frenzied whisperings in the darkness. Joe was right. Michael needed help that Chachi couldn't see him through the way his father could.

He rested his forehead on the coolness of the window and watched the clouds. He couldn't get out of his head what Michael must be feeling and that he might never understand, in spite of his breaking yet another vow, how much he loved him. God, he loved him, he loved him, he loved him… Thinking about it caused a rush of emotions and something seized up inside him, making him grip his armrest like a man gone mad.

"Something to drink, sir?"

He kept his eyes shut and nodded. His breath came in short bursts. He tried to accept the glass, but his hand disobediently wrapped itself around her wrist and the liquid sloshed over the rim. Eyes wide with panic, he began to quiver as tears spilled down his face.

"It's all right," the attendant said in hushed tones, using her free hand to secure the curtain around them. She removed the glass and held his hand, their fingers intertwined so tightly that her long nails dug into his skin. Slipping ice into a napkin, she dabbed his forehead with it.

When he could let go, she poured a fresh glass of what turned out to be bourbon and he drank it.

"Another?" she asked gently, smiling.

He shook his head and, feeling a bit ashamed, offered her a shaky smile in return. He would not forget her. The alcohol had an immediate affect and he let his head loll and fall against the window.

"You rest now," she said.

He nodded and squeezed the hand that lay gently on his shoulder. What was he doing? Michael needed him more now than he ever did. But leaving him was the responsible thing to do, wasn't it?

Jasper, his mother and Papi were waiting for him. He needed this new start to rejuvenate, to heal his soul. But what good was his soul without his soul-mate?

He was overcome with indecision. He struggled to push Michael back into the recesses of his mind, but his heart was already working out the details.

"Anything else I can do for you?" She brought pillows and a blanket. Her smile was like a soothing balm.

"I need to get off this plane," Chachi said, his spirits soaring. "How soon can we land?"

Discussion Questions

1. Throughout history and various cultures, children were often married off at ages as young as twelve. At what age is a person generally capable of handling the mental, physical and emotional challenges of a sexual relationship?

2. Do you think Michael or Chachi's background had anything to do with their decisions?

3. What did you think about Joe and Chachi's relationship? Were they too close for men?

4. Were you surprised to find out who Chachi really was, or did you guess?

5. Did Joe's family and friends enable his anger management problem?

6. Were you upset with the way Joe handled or failed to handle his best friend's relationship with his son? Do you think he would have responded differently if it had happened to David?

7. Being so young, did you think Michael was in love with Chachi or did he simply idolize him?

8. What more could Joe, Chachi and Steven have done to prepare in case their secret got out to the press?

9. Did you admire Lydia for supporting Joe during his grief when Sarah died, or did you criticize her?

10. Did you sympathize with Renee?

11. Do you think Chachi's sexual abuse had anything to do with his abusing Michael?

12. Was Joe obsessed with Michael (as Chachi claimed)?

13. Do you think Michael was mentally ill, or did he really see his dead mother? Do you believe in ghosts?

14. Was leaving Michael the right thing for Chachi to do?

Chicago native, D. J. McLaurin, is the author of the provocative new novel, *What if it Feels Good?* She is a graduate of DePaul University and a Certified Public Accountant. She has worked in various fields including banking and auditing before her current twenty-two year stint in major media. Prior to venturing into the world of writing contemporary fiction, D. J. wrote plays for local venues which are still in circulation today. She resides in South Holland, Illinois, with her husband and the younger of her two daughters, where she is working on her next novel, *Metamorphosis*, the riveting sequel to *What If It Feels Good?*

LaVergne, TN USA
10 August 2010
192771LV00003B/1/A